MAGEBORN:

THE
GOD-STONE WAR

BY
MICHAEL G. MANNING

Dedication

I would like to dedicate this book to my family. They provide a lot of inspiration for me, in particular my wife, who often serves as a role model for some of the feistier female characters in the novels. I'd also like to thank my proof-readers. Their input made this a more enjoyable reading experience for all of us. You know who you are.

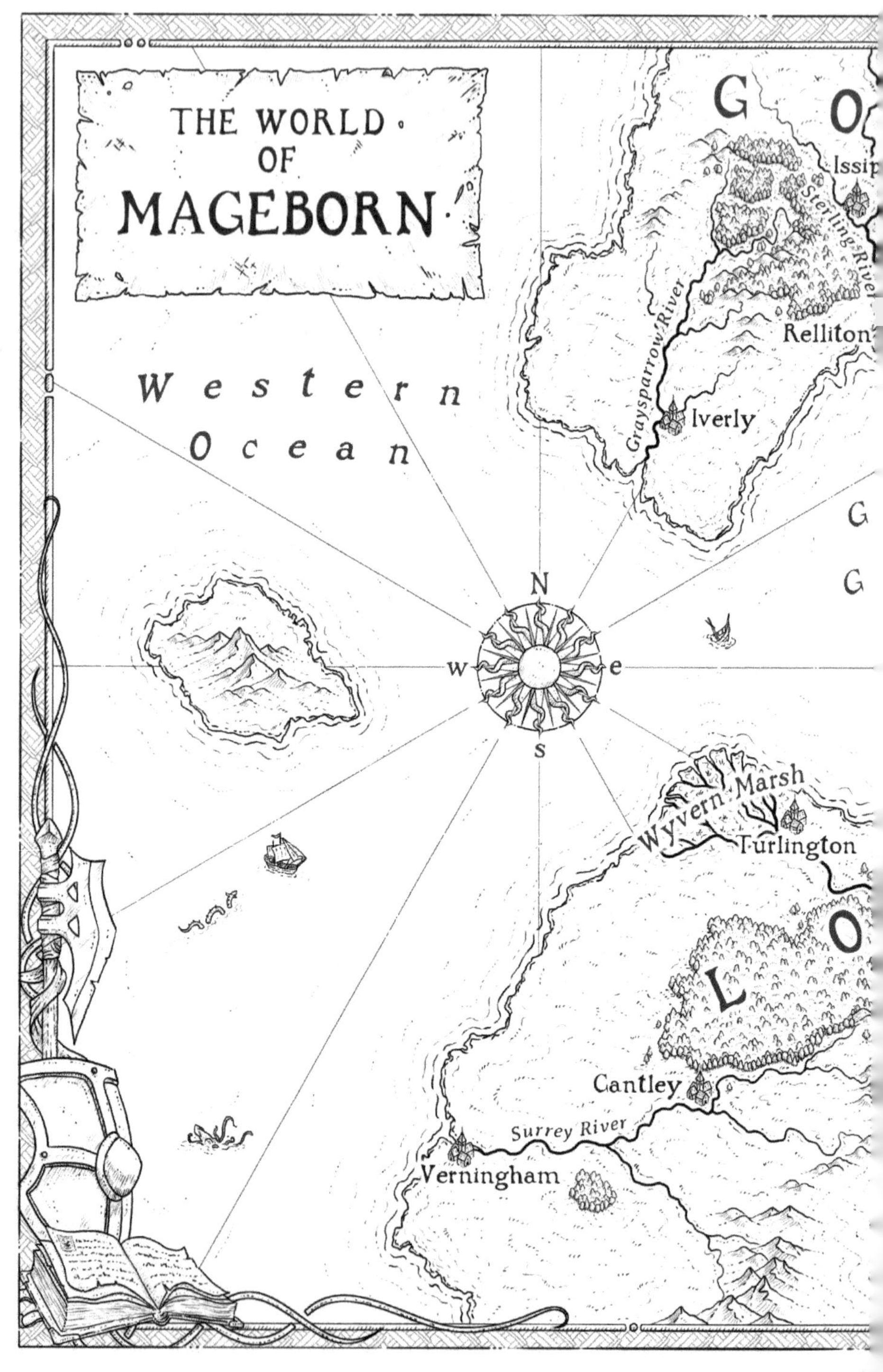

THE WORLD · OF MAGEBORN ·
Western Ocean
Graysparrow River
Sterling River
Issip
Relliton
Iverly
G
O
G
G
N
w
e
s
Wyvern Marsh
Turlington
L
O
Cantley
Surrey River
Verningham

DUNBAR
DODDIN
SURENCIA
Vergil River
Dalensa
Northern
Wastes
of
Ion
Glenmae River
Shepherd's Rest
Cameron
Arundel
Formby
Marsh
Lancaster
Elentirs
Malvern
Trent River
ITHILION
Myrtle River
ALBAMARL
Southern Desert
PLASSE
2015

CHAPTER 1

Storm clouds were brewing to the west, and I could feel the wind drawing them ever nearer to the construction site as I looked down over it. I was standing in the newly completed 'Traveler's Pinnacle.' That was the best name I had come up with so far, though I had no doubt that James or one of his underlings would find a more suitable name for the tower soon enough.

It stood close to two hundred and fifty feet in height with a broad base having its roots atop a massive stone fortress below. To achieve such lofty heights with a wood and stone structure, we'd had to build the bottom floor almost a hundred feet across and tapered it slowly from there as it rose in altitude. Even so, the highest floor was still nearly fifty feet across and boasted a magnificent view from its rooftop balcony. The land could be seen rolling away for miles in every direction. Albamarl was visible in the distance, and the main road went in that direction. Most notably, it was the only paved road that reached the massive construction project that I had named the 'World Road'.

A whisper of wind and damp air brought me back to my more immediate thoughts. Far below the nearby quarry was in a delicate state. Work had begun that might lead to disaster if there was a heavy rain before it could be completed. "Elaine," I said softly to get my companion's attention.

"Yes, Your Excellency?" she said promptly.

I gave her a sour glance. She knew I preferred less formality, and I was not surprised when I saw the hint of a smirk in her expression. She was serving as my 'miellte' today, my watcher or spirit guide might be better terms. The magical remnant of Moira Centyr, the last archmage, was no longer able to assist me. After the birth of her daughter, she had begun to fade, her purpose accomplished. In truth, I was not sure if she still existed at all—I hadn't seen her in years and I left her to her rest, not wishing to disturb her.

"I need to talk to the wind for a bit. Remain watchful," I told Elaine, not bothering to reprimand her for using the formal address. It would only encourage her. I held out my hand and she placed her own within it.

"As you wish, my lord," she replied, dipping her head respectfully. Her soft brown hair had golden highlights in the mid-afternoon sunlight and the wind tossed loose strands of it across her delicate features. Though she didn't have Rose's high cheekbones or Penny's smooth complexion, she had grown to be quite a beauty in her own right, and her freckles had a certain charm. I put those thoughts aside and turned my attention to the sky above—the young woman was practically a niece to me, or at least I tried to think of her as one. I opened my mind to the wind, and soon enough I had forgotten all thoughts of men and women, male and female, as my thoughts were swept up to the rapidly clouding sky.

Drifting, I still retained some sense of purpose and I gently persuaded the winds to shift, guiding the heavily laden rainclouds aside and somewhat to the south of the quarry and active construction sites. A week before I had moved the rain to the north and consequently the south had gotten a bit dry, so I hoped to balance things out a bit this way. As I had discovered, once you began meddling with the weather there were far reaching consequences, the less one interfered the better. In this case though, I had little choice. Otherwise the work would be delayed by months while the quarry workers tried to sort through the mud this rain would make of their recent excavations.

Once I had finished adjusting the weather I withdrew and began contracting my awareness, pulling myself back and rediscovering my limited human self. There was something warm in my hand. I blinked as I stared down at the strange creature standing next to me. After a moment the image seemed to resolve itself as my mind resumed supplying names and labels for what I was seeing. Elaine was standing next to me and the warm 'thing' was her hand. Her eyes were damp, and I could feel a certain poignant sadness emanating from her.

"Are you alright?" I asked, with a voice that seemed foreign to my ears.

She blinked and smiled, "Yes—forgive me. Watching you I find my breath taken away by the vastness of the sky. I could see something of what you felt—the beauty of it is almost unbearable."

I released her hand and patted her cheek fondly as my more paternal instincts returned along with my human emotions. "It *is* unbearable Elaine. You find it so because you are experiencing it as a human—and that is why you have to watch me. When I let my soul drift free like that the winds scour away my human frailties and I become an alien to my own kind. If it were otherwise, the reality of it would destroy me."

"I wish I could hear the wind," she replied wistfully.

"You just did," I answered, referring to her watch over my inner world.

Elaine shook her head, "You know what I mean—directly, for myself, the way you do."

I did indeed know what she meant, but that was one thing I had no power to change. Nor would I have wished to do so. Listening to the voice of the wind, or the earth for that matter, was dangerous. "I am not sure it would be a good thing. Each time I return, I wonder what part of me I may have forgotten or lost this time. Besides, if you were to hear these voices as well, I'd have to find another miellte."

"George will be up to the task soon enough," she reminded me, referring to her younger brother, who had just turned eighteen, "and you still have Father." Her father was Walter Prathion, a wizard and my friend since I had helped rescue his wife and children seven years previously. She and Walter had generously taken turns acting as my miellte over the past few years.

I nodded. "That's true. I'm sure you'll be glad to have more time to yourself, rather than having to follow me around all day," I commented.

Elaine looked downward and her eyes darted to one side in the split second before her face was obscured. "It hasn't been an inconvenience, and I have learned so much under your tutelage."

I had promised Walter I would do my best to train Elaine, and someday George, in whatever I could teach them, but I knew her reply was more than a simple compliment. Elaine was deeply infatuated with me, and I was sure it went well beyond simple hero worship. I also had not the faintest idea how to deal with it.

I stuck with the strategy that had worked best thus far—I ignored it. "Let's go inside. I'd like to get back to Castle Cameron and see if they've reported back yet." Taking quick strides, I headed toward the door leading in and down, pausing beside it until Elaine had caught up with me.

By 'they', I was referring to the latest mission into Gododdin. Since their defeat eight years ago, the population of Gododdin had been decimated by the priests of Mal'goroth. The families of the soldiers I had slain were put to the knife and their hearts' blood poured out on his altars. Eventually this led to a widespread revolt and the theocracy had been overthrown, but they were in no shape to handle the shiggreth when they began appearing soon afterward.

The Knights of Stone, led by my close friend, Dorian Thornbear, had been responsible for rooting out and destroying any hint of the shiggreth remaining in Lothion, and by and large they had been very successful. Unfortunately we hadn't paid much attention to events in Gododdin until it was almost too late. Three years ago James Lancaster, the current King of Lothion, had received a missive from the shaky new government in Gododdin.

The nation had restored the monarchy, putting a man named Nicholas on the throne. Apparently he was the nephew of the last king, Valerius, who had been deposed by the Children of Mal'goroth. By the time James received his message the Kingdom of Gododdin had been largely overrun by the shiggreth. It had begun in isolated villages and had progressed to the point that many mid-sized cities had been completely wiped out before any organized resistance was formed.

By 'organized resistance' I meant the armies of Lothion and the Knights of Stone. The nation of Gododdin was currently not much more than a diplomatic fiction. Initially I had led the vanguard as we swept through the troubled country and our fears were quickly realized. The place was rife with the undead. We moved cautiously at first, for I feared that we might encounter the creature I knew only as 'Timothy', but after months of campaigning we never found a trace of him. I could only hope 'it/he' had died or was still trapped underground where I had last seen him.

The undead we encountered were disorganized, and although dangerous, they were no match for the newly minted Knights of Stone. With my magic and a new arsenal of enchanted weapons that drew upon the power of the 'God-Stone', we cut and burned our way across Gododdin, hunting the fell creatures wherever they tried to hide.

Within a few months the bulk of the fighting was done and half of Gododdin's remaining citizenry were dead. They were cremated in massive bonfires to prevent them from returning or infecting others with their peculiar form of 'undeath'. King Nicholas was allowed to resume control of the country, although James had considered annexing the nation while they were vulnerable. I had effectively vetoed that course by refusing to consider those particular commands valid. It had made things a bit tense between James and me for a while, but he didn't have much choice in the matter.

Today our latest 'patrol' was returning. Patrol was the word we used, but it was a strange choice considering the patrol consisted of over two hundred men along with support, wagons, camp followers, and ten of my hand picked Knights of Stone. It was more of a small army. They had passed their relief, a similar force heading back toward Gododdin, two days ago on the road that led to Castle Cameron. We were still finding more shiggreth, and until we were sure they were all gone, the patrols would continue.

In truth though, the main reason I was anxious to see the returning patrol was one particular man, Dorian Thornbear, one of my best and oldest friends. He had been gone for nearly six months and despite frequent correspondence via my magic letter boxes, I had sorely missed him. Worse still, Rose was beginning to show signs of agitation at his continuing absence, and when that happened Penny soon picked up on it, and when Penny wasn't happy—well you understand what I mean.

Reaching the bottom of the stairs, I opened a door leading into the topmost floor of Traveler's Pinnacle. The room was mostly empty, possessing no furniture and few decorations, other than a tapestry on the wall and a plain rug. Another stair led down into the lower parts of the tower and eventually to the fortress itself. A circle was cunningly worked into the floor as a pattern of darker woods inlaid in the plain golden oak boards.

I stepped into the circle with Elaine and she glanced up at me. I gave her a quick nod to let her know I was waiting on her to do the honors. She already had plenty of practice, but I frequently let her activate the circles since she seemed to enjoy it. I think it might have given her a sense of usefulness, but I wouldn't have suggested it aloud. I felt the smooth surge of her power and our surroundings shifted. We were back in the hall of circles within my house in Albamarl. A short walk put us on a second circle and Elaine took us to Castle Cameron.

The circle in Castle Cameron actually was placed in a moderately sized building in the castle courtyard. Experience in the past had taught me that the circles could just as easily be used by an enemy to gain entry. To minimize the risk, the circles in Cameron and Lancaster were housed in external buildings with a twenty four hour guard. This didn't apply to my house in Albamarl, but it had plenty of 'other' protections.

"My lord!" announced the guard stationed inside the building as he snapped to attention. I nodded absently toward him as we stepped out and made our way to the exit. To my shame, I couldn't think of his name, though his face was familiar. Over the years the growth in the number of my retainers, combined with multiple residences and a busy life had made it difficult for me to keep up with all of their names. I knew it was only natural, but I still felt vaguely guilty about my ignorance.

As we emerged from the building I addressed the guard outside the doors, a fellow whose name I felt relieved to remember. "David, has Sir Dorian's patrol returned yet?"

He had already straightened when I had stepped out. "Yes, mi'lord! Sir Dorian returned early this afternoon," he answered quickly.

"Where is he now?" I asked.

"I am unsure, Your Excellency," he replied briskly. I had to admire the guard's cool professionalism. In his place I would have been tempted to respond with something smart, such as suggesting I should ask the Countess.

I thanked him and headed for the main keep. It was fully repaired now and probably in better shape than it had been ever before. Not that it mattered, since Penny and I didn't really live here anymore. We dined here, we worked here, and much of our daily lives took place here, but one of my most closely guarded secrets was the fact that we slept elsewhere.

Seven years before, Penny and my unborn son were kidnapped and I had never forgotten that lesson. Time and experience, not to mention the removal of one of my enemies had made them safer, but I would never take their safety for granted again. Part of that involved safeguards that no one knew about, things I hoped might even fool the gods themselves if they were to come calling. Some might call me paranoid, but I really didn't give a rat's ass what 'some' might think.

People scattered as they saw us crossing the courtyard, bobbing heads in deference to my rank. Mumbled 'Hello's' and 'Good-day Mi'lord's' could be heard as we passed. I had never required any obeisance from my people, aside from a modicum of respect. As we reached the main entry one of the footmen stationed outside opened it for us. I had many more retainers now. I sometimes laughed to remember the early days, when I had been hard pressed to find even a messenger.

Peter met me as we stepped inside. "Good day, Your Excellency," he said primly. To his credit, not a hint of his deeper disdain for me showed in his voice. Peter Tucker was the grandson of a man I had accidentally slain years before. I had hired him in an attempt to assuage my continuing feelings of guilt. We had never spoken of his grandfather's death and he doubtless thought I was unaware of the connection.

I had initially hired him as a scribe and occasional messenger, but his efficiency and native intelligence had led me to promote him several times. He now served as my chief valet, man-servant, and de-facto chamberlain. I knew for a fact that at one point in time he had planned to kill me, but over the years I suspected that his secret anger had waned. In any case, he did a good job and I thought we had developed a sort of mutual respect for one another. At the very least, I never saw the flickers of anger in him that I had once seen.

"Where is my wife?" I asked without preamble.

"She recently retired to your apartments, my lord," he responded.

I frowned. "And Sir Dorian? I thought she would be entertaining him since he just arrived."

Peter coughed slightly, not from any illness but to signal that he was speaking on a sensitive topic. He continued, "Lady Rose indicated that they needed some time in private before Sir Dorian's more general reunion with everyone. The Countess bade everyone avoid bothering them until dinnertime. She has set the cook to preparing a special feast this evening to welcome him and the other knights."

Considering she hadn't seen her husband in months I wasn't too surprised and I certainly didn't begrudge them their privacy. "Sounds like I should do the same and see my own lady wife first as well," I observed. "I'll be with my family if any needs me, but I'd prefer not to be disturbed until dinner time, if possible."

"Of course, my lord, I will see that it is so." Peter said as he dipped his head deferentially. I moved on, heading for the stairs that led upward to the living areas of the castle; in particular the suites that housed important guests, the Thornbear family, and in theory, myself and Penelope.

Elaine followed closely beside me and I paused for a moment to address her, "You're free for the rest of the day, Elaine. I don't plan to exercise my more esoteric abilities again today."

Her face was a picture of disappointment. "But, Your Lordship, you really shouldn't—I am more than happy to serve," she protested, while at the same time casting her eyes downward. At times her submissiveness was tiring, while at others it was—distracting. She really was a lovely girl.

Girl? Ha! She's grown into a woman. Now, if I could just get her to open her eyes to the wider world around her and realize her own strength, I thought to myself. "I'm sure you have better things to do with your day than follow me around, and I myself am looking forward to some quiet time with my children. Go! I'll see you at dinner," I told her firmly. Turning away, I headed for the stairs, my body language communicating my expectation that she had already acquiesced. Over time I had learned that a large part of the art of command was based upon confidence and learning to project it. Even so, my magesight could see her lips curve into a faint pout as I left her there.

I pushed that thought away and climbed the stairs, my long legs taking them two at a time. I was looking forward to seeing Penny. She and the children were still, and always had been, the brightest part of any day for me. Well most days—I won't lie, she had her bad moments, but then again, so did I.

CHAPTER 2

The heavy oak door in front of me had a guard on either side of it. Neither of them were Knights of Stone. There were too few of them to spare for simple guard duty—even for my family. Instead they were among the more trusted members of my guard, men who would probably be promoted to more senior positions later. Only those who showed potential were selected for this posting. I knew both of them on sight.

"Jerod, Douglas…," I said, to acknowledge their presence. Both of them greeted me and nodded in return. Jerod moved to open the door for me and I stepped into the antechamber of my family's suites, waiting for him to close the door behind me.

Once the door was shut, I moved to the main door, the one that was supposed to lead into our private rooms. At certain times during the day we would leave it open, and any guests we invited into the antechamber could see our rooms. We would also leave the door open for cleaning staff occasionally. The rest of the time, especially in the evening, the door was kept firmly closed—and with good reason.

I lowered my personal shields and placed my hand against the door, allowing the hidden enchantment to recognize me before I grasped the handle and pulled the door open. This was important, for if I opened the door without doing that first I would have found only our mundane and empty apartments behind it. Instead, the doorway opened onto an expansive entry hall leading into my true home, a home I had built in secret, many miles from Cameron, deep within the Elentir Mountains.

Hidden in the doorframe were the runes of an enchantment very similar to the one that made my magical pouches and message boxes function. In this case though, the runes created a much larger portal, one that remained active whenever the door was closed and sometimes when it was opened, but only if the person opening it had been recognized. If the door was opened normally, or if it was forced when it had been locked, the portal would shut down and any would be thief or kidnapper would find only our empty apartments.

The portal was kept active, even when the door was closed, for one express purpose—it allowed us to hear knocks at the door when the staff or a messenger needed us. Thus far I was certain none of the staff had figured out our little secret, although I wouldn't have been surprised to learn a few of them suspected we were sleeping elsewhere.

Stepping into the hall, I took a moment to clean my boots with the brush set there for that purpose. Unlike the castle, Penny was the only person cleaning our private home, and she got rather cross if I tracked mud in. My boots were already clean but I ran the brush over them anyway—she had a sixth sense in some regards, and if I skipped the ritual she would know. I grinned to myself at that thought.

My arcane senses had already alerted me to a small form creeping stealthily up from behind the coat rack, in what should have been my blind spot. Rather than react, I kept to my routine, pretending that I hadn't noticed. Several methods of escape ran through my mind, but I rapidly discarded all of them. Sometimes the simplest responses were best. I waited, seemingly oblivious to my stalker.

After a moment, my attacker leapt upon me in a sudden rush. "Boo!" screamed my son, as he landed firmly upon my back and wrapped his arms and legs around me like some deranged primate.

"What the—holy hell!" I screamed in alarm, as I jumped up wildly, nearly dislodging the small boy on my back. I spun around to exaggerate my surprise, while Matthew laughed and hooted at his victory.

"I got you! You were soooo scared!" he yelled loudly.

I pried him loose and set him on the floor, allowing me to glare imperiously down at him. "I beg your pardon!" I protested, "I am the Royal Wizard and Count di'Cameron, scared is not in my nature." I grinned as I said the words.

"You were scared!" he argued, but there was laughter in his voice as he said it. He knew I was playing. On impulse I snatched him back up and swung him around before planting a kiss on his cheek. He was a gangly boy, all arms and legs, with just a hint of the chubbiness he had possessed in his days as a toddler. Somehow, despite my dark hair and Penny's soft brown tresses, his hair was merely a dark blonde shade.

Before I could set him down another child appeared and charged toward me. "Daddy!" Moira cried, as she slammed into my waist. She began attempting to scale me and the three of us wound up doing an odd dance, as I tried to assist her with one arm while holding onto Matthew with the other. Eventually I managed to balance the load, with one child in each arm, yet even so, their combined weight almost made me stagger as I walked.

I wonder how long I'll be able to keep carrying two at the same time, I thought silently. I hoped it would be a lot longer, but if not I had many ways I could cheat. Magic could be handy.

Moira kissed me soundly on the cheek, and I could feel something sticky on her face. Jam would have been my first guess. She smiled slyly, her blue eyes glittering under wild dark hair, and then she reached over to pat Matthew's arm. "You're it," she declared calmly.

"That doesn't count!" Matthew protested. "I wasn't hiding anymore." His eyes went from his sister to me and back again, as if he was hoping I would rule in his favor.

"So that's why you were hiding behind the coats," I said dramatically, as if a great mystery had been solved. "I'm afraid she's right. You came out of hiding voluntarily to surprise me." I could sense Moira sticking her tongue out at him as I made my ruling.

"You don't win till you find Gram too," replied Matthew, looking past me as he spoke directly to his sister again. Gram was the name of Dorian's six year old son, who I gathered, must be spending time with us while Rose and Dorian were enjoying their reunion. Casting out my senses, I located him quickly. I had missed him at first for he had cleverly hidden himself on top of the fireplace mantle in the nearby parlor. How he had gotten there, without knocking various knick-knacks down, was beyond my wit to understand, nor did I think Moira would ever notice him there. He obviously took his hiding seriously.

I set them both down. "I'll let you two get back to your business. Be careful not to break anything." I worried about what would happen when Gram eventually tried to get down from the mantle, but I felt a duty to keep his secret. Hide and seek was serious business after all. After a bit of bargaining, the two of them split up to search for their hidden friend.

By now I knew where Penny was, so I moved confidently through the house until I had reached her. Entering the nursery, I was immediately reminded of an old painting I had once seen. Actually, the scene that greeted my eyes was better, for this vision included the loveliest woman I had ever met and she had pulled her dress down from her shoulder to expose one side of her chest. The old painting at the Lancaster's had certainly included nothing as risqué as that.

"Obviously you heard me in the hall," I said with a devilish smile, at least I hoped it was devilish. Penny made a face at me as she picked up our tiny daughter Irene and placed the babe to her breast. I responded with a look of mock disappointment, "I thought that was for me."

Penny stroked Irene's soft cheek and cooed at her until she had firmly latched on before responding. Glancing up she gave me a look that held equal parts affection and exhaustion. With a small laugh she replied, "You're going to have to learn to share." I got the impression that particular joke was getting worn out. Given that this was our fourth child, it was impossible for me to guess how many times I had used it. "I didn't expect you back so soon," she added.

"The work is moving along smoothly. Things will probably still get done without me there," I said, giving her my most charming smile. Before I could elaborate, our third child, little Conall, emerged from behind Penny's skirt and latched onto my leg. I gazed down at him with a serious look to complement the thoughtful expression on his face as he stared up at me. After a moment his face changed and lit up with an adorable grin. "Where have you been!?" I asked him with an excited tone.

Conall's warm brown eyes spoke volumes but his mouth only gifted him with one word, "Dad!" The word emerged imperfectly from his lips and then he resumed smiling. Conall wasn't very much for deep conversation yet, but I wasn't in any hurry. Matthew and Moira were already talkative enough for the entire family. I could wait a while longer for whatever words Conall would grace me with someday.

I went down on hands and knees while Conall began to guide me along the floor, showing me his discoveries among the nursery room toys. As often happened, my conversation with Penny was sidetracked while she fed Irene and I tried to emulate an air of serious attention for Conall. The children had enriched our lives in a multitude of ways, yet in others they contributed to a certain feeling of distance between Penny and me, as we found ourselves continually drawn in different directions by their needs and distractions.

A loud crash roused me from my reverie with Conall. There was a distinctive tinkling in the noise as well, a sound almost exclusive to glass breaking. Penny's head came up quickly and her eyes focused on me, "What was that!?" Her sudden movement and sharp tone disturbed the babe in her arms, and little Irene began to cry.

My senses hadn't noted any strangers, so my first thought was of the twins and Gram. "I'll go check," I told Penny calmly, but my magesight had already pinpointed the source of the commotion. Gram had fallen from the mantle. Rising rapidly I left the room and headed back to the parlor. Little Conall rambled along behind me, trying to keep up with my long strides.

As I got closer I could hear Moira crying loudly with a panicked tone in her strident voice. Upon entering my eyes traveled over her. Though I could see she was distraught, I could find no sign of harm to her. I scooped her up, and felt as if a hand were squeezing my heart when I saw her lower lip trembling and the tears running down her red cheeks. She couldn't quite get the words out but she was pointing at Gram, who sat quietly on the floor surrounded by the remains of the large, silvered glass mirror, that had until recently hung on the wall above the fireplace mantle.

Matthew stood beside the younger boy, and though he wasn't crying audibly I could see that something had frightened him badly. There were tears on his cheeks as he looked up at me. "I told him I was sorry. It was an accident! I didn't mean for it to happen!" Matthew told me in a tone bordering on panic.

I set Moira down and turned to my son. "Shhh—it's ok," I told Matthew soothingly as I stroked his hair. My eyes and other senses had already confirmed that the two of them were unhurt so I focused my attention on Dorian's son Gram. "Are you alright, Gram?" I asked him calmly. The boy's features were calm, but there was a certain wildness in his eyes and his face was ashen.

Gram shook his head negatively and his eyes grew rounder, still he remained quiet. I could see that his forehead was damp with sweat and then I spotted his arm. It was bent at an odd angle, and my stomach tightened as I noted the white bones jutting from his forearm. The pain had to be excruciating, which probably explained why he was sitting so still. Even the slightest movement would be agonizing. Despite all that, I had to respect his reserve; Dorian's son hadn't cried out, even though he was clearly in a great deal of pain. The boy was very calm, or perhaps he was in shock, and tears were beginning to well slowly in his wide blue eyes.

"Gram, everything will be alright. I can see you hurt your arm, but it's nothing we can't fix," I said softly, trying to project an aura of reassurance. "Just sit still and I'll try to make it stop hurting. Did any of the glass cut you?"

His head bobbed up and down affirmatively and then he spoke in a whisper, "I want momma."

I nodded, "Of course, and we'll go see her in just a minute, but first we need to make your arm feel better." I brushed some of the glass aside and sat down next to him. He flinched when I touched his arm, but not a sound escaped his clenched teeth. *Just like his father,* I thought to myself, remembering a few of Dorian's childhood injuries. Closing my eyes, I quickly sought out the nerves in his upper arm and blocked them to stop the pain. Gram relaxed visibly when I did, and a long sigh of pent up breath escaped his lips. "There. Does that feel better?" I asked him.

"What happened?!" came Penny's voice from the doorway. As soon as she entered Moira leapt up and ran to her. Matthew followed quickly after. The sight of their friend's arm bones sticking through the skin had thoroughly unnerved them.

Matt and Moira both began trying to explain at once, but it came out in a confusing rush. I interrupted, "Gram broke his arm. Let me fix this and we can sort out the rest afterward."

Penelope had always been quick on her feet, and she took in the situation without batting an eye. Turning, she led the twins toward the doorway. "Let's go to the kitchen while your father takes care of Gram. I think you've both seen enough." Conall toddled after them.

As they left I could hear the children asking whether Gram might die, and I worried that he might have heard them. Sure enough, he began crying as soon as they were out of earshot. "It's alright. You're not going to die. I promise," I said, stroking his hair.

"Please don't take my arm," he sobbed.

Oh hell! I thought. *He's been listening to Dorian's battlefield stories.* The pain hadn't made him cry, but the fear of losing his arm had done the trick. "No, no, no—

Gram, I don't have to do that. It's just a break and I can fix that very easily. No one is going to take your arm," I said, trying to soothe him. "Let's move over there, so we don't get any more of this glass on you, and I'll have your arm back in working order before you know it." As I spoke, I eased my arms under the six year old and began to lift him. He was heavy for a boy his age. Heavier than Matthew despite a year's difference between them. *He'll have his father's build someday.*

I put him down carefully on the divan. Thankfully, the nerve block still seemed to be doing the trick. If Gram felt anything from the jostling, he gave no indication of it. Reaching under his shirt I drew out the pendant he wore to protect his mind from magical influences. Over the past eight years, I had put considerable effort in to making sure that every man, woman, and child had one of the enchanted necklaces. They would enable them to continue fighting, or running, if they came into contact with the shiggreth. "I'm going to put you to sleep Gram, and when you wake up your arm will be all better."

"You won't tell my dad I cried will you?" he asked plaintively.

I gave him an odd look. "What's that got to do with anything?"

"My dad's the bravest knight in the world. If he knew I was a crybaby…," he let the words trail off and he looked as though he might start crying again.

"Gram Thornbear!" I exclaimed dismissively. "Do you think your father never cried?"

He shook his head negatively.

"Well, let me tell you something. Your father cried plenty when we were little, and even a few times after we were grown. Tears are part of life, and they don't make any difference to a brave man. It's what you do that's important, whether you cry over it or not. Do you understand?"

Gram shook his head negatively before replying, "Dad never cries when he gets hurt. I've seen it."

I took a deep breath. "That gets easier as you get older. When your dad was little, he did cry when he got hurt. Now that he's older and tougher he just makes faces and cusses." I twisted my face into a comical grimace and crossed my eyes.

Dorian's son almost smiled but then his curiosity got the better of him, "He cried after he was grown?"

"Yes, but not over an injury," I replied.

"Then why?"

I sighed and tried to compose my thoughts. Obviously Gram needed a full explanation. "Listen," I said slowly, "People cry over two sorts of pain. Physical pain, like the kind you just experienced when you broke your arm, and pain inside, when you are sad—emotional pain. As men get older, they often learn not to cry over physical pain, but everyone cries when their heart hurts, especially good men."

"Why 'especially good men'?"

I hadn't expected this to lead to a deep philosophical discussion, but Dorian's son had always had a somber and serious nature. "Because they care," I told him.

"But why did Dad cry—after he was grown?" Deep blue eyes bored into my own.

It wasn't my place to talk of such things, but Dorian was as much my family as anyone could be, and so was his son. "You know who you're named after, right?" I asked suddenly.

Gram nodded, "Grandfather."

"Well, your grandfather was your father's dad, and your dad loved him just as much as you love your dad. Do you understand?" The memory of Dorian's father brought made my own eyes grow misty.

Dorian's son nodded in understanding and a thoughtful look passed over his face.

"Good," I said, "Now let me put you to sleep so I can fix that arm."

CHAPTER 3

A short while later I sought out Penny in our bedroom. She had calmed the children and set the twins the task of watching over Conall. I had left Gram sleeping after repairing his arm, and by a fortuitous stroke of luck, little Irene had fallen asleep after her feeding. My wife and I were completely alone for the first time in several days.

I closed the bedroom door behind me, and as Penny glanced in my direction, I noted her red rimmed eyes. That was rarely a good sign. Crossing the room, I set my hands on her shoulders and began to knead the muscles there, in an effort to relieve her tension. I waited for her to speak first. The years had taught me that a little patience was often much more productive than fishing for answers.

"Is Gram alright?" she asked.

I leaned forward and set my chin on her head, inhaling the sweet smell of her hair. "He's fine," I started, "It looked bad, but it wasn't anything I couldn't fix easily."

"Thank goodness. I don't know what I would say to Rose if I had to explain that our son had broken his arm," she replied.

I snorted, "Children, particularly boys, do lots of stupid things."

"Some never grow out of it." There was a bit of humor in her voice.

"What did Matthew do?"

Penelope took a deep breath. "Apparently they were playing hide and seek and Moira spotted him up on the fireplace mantle. When he refused to come down, *your* son decided to leap up and grab his leg. You saw the result. Of course, it wasn't all Matthew's fault—Gram should never have climbed up there."

"It did seem like a bad idea," I agreed with her.

She turned, frowning up at me. "Did seem?"

"He was up there when I came home."

"And you left him there?" she said incredulously.

"The twins were excited to see me and I didn't want to spoil their game." Hide and seek was serious business after all.

"You left a six year old up there? Didn't you think something might happen? What if it had been worse?" The intensity in Penny's voice had gone up several notches. I began to suspect I had missed out on some important point.

I studied her carefully, watching her face and body language, while my mind raced to understand my mistake. Over the years, my skill at this crucial marital skill had increased dramatically, but today I came up blank. I returned to my old standby, rationalization, even though my instincts and past experience told me it was a mistake. "We can't protect them from everything, and I don't really think it was that dangerous. They're in more danger climbing that scrawny holly tree outside than they are on a six foot mantle. It was a freak accident."

Over the years Penelope had changed as well. In particular, her temper had softened; or rather she had learned to suppress it better. That wasn't always a good thing though, for sometimes it meant that our problems got swept under the rug instead of being dealt with directly. Her mouth closed and she pressed her lips firmly together before opening again as she replied, with just a hint of sarcasm, "It must be nice to be able to put your fears in a box and examine them so plainly."

"We have different definitions of risk sweetheart, but everything turned out alright. Let's not let it ruin the evening," I added.

A subtle whirl of emotions passed through her. I could see it in her aura and in the faint movements of her lips and eyes. "You're right. I'm tired, and lately everything seems to bother me more than it should." As she spoke, she seemed to almost visibly project her sincerity. If Marcus had been in the room he would have called it 'overacting'.

Taking a step forward, I started to embrace her but Penny sidestepped me. "Let me go clean up the glass first. It's really bothering me." I stopped awkwardly with my arms half out, while she turned and left the room, heading for the broom closet.

Sitting down on the bed, I began reviewing the last few minutes in my mind, while following her progress with my magesight. She had gotten a broom and was now sweeping up the fragments of the mirror that had hung over the fireplace. After a moment she stopped and leaned on the broom. The shaking of her shoulders told me she was crying and I withdrew my senses. Watching was only making me more upset. *Why is she so upset?*

It wasn't the accident. She had dealt with far worse than that over the past few years. That was simply the trigger and the excuse. Perhaps it was the mirror, though that made little sense. I was one of the richest men in Lothion. I could easily buy her another mirror. Where had we gotten that mirror anyway? The question rolled around in my head for a moment before the answer sprang at me like a jungle cat waiting in ambush. *...Her mother. That mirror was one of the few things she had from her mother,* I realized.

Leaping up, I caught her at the kitchen door. It led out to our small garden, and was the preferred exit we used to reach our rubbish pile. She had the glass fragments bundled into a heavy pile within a cloth square. I stopped her by making an obstacle of myself as she tried to reach the door. "Wait, let me have those," I said.

Her cheeks were dry already as she looked up at me. "Mort, let me by. I need to throw this stuff away."

"That was your mother's mirror. I finally remembered a moment ago. Let me have it and I'll fix it for you."

"It would take forever, even for you. It's broken into a thousand tiny shards. You'd never get them all together again. Just let me throw it away. It isn't your fault," she said reasonably. Though she tried to hide it, there was a glimmer of hope in her eye.

I pulled the bag from her hands and she didn't resist much. "There might be a way. Give me some time to think on it. Alright?" I slid my right arm around her shoulder as I spoke and I felt her relax against me. Her own hand snaked around my waist.

"Fine," Penny said at last. "If it will make *you* feel better." There was a hint of amusement in her voice.

"Yes, I think it would. You know how terribly sentimental I am about these things," I answered with a wink.

Dinner was served at the usual hour, but today the keep bustled with increased activity and there was a feeling of excitement in the air. Since the patrol had returned, it meant that two hundred men who had been absent for six months were back home again. The multitude of family reunions as the soldiers reunited with their wives and children made it seem much like a holiday, and in fact, the castle staff was treating it as one. Several pigs had been slaughtered, and my foresters had brought down a few deer as well. The feast would be exceptional tonight.

Penelope stood beside me, dazzling in her beauty. She had spared no effort in her preparations today. Two hours before dinnertime we had returned to our nominal suite of rooms, the part of the castle that we supposedly lived in. The children were gathered up by our nanny, Lilly, and they were now enjoying their dinner in a separate hall with the other children of Castle Cameron. We normally had breakfast and lunch as a family, but the evening meal was usually a more formal occasion.

The woman next to me looked every inch a Countess and I still wondered at my fortune in marrying her. This evening she was wearing a straightforward green dress, but the devil was in the details or in this case the accents. The hem and sleeves were delicately embroidered with dark green leaf patterns, that matched the leaves in a cloth of gold belt that looped around her waist twice at different heights. The net effect was to accentuate her figure and exploit her natural curves. The emerald earrings and the pendant that she wore were simple and elegant but only highlighted the fact that the wearer was, in fact, more beautiful than her jewelry. "Ready?" she asked me.

By that she meant was I ready to make our entrance. Unlike most of those who lived in the castle, we couldn't simply walk in and sit down at the table. We couldn't even be early, for if we were, it disrupted the staff and the routine. Given our position as master and mistress, our arrival signaled the beginning of the meal. Once we entered everyone would rise and wait until we had reached our places. All in all it was a pain in the ass.

Nodding, I took her arm and we stepped out into the noisy feast hall. One of the footmen standing by the doorway raised his voice above the crowd as he announced us, "All rise for the Count and Countess!" The noise in the room died away rapidly, as everyone stood and watched us make our way to our seats at the high table.

Reaching the end of the table I held Penelope's chair for her, before taking my own. The old tradition had been for two servants to hold both our chairs for us and we would sit at the same time, but I much preferred the chance to engage in a bit of gallantry. In the end my stubbornness had prevailed, and a new tradition was born. I spoke as I sat down myself, "Please everyone, relax and enjoy your meal."

The level of noise rose rapidly back to normal, as conversations resumed and the servers began bringing out the pitchers to fill everyone's cups. Our table was long, but it still lacked enough seats to accommodate everyone that might be of a rank to sit with me. I had created twenty Knights of Stone, but since half of them were usually in Gododdin, I rarely had to worry about seating that many knights and their wives.

Since this patrol had just returned, the ten knights who were now back home would be given a few weeks rest before dispersing to their usual posts across the kingdom of Lothion. Each of them had been granted a home and a small allotment of land in whichever part of the kingdom they resided. They lived in those homes with their families during the half of the year that they weren't busy trekking across Gododdin in search of undead monsters. Although King James had been the one to give most of them their grants of land, they still answered directly to me. He and Dorian would accept matters no other way.

Tonight I had Penny sitting at my right and my mother, Miriam, was beside her. On my left sat Dorian, still a bit rough looking after his long sojourn away from home. Beside him was Lady Rose, who almost seven years before had become Lady Rose Thornbear. She was resplendent as usual, in a silver gown. Her hair had been carefully coiffed and piled atop her head, while some of it had been left to spill free in the back, flowing down her neck and across one shoulder. A natural beauty, she was made even more stunning by the fact of her pregnancy, she was quite literally 'great' with child. Given the shine in her eyes and the way Dorian was constantly watching her, I did not doubt the old rumor that many women were more beautiful when pregnant.

Next to Rose sat Sir Harold, the third highest ranked of my knights. Beside him was his wife, Lisette. She had formerly been one of the castle maids, but now she was more properly addressed as, 'Dame Lisette'. Across from Harold and sitting next to Miriam, was Walter Prathion, wizard and these days, Baron of Arundel as well. I had granted the title and lands to him not long after the death of our previous king, Edward. He certainly deserved the reward, and I didn't mind having one of the only remaining wizards in existence as my vassal.

Beside Walter sat his wife Rebecca, now the Baroness of Arundel. Beyond her sat the rest of the Knights of Stone, Sir Egan, Sir Donald, Sir Brian, Sir Daniel, Sir Jeffery, Sir Grant, Sir Lionel and Sir Ian. Only a few of them had families close enough to attend the dinner at Castle Cameron, although two of them were lucky enough that their wives were able to attend. Given the length of the table, conversation wasn't easy. That was probably for the best, since I had forgotten the names of their wives. Penny frequently saved me when it came to such matters.

After everyone had had their cups filled, I stood and looked first down the table and then across the hall. I drew everyone's eyes to me before I raised my goblet and called out to them, "Today we are grateful at the return of our brave soldiers. Let us all raise our drinks in a toast to those who have worked so hard to defend this realm from all who threaten it, and who have risked their lives to protect those who yet survive in Gododdin."

Cries of 'hear, hear!' rang out as everyone stood and lifted their mugs. After several noisy moments, during which people shouted their agreement, I sat back down and the first platters of bread were brought in. A light cream soup followed and the meal began in earnest.

"How is Gram feeling?" said Penny looking across the table to Rose. After his nap we had turned him loose to see his father but we didn't know for sure what he had told them yet.

"You mean his arm?" Rose replied. Her face was smooth, like a still pond with hidden depths.

"Of course."

Rose broke the tension with a smile. "He's fine. In fact, he seems to think that it's magic now, though he wouldn't tell me what sort of fantastic tale Mordecai told him when he healed it."

Dorian uttered a deep chuckle. "A broken arm wouldn't slow him down much anyway; the Thornbears come from tough stock." The large warrior's face had lines now, the product of years spent in the sun. His once dark hair now held a large amount of grey; much like his father, Dorian's hair was turning white early. He also bore a full beard, for shaving was a luxury few bothered with while living on the road.

In my mind, Dorian was still a downy cheeked youth, the friend I had grown up with, but each time I saw him my eyes reminded me that he was no longer a boy. Whenever he returned from one of the long patrols it seemed as though he had aged several more years. It was an unwelcome reminder to me of his mortality.

"I wouldn't have known he was injured if I hadn't seen the bone sticking out," I interjected, "He was so calm and quiet about it."

Rose spoke again, "He obviously takes after his father."

"Speaking of his father, I'm dying to know how things went in Gododdin. I hear there were no casualties this time." The latest question came from my mother, Miriam.

Dorian grimaced, "That is true, but I worry at the cause for our good fortune."

Sir Harold leaned in, "Perhaps we should save this discussion for the meeting tomorrow morning."

"That might be best," agreed Dorian. "I'd rather not start speculating here and create unnecessary rumors."

I nodded, "Your words show wisdom, Harold. Even so, I'd like both of you to meet with me after dinner, rather than wait till morning."

My mother was not quite as content. "Now hang on—when will I get to hear the news?" said Miriam.

"I'll fill you in later," I said soothingly.

Miriam grunted, "You always say that, but later doesn't always come."

As much as I would have liked to argue the point with her, my mother was correct. It was a problem with my new title and station, but it wasn't anything I could fix. Before I could open my mouth to try and apologize she spoke again, "Don't worry about it son. You're the Count di'Cameron, and I am a nosy old woman."

"That isn't true, and you know I value your advice," I said, without a hint of the apology I had considered a moment before.

Having recovered her sense of decorum, she replied, "You're kind to say that, Mordecai." With that she put her attention deliberately on her food and retreated from the conversation. I admired her for her graceful recovery in an awkward situation, but I still worried about her. Since my father's passing she had become more emotional. Penny had suggested that without Royce to anchor her, she was simply showing more of her emotional side to her family (me). I suspected that she was correct. Penny had an uncanny intuition when it came to these things.

The conversation proceeded from there, as Penny and Rose took up the slack in the conversation. Over the past seven years the two had become even closer friends, which was a good thing considering that Rose now resided primarily in Castle Cameron.

"What was that?" I asked. Rose had said something to Dorian, but I hadn't quite caught her words. For his part, my friend looked a bit uncomfortable.

Rose glanced over at me before speaking, "I was telling my husband that it's a good thing these patrols are timed the way they are. If he had been leaving on this one instead of returning, he might have missed the birth of our next child."

The birth of your daughter, I thought to myself. Rose and Dorian had asked me not to tell them the gender of their unborn child, preferring it to be a surprise, but she was far enough along that every wizard that had come into contact with her already knew the sex. "The timing was pure luck, but I'm sure we could have rearranged things if it had worked out differently," I replied.

Dorian spoke up, "If fate smiles kindly upon us, we should see our second child in less than two months." His optimism sounded a bit forced.

"Perhaps if fate were truly kind, you would not need to lead the next patrol," Rose answered acerbically. She looked at her husband as she spoke, but the words were clearly directed at me.

A split second passed as the words hung in the air. Penny had reached across to clasp her friend's hand with an encouraging look. Glancing in my direction she clearly thought it obvious that I would excuse my friend from the next patrol. In fact I had already considered doing so, but the look on Dorian's face gave me pause. Having known him for most of my life I could see that he had no intention of passing his duty on to someone else. I could also see that he had probably already had this conversation with Rose in private. She had brought it up again to put him on the spot, certain that my approval would leave him with no choice but to stay at home.

All of this occurred in one breathless pause, and then I lowered my eyes, rubbing my forehead with one hand to give me a moment to think. Penelope frowned as she saw my hesitation, and of course Rose was equally observant, meanwhile I spotted a flash of hope on Dorian's face. *What the hell kind of man wants to leave his family to pursue undead when he had a newborn at home?* As a father myself, I found his devotion to duty abnormal, and yet I had known he would be this way. It was a large part of the reason I had chosen my friend to lead the Knights of Stone.

If I gave public approval to their plan to keep Dorian at home, he would be in very hot water if he chose to go anyway. Yet, if I ordered him to go, I would face the wrath of Penelope later. Taking a deep breath I spoke, "I cannot in good conscience force Cyhan or Harold to take up an extra patrol at this point. If there are other options I may consider them later, but it will depend upon our meeting tomorrow and on Cyhan's report when he returns in six months."

None of them had expected that response, and I didn't like the look on Penny and Rose's faces. Penny in particular opened her mouth to argue with me before closing it again. She had learned quite a bit of tact over the years. When she opened it again, she had a cooler reply, "I'm sure you have your reasons, *husband*. We can discuss them later."

Dinner was noticeably quieter after that.

CHAPTER 4

Feel free to explain your extremely clever reasons for not putting Rose and Dorian's minds at ease about the next patrol," said Penny, as we closed the door leading back to Castle Cameron. Her expression left no doubt regarding her personal opinion.

Now that we were alone, I had no reason not to give her my real justification. "First I will have your promise that this remains between the two of us," I told her.

"Why?" she asked shrewdly.

I sighed. "If my reasoning gets back to Rose then it will defeat the purpose."

She shook her head in resignation, "At the moment you aren't in her good regards anyway."

I held my ground. "Promise?"

Penny stared at me, "You really don't want me to tell Rose?"

I nodded positively.

"Fine."

"Dorian can't help himself. As long as he feels he could be doing more, he will. I'm just trying to make things easier for him with Rose," I said at last.

My lovely wife stared at me intently for a moment before she replied, "You really surprise me sometimes. Over the years you've learned a lot of tact and subtlety. What really amazes me is that you can be so complex and yet still make so many mistakes." Her face was thoughtful and one of her eyebrows twitched awkwardly.

And you my dear, have come a long way in mastering your temper. Years ago you would have simply called me an 'idiot' and the fight would be on, I thought silently. "You still haven't mastered the art of lifting one eyebrow," I said instead, raising and lowering my right brow to illustrate the point.

Penny smirked. "That doesn't change the fact that you picked the wrong side this time. Dorian is about to be a father again. I know you well enough to know, you couldn't possibly think he should be out in the field rather than at home with his children. You should be trying to beat that lesson through his thick skull, rather than making it easier for him."

She had me, but I didn't intend to admit her point yet. "The danger still exists; otherwise Dorian would not be so keen to find the shiggreth."

"You have many other knights who are capable of managing the task for now."

"There is only one Dorian."

"His children deserve a father, and he deserves a family life," she countered smoothly. "Only he can do that for them. Other knights can lead your patrols."

I crossed my arms, a visible sign of my stubborn intent. "I believe he wants that as well, but I trust his instincts. If he thinks he needs to keep going with them, I won't hold him back."

She pursed her lips, staring up at me. "You'll pay a price with Rose for this. Don't think she'll let you off, now that you've set yourself as the obstacle to her happiness."

"What about you?" I asked.

Her hand slipped into mine and we resumed walking. "I think you're wrong, but it isn't worth fighting over."

"Rose is your closest friend. Will she hold my decision against you?"

The most beautiful woman I had ever met looked at me from the corner of her eye. "I intend to let her think I'm making your life miserable at home as matter of female solidarity. Make sure she doesn't doubt me or I'll make the ruse into reality."

That deserved a kiss.

The next day I met privately with Dorian after breakfast. I had considered having him eat breakfast with us, but Penny had vetoed that idea by telling me that he needed to spend the time with his own family.

Since it was just the two of us, I thought we could use the time more productively if I showed him the progress on some of my projects while we talked. I was too often forced to sit in chairs to want to spend my morning that way. So it was that we found ourselves walking down a corridor leading to a stairway.

As we walked, Dorian asked with a grin, "Aren't you supposed to have a babysitter or some such with you?"

I gave him a sour look to reward his witty remark. "If you mean a miellte, then yes I probably should, but I gave Elaine the morning off."

"I thought you said they were supposed to keep you under twenty four hour watch."

I was beginning to regret sharing some of the information that Moira Centyr had given me years ago. According to her, an archmage with my extreme sensitivity should be monitored constantly, even while sleeping, to avoid unfortunate 'accidents'.

"There are only three other wizards in existence currently. I can't afford to keep them all occupied simply watching me," I replied. Of course I was referring to Walter, his daughter Elaine, and his son George who had just turned eighteen, hardly a good age for the boring duty of following me around all day. "Besides," I added, "I'm not planning to do anything remotely magical this morning, and I thought we might need some privacy for your report."

"I'm sure Elaine was disappointed," my friend replied, with an amused expression.

"Are you planning to tell me about your trip through Gododdin, or do you just plan on reminding me of all my other problems this morning?" I answered, slightly annoyed.

Dorian's brow creased as his thoughts returned to the main purpose for our walk. "I don't have very much to report, which bothers me." As we began descending the stairs leading into the cellars beneath Castle Cameron, he said, "We saw absolutely no sign of any remaining shiggreth in Gododdin this time."

"Which doesn't mean they aren't there," I responded, "since we have no way of detecting them yet."

"You keep saying 'yet', but you've been trying to solve that problem for years now. You should put your time and energy into something more productive."

I ignored the subtle reproach in his statement. "I'll find a way eventually. What do you think they are doing?" I asked. At the same time, I raised my hand and placed it against an unremarkable stone in the wall on one side of us. Hidden runes lit up in my magesight, and part of the wall slid away to reveal a secret corridor.

Dorian followed me through the opening without pause; he had been this way several times before. "I have no way of knowing," he said, as the stone door closed behind him, "but my gut tells me that they've moved north and east, around the Elentir Mountains."

"To Dunbar, eh?" I remarked. Dunbar was a kingdom to the east of the Elentir Mountains. Given the difficulty traversing the Elentirs, Lothion and Dunbar had had little commerce in the past, but historically they had had some trade with Gododdin.

"That's what I'm afraid of."

"James has given them ample warning about the threat. They closed their border with Gododdin years ago. They should be ready," I observed.

My friend sighed. "You know they can't keep them out. There's no way to close the entire border. Without magic and the proper tools they will be overrun no matter what they do." He patted the enchanted sword he wore at his waist. He wasn't wearing the magical plate today; six months on the road had given him a strong desire to avoid armor for a while.

I led him through another door, this one over a foot thick and composed entirely of iron. It opened into a spherical room that was fifty foot across from side to side and twenty five foot from floor to ceiling. In fact, the floor was a wooden platform that had been built across the middle of the chamber. Below the wood at our feet, the thick iron walls extended downward another twenty five feet. We stood inside a perfect bubble of iron, deep below Castle Cameron, a bubble with walls a foot thick.

Dorian gazed around us at the foreboding black walls. Naturally his eyes could not see the runes and patterns etched into the iron, but then again, neither could mine. I had designed the enchantment using a similar structure to the one that hid the secret room within the

Illeniel house in Albamarl, with a few distinct and very important differences.

He spoke again, "You never told me where you got the iron for this thing. It must have cost a fortune."

I smiled. "It didn't cost a thing. The earth itself provided the materials." By that, I meant that I had used my abilities as an archmage to coax the earth into providing the raw iron. I had brought the metal up from the hot mantle miles below us. In a very similar manner to the way a bubble of air rises in water, my iron bubble had arisen through earth and stone before settling here.

Shaking his head in disbelief, Dorian replied, "You could be the richest man in Lothion, no, in the world, if you used that trick to your advantage."

I didn't bother telling him it would be almost as simple to bring up vast quantities of other metals. Though iron was the most common metal, I could easily have produced enough silver and gold to destroy the economy and render the precious metals much less precious. "There comes a point my friend, when money is no longer a goal, just another tool, another means to an end. Besides, my wife and children, and friends like you—I am already the richest man in the world."

"Ha!" he exclaimed, which I took to mean Dorian couldn't think of a good reply—either that or he was simply too embarrassed. After a moment he changed the subject. "You never explained the full reasoning for this massive underground chamber. Will all this iron really protect the 'God-Stone' from the other gods?" God-Stone was the name we had taken to using for Celior's jewel-like prison.

I stared hard at my friend, considering how much I should tell him. I had hidden my true reason for constructing the 'Ironheart' chamber. That was the name

I had given the room when I first demonstrated it to the Knights of Stone. Standing at the exact center of the room, on a small pedestal, was a large pulsing yellow gem. The light shining from it was so brilliant that it was difficult to look at without shading your eyes. It was encased within another stone; an orange citrine colored stone that I had convinced the earth to grow around it. The light emanating from the stone within was so great that it was impossible to tell that it was actually a stone within a stone just by looking at it.

The outer gem collected the excess power from the stone inside it. It also provided the means for siphoning off that power and using it productively. I had broken pieces of it off and mounted them in many items; particularly in the newer swords I had crafted for the Knights of Stone. I had designed those swords to channel the energy they received, producing great gouts of flame upon command of the user. The blades themselves were designed to serve as rune channels. Thus the magical flame they produced could be used to reduce any shiggreth unfortunate enough to encounter them to cinders within seconds.

All of my knights bore the 'sun-swords' now, well— all except for Dorian. His unusual nature, as a stoic, prevented him from activating the enchantment that released the divine fire. In order to prevent the swords being stolen and used against us, I had keyed each one to its owner and it relied upon a tiny amount of the wielder's aythar to activate the enchantment. Because of Dorian's special nature, he was utterly unable to channel even the tiniest amount of aythar.

Returning my thoughts to his question, I considered the iron walls around us. I had told no one of their secret purpose; not for lack of trust, but for fear of discovery. I could not be entirely certain how great the shining gods' information gathering skills were. I believed that they were limited to knowledge gathered by their followers, either directly or indirectly, but I couldn't be perfectly sure. "I thought I explained it all to you previously," I said at last.

He shook his head, "No, you went on and on about the stone and those fancy swords that won't work for me."

"This chamber is completely undetectable when the door is closed. Even the gods could not find it. It serves to protect the hiding place of our divine prison," I said, pointing at the glowing rock in the middle of the room.

Dorian grunted, "I can think of at least nineteen other people who know where it is located." He was referring of course to his fellow knights. I had brought each of them down to see the source of power for their swords.

I smiled, "I trust them implicitly."

"As do I," he replied, "but men are men and tongues will wag."

"It has already been several years, and still they have not come. Either our secret is safe, or the gods fear to confront me," I argued.

"You have me there," said Dorian. "But if they do come for it, do you really want the confrontation to happen here, beneath your very home?"

"I cannot keep a close eye on it if it is kept far away. And I have made preparations to protect our families, you know that."

"Aye, but I just want to make sure you've still got it in mind," he answered, and then his expression changed. "I've been meaning to ask you but I never seem to get around to it." His eyes drifted to the stone again.

"What?"

"Why does it look different?"

"What do you mean?" I asked.

He pointed, as if that would make his meaning clearer. "The stone; it looks different than it did when you first defeated him."

I sighed. "That's easy enough, depending on exactly what difference you are referring to—either the encasing stone, or the overall glow."

Dorian waved his hand, "Nah, I understand about the stone that encases it. You explained that already, but the glow does seem different."

"Look here," I said, gesturing to a small crystalline arrangement of stones that rested beside the central pedestal. There were ten thumb sized stones in a row and each of them had a column of nine small stones beneath it. Currently nine of the large stones glowed with a yellow light. Beneath those nine stones the smaller stones also glowed. The tenth stone was unlit, as were all but one of the small stones.

"You showed me the gauge thing before," he said, dismissing it.

"Then pay closer attention this time," I said with some irritation. "When I first created this device, all ten stones were lit. I call that value '1 Celior'."

"I still don't understand why you measure a god's power using his own name," said my friend grumpily.

"He was the first thing I tried to measure, so I used his name—now listen. The power the stone contained at that point in time I have labeled, '1 Celior'. I don't want the stone to contain more than that, because I don't know for certain how much it will hold before it breaks. So, I use one Celior as the limit beyond which we know that things are no longer safe," I told him.

"So exactly what does it mean, when it looks like this?"

"Nine large stones being lit denote nine-tenths of one Celior in charge. The extra small stone there shows another one-hundredth. That means the total power stored within the God-Stone is currently at ninety-one-hundredths of a Celior, or you could say it is at ninety one percent," I explained.

Dorian smirked, "He's not going to be happy when he finds out you've turned his name into a unit of measure. What does all that have to do with the stone looking different?"

"Well—it changes the brightness and color slightly, though I'm amazed you can see the difference. Most people are so dazzled by the light, that they have trouble seeing small differences," I replied.

Dorian made an odd noise, a sort of 'harrumph', which indicated he wasn't that impressed. "It has never looked particularly bright to me."

He can't see the magical light, I realized. Over time I had learned that some things which were visible to me were difficult for normal people to see, and other things were downright invisible to them. What I hadn't considered, was the fact that because Dorian was a stoic, there might be some things that even normal people could see that he could not. In this case, his utter inability to see any magic at all left him seeing only the most mundane light, produced as a side effect of the concentration of Celior's power. In other words, the stone only appeared to glow moderately to his eyes. As a result, he could see the actual physical stone, while most people couldn't see past the intense glare; even worse he had noticed a difference.

"I forget you don't perceive some of the magical glow that other people see," I told him, in a bored tone that was entirely feigned. "It does look different though, even to your eyes, as the power level stored within it varies over time. I don't know how else to explain it."

He rubbed his bearded chin. "It probably doesn't matter. I just wanted to make sure you had noticed. You know a lot more about these matters than I do, that's for certain."

I smiled and put a hand on his shoulder. "Speaking of matters I know better than you—have you really considered the consequences of continuing to lead patrols? Your wife is not going to be happy if you keep trying to wipe out the shiggreth single-handedly."

Dorian gave me a wide eyed glance, as if I had already betrayed him. "I thought you understood, and I'm not doing it single-handedly. There are always at least nine other knights with me, not to mention the men at arms."

I used my extra inch of height to look down my nose in what I hoped was a paternal glance. "You have one child now and another soon to arrive. What is your greater duty, fatherhood or knighthood?"

He frowned. "Considering I am *your* knight, I should think you would prefer I prioritize my knightly vows over other considerations—and I only go every *other* patrol."

"I'm going to pretend I didn't hear that. We were friends long before I became a noble or you a knight. As a father myself, and as your friend, I cannot help but think you are going about things ass-backwards," I said brusquely.

"If you truly feel that way then why did you tell Rose you still wanted me on the patrols?" he asked suspiciously.

"I know how stubborn you are. I was hoping I could talk some sense into you rather than give Rose good cause to make your life hell." My stare was piercing.

Dorian looked back without flinching. "I want to be here, for Rose, for my children, but I can't rest yet, Mort."

"That's not..." I started to interrupt but my friend held up his hand.

"Hear me out," he said, and once I had closed my mouth, he continued. "I can't explain this as well as you might. You've always had the words, you and Marcus both, but I don't—so be patient and listen." He took a deep breath and stared at his hands before holding them up for me to look at them. "I'm a man of my hands, Mordecai. I don't always know what to say, but these hands always know what needs doing."

Staring at them, I noted for the hundredth time the multitude of scars that marked his large, rough hands. Dorian had had large hands and feet even when we were young, and much like a puppy he had grown into them. Now there was little about him that was small, from his broad shoulders to his powerful legs, yet in my mind, I still saw that awkward youth, tall and gangly, with oversized hands and feet. Time passes too quickly, and in doing betrays us all. My friend and I were no longer children, but men with children of our own.

"They're out there Mort, somewhere, and not as far as we'd like. They know you, and they know me. They know where we sleep and where our children play. They are neither alive nor dead and they will never rest until they have had their vengeance, upon us and every other man, woman, and child alive." He stopped for a moment and then repeated himself, "They will never rest—and neither will I, not until they are dust, or I am."

A long minute passed before I replied, "There will always be an enemy or threat. Once the shiggreth are gone, we will still face the shining gods, and after them the dark gods, and after them—who knows? We can never be completely safe, and if we spend our entire lives trying, then we'll wake up one day and find our time spent and none of it on the things and the people we loved."

The massive man who had grown from my weedy childhood friend, gave a deep grunt and looked at me from beneath dark heavy brows. "Men I can fight, and thanks to you and this sword, the dead as well. Gods and their kin I leave to you. Once the shiggreth are done, I will stay home and tend the hearth, until you command me to rise again, whether against human foes or for some other purpose. But until the dead stay in their graves, I will not rest."

"And if I command you to set that sword aside and stay home?"

Dorian's jaw clenched. "Don't do that Mort. I've never broken my word or vow, but if you force my hand…"

Letting out a deep breath, I stepped forward and hugged the stubborn giant. "I was just making sure my friend. If this is really your choice, I will not keep you from it. We'll find a way to end this quickly, for both your sake and the sake of your children. Until then, I'll take the blame from Rose. I can do that much for you easily enough."

CHAPTER 5

Later, I filled Penny in on my conversation with Dorian. She didn't agree with his decision, or with mine, but we had already agreed to disagree anyway. Over the years the tempestuous woman I had married had mellowed into the most agreeable person I had ever argued with. I told her as much and she responded with a different viewpoint.

"It isn't so much that we've changed, but more that you never seem to change. I've simply given up the hope of reforming you of your stubborn ideas," she explained with an expression that bespoke both affection and amusement.

Sounds like the very definition of 'mellowed', if you ask me, I said silently to myself. *You're just too stubborn to agree with me.* Rather than say that aloud I gave her my most innocent smile.

"Sometimes I'd like to wipe that smug expression right off your face. Don't think I don't know what you're thinking!" She took a threatening step toward me.

Never fearing a challenge, I caught her around the waist and after a few playful seconds I stole a kiss. The moment didn't last however—a cry of dismay erupted as Matthew walked in and saw us.

"Ewww—ugh! Moira! They're kissing again!" he cried. I never understood why he called for his sister at such times, as though she could save him. Personally I think he just liked sharing the trauma.

Moira appeared, followed by Conall, and any hope of a private moment vanished. I gave Penny a mournful look before replacing it with a smile, then I released her and turned to chase the children, threatening to curse them with kisses as well.

***

That afternoon I went back to my rooms and checked the message boxes again. After my first box had proved so useful years ago, I had seen fit to make many more. Of course, so many boxes were inconvenient to carry about, so most of them we kept in my study where I could check them once or twice a day. It had gotten to be a bit of a chore and I worried that someday I might not be present to get an important bit of correspondence, but I had yet to change the arrangement. Just a year past, Genevieve, now Queen of Lothion, had suggested a better solution during a brief visit.

Her idea had been to set up a messenger's office and staff it with a trusted clerk. It was a wonderful idea in my opinion, but I had yet to find the time to make it a reality. I also wasn't sure if some of the boxes should be trusted to other people's hands and eyes. The messages sometimes contained sensitive material, as a result I was still putting the idea off to *sometime* in the future.

As I stepped into my study, I noted two of the boxes had gems glowing on their lids. One I expected; it was the daily report from the patrol Cyhan was leading into Gododdin. The other box was the mate to the one that I had given to Marcus. He was still living in Albamarl and it was handy to be able to communicate with him now and again without having to make a trip to see him.

Taking a seat at the desk, I checked Cyhan's field report first. As expected, it was dry and impersonal, much like the man who had written it.

My Lord,

We are now two days past the border of Gododdin. No contact with locals yet. We should reach Dalensa tomorrow. From there, we will proceed upriver from there to Surencia to make contact with King Nicholas. Everything has been normal thus far.

Your Servant,
Cyhan

I thought about my reply for several minutes before dipping my pen and touching it to paper.

Sir Cyhan,

I've had time to discuss matters with Dorian, and he has convinced me that the shiggreth may have moved north and east, skirting the mountains and heading to Dunbar. After paying your respects with King Nicholas, please continue upriver. Do not bother heading west to check Issip this time. I want you to head for Dunbar and renew our warning to them. If they need assistance, be ready to continue onward and render any and all aid necessary.

Mordecai

I dried the nib of my pen before scattering sand over the sheet of paper to blot any excess ink. Once that was done, I carefully folded the paper and placed it into the box that would transport it instantly to Cyhan. After that I reached into the box that held Marcus' note and withdrew it. Leaning back in my chair I began to read.

Mort,

You need to visit as soon as you have time. Partly for social reasons, as we have a lot of catching up to do. I have been working on a book; part philosophy and part compendium. I hope to lay a clear description out for those trying to understand magic and the nature of reality. When you first started learning about your gift, we understood so little of how things worked. Things that were once common knowledge are now forgotten. Perhaps in the future my book will help to educate someone who doesn't have a tutor.

Anyway, I need to pick your brain a bit. I also need to tell you about the things I have recently discovered. The archives of Celior held many secrets and some of them might interest you. I also found a few things of interest here in your family library.

Marissa would like to see you as well. She wants me to tell you to plan on eating dinner when you come. Try to give me some notice though, so she will know when to cook for you.

Don't wait too long. Some of my news won't keep very well, if you take my meaning.

Your friend,
Marcus

Interesting, he had mentioned the desire to write a treatise on magic before, but I didn't realize he had actually started on it. Some might think it an ambitious project for someone who wasn't a wizard, but I knew how keen Marc's mind was, and he had also had far more exposure to magic than most people. I also wondered if his perspective might make him more objective, considering that he had been one of the rare 'chosen' who had acted as a vessel for one of the gods. Not many men had been given such a rare honor, and fewer still had then later rejected it—none that I knew of, though there may have been others in the past.

His last line had hinted that his news was urgent, and I trusted Marc's judgment. Flamboyant in person, he had a tendency to understate things when he put them in writing. I started a second letter.

Marc,

I'd be glad to join you this evening. Tell Marissa I look forward to her cooking.

Mordecai

I put the letter in the box and went to tell Penny. The thought crossed my mind that she might want to join me. Elaine was waiting for me in the hall outside our apartments.

"Where's your father? I thought this was his day."

She smiled, "He was busy, so I offered to take his turn."

I could tell it was a terrible hardship for her. "Have you seen Penny?" I asked. I was fairly sure already that she was with Rose, but since I had just entered the keep through the portal from my apartment, I hadn't had a chance to locate her yet.

"She and Rose went for a walk I believe."

My mind found the children. The twins and Conall were with Dorian and his son, Gram. They appeared to be attempting to drag my large friend down to the ground in the castle courtyard, much like a pack of hounds on a boar. At a guess, the ladies had left him in charge of the herd while they enjoyed a quiet chat. "Did they take a guard with them?" I wondered aloud.

"I would assume so," replied Elaine, though I hadn't actually meant to ask her.

I decided to check on Dorian. As I walked, I double checked to make sure our youngest, Irene, was with Lilly Tucker. She had helped Penny frequently over the years, first as a maid and then more recently as a nanny. We had debated the subject carefully before we let her help with the children, considering her past. The only other people in the castle who knew of Peter and Lilly's grudge against me were Penny, Rose, and Dorian.

Over the years we had gradually come to trust her, though she never knew that I was aware of their secret grievance with me. Penny had been the one to make the final decision several years ago. "Peter *might* still want to stick a knife between your ribs, but neither he nor Lilly would hurt the children," she had told me. Naturally I had questioned her certainty. "Trust me. My intuition is never wrong. I would know if they were a danger." She had been pointing to her forehead as she had said that, a particular reminder to me that she frequently had visions of the future.

Sure enough, Irene was safely tucked in Lilly's arms as she walked her around the castle nursery. Sometimes it was handy being a wizard. It had taken me less than half a minute to locate each of my children, an ability I imagined most parents would envy.

When I reached Dorian, he was still in the midst of a heap of squirming children. "I don't suppose you've seen our children anywhere have you?" I asked him drolly.

He grinned at me, his face half covered by Conall who seemed to be doing an impression of a hat. "Nah! I haven't seen 'em all day. I've been busy taking care of all these wild animals."

I laughed, "You do seem to have quite a herd of them. Can you tell me what sort of beasts these are?"

"Easily! This one up top is a baby bear. I just found him in the woods earlier today. I haven't decided what to call him yet." As he spoke, Dorian put a hand up to steady Conall, who had almost slipped and was now clutching at his hair and beard. It looked distinctly painful, but my friend didn't show it. "This one is a wolf cub I found last week; I call him 'growler'," he shook his left leg to indicate he meant Matthew. Continuing, he reached down and pulled Gram up from where he was clinging to his right leg, "And this one is a mountain lion I've had for a few months—I named him 'Percy.'"

Gram hissed to display his displeasure at being named 'Percy'. Clearly it wasn't a name fit for such a fierce animal.

Moira was crawling around at his feet so I pointed at her next. "What's that one?"

Dorian reached down to pet her carefully. "Oh this one's not wild at all. This one is my favorite pet, 'Fluffy'. Isn't she just the sweetest kitty?"

My daughter purred and butted his hand with her head.

Dorian Thornbear didn't look particularly warlike as he stood there, covered in children. In fact, with his baggy shirt and crouched posture, he could have been mistaken for a heavyset baker, or perhaps a broad shouldered porter. I doubted anyone could confuse 'Uncle Dorian', as my twins called him, for Sir Dorian, the deadly warrior that led the Knights of Stone.

"That truly is a beautiful kitten you have there," I said encouragingly. Moira let out a loud 'meow', to let me know she approved of my remark. "I hate to disturb you, since you obviously have your hands full," I waved my hands to indicate all the 'animals', "but I wanted to let you know I'm going to visit Marcus this evening. Do you think you and Rose might want to accompany us?" I knew he hadn't seen our mutual friend in almost a year.

My large friend grimaced, "I'd like to, but Rose and I already have a prior commitment this evening. In fact I was going to ask if you'd mind sending us to Albamarl later. We're planning to visit her family in the city for a few days."

Requests such as this were a daily occurrence—so much so, that I had restored the large circle at James Lancaster's private house in Lancaster. Since he had become our monarch, James had little use for the house, so we used it and the storage buildings there for moving goods and people to and fro, between Castle Cameron and Albamarl. It had gotten to be such a frequent need, that Walter and I had set up a schedule, and nearly every day one of us would ferry people and things back and forth between the two circles, usually around noon. The possibilities created by instantaneous travel, and the increase in Washbrook's prosperity, had been the inspiration for the giant World Road project that consumed so much of my time currently.

"I don't mind at all," I answered him. "We can use the circle to my house in Albamarl."

Dorian nodded, "Sounds good, that way Rose and I can at least say hello before we traipse off to see Lord Hightower."

CHAPTER 6

Itook another spoonful and felt a burning sensation spreading from mouth to stomach. In my bowl, the broth looked deceptively tame. The soup was light brown with small bits of meat and vegetables swimming in it. The flavors were delightful, but I was fearful of what consequences might result from the powerful spices it contained. I reached for the bread, hoping to calm the fires in my mouth.

"Is it good?" Marcus asked me. There was an almost hidden smirk on his lips as he spoke.

"Quite," I managed to say. Sweat was beginning to bead on my forehead. I really did like the dish, but I was afraid to admit that its heat might be too much for me. Marissa sat across the table from me, and I didn't want to offend her. She was such a demure woman, her eyes rarely left her plate to meet my own.

"What was it called again?" Penny asked. Her bowl was already empty. As Marissa had been ladling out the portions, Penelope had been honest enough to admit her palate could only take so much spice and our hostess had given her a very small portion. As a result, she was now enjoying the more moderate parts of dinner, while I was still struggling with a bowl full of liquid fire.

"My people call it *dag'n sufir*," Marissa responded modestly. "It is thought to give strength and passion to those who eat it, and because of that, is one of our most popular recipes."

Penny's curiosity was piqued, "I thought you were from Albamarl."

"I moved here after joining the Church of Celior, but I am originally from Agraden," answered our hostess. As usual, I felt slightly uncomfortable at the mention of Celior, since I was directly responsible for the imprisonment of her god, as well as the banishment of his priesthood from the capital. Marc had frequently reassured me that she had come to terms with the reality of the situation, but I still wondered if she might have some secret resentment.

"Isn't that where Cyhan is from?" Penny said, nudging me from my unpleasant thoughts.

Though he almost never spoke of his origins, much less his birthplace, I did know that much about the deadly man who had become one of my most trusted knights. "Yes, at least that's what he told me, Agraden, the jewel of the southern desert." It was known as the 'jewel' of the southern desert because of the large oasis that it was built around. It was a lush, almost tropical city in the midst of an arid wasteland.

I managed another bite of the soup. *If only Dorian had stayed for dinner. I would have dearly loved to see his face as he tried to eat this.* While I considered myself to have an adventurous palate, our childhood friend was entirely the opposite. Dorian had been known to blanch at overly spiced potatoes, and by 'spiced' I meant salt and a pinch of pepper. Marc grinned at me as if he could read my thoughts. Glancing at Marissa to make sure her eyes weren't on me, I mouthed the words '*you bastard*' at Marc.

"Your bowl is almost empty. Did you want some more?" he asked immediately.

"I'm afraid I might not have enough room for dessert if I eat any more," I responded, keeping my face neutral. Marissa's eyes were on me now.

"No need for modesty, Mort! I can tell you want more, here…," he leaned over and spooned the last portion into my bowl.

I briefly considered doing something seriously unpleasant to my childhood friend, but before I could decide on the specifics, Marissa spoke, "I am amazed at your appetite. Even my family limit themselves to one portion normally. Not many can handle such strong flavors."

It was a good bet that *I* could not handle such strong flavors either, but I wasn't about to hurt her feelings. "I may regret it later, but right now I can hardly restrain myself," I told her. "We have nothing like this in Washbrook."

"I could give you the recipe if you like, Countess. Perhaps if you passed it along to your cook he…" Marissa began, addressing Penelope.

Penny interrupted her, "Penny. Call me Penny and don't be silly, if you're willing, you can teach me the recipe directly. I'd love to make it for Mort myself."

"Would you like to help me with the dessert? I can show you the spices I use while we are in the kitchen," said Marissa.

Marc and I were left sitting alone, and I gave him a hard stare. Rising quickly, I took my remaining soup to the front door and used my magic to clean the bowl out, sending the spicy stew down the nearest gutter. He said nothing as I returned to my seat, but his smile spoke volumes.

"No wonder you haven't gained any weight," I commented.

"I love her cooking, but that stuff will scour the very flesh from your bones, my friend. It's a mercy she only makes it for special occasions," he said with a laugh.

"You could have warned me!"

"That would have ruined the fun. Plus, I had hoped we would be able to draw Dorian into the trap as well. I would have dearly loved to see him attempting what you just ate. I'm impressed at how far you made it."

I shook my head in wonder, "You really do have a cruel streak. When are you going to have some children to teach your bad habits?"

A shadow passed across Marc's face. "I'm pretty sure I can't have children, Mort."

"Why?" I said, without thinking. Then I wondered if perhaps his time as Millicenth's avatar had sterilized him.

"I have no idea, but it isn't because of the goddess, if that's what you're thinking. I was taking chances long before that happened, but nothing ever came of it," he replied.

Before he had been chosen by the goddess, my friend had been an absolute plague upon the young noblewomen of Albamarl. If he hadn't taken any precautions then... "Are you certain?" I asked.

"As certain as I can be. Marissa and I have tried, and I wanted to give her a child, but it seems that the fates have decided otherwise. It's probably for the best anyway," he said, with a dark note to his voice.

I didn't like the sound of that. "What do you mean?"

He looked toward the kitchen. "They're returning. I'll explain later."

Marissa led the way carrying two elegant glasses filled with a thick yellow cream. Penny was close behind her with two more glasses. "You're going to love this," said Penny. Her eyes were wide in an expression that told me she had just discovered something incredible.

I accepted the glass that Marissa handed me and was rewarded with a delicate lemon scent rising from it. "What is this called?"

"Lemon syllabub," Marissa replied with a mysterious smile. "You haven't had it before?"

I shook my head to indicate that I hadn't.

"Then you are in for a treat," she said and Penny nodded her head in enthusiastic agreement.

Marc had already started on his, so I saw no reason not to follow suit. Taking spoon in hand, I took a mouthful of the thick, creamy substance and hoped for the best. I was not disappointed. "Sweet mother!" I exclaimed, forgetting my manners for a second. The taste was light and airy, a combination of sweetness with a hint of lemon and the smooth texture of whipped cream. The aftertaste left a sweet tang in my mouth that reminded me of a fine wine. "That is simply incredible! What is it made with?"

Marissa smiled. "I will keep the preparation a secret for your wife's sake, but I am sure your taste buds can identify most of the ingredients."

"Welcome to the conspiracy, Penny," said Marcus. She grinned and winked at him.

"I take it you've had this before?" I queried him.

He nodded. "Yes—and ever since that day, my sweet lady has held it over my head. I fear I have become her slave now for fear of having the dessert plate withheld."

I plied Marissa with compliments for several minutes, but she steadfastly refused to divulge her secrets. Eventually I gave up and the conversation finally turned to more serious matters. "So, what did you have to tell me about? Your note hinted that you had found something important," I asked.

Marc's face grew serious. Rising from the table he gestured toward the parlor. "Let's go sit down where we'll be more comfortable. I'll go get what I wanted to show you. Marissa, would you mind pouring some after dinner drinks for everyone?"

He headed upstairs to the Illeniel—to my—library. Part of the reason I had let him set up house here with Marissa, was because I wanted someone to keep my city home in more livable condition, but the more important reason was because he and Marissa were actively researching the history of both wizards and the gods.

As we moved into the parlor, I motioned for Marissa to sit down. I knew very well where the liquor was stored already. "Let me do that Marissa. Take a seat and relax, the meal you made was wonderful. Let me serve you for a change." She and Penny found seats, and I poured a sweet sherry into four glasses, one for each of us. Marc returned just as I was sitting down myself. I handed him the last glass, and he held out a large wooden case toward me.

"That's what I wanted to show you."

I took a slow sip before setting my glass aside and putting the box in my lap. "Where did you find this?" I asked absently.

Marissa spoke first, "It was in the archives."

"The Karenthian Archives?" Technically the archives belonged to all four churches of the shining gods, but the priests of Karenth the Just were primarily responsible for maintaining them, hence the name. After the battle with Celior, I had acted as a secret stand-in for King Edward for several months, and during that time I had banned the churches from the capital. The archives had been confiscated and the priests forced to relocate. In actuality that meant the archives had stayed where they were—I had just forced the priests to move.

Once James had taken over, he had kept the ban in place, though he had acted to repair some diplomatic ties with the three remaining functional churches. It was one of many things we had disagreed upon, but since he was king and I was not, I learned to live with the difference in opinion.

Marissa had been a church scholar, and a priestess of Celior, which was how Marc had originally met her. Since that time, he had somehow convinced her to change her views regarding the deities that had previously ruled her life. Well, I assumed he had anyway—since she was now married to the most well-known heretic in the kingdom.

"Yes. I stumbled across it locked in a chest in one of the oldest parts of the archives. I don't think it has seen the light of day since the Sundering," she answered.

"That's rather odd," I pronounced, "since it bears the Illeniel family crest on the case." Looking closer, I could see that it had also at one time been warded, though the runes had long ago lost their power.

"From what I could gather, it was stolen from your family. Probably during the chaos immediately after Balinthor's defeat," she added.

"Thank you for returning it then," I told her, perhaps unnecessarily.

Marc broke in, "Don't thank us until you've had a look. I think it may prove to be useless to you."

Penny interrupted, "Do you know what's inside?" She was leaning over from my left side to get a closer look at the box herself.

Marissa shook her head negatively as Marc answered, "We examined it, but it's written in a language neither of us has ever seen." That was actually quite an admission coming from him. My friend hid it well, but his education had been very good. I hadn't thought there were any languages he wouldn't at least recognize, aside from perhaps Lycian. His wife was even better educated in that regard. Much of her adult life had been spent deciphering and translating older tomes into more modern language.

"That's discouraging," I said, and then I pulled the lid away to reveal the interior. Inside was a large square rectangle of some hard black material.

It appeared to be about eight inches wide and perhaps twelve in length, but it was less than half an inch in thickness. The edges were decorated with intricate carvings of leafy vines, or perhaps trees. The rest was covered in delicate patterns that reminded me of letters, but it was difficult to be sure, for they were all connected. I stared at it in shock, and for a moment it felt as though the universe itself stood still beside me, looking over my shoulder.

In my mind's eye, I could see an older man holding it in his hands as he spoke to me. "This is the accord, my son, the binding trust between our race and the She'Har. You must keep it safe." The man was my father, that I was sure of—though he did not resemble the paintings I had seen of Tyndal, nor did he look like Royce. As I watched, the man began to change, gradually transforming into a colossal tree, the size of which I had never seen before.

"What do you think it is made of?" came Penny's voice at my side, and for a second I felt as though I had splintered into two separate people. A whirl of images and knowledge passed through my mind, as though a door had opened letting another life spill into my head. I was caught up in a sensation of drowning, as the visions threatened to overwhelm me, and then with strength I had not known I possessed, I somehow closed the door within.

"It is made of a rare type of wood, known as *Eilen'tyral*, which means 'heart wood' in their language," I said quietly.

Marc looked at me with interest, "You're familiar with it then?"

"Whose language?" added Penny.

"The She'Har."

That got everyone's attention. "How do you know that?" said Penny.

"I'm not sure," I said hesitantly. "It feels like a memory. I can remember someone giving me this tablet." I closed the box, protecting it again from the outside world.

"Wait, don't you want to read it?" said Marc.

I shook my head, "I already know what it says."

"That doesn't make any sense," my dear wife added. I had to agree with her.

"I don't understand it either. I just *know*. I have these—I guess they're memories—of receiving the tablet, of reading it, and I think there's more," I stated uncertainly. Seeing it had awakened something within me, as though I had once been another person, a person with an entirely different set of memories.

Penny's face was set in an expression of deep concern, but she held her questions for a moment. It was Marc who finally asked the practical question, "So what does it say?"

I had already closed the door within, the one that led to those other memories, but I still retained the knowledge of the tablet. "It is a physical record of the first accord between the She'Har and mankind."

"A treaty?" he pressed, wanting more detail.

"Of sorts. They were a civilized race long before we were. This is their original acknowledgement that we were sentient beings. This was their promise that we would be treated as equals. Before this, we had no more legal status among them than a horse or cow does today in our courts," I explained. There was more—hiding in the back of my mind, but I dared not look at it. There was something dark there, something terrible in those memories, and I did not want to see it.

"Sounds as if they were rather full of themselves," Marc commented.

I shrugged. "You have to understand; they were building cities when we were living in small groups in the wild, hunting small game and foraging for food. They weren't even aware that we had language then, we appeared little better than apes to them."

Marissa spoke up, "You sound as though you were there."

"I think maybe I was, somehow, some part of me at least."

Without bothering to wonder at the 'how', she leapt on me with a scholar's question. "You said they built cities, yet no historian today can point to any remains of their civilization. Where were the cities? What happened to them?" she asked intently.

"They were wood. Everything they built was made of wood, or rather it was grown. Their cities were…," as the words left my mouth a vision of fire and darkness rose in my mind. I clenched my eyes shut, hoping to shut out the sight. "Can we talk about this some other time? There's just too much for me to manage at one time," I said softly.

A look of disappointment crossed Marcus' face. "Just promise me you'll write whatever you know down—eventually."

"I'll tell you when the time comes. You can add it to your book," I said simply. I had already turned my thoughts away from the dark memories. I could sense them there, staring at me from the back of my head, but as long as I didn't look at them, I could pretend they weren't there.

"Perhaps," he said. "Things don't always work out the way we want them to. Just promise you'll write them down when you can. You never know what will happen."

"Fine," I answered, "Have it your way."

Penny was not so easily satisfied. "I for one don't like the thought that my husband has some other man's memories jumbled about in his head."

"I have other news, if you think that might help to distract…," began Marc with a mysterious smile.

"I'd love to hear it," I said, grateful for anything to change the focus of our conversation.

"Thought so," he replied. "I've kept skimming through the books in your library and found a mention of the Gaelyn family."

"I'm sure there are more than a few 'mentions' of them. You must have found more than that if you are bringing it up," I replied acerbically.

Marc graced me with a sour expression, "Well, aren't you a wise-ass tonight? As a matter of fact, what I found is a specific reference to the movements of the remainder of their family after the sundering."

"How specific?"

"They moved to Agraden," he said immediately.

"When?"

"Less than ten years after the Sundering," he replied. "They established a large family stronghold there, not far from the oasis city itself."

I looked at Marissa, "Have you ever heard of this?"

She shook her head negatively. "No, but then I have not lived there since I was a teenager."

"Do you think there could be some of them still alive there?" said Penny.

"Unlikely," Marcus said quickly. "The book I found this in was a history of the wizard lineages. The last entry on the Gaelyn family was made by Jorlyn Illeniel over a hundred and twenty years ago. According to that entry, the last remaining scion of the Gaelyn family line died in a fire that consumed their family dwelling."

"I would like to study that book later," I remarked.

Marc smiled, "I left it on your desk in the study. I knew you'd want to examine it carefully."

The study was a private office-like area that was connected to the master bedroom, my parent's bedroom originally. Though I had let Marc and his wife set up housekeeping here, they had decided to leave that room for Penny and myself, since the house actually belonged to me. "Thank you," I told him.

Marissa gave Marc a pointed look and gestured toward us. Clearly there was something else she was waiting for him to tell us. He leaned over and whispered in her ear for a second before straightening and addressing us directly, "Part of my reason for bringing up the matter of the Gaelyn family, is that it coincides with a few other things."

Penny looked at me, and I stared at my friend for a moment before it dawned on me what he must be working toward. I glanced at Marissa. "Do you still have family in Agraden?"

She nodded affirmatively.

"That is a rather long trip and I have no circles there," I commented.

"It's actually a shorter distance than that between here and Lancaster," my friend noted.

"Which is a trip involving good roads with many villages along the way. Agraden isn't even properly part of Lothion, I believe they have their own ruler or some such," I told him. I didn't like the sound of this trip.

"He is called a 'shah', but it is simply another word for king," Marc informed me.

"More than half the journey is through dessert, with no chance of finding a friendly inn along the way," I reiterated.

"It isn't nearly as difficult a journey as you make it sound," he replied.

"You also have to consider the return."

"We plan to live there. Marissa still has a prosperous uncle there who is willing to help us until we get acclimated."

"You're moving there?" I said, a bit more loudly than I had intended. Without realizing it, I had risen to my feet.

Penny's hand was on my shoulder. "It hardly matters Mort. Once you've been there and created a circle it will be just as close as Albamarl."

"I don't have time to travel into the desert right now. I have to oversee the construction of the World Road, and when I'm not doing that, I have to figure out how to root out the last of the shiggreth. All this goes without even mentioning the fact that I have to keep up with *your* father," I said darting my eyes in Marc's direction.

Marc gave Penny an apologetic look. "Would you mind if I spoke to Mort alone for a few minutes?"

She gave him a curious stare before replying, "No, I don't mind. I've been hoping for a chance to talk to Marissa for a bit anyway." I knew there was nothing further from the truth, but my wife had become an experienced noblewoman over the past seven years. She knew how to play the game.

After the two ladies had left the room, I turned back to Marc. "Alright, you can be honest now. There's no way in hell you'd suddenly decide to move to some backwater in the desert. What's going on here?"

My friend's eyes bore an expression of sadness so deep that it sent a sudden chill down my spine. His voice was soft and yet also matter of fact as he answered me sadly, "I'm dying, Mordecai."

CHAPTER 7

My first impulse was to call him a damn liar, but his eyes had already told me the truth. My second impulse was to laugh and lie to myself. Surely he was mistaken. "You're full of horseshit." I included a sickly smile and a poorly executed laugh with my declaration. It sounded pathetic even to my own ears.

"I haven't felt well for a long while now. I couldn't be sure at first, but I've done a lot of research into this…," he started, but I interrupted.

"Research?" I mocked. "You're no physician, and you haven't the first idea what might be wrong."

He drew a patient breath, "I have a very good idea what is wrong. Let me finish."

I sat back and glared at him. "Alright, I'm all ears. Let's hear your diagnosis." Even as I spoke, I was refocusing my senses, searching within him for any sign that something might be wrong. Given my anger, I wasn't at my best, but I could easily rule out any major problems immediately. His heartbeat was steady, respiration normal, all of his innards were in their proper places and there were no large abnormalities, like growths or tumors. I couldn't be entirely sure though. It would take at least ten or fifteen minutes, and a calm mind, before I could dismiss the possibility of more subtle problems. Even then I could never be perfectly certain. One thing that did bother me however, was his vitality, his aythar itself; it was noticeably dimmer than that of most normal people.

"It's called the 'grey wasting'," he said carefully.

I narrowed my eyes, "Did you invent the name yourself?"

My needling finally roused his ire. "Would you stop acting an ass and listen to me!?"

He was right. Taking a deep breath, I answered, "Alright, tell me what makes you *think* you're dying."

"I didn't have any specific symptoms at first, just a general malaise. There was never anything specific I could point to as the source. I thought perhaps it was just a normal part of getting older."

I suppressed a laugh. We were only twenty seven, so I wondered how long that theory had lasted.

He went on, "While she was searching through the archives, Marissa came across a physician's textbook that documented a case similar to mine. The physician was a priest of Karenth, and his case revolved around a fellow priest, a man who had once been 'chosen' by their god, much as I was by Millicenth. On this occasion, the chosen vessel had been occupied by his god for over ten years before Karenth decided that he was no longer needed. In effect the priest was retired from his direct service to the god. Unlike me, he was not declared a heretic and cast out; he simply was no longer needed." Marc paused and took a long sip of his wine before continuing.

"He died a year later at the age of forty two. His friend and physician carefully documented his decline. No cause was ever found. The priest simply grew weaker until one day his heart no longer had the strength to continue beating."

I broke in as he paused, "It has been almost eight years since you and Millicenth parted ways, and that is beside the fact that your story shows no definite connection between the god leaving him and his eventual demise."

Marc lifted one eyebrow and I knew he must have more. "True, by itself that story would be nothing more than an isolated anecdote, but after his friend's death the physician began researching similar cases."

"What was this physician's name?" I asked.

"Thomas of Cantley," Marc replied, "not that it matters."

I didn't know much about medical history and the name didn't stir any memories, so I nodded for him to continue.

Marc began again, "He found three cases of similar circumstances over the previous century, and going even further back he found many more, though they were too remote for him to get much in the way of firm information. Eventually he named the condition *kaltrin atrophie*, which were simply his words for 'grey wasting'."

I drained my glass and stood up to pour another from the bottle. I picked up Marc's glass and topped it off without waiting for him to ask. Turning back I addressed him, "In spite of all that—it has still been nearly eight years, and yet you are still among the living, my friend."

His face took on a sad smile. "One of the cases he documented lasted almost ten years. It bore a striking similarity to mine. The 'host' had only been blessed by the god—in this case Celior, for a period of a few weeks before he was cast aside. In fact, in most cases there was a direct relation between the length of time the person had hosted their deity, and how quickly they died."

Despite my strong urge to rail at him, to deny his argument, I could not help but feel the resonance of truth within his words. As I suppressed my emotions we locked eyes; and in that moment, I saw the degree of his conviction. We had been friends since a very young age, and we sometimes communicated more in a glance than an hour long discussion. He had been studying this for a while, trying to find a way to dismiss what he had found. He had already gone over all the arguments I might present.

"None of those men who died before had a friend that was an archmage," I stated simply.

"Several had friends who were wizards," he replied, "and one of them went so far as to form the bond with the man that was dying."

That surprised me. "Why?"

Marc raised his glass and took a slow sip. "It was a case not long after the Sundering and the man that had been put aside by his god was close friends with a wizard named Samuel Mordan. Apparently, they developed a strong kinship during the war against Balinthor and the shiggreth. Samuel was a notable healer, and his theory was that while the god had occupied his friend, it had somehow damaged what he called the 'wellspring of vitality'."

"I can only assume you mean his body's means of producing aythar," I commented. All living beings produced aythar in varying degrees. It was also the main reason Moira Centyr's living shadow was slowly fading, if indeed she still existed at all. When the original Moira had created her copy, she had given it a fixed amount of aythar and over time it had dwindled. When I had first met her, I had unwittingly provided the 'source' she needed in order to manifest; she had already become too weak to act on her own.

Marc nodded. "If what Samuel, and later Thomas of Cantley, had theorized was correct, the occupation of a living human body somehow damaged the aythar source of the human occupied. Over time, depending upon how severe the damage, the person would gradually weaken as they used up their remaining aythar and were unable to replenish it."

Now I understood the reason Samuel Mordan had formed a bond with his friend. A wizard and his Anath'Meridum shared their aythar through the bond. Samuel had hoped that the bond might provide the vitality his friend needed to survive. "So what happened with Samuel and his friend after they formed the bond?"

Marc's eyes bored into my own. "They both died a few weeks later."

"I have a better idea," I began, but he stopped me before I could finish.

"It isn't your decision, Mort."

I waved my hands dismissively, "I won't risk myself. Listen, I'll create a bond with the earth. That will provide more aythar and even if it fails, no one else gets hurt. There's no reason not to try at least. Hell, I might be able to repair the part of you that generates your aythar. That Samuel person you spoke of was only a wizard. I can go deeper. If I enter your body, as I did with Penny, it might be possible for…"

"No."

"I don't understand."

Marc lowered his head a bit, as if speaking to a child. "You damn well 'do' understand," he said, emphasizing the word 'do'.

"You're worried I'll get myself killed?" I suggested.

"No. You should know well enough that I respect your freedom to do stupid things and get yourself killed if you want to, even though you have a family and children and a hundred other reasons not to take idiot chances with your own life," he answered.

For a second, his rebuttal struck my funny bone and I laughed. "Now you have me wondering at the wisdom of all my past choices."

He smiled. "You're the biggest fool I've ever known, aside from myself. I know you would do anything to fix this, but I'm still not going to let you experiment on me."

"Why?"

"You remember our promise?" he asked suddenly.

I knew exactly what he was referring to—a promise I had forced him to make with me years ago, when he was first struggling to deal with the loss of his goddess. I had made him swear never to take his own life, unless he enlisted my aid. "I thought perhaps you were past that. What about Marissa?"

His face hardened when I mentioned his wife. "I love her Mort. More now than ever, but I can't change this. The pain is still there. I've struggled with it every day, and if it weren't for her, I doubt I would have made it this far."

"She'll be devastated without you."

"She deserves better than I can give her. I can't even give her children."

Something clicked into place as he said that. "That's why you're moving to Agraden, her family is there," I observed.

"She'll need them," he said, "afterward… She's still young Mordecai. She can still have children if she doesn't wait too long."

I glared at him while tears formed in my eyes. "Perhaps you should ask her that. I suspect she'd have a few opinions on that topic you might want to consider! In fact, maybe I should ask her myself."

Marc didn't bother trying to stop me, for I never rose from my seat. He simply said, "Don't."

I growled at him from between clenched teeth, an inarticulate sound without words, a mixture of tears and frustration.

He stood and crossed over to stand before me. "You promised to help, no matter what I chose. You can't stop this, so help me make this easier for her."

I rose and hugged him, hard, and then I answered, "What do you need me to do? It sounds as if you've already got everything figured out."

"When the girls come back, they'll want to know why you're crying. We'll tell them we spoke about your father. Later I want you to support my decision to move to Agraden—for research into the Gaelyn family. I'll also need your help with finances. Relocating probably won't be cheap," he told me softly.

I pushed him away. "I'll help you with the finances, but I haven't given up hope yet."

He laughed, remembering the joke he and Dorian had made of Penny and me years ago, and then he hugged me again. "You've already been a better friend than I ever deserved. Let me do this my way," he answered in a voice thick with sorrow.

Penny returned after a few minutes, but I had dry eyes by then, so we didn't have to resort to Marc's excuse. That was probably a good thing—I'd never had much luck lying to Penny.

CHAPTER 8

The next day I planned to check on the work at the World Road. Most of my work on the actual project was already completed. The runes for the great gates had all been carefully laid and etched into the stone, but I still needed to make sure that the rest of the design was completed properly, before the enchantments could be activated. My best estimate was that the massive construction project would take another year or two to complete all the stonework involved in the design.

Most of that stonework had little to do with the magic itself, but was purely for control and defense purposes. Once the gates had been activated, the World Road would connect even the farthest portions of Lothion, allowing farmers and merchants to get from any part of the nation to its capital, with no more than a couple of days travel at most. It would also allow the king to move troops rapidly to any place in the kingdom that might be threatened.

The World Road itself was actually being built underground in a shape similar to a wagon wheel. The hub at its center was the fortress that the Traveler's Pinnacle was built upon. Circling that fortress was the main road itself, with a circumference of nearly a mile and two thirds. The road bed was built upon dressed stone laid some fifty feet below the surface. To create it, we had excavated a massive trench before laying the base of the road directly upon the bedrock and building the walls of dressed stone. The ceiling was built of massive monoliths that stretched twenty foot across, from one side to the next.

Once it was completed, the entire thing would be covered over again with earth. Hopefully, there would be little sign above ground of where the actual road lay, aside from the fortress at its center. There were two roads that led from either side of the circle to enter the fortress itself, and massive iron portcullises and oaken gates protected the entry ways to it. More portcullises subdivided the road after it entered the fortress. Several others were planned along the main outer road as well, to control the traffic there if an invader ever sought to use it to invade Lothion.

Along the outer circumference of the World Road, were the magical gates that everything else had been built to protect and manage. Each of these massive gates would, when finished, permanently connect to a similar gate near the various cities of Lothion. Those gate destinations would each be protected by a modest fortress, not to mention the other more basic 'structural' defenses I had built into the design.

More interesting, to my mind at least, were the wider possibilities. The structure we were building had room for twenty three gates eventually, but only seven had been designated for locations in Lothion. Someday, given stable enough political and economic conditions, we might open gates to key locations within other nations, such as Gododdin or Dunbar, or possibly even to small city-states like Agraden.

Having seen the effects of easier trade and transportation upon Washbrook and the Cameron lands, I could only imagine what the implications of a larger system of full time gateways might be. My hope and dream was that it would prove to be one of the greatest boons to the economy of, not just Lothion, but all nations. The world of men had been a place of wonders before the Sundering. A world of prosperity, one in which magic was common, and many of the ills of the present were easily handled. The World Road would be a grand step to returning mankind to those days.

Today was almost my first day with George, Walter Prathion's son, as my miellte. At eighteen years of age, he was a tall young man with a slender build and light brown hair. Over the past few years I had spent some amount of time helping him to learn the careful use of his abilities, but I still had my doubts about whether he would be very useful as a miellte. The task required patience and observation—in spite of the fact that it was incredibly boring. Even I could admit that. Following me around all day and keeping an eye on my mental state was a tedious job for anyone. Hell, I didn't even like trying to keep up with my mental state.

Though I hated to admit it, that was one thing about Elaine that made her better suited for the job. Her infatuation with me made it much easier to spend a large portion of her time watching my mental condition. Even so, George was a quiet lad and he hadn't shown too much in the way of youthful recklessness yet. I was quite sure that in his place, and at his age, I would have been a poor fit for the job.

George was trying to inconspicuously pick his nose when I spoke to get his attention. "George, are you sure you want to spend all day following me around?"

He glanced up before answering, with a face almost devoid of expression, "Nope."

His honesty caught me off guard. The boy had a combination of frank honesty and sarcasm that, when mixed together, often left people puzzled. I didn't mind though. I had been an arrogant young man myself once. Most would say I wasn't too far from it even now. "Glad to hear it," I responded with a grin. "I feel much the same way."

His lip twitched into an almost awkward smile, which I took to be a good sign. Without further ado, we took the teleportation circles, and soon we were standing once again in the Traveler's Pinnacle. I led him up the stairs to take in the view from the highest balcony. Before we reached the top I sensed the presence of another person, a guard or messenger at a guess, based on his clothing. Stepping out, we saw the man standing near the edge, taking in the view. He turned back as he heard us on the stairs.

"Your Excellency, I have a message for you from the King," he told us, adding a deep bow of respect.

I gave George a sideways glance before answering, "The balcony is rather an odd place to send a messenger."

The messenger blushed with embarrassment. "I was told to wait for you at the teleportation circle, mi'lord, but I could not resist the urge to look out from the pinnacle."

"No harm done. Anytime I use that circle it is because I am coming up here for a look, so you might as well wait here. The view is certainly a cure for boredom," I said with a smile. "How long have you been waiting?"

"Since daybreak, mi'lord."

"Give me your message then," I told him. Dawn had been three hours ago.

He straightened as he performed his duty. "The King requests your presence at your earliest convenience. Being aware that you might not check the message box until late in the day, he sent me and several others to wait at circles you might use, to deliver that message to you as quickly as possible."

Technically, the King of Lothion didn't have to 'request' anything. Given our long relationship and the fact that I had played kingmaker in setting James on the throne however, he tended to be very polite when it came to ordering me about. Still, his reason must be fairly urgent if he hadn't wanted to wait until I checked the message boxes this evening. I walked over to the stone wall and looked out between the merlons. "Come enjoy the view with me for a moment, and then you can take the circles back to the palace with me. I'm sure you don't relish taking the stairs all the way back down again."

The messenger let out a grateful sigh. The stairs leading up were hundreds of feet in length before reaching the room with the teleportation circle. The final stair we had just taken was less than twenty five feet.

The view was spectacular, as usual.

"I'm glad one of the messengers found you so soon," said James, as we retreated to a private chamber to talk. Whenever possible, he preferred to meet with me in less formal settings. Neither of us was entirely comfortable with the nature of our relationship in public.

Once the door was shut and we were truly alone, I stepped forward, and ignoring his outstretched hand I embraced the man who was something of a surrogate father to me. "Don't be so damned formal," I chided him.

Relaxing, he finally ended the hug with a solid thump on my back. As we parted he spoke again, "I wasn't quite sure where we stood." He was referring to our last argument, over the nature of our 'aid' to the Kingdom of Gododdin.

I gave him a dour look. "That was business, even if I do think you were wrong. We're family after all." Technically James was my uncle, but the relation was through his wife. In reality I felt a kinship to him more because of my childhood and my close friendship with his son, Marcus. "What did you need?" I asked.

James had a curious expression on his face, somewhere between boyish grin and subtle embarrassment. "It actually involves Gododdin. Your knights have done such a remarkable job driving out the undead, that King Nicholas has found the time and wherewithal to make the journey here."

I raised one eyebrow. "He came here? How much warning did he give you?" I had only met Nicholas once a few years back, when we were 'informing' him of our intention to cross his borders to fight the shiggreth. At the time he had been desperate for aid, so permission wasn't a problem.

"Almost none," said James with an audible cough, a sure indicator of his annoyance. "Presumably this was to ensure there would be little chance for assassins, or other enemies to attempt to waylay him. He arrived with only a small escort."

With a light laugh I replied, "That's as may be, but I'm sure he had more reasons than that."

"Certainly he also hoped to catch me off guard; to see what he might learn from an unexpected visit, though he cannot afford to damage relations between our nations. It is a fine line Nicholas walks in arriving here unannounced," James stated bluntly.

"I'm certain he still needs to court your favor, unless he is a fool, and I certainly didn't get that impression the one time we met," I said, by way of agreeing with him. "You still haven't told me how this applies to me," I finished.

James grimaced. "He wants to meet you, to thank you for the work the Knights of Stone have done for his country. He is also hoping you'll give him a tour of the World Road."

"I should have known!" I exclaimed loudly. "I thought we agreed I wouldn't be giving any more 'tours' until next year." I was a bit annoyed. Although I understood the need to show and explain the purpose of the project, in order to drum up interest and maintain firm support amongst the nobility, James had agreed to leave me alone for another year before setting any more 'visiting dignitaries' in my lap.

He held up his hands, "This isn't just any diplomat, Mordecai; this is the ruler of Gododdin."

"Only because I'm still patrolling his borders," I snapped back, "otherwise either the shiggreth would have taken them all, or Dunbar would have annexed them."

James smiled wickedly at me as he answered, "You were the one who wanted to take the high road and restore him to his throne. As I recall, I wanted the support of your knights in claiming Gododdin for Lothion."

I glared back at him, attempting to use the stare Penny used to burn holes in me when she was angry. Unfortunately, I had never come close to perfecting the look. "The Knights of Stone were not created to invade and conquer," I shot back, repeating my argument from years past.

"Then you'll just have to face the consequences and entertain our guest a little bit. It shouldn't take more than a few hours of your time to satisfy him," said the King of Lothion, as he firmly drew his verbal trap shut.

I had been outmaneuvered. "Alright, have it your way. When would you like me to start my dog and pony show?"

"Tomorrow morning, about ten I should think," James said smugly, as if he had known I would agree from the start.

"You already made the arrangements with him, didn't you?" I remarked in a moment of insight.

Marcus' father had taken to kingship as easily as a fish takes to water. With a wink he spoke again, "Of course not! Really Mordecai, you should learn to trust more. I am your monarch after all."

With a sour expression I told him, "I'll see you in the morning," and taking my leave, I stepped outside and collected George. I had left him waiting while I spoke to the King privately. Whenever other people were present James and I had to maintain a much stricter protocol.

As we left, I muttered under my breath, "Wily old bastard...," and George's young ears caught my words.

"What did you say?"

"Nothing," I groused, but my magesight could see George's smile as he followed behind me.

⟞⟝

The next day I arrived bright and early. I had gotten better at being a morning person over the years, but I still found dawn to be a terrible chore. That was quite possibly the very reason James had chosen ten in the morning before consulting me—he had known that anything earlier would be courting disaster.

Elaine was beside me today. George had been scheduled to escort me the rest of the week but everyone agreed that his sister would be a better choice for entertaining a king, and her appearance today certainly held up that belief. She had dressed in an elegant yellow dress that highlighted her shimmering golden hair. Penelope had even gone so far as to lend her one or two pieces of jewelry to accent her appearance.

She might only be the daughter of a minor lord (born a commoner), but I didn't want any foreign royalty looking down on one of the few remaining wizards in the world. Someday I would be gone, and the impressions created by my children and Walter's children would have a lot to do with the places they occupied in the future. I wanted to make sure those were places of respect and authority. The days of wizards being crippled and slowly eliminated by the church were over.

I had spent the rest of the previous day working on improving George's magical prowess. I had planned to take it easy on him, but after my conversation with King James, I had needed an outlet for my frustration. We spent the afternoon using our powers to aid and assist the stone masons working on the World Road. To be fair, I had done just as much work as George, but due to my greater ability, I was far less tired when we finished that evening. In terms of brute magical strength, George fell somewhere between his father and his sister, but he lacked quite a bit compared to either them if you considered their superior finesse.

Elaine and I were in a side room near one of King James' reception parlors, waiting for our summons. We had been there for nearly thirty minutes before the door opened, and Adam, the chief chamberlain, looked in on us. "His majesty is ready for you now, Your Excellency," he told me with a dry tone that concealed any familiarity there might have been between us. Adam knew me from my first stay in the palace years ago, and many times since, but he was far too professional to show it.

I held out my arm for Elaine as I rose from the cushioned chair I had been relaxing on. "Thank you Adam," I responded, resisting the urge to tease the man. We followed him into the parlor where the two kings were seated and enjoying light drinks of fresh pressed juice, by the color I judged it likely to be apple.

"Lord Mordecai Illeniel, the Count di'Cameron, and the Honorable Elaine Prathion, Your Majesty," announced Adam as we entered the room.

Elaine and I bowed deeply, then waited quietly before the two monarchs. Protocol dictated that we were not to speak or approach until we had first been addressed by King James, and acknowledged by his guest, and visiting head of state, King Nicholas. After a very brief but noticeable pause, James spoke, "Lord Cameron, please approach and be welcome." Gesturing toward me, he addressed Nicholas, "Allow me to present the noble Lord Cameron and his companion, Elaine Prathion. Elaine, please come forward as well."

With that final statement she moved forward to join us, though we still held our tongues, awaiting Nicholas' first words. *Etiquette will be the death of me,* I thought silently. A few short years before, I would have had no idea how to proceed in such a tricky situation; fortunately James had trained me well in the particulars of social protocol.

Taking a slow breath, Nicholas finally spoke, "Lord Cameron, we have heard far and wide of your daring exploits. We are also grateful regarding the particular elements of your actions that have saved so many of our people."

I bobbed my head in a second, though smaller bow, "Thank you, Your Majesty. I am honored to have been of some small service to your people."

Nicholas turned his gaze upon my companion. "Elaine, we are given to know that you are the daughter of Lord Walter Prathion and a wizard in your own right. Is this true?"

She lowered her head gracefully, "Yes, Your Majesty."

"You bear your power and position well for one so young," the foreign king replied.

"Thank you, Your Majesty."

James gestured toward several empty chairs, "Please sit and be at ease."

Elaine and I found our chairs and stood beside them. King Nicholas spoke next, "Lord Cameron, I would prefer to dispense with the normal formalities. Please feel free to speak informally since we are in a private setting."

I glanced at James and watched for his nod of agreement before replying, "If that is your wish, Your Majesty. Please call me by my given name."

Nicholas smiled, "Then you must call me Nicholas and no more 'majesties'. James has already informed me that you are his kin, so you should be used to addressing kings with familiarity."

"You do me a great honor—Nicholas," I said carefully.

The King of Gododdin answered warmly, "And you *should* be honored. Were it not for the assistance of your knights, I doubt I would still have a kingdom."

I gave another bow. "I and my knights answer to our king. It is he who deserves your thanks." As I spoke, I glanced at James, to make sure he was aware of the irony.

"No ruler can succeed without the service of wise councilors, and it was your advice, Mordecai, which counseled my decision to aid Gododdin, and your men that acted upon my will. Come sit down. We're beginning to sound like old men, spending our time praising one another," James said at last. He handed me a drink as well before offering another to Elaine.

Elaine accepted the glass while Nicholas turned the conversation to his present desire. "I have been asking

James about the construction project you have been about these past few years. I fear I do not fully understand the workings of magic, but he says you will be able to connect the farthest reaches of your nation with but a short one mile road."

"The World Road will be closer to a mile and a half in length, Your Majesty," I corrected out of habit. *Fool,* I cursed myself silently. One does not correct a monarch idly, even if it isn't your own.

Nicholas frowned, "I thought we would dispense with formalities, Your Excellency." His remark was a pointed reminder that I had referred to him as one would a king.

It was a relief to realize he was chiding me for being formal rather than for correcting him. "I'm sorry, Your—Nicholas. Old habits are hard to break." I laughed inside as I gave that last explanation. If anything, the ways of nobility and royalty were most decidedly 'not' old habits for me, but rather the result of extensive practice and coaching from James, Rose, and Marcus. My true intention was exactly what I had presented, the appearance of a noble having difficulty putting aside the trappings of respect and etiquette.

James was smirking faintly since Nicholas' eyes were on me. He knew quite well how easily I could revert to casual speech. "Mordecai, I have a favor to ask of you, regarding the World Road."

"You have but to ask," I told him.

"Nicholas is curious about our project, and considering we may wish to someday include other nations within its reach, I thought you might like to show him your progress and further explain the details of how it will operate."

None of this was news of course. Throughout our conversation, Elaine had been watching carefully. Her expression suggested that, aside from her youth, her quick mind understood far more about the undercurrents than might be expected. Turning my thoughts back to the question, I replied, "It would be a pleasure. Do you mind if Elaine accompanies us?" I addressed the question to Nicholas himself.

"I can think of no more pleasant way to spend a few idle hours," he responded, before standing and extending his arm to the young woman. With a quick curtsey Elaine blushed and then draped her hand across his proffered forearm.

Less than half an hour later we were back in the Traveler's Pinnacle, stepping away from the circle that Elaine had just teleported us onto. We had also gained a small honor guard consisting of two of Nicholas' men at arms. James had declined to bring any men of his own, stating that Elaine and I, as his vassals, would serve as more than adequate protection. I decided that was probably a compliment.

Staring down from the highest balcony, Nicholas was obviously impressed. "How high are we?" he asked.

"Slightly more than two hundred and fifty feet," I answered in a matter of fact manner.

His sharp brown eyes caught me, "Is there a purpose to such great height? Is it necessary for the magics?"

A good question, I thought to myself. "No, the height is purely a matter of defense, and perhaps some small vanity on my part. For such an important structure, I felt that building the world's tallest tower would be appropriate."

The foreign king nodded to himself, "I see. So what is the purpose of the central fortress, merely defense?"

"In large part, yes," I said. "It shields the central crossroad, preventing those who will travel the World Road from exiting here near the capital if they are hostile.

It will also house the troops that will be vital in protecting the road itself if it should come under attack from without."

"Does a road need to be defended so carefully?" Nicholas asked with knowing eyes. He knew the answer already; he simply wanted to hear my explanation.

James interrupted, "Well of course…," but he stopped abruptly, looking at me. "Go ahead and give him your rationale, Mordecai."

I nodded, taking a deep breath. "The World Road will connect all of Lothion and enable free trade between every part of it. It will revolutionize commerce and become a vital part of our economy. If it were to be misused, it could transport an enemy army from any part of the kingdom to our doorstep in a matter of hours, or anywhere else for that matter. Because of this, the road will have immense military importance. This fortress will control and protect the actual road itself, although there will be only one egress and ingress here, that which leads from the center out to the capital itself."

Leaning out between the merlons, I pointed at the road being constructed below us encircling the fortress, "The road itself will be entirely underground once it is finished. This will prevent those using it from exiting without passing into this fortress first. It will also make possible some of our stronger security measures."

"Stronger measures?" said Nicholas questioningly.

I glanced at James and saw him nod before I continued, "We will be able to flood the entire road if necessary to stop an enemy using it against us." *Or simply a quarter of the road,* I added mentally. There were four stone locks that would seal the road off into sections, allowing us to flood whichever portion necessary, while continuing to use the rest. I didn't feel it necessary to give King Nicholas that much detail though.

In fact, the underground design would allow us to flood the road, in part or in whole, without causing water to spill out into the surrounding countryside—salt water. Four entry portals would connect to matching stone portals in the sea itself; portals that had been sunk to the appropriate depth to allow them to fill the World Road, without causing the water to rise above ground level if we were somehow unable to close them. When we desired to drain the water, they could be sealed and complementary drain portals would open at sea level along the coast, allowing the seawater to rejoin the ocean.

Even more interesting was the second set of portals that were never meant to be used. They were connected to a portal deep underground, one that led to a massive magma chamber. Opening that set of portals would fill the World Road with lava, effectively sealing and destroying it entirely, if our need were ever that dire.

"Your design seems to be extremely defensible," Nicholas noted.

I smiled. "That was my intention. Not only will we be able to seal the road itself and submerge it if necessary, but each gate that opens onto it will be housed within a small fortress at its destination point. The guards at each of those locations will be capable of deactivating or destroying the gate their keep protects if they deem it necessary, to stop an enemy from entering the road."

"No one can fault your thoroughness," replied Nicholas.

"Why don't you take us down to see the road itself, Mordecai," said James to fill the pause. "You really get a feel for the scale of it when you see it up close," he assured the King of Gododdin.

A short walk down the stairs took us to the circle, and a much longer flight of stairs then took us down to the fortress itself. It was unusual as castles go, in that it wasn't built around a central keep. Instead it was built around a large, circular courtyard, with one main gate leading out to the north, toward the Myrtle River and the bridge that led across it to Albamarl. Above the gate was the massive bailey that Traveler's Pinnacle was built on top of. The rest of the fortress consisted of a fifty foot thick wall that encircled the courtyard, punctuated every thirty yards by a small guard tower.

The central courtyard itself held two ramps leading down and under the walls. Those ramps each led a quarter mile out to the eastern and western-most points of the World Road itself, which was underground. Once we had reached the level of the courtyard itself, I led the two kings and Elaine out and down the eastern ramp.

I called it a ramp, but in truth it was a part of the road, paved and leading downward at a gentle grade. We were quickly enclosed in stone, but above our heads were enchanted globes providing a steady glow. The overall illumination level was less than full daylight, but bright enough to read if someone were keen to do so.

Nicholas was already impressed. "Those lights—are those magical as well?" he asked.

I nodded.

"Did you make all of these? If this road travels a quarter of a mile in each direction and then another mile and a half around the circle—there must be thousands of them!" he exclaimed.

"Indeed," I answered smoothly, "though I did not make them all by myself. Elaine and her father and brother have all spent time helping to construct the enchanted globes." In fact, I had chosen the eastern road because the lights weren't finished yet to fully light the western side. George and his father would be working on some of those even as we spoke. We all took it in turns to produce some of the lights, and even so it might be another year before we had finished them all.

We continued onward. The distance along the eastern road was almost a quarter of a mile before we reached the point at which it joined, what I thought of as the World Road itself. A massive iron portcullis marked the ceiling above us about ten yards from where the two roads, or at this point, 'tunnels', met. Nicholas remarked upon it, "I see a portcullis above but no gate. Is that intentional?"

I chuckled. "There's a gate, you just didn't see it." I pointed back along the road we had just trod. "Over here," I said as I walked back twenty yards. "See these two parallel lines?" The lines I had designated were about five feet apart and crossed the entire road. They also continued up each wall and across the ceiling.

"Yes."

"The stone in the floor can drop about two feet and the stone in the walls can recess a similar amount," I indicated the area between the lines on the floor and both walls. "When that happens, the stone in the ceiling slides down at a rapid, but controlled rate, creating a sheer stone wall that fits into those grooves and completely seals the road. That is our 'gate', but we refer to it as a 'lock', since one of its purposes is to prevent water from flowing up this road if we decide to flood the World Road."

"How is it operated?" he asked.

"Well, normally such a thing would be worked using gears and winches, turned by either men or draft animals, to provide the power. In this case however, the weight of that much stone made such an arrangement extremely impractical," I said. *Not to mention that there are far too many of these locks to keep men at them twenty four hours a day,* I added mentally. "Instead, the mechanism is driven by an enchantment I designed, and it is controlled by a set of levers located within the main keep."

I neglected to add certain details, like the fact that there were such locks at both ends of the eastern and western access roads, along each quarter section of the World Road, and in front of each of the twenty three portals. The World Road could be sealed into four separate sections, or even six if you counted the eastern and western access roads.

King James' main stipulation, before committing resources to building the road, had been that it should never become a threat to Lothion itself if an enemy gained access to it. The locks, the flooding mechanism, and even the ability to destroy the entire road with magma, those had been my answer to his requirement. Even more importantly, the enchantments that controlled the locks, the portals, and lighting, could all be activated and controlled by means of levers, providing the user knew the appropriate command words. That meant that the road could be managed and defended by anyone given the proper knowledge, wizard or not.

Nicholas' face grew thoughtful before he asked another question, "I am no expert on magic, but surely these things must take power to operate. Where does that power come from?"

My estimation of Nicholas' intellect went up a notch. I also wondered if he might be hinting at the whereabouts of the God-Stone. After defeating Celior and imprisoning him, I had generally kept the existence of the stone a secret. Some naively believed I had slain him, while some still worshipped him, ignorant of the fact that he was no longer answering prayers. King James and some of the greater peers of Lothion had been informed of the truth, including the existence of the God-Stone, but the general public was still in the dark. It was quite likely however, that Nicholas had learned of it through his own network of informants, which was a polite way of referring to spies working for a friendly ruler.

He had missed the mark this time though; the stone wasn't required in the slightest for any of this. I drew a deep breath before answering, "The lighting doesn't take much power, but you are correct that the locks do take a more considerable amount. What you might not realize though, is that that power is only drawn upon once."

Nicholas frowned, "You'll have to clarify for me. I am no expert in these things."

"It comes down to the basic difference between what wizards refer to as 'wards' and 'enchantments'," I explained carefully. "Both are constructed using symbols that we refer to as 'runes', but in practice they use power in different ways. Wards can be created simply and quickly, but they do not retain power indefinitely, and over time they wear out. Enchantments are made using specific geometric alignments that result in their power being conserved indefinitely.

In the case of these locks' for example, the power built into the enchantment is enough to move the stones and lower the primary gate stone into place, but once that action is accomplished, the power is not lost. Rather, the potential energy that was released as the main stone descends, is stored within the enchantment, and when it is activated again, that power is applied in reverse to raise the stone and restore the wall stones to their position holding it up." I finished the explanation and waited to see if he had any questions and he didn't disappoint.

"That hardly seems possible. Isn't some energy lost during the process?"

Very astute, I observed silently, *someone has studied basic science and engineering.* "That is true, both in normal machines, and in magic, such as the 'wards' I described a moment ago. However, enchantments are perfectly balanced constructs; they store aythar in three dimensional arrangements that can include movement between two states, in this case essentially 'up' and 'down'," I told him.

"The great philosophers say that we live in a world defined by four dimensions, not three," the King of Gododdin replied, in a manner that made me feel as if I had fallen into an academic debate.

I grinned, "You mean time?"

"Yes, time," Nicholas remarked, as both Elaine and James watched our discussion with confusion on their faces.

"You've hit upon the crux of it. The geometric structure of an enchantment is such, that it forces the aythar within it into a state that is independent of the fourth dimension. It is essentially isolated from time itself," I said, with some enthusiasm. I was warming to my subject, and glad to finally have an audience that might understand. I had taught the Prathions the methods to produce some of my enchantments, but they had yet to really understand the underlying rules.

"I didn't think time could be either stopped or reversed…," said Nicholas a bit hesitantly.

"The other three dimensions can be traversed in both directions, there is no reason to think time should be otherwise," I said, slightly impressed with my own logic. I hadn't fully thought the logic through like this before. The geometry and the rules it had to follow had come to me almost intuitively, but until now I hadn't fully understood the implications. *Now the stasis field effect makes sense,* I realized. A stasis enchantment included a physical space within it, and isolated it in time in the same way that other enchantments isolated themselves from the arrow of time. A lot of things began falling into place in my mind, like pieces of a puzzle.

Our conversation died off after that, and so we simply walked, following the curve of the World Road until we reached the first of the portals. It was a magnificent stone structure along the outside wall of the road, a stone arch twenty foot high and twenty foot from side to side. The stones were covered in massive, yet utterly perfect and precise runes. I had etched them there myself, nearly a year ago. A flat tablet set above the arch named the portal's destination, 'Verningham', one of Lothion's three largest port cities.

The archway itself held a flat stone surface, for the portals were still inactive. James ran his hand across the smooth granite. "How long before you will be able to activate them, Mordecai?" he asked, more for our guest's benefit than his own.

"All six of the Lothion portals are capable of being opened when we are ready for them," I responded, "but their respective fortresses are not yet finished. Aside from that, the other half of the road is still incomplete."

Nicholas spoke up, "What destinations will the portals connect to? I see this one will go to Verningham."

"Verningham, Cantley, Turlington, Malvern, Lancaster, and Arundel," I replied quickly. "In the future we hope to connect many more destinations, provided we can establish a significant level of trust."

"I assume you mean Gododdin," he said intently.

"Surencia, Dalensa, Relliton, Issip, and Iverly, are all cities we think might benefit greatly," James added, naming the major population centers of Gododdin.

The King of Gododdin looked distinctly uncomfortable. "I hate to belabor the point, but I'm sure you realize that creating portals in all the major cities of Gododdin would put us entirely at the mercy of Lothion, or whoever controlled the World Road in the future."

You are already completely at our mercy as it is. "The fortresses constructed at each destination serve a dual purpose," I began. "They protect the World Road, but they also protect the region where they are located. Any future portals constructed in a foreign nation, such as Gododdin, would include the ability to deactivate the portal from either end. This would enable you to seal your borders completely if needed."

"Your words are reassuring, as I am sure they are meant to be, but still you must understand the hesitation I would feel; even as I simultaneously thank your country for its recent and continuing assistance with the shiggreth." Nicholas managed to convey a tone of both diplomacy and caution, without giving offense.

James took up the debate at that point, sparing me from arguing over matters of state. "Beyond our historical issues, our two nations have a lot in common, Nicholas, and neither of us had any vested interest in the previous conflict." He reached out to touch the King of Gododdin's elbow in a friendly gesture.

Nicholas didn't withdraw physically from James' overture, but his words did that for him, "You know as well as I do James, the future cares little for our friendship. Politics and world events could easily set us against one another someday, and even if we avoid such hurdles ourselves, we have to think of our future successors. Could I put one of them in such an untenable position, completely at the mercy of whoever rules your nation?"

As the King of Gododdin spoke I couldn't help agreeing with his reasoning. His arguments were entirely valid, but James was not one to give up so easily.

"You make a good point," said James before beginning his rebuttal, "but you fail to consider the impact that this road will have upon the future economies of our respective lands."

Nicholas set one hand to his hip and faced James squarely, giving him his full attention. "Pray continue."

"Once the World Road opens, Lothion will experience an economic boom, as traders, farmers, and craftsmen begin to take advantage of the vastly improved travel and trade between all parts of Lothion. At the same time, Gododdin is still recovering from the devastation wrought upon it by the Children of Mal'goroth, followed by the infestation of the shiggreth," James elaborated.

"I see where you are leading, but there will be more time in the future to rethink the decision, if things do work as you suppose they will," the other king responded.

"There is more to consider than just Gododdin and Lothion," James replied, with hands held wide in a gesture of resignation. "Dunbar to the East will likely be very interested in a method of easy trade across the Elentir Mountains. The city-state of Agraden would also benefit greatly. Beyond those lie the possibilities of trade with nations even further removed. Where would that leave Gododdin? It would be destined to become a stagnant backwater, eclipsed and overshadowed by its neighbors. What option is that?"

A muscle twitched in Nicholas' jaw, and I began to feel an uncomfortable tension rising. The King of Gododdin spoke again, "That sounds uncomfortably close to an ultimatum, but I will answer the question. The choice seems to lie between stagnation, and becoming a vassal state attached to Lothion's rising star. Do not put my back to the wall, James."

I watched the former Duke of Lancaster as he dealt with the King of Gododdin, as a student might watch a well-respected teacher, with a mixture of awe and admiration. Thus far he had dealt admirably with his fellow head of state, but it was his final twist that made me realize that a lifetime of negotiating had given his diplomatic skills a masterful polish.

James assumed a look of great consternation as he answered, "Don't mistake me Nicholas. It has not been my intention to pressure or intimidate. I am simply speculating on the future; and based on my opinion, I have chosen to offer you the first opportunity to enjoy the benefits that this road will bring, *before* offering it to Dunbar." In one stroke he had turned what might have been interpreted as a threat, into a friendly offer. He had also given Nicholas a way to escape the argument without losing face.

A pregnant pause settled on the air as the King of Gododdin mulled over James Lancaster's words. After a few seconds that seemed like an eternity, he smiled and put a hand to his brother monarch's shoulder. "Forgive me for seeming tense James, my remark was ill-considered. I did not mean to imply that you would use such strong-arm tactics against me. Nor did I think on the potential advantage you were kindly offering me. Give me some time to consider it and I will give you an answer soon after I return home."

James grinned and clapped Nicholas upon the shoulder, "A fair answer my friend. Let us leave these matters for now!" Turning he addressed me directly, "Mordecai, I understand you probably have much to see about this day, would you dine with us this evening?"

"Certainly" I answered quickly.

"Bring Dorian with you as well, I haven't seen him in ages," James added.

Nicholas nodded agreeably, "Yes that would be perfect. I have been looking for a good opportunity to discuss matters with the headmaster of the Knights of Stone. It would also allow me to publicly thank him for what he has done already for my people." He glanced at Elaine and added, "Be sure to bring Elaine as well."

Elaine blushed and I began to have an entirely new set of worries. The somewhat young King of Gododdin was still unwed after all.

CHAPTER 9

The dining hall within the royal palace of Albamarl was of such quality that it made my own look rather squalid. Where the hall at Castle Cameron was constructed with dressed granite stone and heavy oaken timbers, adorned only with tapestries and occasionally fresh pine boughs, its counterpart at the royal palace was entirely different. While most of the palace was constructed of rose granite, the constant pink color grew tiresome quickly. Instead, the walls inside the palace were dressed with a variety of different marble hues, and in some places they were wood paneled. The dining hall was no exception, the walls having been covered in white marble.

Though the hall was far inside the palace, windows were cut high along the walls near the ceiling, and panes of thinly cut alabaster allowed a pleasant light in during the daytime. In the evenings, the hall was lit by my enchanted globes. I had replaced the oil lamps several years ago, and the King had been kind enough to deposit a sizeable sum into the Cameron accounts to repay me.

We sat at a long table with James at the head and with Genevieve at his right hand. I was next to Her Majesty and Penny sat beside me, followed by Dorian, Rose, Walter, and Elaine. Yes, Walter had come to keep an eye on his impressionable daughter, or perhaps he had come to encourage a match, I wasn't really sure.

Sitting directly across from me was King Nicholas, and next to him was his chief knight, Sir Barnabas. Beside them was Lord Gerald Winfield, who still retained the position of Lord High Justicer, a position he had had for years. In fact he had been the man to preside over the grievance brought against James by the Duke of Tremont after I had killed his son some seven or eight years ago. *Thank goodness Tremont isn't here,* I thought to myself. That would have been the pinnacle of awkwardness.

Not that I really ever worried about the Duke of Tremont appearing in court. Since James' ascension to the throne and my subsequent rise in prominence, he had effectively retired from dabbling in court politics.

The soup course had already come and gone. Servers were bringing fresh bread and a new wine to prepare us for the main course. I had been told it would feature wild duck and a smattering of small game birds, served with wild grasses and some sort of cream based sauce. I had learned a lot about epicurean delights over the past few years, but most of my knowledge involved the part with me holding a fork. All that aside, the royal kitchens were the best in all of Lothion and I was looking forward to the rest of the meal.

"Where did you get this wine?" Nicholas asked, after a server had replaced his glass.

James started to speak before lapsing into a frown. Genevieve took note and spoke on his behalf, "It's from Turlington, Your Majesty. They call it 'Wyverlin White', because it is accented during the fermentation with a marsh plant that grows in that region." James looked on his wife with visible relief. Though he was a man of considerable charm and power, it was obvious that his wife had many talents of her own.

The King of Gododdin raised his glass in a silent toast to the Queen and sipped it appreciatively. A moment later he addressed her directly, "I must confess, this is the first time I have ever tasted something like this. I am afraid it puts my own gift to you and your husband to shame."

She smiled, "I am sure you are simply modest."

James broke in, "Nicholas brought a wagon loaded with select Dalensan reds, my dear."

I had been considering whether I should attempt to enter the conversation, a chancy prospect when you are dining with royalty, but Lady Rose beat me to it. "I absolutely adore the sweet red they produce there, though I can never remember the name…," she began. I suspected she was lying; Rose had a mind like a steel trap and rarely forgot anything. She was merely creating an opening to continue the conversation.

The King of Gododdin leaned forward to answer Rose's question, and as he did I could not help noticing the silver glint of a necklace at his throat. I missed his reply to her, as the jewelry caught my attention, for it was tucked into his shirt. There was certainly nothing unusual about royalty wearing jewelry, but normally it was openly displayed. Without thinking I let my senses explore, following the chain and examining the shape of the pendant it held.

It was the likeness of a balance, the symbol of Karenth the Just. It wasn't unusual, Karenth had been the most popular deity among some nobility and many rulers, but I hadn't realized that Nicholas was still a devotee. Considering what had happened in his country; the execution of his royal uncle by the Children of Mal'goroth, and the horrors that had followed, I had thought perhaps Nicholas might have abandoned his faith.

After all of that, the dark god had put half the populace to death on his bloody altars. Though the Children of Mal'goroth had been deposed by the revolt that followed, the shiggreth quickly turned victory to despair. If it hadn't been for the intervention of the Knights of Stone, at the behest of the 'godless' Count di'Cameron, there wouldn't be much left of his nation.

I kept my observations to myself and turned my ear back to the conversation just in time to catch Penny thanking Nicholas. "Of course my husband and I are both honored that you thought of us," she said. Her foot jostled mine as she sought to bring my attention back to matters at hand.

Mentally I reviewed the last few sentences they had exchanged and luckily it was enough to keep me from making a diplomatic blunder. "You have me at a disadvantage, Your Majesty," I told him, "for I have nothing prepared to compare to such a gift." Along with a dozen other selected vintages, he had just brought up the fact that he was giving us two bottles of Dalensan Instritas, a very expensive and highly sought after wine, especially since the winery that produced it had been unable to resume production for the past two years.

"Think nothing of it!" he insisted. "It is but small thanks for the blood you have shed on our behalf, and a small apology for the terrible wrong that was done to both our countries." He was referring to the ill-fated invasion by the army of Gododdin. Mal'goroth had forced the war upon them and I had responded by wiping out the entire invasion force, a group of soldiers and support staff numbering over thirty thousand strong. "I would be honored if you would drink a glass on the eve of your annual celebration," he added.

I was mildly embarrassed at his mention of our annual celebration. Since the defeat of the Gododdin army, the people of Lancaster and Washbrook had begun holding a yearly holiday. There was even some sign that it might be catching on with the rest of the kingdom. Given my mixed feelings about the actual event that the holiday was based upon, I tended to avoid the jubilation that went on, but hearing about it from the mouth of Gododdin's present king was even more awkward.

My eyes were serious as I fixed them upon him, "Although the people find comfort in celebrating that day, I take no comfort in what I did. Tens of thousands died that day, and while some might defend my action by saying it was necessary, the fact still remains that I slew tens of thousands. If I could wipe the event from the minds of men, I would, but my guilt would still remain." Penny's hand tightened on my arm as I spoke.

The King of Gododdin looked upon me with something approaching sympathy in his gaze. "Pardon me for reminding you of that day. I had no idea you held such sentiment. As you know, my father was long dead before the attack was decided upon, and I was in hiding. Though you slew my countrymen, I do not hold you to blame. You did what was necessary to protect your people. Those men knew the risk when they joined Mal'goroth's army."

Something in his last words struck a chord in me. "Did they really? I suspect many joined out of fear, and even if they didn't—what of their families? Many more died than just those I slew personally." I was referring to the slaughter of the wives and children of those who died attempting to invade Lothion.

A fire kindled in the foreign king's eyes. "You seem quite sympathetic to those whose only goal was to remove your head from your shoulders. Perhaps you should give yourself more credit. Those men were not entirely innocent. Had they kept faith with the true gods none of this would have occurred."

"You refer to your uncle's death, I presume. Did you know that he exchanged letters with my father?" I asked, a bit tensely.

"I did not," Nicholas answered. "Still it does nothing to change the fact that it was the lack of faith amongst the commoners that allowed Mal'goroth's followers to depose my father and to do such damage to my kingdom. Their defeat at your hands, and the slaughter that the priests wrought afterward, were the catalysts that showed the dark god's true nature, and once it was seen for the unforgivable abomination that it was, the people finally rose up and threw off the shackles that bound them. You may lament your action, but my people would still be in chains without it, and I would not be sitting on my throne." As he spoke Nicholas' voice rose in intensity.

"I am impressed with the fact that you can accept their loss so stoically, yet I have to wonder how much choice they had, and even if they had choice, should people be made to suffer for their gods? Whether you consider it the divine justice of the dark god, or the proper penance for their lack of faith in the Shining Gods—should men and women be put to death for failing to pick the winning deity? It reminds me too much of betting on horse races," I replied with some bitterness.

"Your impiety is well known," Nicholas responded. "Despite your power and opportunities, you deny the goddess that sheltered you before you reached the privileged position you hold today. Having seen Mal'goroth's madness first hand, how can you deny the gods of our people?"

"A valid question," I noted angrily, "I was raised, like most in the vicinity of Lancaster, to revere the Goddess of the Evening Star. Some there still worship her, but I feel a god or goddess should owe their followers the same due a liege owes his vassals. A priest of the Lady poisoned my father, along with the entirety of the Cameron household. That same priest almost poisoned the Duke of Lancaster's household."

"You cannot blame the actions of a single man upon his god."

If my emotions were any gauge, there were sparks shooting from my eyes by that time. "I am certain his actions were ordered by his goddess. She later refused to heal my wife when she was gravely wounded, and action that caused even her greatest champion to forsake her," I said, bringing up Marc's defection, "but that was not her greatest crime…"

"Thus far you have said only that she failed to bless those that already doubted her," Nicholas started, but I was far too incensed to let him continue.

"She resurrected the shiggreth! Is that crime enough for you?" I nearly shouted. The conversation at the table had nearly halted before my outburst, but now a heavy silence lay over the room.

"No one could believe that," Nicholas replied angrily. "Where could you have gotten such an idea?" To his credit, he kept his reserve better than I had; his voice was still at a much more reasonable volume.

"It came straight from the mouth of one of the shiggreth. I'm pretty sure they would know," I retorted in a strained tone.

By that point I was ready to throttle the presumptuous King of Gododdin. In part because he had made me lose my cool and no matter how things turned out now, it would reflect badly upon me. A host of clever arguments passed through my mind, but before I could utter any of them, destiny took a hand and completely disrupted our already tense dinner.

Several of the guards had approached the table at the sound of our argument, ostensibly to be close at hand should one of us (me) need restraining. Given the nature of the guests at our table though, I should have realized that no ordinary guard would dare to intrude on an argument between a foreign king and one of the most influential nobles in Lothion. Once again my peasant upbringing led me to miss something that would be more obvious to the noble born.

Dorian was more observant, as were both James and Sir Barnabas. Everyone else was too caught up listening to the argument to have paid heed to the approaching guards. One stood behind me, looming ominously, while the others stood behind King James, King Nicholas, and Walter, respectively. Before I could do more than feel slightly sheepish at having created a disturbance they drew sharp swords from their cloaks and all hell broke loose.

The second their weapons came clear, a word of power cracked out across the room in a language that even I didn't recognize (it wasn't Lycian), and each of their weapons were limned in a purplish, magical glow, the sort that indicated a spell to enhance the edge. A spell that would allow an ordinary sword to cut through the type of shields I habitually kept around my person.

Without uttering so much as a threat or battle cry, the four assassins struck simultaneously. The one behind Walter drove his sword through the older man's back, sending blood spattering forth across the table while Elaine gaped. It had happened so quickly she barely had time to register their presence before seeing her father impaled.

King Nicholas might have suffered a similar fate but for the loyalty and quick thinking of his companion. None of us were armed or armored of course, dining in a royal hall, but Sir Barnabas never hesitated. As the assassin's blade dove toward his monarch's unprotected back, he surged up from his seat and threw himself sideways; and even so, he was almost too late. The blade was driven off course by his momentum, and instead it cut a bloody swath across his back and side.

James Lancaster was better prepared, and before his foe could strike, he had already come to his feet with a roar, causing his chair to fly backward and throwing his foe's attack out of line, as the man nearly stumbled over the heavy furniture.

The ensorcelled blade driving toward my back had a clear path, and while my senses had registered it, my surprise had slowed my reactions far too much. Penny's eyes were caught by the spectacle playing out with King Nicholas across the table from us, for she had been caught just as off-guard as I was. The assassins had played their hand well. They had prepared and executed their scheme flawlessly, and if the universe were fair, I would have been skewered by the blade coming at me.

The universe isn't fair however. I can attest to that after the many trials I have endured. Although I had been caught with my proverbial pants down, I had already stacked the deck; for the man sitting beside Penny was Dorian Thornbear. I could give a ten minute description of how acutely deadly my dear friend is, but in the end, his deeds have always been the best testimony, so I won't bother.

The first sound I noticed was a crack, rather like thunder. I discovered later that it had been caused by Dorian's chair breaking into several pieces after it struck a marble pillar positioned a good ten feet behind where he had been sitting. That was how violently he had arisen.

Dorian was of course, completely unarmed, just like the rest of us, and dressed in a lovely outfit that consisted primarily of maroon satin and soft doe-hide; yet none of that mattered in the least. He managed to cross a distance of some four or five feet in the space of a heartbeat, and his hand swept up, catching the assassin's arm by the wrist, and sending the sword clattering to one side, as the man's wrist broke.

The would-be killer gasped as Dorian's hand crushed his forearm, but he was committed to his task. With his free hand, he reached for the dagger at his waist; probably hoping to gut Dorian. He never got the chance. Stepping forward, Dorian's right hand caught the man's face as his heel slipped behind the assassin's foot. Thrusting out and downward he slammed the killer's head against the floor with such force, that it cracked the marble tiles even as it crushed the back of the man's skull.

Those events passed in the amount of time it took me to stand and take in what was occurring around me. Nicholas had tumbled from his chair as Sir Barnabas fell over him, and both men wound up tangled on the floor. It seemed unlikely either of them would recover in time to avoid their attacker's next stroke. Meanwhile, I was caught by the vision of Elaine's beautiful face, as her mouth formed an 'O' of horror and surprise, and I could see several drops of her father's blood on her cheek. The assassin's sword was now rising above her. I doubted she would rouse herself from her shock in time.

"Borok Ingak!" I shouted. It wasn't the best spell I could have used, but I hadn't had the luxury of much time to carefully consider my choices. It was the same spell I had used in the past to shatter doors and destroy gates. The poor bastard standing over Elaine disappeared, as a force

similar to an invisible battering ram sent him flying across the room to fetch up against the far wall.

Glancing to the side, I discovered that Penny had fallen into bad habits again. While she had initially been taken by surprise just as I had, she recovered from it quickly. She had leapt across the table, and snatching up a platter full of duck and other succulent fowl, she flung it into the face of the assassin attempting to take King Nicholas' life. Her opponent side-stepped the makeshift missile and reacted by throwing a dagger toward her.

The bastard's reflexes were fast. He had snatched the dagger from his belt so quickly, I barely saw the action. If he had been aiming at some dowager duchess or helpless damsel, it might have caused serious harm. My Penny has been described as many things, but it had been a long time since anyone called her a 'helpless damsel'; today was no exception. The silver platter was still in her hands and she deftly swatted the blade from the air before charging forward to engage the man in direct 'platter to sword' combat.

She was fighting a man with excellent sword skills and superior strength, for she was no longer my Anath'Meridum. On a good day, I might have given him a fifty-fifty chance, but only because he was armed, and her weapon was a makeshift serving platter. Penny had continued to make it a habit of practicing with the soldiers of Castle Cameron, until I had insisted that she stop. It wasn't really becoming to have the Countess di'Cameron drilling in the yard with the men at arms. She hadn't given up though, and she continued to practice in private with Harold, Cyhan, or Dorian when they were at the keep.

I spotted Dorian as he was about to intervene, for he had already dismembered the remaining assassin, the one that had threatened King James. Holding up a hand, I signaled for him to wait rather than interfere. "She's got this," I told him. I secretly worried she might not, but I didn't want to be the one to steal her glory. Instead I watched carefully, that I might intervene if things went badly.

We needn't have worried; in the span of less than a minute she had completely demoralized her opponent. The fight was over when she slammed the edge of the platter into the bridge of his nose, sending blood spurting forth while he collapsed on the floor. All told the entirety of the fight, from the moment of surprise until Penny's victory, was less than a minute and a half.

King James was surrounded by armed guardsmen now, as was King Nicholas, but if there were more assassins, they had chosen not to make their presence known. "Stand aside," James yelled at two of his bodyguards who were obstructing his view of the room. "Who were these men? I want names! I want answers!" He was pointing at the recently deceased men, who were all conveniently clad in his own arms and livery.

Ignoring the uproar and interrogation, I went to my friend Walter first. Even without using my senses, I could see he was quite clearly dead, the sword had passed completely through him and my magesight confirmed that his heart had been neatly pierced. He had died almost instantly.

Elaine was still in a state of disbelief, but as I approached, her eyes lit up with hope. "You've got to save him! He's dying!" They were the words of a desperate child, unable to accept what was plainly in front of her.

"Go help Sir Barnabas. I'll see to your father," I told her, with a calm that I didn't truly feel.

"No, we can save him," she repeated stubbornly.

"Know your limits. Tend to the man you can aid, so that I can see to Walter," I said harshly. She hesitated, but

I was devoid of sympathy. "Now!" I barked in a tone of cold authority. I was doubtful that anything could be done, but if it could, I wouldn't be able to manage it with her crying over my shoulder.

Her face blanched at my sharp words, but she rose and did as I had ordered. I took her place beside Walter and began a more thorough examination of his body, both within and without. It was as bad as my first impression had suggested. His heart had been seriously damaged and it had probably been more than a minute since it last beat. I looked upward and found Penny standing beside me. "Make sure no one disturbs me," I told her. "If I don't awaken on my own within a few minutes, or if I stop breathing, let Elaine try to wake me."

Penelope's eyes locked on my own for a brief but intense moment. I saw fear and doubt within them, but she merely nodded.

Stretching myself out upon the cold marble floor, I drew Walter's still form close beside me, and then I closed my eyes. Letting my mind expand beyond my own body, I tried to focus my awareness on the still shape lying next to me. *It has to have been nearly two minutes since the sword passed through him*, I thought for second, and then I pushed those thoughts aside.

For a moment I felt myself failing, I couldn't force myself into Walter's dead body. *I have to listen.* Stilling my inner turmoil, I let go of my doubts, and soon I began to hear the song that was Walter's physical form; and within it, the melody of his now dwindling spirit. I had once sent my mind into Penny's unconscious form when she was dying, but this was different. I wasn't simply entering his body; I was assimilating it within myself. In part it was necessary, for Walter was no longer truly attached to the flesh and bone that had housed him for so long.

Somehow I had to assume responsibility for his corpse long enough to reanimate it, and simultaneously I needed to keep the spark that was truly Walter from departing before I was done. It was a task that defied conscious thought, which was the very reason that the waking rational mind was incapable of such a task.

Searing cold tore through me, my heart was no longer beating, my blood was cooling, and around me I could sense little more than darkness. I had become a flame, a burning light in an endless void, and yet I could still feel the dying flesh around me. In the distance there was another light, but it was flickering, drawn away as if caught in an inexorable and frigid wind.

No.

Pushing—I expanded, a searing light flaring within an empty hall, and the darkness receded. Pain tore through me; the sensation of a torn back and hopelessly damaged heart. I was driving his heart to beat, forcing his blood to move, while my thoughts were like fire along his damaged nerves. I imagined his heart whole and I felt the flesh knitting as his body struggled to conform to the imposition of my will.

Even as his body mended I could see the light that was Walter receding. He wavered, on the verge of going out. Reaching out I tried to grasp him, but the distance between us seemed impossibly great. I was holding two bodies now, his and my own, and the effort to keep them both alive was greater than I had imagined. While the effort in terms of pure power was negligible, the complexity of the human body is staggering. All the things our bodies normally do automatically, I was attempting to do deliberately, for him as well as for myself.

In the end I failed—but I refused to accept defeat. Instead, I released my own form and took up sole residence within Walter's, letting my instincts keep his body alive, while I bent my conscious will toward the tiny light that was almost gone now. *Goddamnit! You will not be allowed to go quietly. Come back!*

There was a sense of connection then, and I felt Walter's mind respond for the first time, with a bewildering rush of fear and confusion. We were standing together at the edge of the abyss; a place where light twisted and turned, taking another direction—transforming into something so dark I couldn't see it directly. It reminded me of the shiggreth. *The void—this is the void, the place from whence they have returned.* Even as that thought struck me, I could see myself eroding, as the source of my own light began to lose coherence. *How did they survive this?*

I had no time for wondering though, using the connection we had somehow forged I drew Walter away, pulling and dragging him with all the energy I had left to me. For what seemed an eternity I struggled, until it seemed I had no strength left, until at last, with a snapping sensation, I felt Walter's spirit reattach to his body. His heartbeat stabilized and I withdrew to make room, as his spirit bloomed to life within his once still form.

"He's breathing!"

I heard the voice, but I couldn't be sure whose it was. I was exhausted and all I wanted was sleep. The endless night around me was warm and comforting, and I felt myself drifting.

"Mordecai isn't!"

That sounded like Penny, but the voice was muffled, as if it came to me from a great distance. She said other things as well, but I could no longer make them out. I just needed rest. I would ask her what she had said later.

Mordecai! Come back! We need you. Elaine's voice was loud and annoying and it cut across the distance that had muffled the others with no loss of volume.

Shhhh, I thought back at her. *I'm trying to sleep.*

You mustn't sleep here. Your body is dying. You have to return to it, came her anxious reply.

Make me, I replied rebelliously. Her continued presence wouldn't let me relax.

I can't. I can't see you Mordecai. I can't follow you there. You have to return. Her thoughts sounded almost frantic now.

Fine, I thought back. *If it will shut you up. One of these days I'll find a way to convince people to let me get some decent sleep.* Angrily I focused my awareness and once again I felt my body close by. Seeing it from the outside, it seemed foreign to me, and a great lethargy had sapped my energy. With slow effort I began trying to re-enter, but it felt as though a shield of some sort prevented me from reaching my goal.

I saw myself then, a fragile light beginning to fray and fade at the edges, like old cloth. I made one more desperate push. With a sudden 'pop', I broke through and once again I felt flesh enfold me. Drawing breath again for the first time seemed like a monumental task. My heart leapt to life in my chest, and I found myself lying on cold stone, gasping and coughing for air.

Penny held me now and I felt her tears on my face. As she cradled my head, she said nothing and for a moment we were both content. Her lap was a peaceful place, and her hair filled the air around me with a sweet scent. All in all, I could think of no other place I might prefer to be— except for all the crying.

"You're going to drown me," I told her, in a weak attempt at humor.

She looked at me with tear streaked cheeks, "It would serve you right, you bastard. You nearly died this time."

I smiled weakly, "You should see the other guy."
"What other guy?"
"Exactly," I agreed.
She frowned at me, but I heard Dorian chuckling behind her. At least he understood my humor.

CHAPTER 10

The next few days passed slowly. My experience on the edge of death had exhausted me far more than I had expected. Worse, I had begun hearing a faint song, one that I had never noticed before, a dissonant sound. I avoided thinking on it directly, but it bothered me.

After a week had passed I returned to Albamarl, to see my friend Marc. Since I had been convalescing over the past few days no one expected to see me out and about, so I took the opportunity to sneak out and visit him without any of my usual escorts.

He was surprised to see me when I turned up one afternoon. I had teleported into the house in Albamarl, and after a brief search I found him downstairs. He appeared to be organizing a chest of clothing and other sundries. "You're going to leave that soon?" I asked suddenly.

"Holy!" he exclaimed, as he jerked and fell away from me. "Damn Mordecai! You scared me within an inch of my life."

"That was my plan," I retorted.

He grimaced before standing up and embracing me. "I heard you nearly found an early grave yourself."

"The rumors of my demise are greatly exaggerated."

"I'm sure Penny didn't appreciate your close call," he observed.

I snorted. "I probably would have passed on, but she wouldn't give the grim reaper permission to enter the room. Did you hear about her battle with the assassin who tried to kill King Nicholas?"

Marc laughed, "Yes indeed. For a woman who is no longer your Anath'Meridum she still has the instincts of a rabid tigress."

"You try chasing four children around all day—the man is lucky she was in a good mood," I replied.

"He survived?"

"No, her final blow broke his nose and killed him near instantly. If she had been in a bad mood, she might have drawn things out for a while," I explained. "The one good thing that came of the whole thing is that the King of Gododdin now regards her as his personal savior."

Marc grinned, "You can never have too many friends."

Those words and his smile sent a shadow across my heart, as I thought of his words at our last meeting. *There are some friends you can never replace,* I thought silently. "Where is Marissa?" I asked, hoping to distract myself from those thoughts.

"Shopping," he replied simply. "There are a hundred different things we need for our journey."

"So we have the place to ourselves?" I said amiably. "Like a couple of old bachelors."

"Hardly," he remarked. "You haven't been an old bachelor since—hell, you were never an old bachelor! You went straight from teenager to married life."

"You have me there," I admitted.

He shrugged. "Stop changing the subject. Did they ever figure out who tried to assassinate you?"

"James had the palace searched from top to bottom," I began, "and by the time it was done, they found two more accomplices hiding in the wine cellar, not that it did us much good. We still aren't even sure who their primary target was."

"They wouldn't talk?" Marc frowned.

I shook my head, "They took poison. They were dead within half an hour of being captured."

"Fanatics," Marc noted. "You had best be careful my friend."

"That seems like a snap judgment," I offered.

"Not many will take poison."

I thought for a moment, "Perhaps they preferred that to torture."

"Did they find out how they got into the palace?" he asked.

"According to the seneschal, they were all hired as guardsmen over the past year. They didn't have to 'get' in, they were supposed to be there," I said, relating the news I had heard from Dorian two days before.

"And they all had guard duty in the dining hall on the same day?" Marc asked with a curious tone in his voice.

"Of course not," I said dismissively. "As they soon found out, they slew several of their fellow guardsmen and took their places on the roster that evening. They found the bodies hidden in the stables."

"You're lucky there were only six of them," Marc observed. "From what I heard described, they nearly killed Walter and King Nicholas both."

I nodded, "That's one thing that still has me puzzled. Why didn't they have all six of them attack us in the dining hall? Only four of them came at us there, while the other two were found hiding in the cellar."

Marc stared back at me. "You're right. If they weren't participating in the attack, why hide at all? They could have made a second attempt later. It isn't as if anyone knew they were associates of the assassins in the dining hall."

Something tickled the back of my mind but I couldn't lay my finger on it, and after a few minutes of musing over it I decided to worry about it later. Often my mind needed time to work on things in the background before presenting me with a fully formed idea after a few days.

"On another note, I came by to ask you about your book," I said suddenly.

Marc squinted at me. "You say that as if you have some purpose."

I smiled. "I do. I think I've figured something out." Over the past few years, Marc and I had begun having detailed discussions regarding the nature of magic. I had shared most of my observations about the workings of magic, wards, runes, enchantments and how they relate to language and thought. Marc for his part had already had quite a bit of experience with magic while he was occupied by his goddess, or rather, his ex-goddess. His initial search to find a method for defeating the gods had been futile, but during the course of our talks he had decided to compile our observations into a tome; a guide to those who might come after us someday, curious about the nature of magic.

I had scoffed at the idea in the beginning, but after reading the first few chapters and comparing them to what I had learned via other means, it was easy to tell that he had something valuable to offer. The distillation of our hard won experience in plain language might not be necessary to us, but someday it would be invaluable to others.

"Pray tell," he prompted.

"Before the attack, I helped your father by giving King Nicholas a tour of the World Road, and while we were there he asked a number of questions. While I was answering one of them I had a flash of insight."

"What were you discussing?" he asked.

"Enchantments, more specifically, the reasons why they don't require a constant input of energy," I said leaning forward intently.

"In the past you stated that the rune structure was balanced properly to contain the magic without loss."

I nodded. "I did, but as I was restating it for Nicholas, I saw it from a different angle. Magic works in four dimensions, the three of space and one of time, right?"

"Yeah, but…"

"No. Listen," I interrupted. "The geometry of the runes is set precisely to isolate the magic with respect to the fourth dimension. While it may involve some constraints, for practical reasons, in regard to the three spatial dimensions—it is the fourth dimension, time, that the structure controls most particularly."

My friend was one of the most intelligent men I had ever known, but even his brows furrowed after the mouthful I had just regurgitated at him. "Wait, what?" he said articulately.

I reached into the special bag at my waist and drew out my staff. It was one of the earliest enchantments I had done, and in many ways one of the simplest. "Alright, we talked about this one before," I began, "but the staff has an enchantment built along the wood called a 'rune channel'."

He waved his hand at me, "I remember—what about it?"

"The rune channel has a structure that allows magic to be focused along its length, for purposes we have discussed before. Because of that, the runes are built into a structure that resembles a hollow tube, which constrains the magic along two physical or spatial dimensions, right?"

He gave me a quick nod.

"But the structure does more than that," I added. "It also controls the magic completely with regard to the fourth dimension, time."

"No it doesn't," Marc argued. "Once you channel a line of focused power through that staff it strikes something and dissipates. It doesn't stick around forever."

"Touché," I replied, "but you miss the point. The magic that is contained within the staff's runes does not dissipate. The aythar that is channeled along the length of the channel, also temporarily becomes immobile along the time axis, until it interacts with something else."

Marc looked doubtful.

"Perhaps the staff was a bad example," I admitted. "But it occurred to me because of the shiggreth. In the past they have proven almost immune to all normal magic, except for magic that had been channeled through something like my staff. Now I understand why—because that magic is temporarily immobile along the axis of time."

"Give me a different metaphor," said Marc.

I thought for a moment. "Ah!" I exclaimed at last, "The stasis enchantment!"

"The one that kept Moira alive for over a thousand years?" he answered.

"Yes. In the case of the stasis enchantment, the magic is not simply being isolated along the time axis to preserve a physical effect in three spatial dimensions; the enchantment itself is built entirely to exploit that effect upon a set area. In that case, it was built so that an area the size of a cradle was entirely within a space quarantined from normal time," I explained. "Normal enchantments do the same thing all the time; they just don't affect the time axis for anything except themselves."

Marc's face lit up as he caught on.

"We can do the same for you," I added.

"What?"

"I'm starting to understand a lot more. You heard about Walter right? He wasn't just wounded, Marc. He was dead. Now granted, he was just barely dead, and his spirit was still there, but even so, I was able to repair his body and hold him there until he reconnected with it. There may be a way to do something similar for you." There was a desperate fervor to my words.

"What does that have to do with the stasis enchantment?" Marc asked.

"I can create one for you—to stop your decline long enough for me to figure out how to repair whatever is causing it."

He laughed, "So you want to store me, like salt pork, with the intention of reviving me later?"

"Well I wouldn't have chosen those words exactly, but—yes," I admitted.

The look in his eyes was anything but humorous, despite the tone of his words. Marc stepped close and put his arms around me again. "I'm sorry brother, but no."

Tears stood out in my eyes, though I have no idea how they appeared so quickly. "Why!?" I demanded. I refused to hug him back.

Pushing me out to arm's length, he studied me carefully. "My illness isn't a matter of a damaged body or a disconnected spirit. The very wellspring of my life is dwindling, like the atrophied muscles on an old man. There's no way to fix that, at least not with what you have told me about so far."

Rationally I agreed with him, but I still held hope that I might figure out a method later. "It's as if you're trying to die."

"I'm tired Mordecai, and nothing has really changed since our promise all those years ago. Now that matters are well and truly out of our hands, I would rather accept it gracefully," he said solemnly.

"I wonder how Marissa would feel about this?" I asked aloud. "Perhaps we should include her in this discussion."

"I wonder how you'd like a split lip and a broken nose," Marc answered pointedly. It was an empty threat of course, given my shields, but his voice was angry.

The fight drained out of me suddenly and I returned his hug at last. "I hate you sometimes," I told him.

I sensed his grin even though his head was over my shoulder, "I hate you too, brother." Both of us remembered the conclusion of a fight long ago between Penny and me, when we had all admitted our hate/love for one another. After a moment he let go of me and we stepped apart. "I have one final question for you though," he said.

"What's that?" I asked curious.

"Is there anything I can do for you? Anything at all…," his tone was sincere. "We're leaving in less than a week so I want to make sure. If there is anything you need, that I can provide, tell me now."

I fought to maintain my composure as I smiled. "You're an idiot. I'm a Count now, and a wizard, I have everything a man could want—a home, children, Penny. I'm fine. The only thing I'd prefer is for you to stick around."

"That's one thing I cannot do. I need to get Marissa back to her family. You sure there isn't anything else?"

"No." I said simply. "How about you? Won't you need money for this trip?"

"You already paid for it," he smirked.

"What—oh never mind, I don't want to know," I said with some exasperation. "Actually, there is one thing you could help me with," I remembered suddenly.

"Hmm?"

"The other day, when you showed me the 'First Accord', the treaty between men and the She'Har, I wasn't entirely honest with you," I stated.

"I knew that already," he said. "You ready to talk?"

"Something awoke that day, inside me," I told him. "It was as if I had lived another life, one that I had forgotten completely until that moment. It's as if I have been two different people," I said, struggling to explain myself.

"So who is this other person?"

"I don't know," I admitted.

"What?!"

"Well, I do know—somewhere, but I haven't let myself look at it yet," I said.

He sighed, "Why not?"

"There's something dark there, Marc. Whoever that other person was, whatever he did, whether he is me, or whether he is someone else—he did something terrible, something so awful I can't bear to look at it directly—not yet at least." A shiver ran down my spine, as I finally said the words I had been keeping within.

Marc chuckled suddenly. "Something *you* can't face Mort? I doubt that. After the things you've done, I doubt any amateur could compare."

"What do you mean?"

"The war with Gododdin." He was referring to the thirty thousand men I had slain to end that war.

I glared at him. "That was the most terrible crime I have ever committed, murdering those men, and you want to make a joke of it?"

"That's the point," he explained. "You did that, and it wasn't murder, it was necessity. No, I'm not going to argue that point now!" He waved his hands to keep me from interrupting. "My point is that you have already done what you consider the worst thing imaginable. What could this stranger's memory have to compare to that?"

It was a valid argument, so I took a moment to consider it and then I allowed myself to peek at the emotions that dwelled within that foreign memory. Comparing them with my own, it was easy to see the difference. Swallowing I looked at him, "It's worse—whatever it is—it's much worse."

Marc's face fell—he had been betting on that argument to cheer me up. "Damn—really? What was it?"

I shook my head, "I don't know, and I can't look, not now."

"Then why are you bothering to discuss any of this?" he said bluntly.

Marc always had a knack for getting to the heart of matters. "I need your advice. I'm trying to approach this logically from the outside, before I delve into what seems to be a morass of painful memories," I explained.

"The fastest answer would probably come from facing whatever you've got collecting dust in the back of your head," he noted.

"I'm afraid I won't be *me* anymore."

"That's just stupid. You're you—nothing will change that. Whatever those memories contain, they're from someone else," he said, with a certainty that I wished I could emulate.

"How can you be sure?"

"I grew up with you, if that counts for anything. I happen to know you didn't commit any horrible atrocities while we were children. Whatever is in your head came from somewhere else—either by magic, or as a side effect of your magic."

I couldn't see it as a side effect, but I grasped at the other possibility. "You mean someone may have implanted the memories within me?" It was an attractive idea, especially if it absolved me from the guilt of whatever lurked in the knowledge in the back of my mind. "How and when would that have happened?"

"Perhaps a spell cast upon you by your father?" he suggested.

"I have trouble imagining a father inflicting this upon his child," I said.

Marc shrugged, "Some people don't share your conscience."

"Reincarnation would be easier to accept," I responded.

"Trying to take the blame anyway?" Marc replied. "If reincarnation were real, there would be more people complaining about *their* resurfacing memories."

"Unless memories don't make the transfer, from one life to another," I countered.

"Again—then where did these memories come from? And quit trying to find some method to take blame for whatever bad there is in them, they're not yours," Marc said.

"Well a spell makes no sense," I stated, "the memories come from a period of time that has to be at least a couple of thousand years ago—so my father couldn't have cast the spell."

"Unless it was passed on to him first," Marc observed.

"Or perhaps it is some sort of bloodline memory, like an inherited spell—or curse," I said suddenly, and then I *knew.* The hair stood up along my arms and neck as a cold chill swept across me. *Illeniel's Doom—no—Illeniel's Promise—this is part of it.*

"You alright, Mort?" Marc's face carried an expression of concern. "You look as though you've seen a ghost."

Or as though I carry one... "No, I'm fine," I said slowly. "But I think I have a feel for this now."

"A feel for what?"

"Illeniel's Doom—it's a part of me—a part of these memories. No, that's not right—it's somewhere else...," I answered. *Down below, behind the stone door—beneath the house.*

"Stop being so cryptic and just spit it out!" Marc's voice was full of frustration.

I closed my eyes, squeezing them tightly shut. I couldn't do it. I couldn't look at it, not yet. "No, I'm sorry Marc. This will have to wait."

Marc let out an explosive breath, "What the hell?! I can see now why you and Penny fought so much in the beginning. You must have been a real pleasure to deal with." His comment was riddled with sarcasm.

"If you let me put you in stasis, I'll be happy to explain it all to you later once I've dealt with my internal issues," I offered with a cynical smile.

"Is that how you proposed to Penelope?" Marc shot back. "I already told you no."

"Then you may just never find out the answer," I teased, with a humor that didn't fully touch my eyes.

"I'll come back to haunt you," he retorted.

I'm sure you will.

CHAPTER 11

After I left Marc, I went to see James. The King had been understandably worried about me after the assassination attempt at the palace; in part because we were family, and in part because without me the foundation of his rule would be considerably more uncertain. That wasn't fair, I chided myself. The man helped raise you, don't let politics cloud your opinions.

The palace guard was noticeably more formal. The events of a week past had shaken everyone, and new measures were being taken to ensure that there were no more secret assassins among them. New scrutiny had been placed upon them, especially those who had taken service in the last two years, but so far nothing had come of it.

"I'm glad to see that you've recovered," said James, after I had been ushered in to see him.

I looked down, surveying myself deliberately. "I still seem to have all my fingers and toes, Your Majesty. How have you been?"

James grunted, "Ha! I hurt myself worse than the assassin managed; bruised my leg kicking a chair out of the way."

I chuckled, "It's the small things like that, that you never hear about in romances and adventure stories."

"Everyone is younger in those tales. Men at my age aren't supposed to be assaulting furniture and fighting assassins," James suggested.

"You are hardly old yet," I countered. James was in his middle fifties now and still fairly robust.

"Easy for you to say," James replied. "How is Walter doing?"

"Still recovering, but I think he will be fine," I answered.

The King smiled. "Nicholas was quite taken with Elaine, but now he speaks of nothing but your wife. He's been calling her his 'angel of deliverance'. Poor Barnabas is probably mortified knowing that a woman saved them both."

"He acted bravely, throwing himself in front of that sword. He had nothing to be ashamed of," I responded immediately.

"Some men have a different view of chivalry."

"He'll have to get over it." *Otherwise I'll tell Penny, and let her knock some sense into him.*

"Don't misunderstand;" said James, "He's not a lout. He's grateful—just a bit embarrassed."

"Speaking of which, I should apologize to Nicholas for my words. I had not meant to argue with him. I think I was just a bit oversensitive about the topic."

"He's leaving tomorrow. I was thinking of offering your services transporting him and his men back to Lancaster, to shorten his journey…," James suggested.

"Castle Cameron," I corrected. "He can spend an evening with us, and perhaps I can win him over with our hospitality."

"Even better," said James.

"You vanish like a stray cat, and then when you reappear, this is what you bring me?" Penny was a bit annoyed with my disappearing act. By 'this' she was referring to my

140

announcement that the King of Gododdin would be spending an evening with us.

"Are you comparing King Nicholas to a dead bird or lizard?" I said, extending her analogy a bit further.

She ignored my clever remark. "Do you know how much needs to be done before we can host royalty here?"

In fact I had a good idea, but I pretended ignorance. "Just wave your hands my dear, and the entire castle will be leaping to do your bidding."

"Good luck with the children," Penny replied with a wry smile.

"Wait, what?"

"If I'm to organize this place for a royal visit, I won't have time to manage them this afternoon."

"But I need to check on the progress at…," I started.

"It can wait another day," she interrupted.

"Where is Lilly?" I asked. I hadn't seen her yet. Normally she was at hand to help with the children.

Penny handed me little Irene. As usual her large blue eyes were focused on my beard, and grasping hands kept trying to pull it out. "Lilly has taken ill today. You'll be on your own. Don't worry though; I'll stop in to feed her in a few hours."

I was perfectly comfortable with our older children, and I had no fear of infants, but three plus Irene would be a handful for me. "Perhaps Rose is free…," I suggested.

"She'll be busy helping me. Perhaps Dorian will take pity on you."

In the end, I elected to take on the chore without assistance, more as a matter of pride than for any other reason. We had effectively gotten through dealing with two infants at once years before, so I was well acquainted with the messier side of babies—and in fact with Moira and Matthew to assist in keeping an eye on Conall, I'd have plenty of attention to focus on little Irene.

That was the plan at least—until Dorian showed up with Gram in tow an hour later.

"Did you come to see the circus?" I asked him with a grin after opening the door.

He looked at me a bit sheepishly, "Actually, I came to ask a favor."

"What's that?"

"Your wife has stolen Rose for her projects, and I need to start preparing the security measures for tomorrow if King Nicholas is really going to be staying with us...," he glanced down his arm at his son and then back up at me.

The day was effectively over for me at that point. The twins were already bouncing with excitement, as Gram left his father and began chatting with them. In general, the addition of an extra child threw the balance out of whack, and I'd now have to keep an eye on Conall—the older children would ignore him.

My prediction was on the mark. The one bright side to Gram's presence was that all three of the older children disappeared outside to play. Although our house was connected to Castle Cameron, its actual location was in a scenic mountain valley in the midst of the Elentirs, a place so remote I doubted anyone had ever been there before we built our secret home there. Conall stayed inside with me while I tended to Irene, and I had to admire his behavior, not many children were as easy to please at age three as he was.

After an hour or so, I managed to get Irene down for a nap, and that let me focus my attention more fully on Conall. I rarely had time alone with him, so I did my best to enjoy the time building things with him out of his extensive wooden block collection. The truth of the matter though, was that I was utterly bored. Thankfully, Conall didn't seem to notice my lack of enthusiasm.

The peace was short lived. Matthew and Gram reappeared, followed closely by Moira. The three of them had encountered some utterly new form of lizard out in the meadow, and after many heroic attempts, had managed to capture it. They broke into the nursery with all the peace and serenity of an avalanche, shouting and waving their catch at me. Irene promptly awoke and began to cry.

I could feel a headache building between my ears, but it was hard to be sure with all the noise. I yelled, "Be quiet!" to give me a moment to see if it had been my imagination. Yep, I definitely had developed a headache. The three children stared at me in utter silence for a moment, while Conall stared intently at the lizard they had brought. After a few seconds they all began chattering again.

"Kyrtos," I said abruptly, and silence fell across the room, as Matthew, Moira, and Gram discovered they could no longer speak. I picked up Irene and began rocking her in my arms while Conall took the lizard from Matthew's unresisting fingers.

The three of them were staring at me while their mouths worked uselessly. I winked at them while I cooed at Irene, trying to soothe her. "There there…" I said softly, "that only happens to noisy children. You are far too cute for me to put a spell on." Something was working; Irene had stopped crying now and was staring intently at me.

"T'ank you," Conall told his older brother, as he stroked the lizard's head.

After a minute I looked at them and felt a momentary pang of guilt. Moira had her fingers in her mouth, trying to discover the source of her vocal paralysis, while Gram sat sullenly in the corner staring at one of Conall's toys.

Matthew on the other hand, was looking straight at me, his blue eyes welling with tears. I had betrayed him.

"Keltis," I said immediately. "Are the three of you ready to behave?" I asked, using a tone that hid my guilt feelings. I had learned long ago never to show weakness in front of the natives—they'd sense it and tear you to pieces if you did—or something like that.

Matthew was the first to nod a slow 'yes', and the look on his face made me want to hug him tightly and apologize, though I resisted the urge; Moira, in contrast, simply asked, "How did you do that?"

"Magic," I said, giving the answer that usually was enough to finish most conversations. Today however, I was struck with an inspiration. "Which reminds me, I know a better spell that doesn't make you silent, but which requires you to stay quiet for it to work," I told them.

Matthew didn't take the bait, but he might have realized I was attempting to win him back over. Moira's face lit up with curiosity, though it was Gram that spoke first, "Better how?"

I grinned with enthusiasm. "It makes you as light as a feather, but only as long as you remain quiet. Would you like to try it?"

He gave me a suspicious look, but luckily Conall volunteered, "I want to!" The look on his face was positively angelic. I glanced at the other children to make sure I had their full attention, and then I place my hand on top of his head while I intoned a few words in Lycian. The spell was a simple one that I had used in several variations over the years. Its primary effect was to essentially reduce the overall mass of an object, and when I say mass, I mean mass, not just weight. Inertia and momentum both become smaller as mass decreases, effects that Dorian had complained about with his original lightweight, enchanted chainmail. I had later gone with a much more complicated system for the plate armors that I made for the Knights of Stone, but for what I intended today with my children, this was the perfect spell.

Removing my hand I looked at him carefully, "Do you feel different?"

Nodding, Conall stepped back and promptly bounced up several feet from the floor. His first response was to let out a 'whoop' of excitement and surprise, and as he did I silently adjusted the spell to make him heavier. Ordinarily, manipulating magic without using words required more energy, due to a loss of efficiency, and the same was true here. However, the amount of aythar required, relative to my own strength, was such that I could easily afford to do so without verbal language. It also kept the twins from realizing I was adjusting the effect deliberately.

"See there!? You were light as a feather until you let out that yell," I observed intelligently. I could see understanding dawning on their faces, and I smiled inwardly. *This will be the greatest silent game ever,* I thought to myself.

Soon enough I had spelled each of them so that they were able to bounce about the room lightly, almost floating, as if they were no heavier than soap bubbles. At first I watched them closely, making them heavier if they spoke or got noisy before returning them to their near weightless state if they stayed silent for a while. Needless to say, my plan worked brilliantly, and soon they were all entirely quiet as they smiled and pushed off from floors and walls, flying effortlessly from one side of the room to the other.

Irene was giggling in my arms as she watched her siblings and Gram cartwheeling through the air. Since she seemed happy enough, I set her in her cradle to watch them, while I sat down in Penny's rocking chair. I had forgotten how comfortable it could be, with its padded arms and seat.

At some point, before I realized it, I fell asleep. Dealing with young children took a bit of energy, and it was quite pleasant to doze as they played around me in the nursery. I had already warned them not to leave the room, and there seemed to be little harm they could do in their near weightless state. With my chin on my chest, I dozed and dreamt of sunny days and simpler times.

"What in the world!?" Penelope exclaimed loudly, startling me awake. My heart was racing at her sudden cry, and my eyes fought to focus on her as she stood in the doorway. A surge of adrenaline shot through me, and I saw her eyes focusing above me, where Matthew and Moira were sailing over my head, holding little Irene between them.

"Momma!" cried Moira excitedly, and then she lost her grip on her younger sister, causing Matthew and Irene to tumble awkwardly while Moira sailed off in another direction. Irene still had her full weight, and though her brother struggled gallantly he lost his grip on her as well.

Looking upward in shock and surprise, I caught my giggling infant daughter as she fell. It was a catch born of pure reflex and parental good fortune, for I was utterly unprepared. My face was a study in bewilderment as I met Penny's gaze. "I can explain," I stuttered out immediately.

As it turned out, my explanation was rather unimpressive, or at least that was my impression based upon Penny's disapproving stare. It didn't help that the children were still bounding up and down around us while we talked. With a wave of my hand, I canceled the spell on them.

A unanimous cry of, "Awwww," went up around the room.

"Go play outside," Penny told them, ignoring their dispirited tones, "and take Conall with you." We watched them troop out of the room, and after they had closed the door she looked back at me. "I can't believe you."

"I didn't intend to fall asleep…," I began, but she interrupted me almost immediately.

"This isn't about that Mort. We're both human. How many near misses do you think I've had? I'm not immune to fatigue either. This is about your promise not to use magic on the children," she explained.

"I don't think that this really counts. I just reduced their mass so they could bounce about," I responded with some relief. I had actually thought she'd be more upset about our falling daughter.

She stared agape at me. "Doesn't count? Were you dropped on your head as a child—like our daughter nearly was? Our children were flying about the room like butterflies! How is that not using magic on them?"

Obviously it was too soon to count on her overlooking the falling child portion of the incident. I decided to forge on. "When we discussed the topic of magic, we agreed that we wouldn't expose them to any potentially harmful magic," I countered, "This wasn't harmful, with the possible exception of them dropping Irene after I fell asleep."

"How do you know? Does anyone know? No one has the faintest clue what sort of lingering effects magic may have. That is why we agreed that you wouldn't use *any* magic upon the children, at least until they are adults," her voice sounded somewhat exasperated.

Even so, that wasn't how I remembered our past conversation. "Hold on, Penny, before you get too far into that. We agreed that we wouldn't expose the children to any harmful magic, not shelter them from *all* magic. Do you really think I would do something that was intrinsically harmful to them?"

"You don't always know what will be harmful and what won't!"

My nap had put me in the mood for a debate. "Give me an example," I retorted.

"Remember the rocks you used to 'incapacitate' the men that ambushed us on the road?" she shot back immediately.

I flinched at the memory, and I could see a flicker of guilt in her own eyes as she mentioned it. Years ago I had created a spell to send small rocks flying unerringly at the heads of enemies. My intention had been to knock them senseless, but the reality had turned out differently. My stones had struck with enough force to shatter their skulls. I had continued to use the spell after that, but only when my intention was to use lethal force. That first mistake was but one of several that still haunted me. "That wasn't fair, Penny," I warned.

"Fair can go hang! This is about our children, Mort. One mistake and we could be ex-parents. How 'fair' would that be?" she said heatedly before countering, "Name one use of magic that you think is completely harmless."

"Healing," I said immediately.

"Marcus," she replied with one word.

I had long ago shared with her the effect of Millicenth's choosing Marcus to be her avatar, though I still hadn't told her about the more recent news—that it might be fatal. Somehow I didn't think that would help my argument. "His addiction resulted from the abuse of the goddess, not merely the act of healing," I replied.

The conversation devolved from there, and eventually we were forced to call a truce, a truce that hinged upon my agreeing to refrain from any further magic involving our offspring. I agreed reluctantly, but I was still sore on the topic when we went to bed that evening.

That might have been the reason it took me several hours to fall asleep. Either that, or I had had too much of a nap earlier. No matter the cause, I tossed and turned for hours before finally drifting off into a troubled slumber. My dreams did nothing to improve the situation.

———————

I sat astride a massive charger while staring across a sullen and brooding landscape. The sky was dark and heavy with clouds that appeared on the verge of producing rain, though none fell. A brisk wind whipped my face while I watched the sky grow ever darker. As I watched, the thunderheads grew and covered the sky completely, leaving the land in a darkness illuminated only by the glow of the clouds themselves, punctuated by occasional flashes of lightning.

It never occurred to me to wonder where I was, somehow I knew. This was the borderlands, the space between the world and *elsewhere*. The interface between the realm of men and the rest of—whatever else there was. Even in dreams I was unsure of what else might exist out there.

What was truly unusual was the weather. This place was normally one devoid of anything beyond bare rock and relentless wind. Thunder and lightning, much less clouds, were unusual and unwanted intruders here. *Something is happening,* I thought, *worlds are about to collide.*

The weather was a harbinger of something ominous. That I could feel, right down to my bones, and the electric tension in the air made even the roots of my teeth ache. I watched and waited, for I could think of nothing else to do. There was no course of action available to me here. I could only observe—and wait.

After what seemed an interminable wait, I felt, as much as saw, the sky crack. It was preceded by a darkening of the already black sky, followed by a thunderous flash of light, and a roaring noise that reminded me of thunder while being completely unlike it. It was the sound of reality being torn forcibly apart. In the wake of that terrible sound and the light that accompanied it, I sensed three incredible beings passing through. They were creatures of such power and magnitude, that I could not help but be left in speechless wonder and awe.

Deep within, my primal instincts urged me to dismount, to genuflect, or even lie face down, so great were the powers I sensed. These were gods, and while they were probably not even aware of my presence in the distance, my primitive hindbrain still yammered at me in mindless fear. I ignored it, and after a moment my stubborn nature and more rational forebrain silenced the raw emotion.

As my reasoning faculties began functioning again, I paid closer attention to the information my senses were bringing to me. A rift had been torn in the world, and three beings of enormous power had passed through, but they had not lingered. In fact, they had moved with a haste that left me wondering. The rift stayed open behind them, though it should have closed already. Such things were unnatural and could not sustain themselves, once the power that created them was withdrawn.

A cold sensation passed over me, while simultaneously the air grew still, as the endless ravening wind of the borderland came completely to a stop. In that pregnant pause, the light pouring from the rift died away as something dark occluded the opening, something ominous. A dark power issued through the tear in reality, and as it emerged, I could feel sweat standing out on my skin. This was a force far beyond the powers that had so recently passed, and while they were bright and indifferent, this power was undoubtedly malignant.

While I stared, I saw the dark mass turn, and somehow I could sense it was shifting itself to face me. An enormous eye appeared and I felt tiny in its gaze—fear shot through me as I realized it could see me. It was aware. *Mal'goroth!*

Sitting up in my bed I found myself cold and panting, as though I had run a hard mile and then been doused with cool water. My dream was still clear in my mind, and worse, I was certain that it was far more than just a night terror. My ears caught the sound of labored breathing, and I realized that Penny was twisting in the bed beside me. Her body curled and fought with the sheets she had wrapped around herself. *That explains why I'm cold.*

The thought barely registered though, I was more concerned with my wife. Her eyes had opened and she was staring rigidly at the ceiling, as though whatever her gaze had fixed upon left her paralyzed with fear. "Wake up," I said, putting my hand on her shoulder.

Worried, I began to shake her, hoping I could snap her out of the dream, when something that had never happened before occurred. Her eyes fixed upon me, focusing, and then her lips moved, "Don't."

"Are you awake?" I asked. Her voice sounded odd.

"No, but I will be if you keep shaking. You mustn't do that Mort. Let me finish talking to her," as she finished that statement her eyes closed.

"Talking to whom?"

"To the Penelope of the present," she answered softly.

Well that reply left me dumbfounded. I had thought *I* was talking to the Penelope of the present, whatever that meant. Her body had grown still and calm, so I felt better at least. Until her lips began moving, while she mumbled softly to herself, never quite clearly enough for me to understand. Penny had had a number of important visions over the years, and quite a few minor ones, but they had never been like this. In most cases she went limp, still, or appeared to pass out. Once or twice she had begun shaking, but tonight she seemed to be holding an internal dialogue while being not quite truly asleep.

"I really hope you aren't going to start giving cryptic messages when you wake up. I've had just about enough of those for one lifetime, thank you very much," I said, without much hope of being heard. It was doubtful that her conversation partner cared much for my opinion anyway.

She looked at me again, "That isn't always easy. Sometimes you think simple statements like, 'help the twins change their clothes,' are cryptic. How should I know what you'll understand and what you won't?"

I stared at her uncertainly, "Am I addressing Penny of the present or 'Penny the unknown'?"

She frowned, "What makes you say that? Were you watching my vision?"

"No, you told me to stop bothering you, and when I asked who you were talking to, you told me 'Penny of the present'," I informed her. "I got the distinct impression that you weren't quite yourself."

The expression on her face spoke volumes. Unfortunately, much like her previous mumbling I had not a hope of understanding what it was saying. Finally she spoke aloud, to put an end to my confusion, "You aren't going to like this, but I've had another vision, and this one is unlike any of the others I have had so far."

"Uh huh," I nodded sagely.

"I saw a portent of dark times to come. The gods walk the earth directly, and we are all in danger...," she began.

"I already knew that part," I said interrupting, "I had my own dream."

Penny gave me a waspish look. She rarely liked being interrupted. "Fine, then I can move on to the important part. I met myself and I've been given a message for you, as well as a choice."

"Penelope Cooper, I swear on my father's grave, if you give me some weird and unintelligible message, like, 'Beware the man that casts no shadow, for he fears the wind,' it will be the last thing you do," I told her gravely.

She shook her head, which made her already loose bun fall apart. Brown hair fell about her in untidy curls. "No, there's nothing mysterious about this one—if you'll just let me finish, and my name is Penelope *Illeniel,* if you recall. We're married."

"Not if you don't tell me the full truth," I said a bit petulantly. "Seven years ago you left me thinking you were dead, and it nearly killed me. I don't care what your prophetic powers warned you about; you'd best tell me all of it this time."

Penny's eyes crinkled a bit, full of sympathy. "I will. There's nothing hidden, at least nothing in the present. I can tell you everything that I know."

Before she could continue I put in, "What do you mean, the *present?*"

"If you'll shut up, I will tell you!" she snapped back.

I was already riled, up but I paused for a moment, and after giving it some thought, I decided she had a point. I closed my mouth without further comment and waved my hands indicating she could continue.

After a moment she did, "I'll start at the beginning. Like you, I saw the gods tear a hole in the fabric of the world allowing them to cross over completely, but unlike when Celior crossed, this time they were able to manage the crossing without any aid from our side."

I bit my lip. It was plain that her vision had included a lot more detail than mine, but I didn't dare ask questions yet. I made a mental note to bring it up when she was finished. *It shouldn't be possible for them to cross without the aid of someone of power on this side.*

"All three of the remaining Shining Gods have entered our world, and they were followed by Mal'goroth. The meaning of that I am unsure of, but I'm certain that it can't be good," she told me.

I nodded, doing my best to let her finish. *I've been waiting for their retribution for seven years, since the day I imprisoned their brother,* I noted mentally, *but I always hoped it would be one at a time—not like this!*

Penny took a deep breath, "This is the part you may not like."

"Why?"

"Because I don't know much else, my vision was interrupted by someone, and I was given a choice: knowledge without the ability to affect the outcome, or ignorance with the hope of protecting those I love." She stopped after that, waiting for my reaction.

I had a better handle on myself by then, and I answered in a more controlled fashion. "First, I'd like to know more precisely who you were talking with."

"Myself," she replied. "I spoke with a future version of myself, one that had seen the vision I was about to see."

"I thought she seemed familiar," I muttered. "So, why would you interrupt your own vision?"

"It was my only remaining choice. Things hadn't gone well for that other me. She was somehow able to warn me, to start over. For some reason, ignorance may offer more hope than knowledge," she answered.

I could sense the hesitation in her voice. "Does this mean our actions will alter her future? Or is she from a different future?" My head was whirling with possibilities.

Penny put her hand on my chin. "Pay attention. Don't let that big brain of yours lead you astray. The important thing is that she gave us a chance to make better choices. According to what she told me, we have at least a week or more, and if I had accepted the full knowledge the vision would have laid before me, my choices would have been fixed, and we would most certainly have lost some, or maybe all of our children."

"What!?" I said, with some alarm. Apparently my safeguards weren't sufficient, which despite the situation was a surprise. I had spent a considerable amount of time planning contingencies. Any man fearing the gods might seek vengeance through his family would do likewise—if he had the resources at my disposal.

Penny's hand on my arm stilled me for a moment. "That won't happen, Mort. I chose a different path. Taking my other-self's advice, I was able to end the vision and deny myself that knowledge. My choice now is simply to prepare, with you, for what we know must be coming."

I shook my head in bewilderment. "What can you do Penny? Not that I ever liked your visions, but knowledge was your only advantage." I stopped myself before adding, 'you're helpless'.

"I know what you're thinking," she said suddenly, "and you know there are other options. Give me power

Mort. Let me protect our children." Her eyes were emphatic as they bored into my own.

"You know better than that. I'll never remake that bond, Penny," I said flatly.

She put her hand in my hair. "Not that bond—the earth bond; make me as your Knights of Stone."

"There's a limit to what I can do…," I began. "I can only create twenty of them."

"Don't feed me stories Mordecai. You picked that number out of the air. I'm certain you can manage another if you really feel it to be necessary," she argued.

"Just a few hours ago you were angry that I used magic on the children. Now you want me to do something far more serious to you. We don't know what this might do. What if you could no longer have children? What if they were stillborn?" I said, and in my mind were visions of hard rocklike children.

"I am not one of the children, and if you don't give me the power to defend them who will?" she replied passionately.

"I will!" I barked back at her. "You've seen what the earth bond does to people. I've already had to release and replace three of them."

"You can't protect everyone, Mort! We learned that lesson already, and all of these plans and contingencies you've created over the years are just that—plans. When they come for us all, your plans will dissolve into chaos in a matter of moments. I need the ability to protect our children, and frankly I don't care what the costs are. We have four children now, and I would rather keep the ones we have than worry about whether we'll be able to have more in the future."

When she finished she simply stopped and her eyes bored into me. I could see desperation there, the same desperation I would have felt if I was facing our current situation without any power of my own. I felt my love for her grow, as it always had, and without hesitation I reversed my stance. I knew my objections were based purely on fear, fear of losing her, but we both feared something worse—losing our family. It was a moment of ironic tragedy and camaraderie, both at the same time. The tragedy was my realization that I was willing to trade her safety, her life, for our children if necessary. The camaraderie came from the fact that we both shared that decision, that if necessary, they were more important than either of our lives. We had each become secondary to their safety.

"I could never have chosen a better mother for my children," I said abruptly, putting my hand against her cheek. Her face grew curious at my change in demeanor, so I explained, "I loved you more than my own life, more than I thought I could love anything. Then we had children, and somewhere along the way, without realizing it, I grew to love them so much, that I am now willing to risk your life for theirs—and somehow I still love you even more than I did before."

I felt tears welling in my eyes, but somehow Penny had still begun crying before me, her face was already wet when she answered, "That's not fair Mort. You can't just stop and say something like that in the middle of an argument." She wiped her cheeks. "Look at what you did."

I drew her close and we stayed quiet for a while, simply breathing and taking comfort in each other's arms. "I will give you the bond," I told her at last, "but I won't make you one of my knights."

She nodded, glancing up at me. "I never asked you to make me a knight, but since you brought it up—why not?"

"I don't want you beholden to any oaths, not to me, not to our people, or anyone else. I will give you strength, but I want you to use it purely at your own discretion, and by that I mean, that if you need to abandon everyone and everything else to save our children—I want you to do so," I explained.

"Thank you," she said, squeezing me even harder.

"Don't thank me," I told her. "These are desperate decisions, and eventually we will pay the price for them. I just wish you didn't have to pay with me."

We didn't waste any more time, and that night in our darkened bedroom, I bound a part of the earth to Penny. It wasn't a decision I could change, but I still felt as though I were damning her to some terrible fate. Afterward, we lay silent and waited for sleep that would not come.

CHAPTER 12

The next morning arrived as it typically does, regardless of my wishes on the matter. Somehow, despite my lack of quality sleep, I wasn't as tired as I might have otherwise expected. Penelope by contrast was positively energized. She was attempting to remain casual, but it was easy to tell that she was excited about the earth bond. There was an extra bounce in every step, and she went out of her way to move heavy items that she otherwise had no reason to move.

She was testing her new strength. Fortunately, since this wasn't her first time dealing with enhanced physical power, she didn't make any of the usual mistakes (as she had when she first became my Anath'Meridum).

"What are you doing now?" I asked as she dug through one of our older wardrobes.

"My armor," she answered immediately. She was referring of course, to the chainmail byrnie I had enchanted for her long ago, when I had expected her to have to defend both of our lives regularly.

"It's not in that one. It's in the chest over there, near the bottom," I indicated one of our heavy oaken trunks that stood in the corner of the room.

"Thanks," she replied, as she stopped searching and went to open said box. As she pulled out the armor, she made an observation. "You really are frightening sometimes, Mort. I know you can sense objects at great distances, as well as being able to see inside of things, but how on earth can you spot something like this within a room full of so many other things so quickly? It doesn't seem human."

A smirk crossed my lips while I considered leaving her with her mistaken impression of my ability. Finally I decided honesty was the best policy. "The armor glows in my magesight, so it and the other enchanted items in the room stand out like fireflies."

"Oh," she paused. "I should have realized."

"You aren't planning on wearing it now are you?" I asked with some concern. I didn't look forward to explaining the change in her physical prowess just yet. In fact I preferred to keep it a secret. The past had taught me that surprise was sometimes the best advantage one could have. Consequently, I now kept more secrets than anyone was aware of, even Penny and Dorian, though I had convinced myself that it was for their own good.

She gave me a knowing glance. "Worried?" The one word question held a host of layered meanings.

"Yes."

"Me too," she admitted, before leaning over to give me a kiss, "but I don't plan on wearing it yet. I just want it close at hand when the time comes."

That was a sentiment I could definitely agree with.

After that the day got underway. Shortly after breakfast we left the house and switched to our apartment within Castle Cameron. Lilly arrived at her normal time. She was feeling better and ready to resume her duties, for which I was very grateful. Penny left soon after, intending to start early. She still had a lot to do to prepare for Nicholas' arrival later in the day.

My only duty for the morning was meeting with Dorian to discuss his plans and inform him of our new information, which wasn't something I relished doing. As I was getting dressed Matthew found me.

"Dad, I have a question," he began, which was his usual method for starting a conversation.

"As usual," I muttered sardonically.

"Can I stay with Gram today?" he continued without noticing my remark.

That was a simple one, I thought to myself. "That should be fine. You can walk with me. I'm going to see Sir Dorian anyway. We can ask him when I find him," I answered.

He nodded and I assumed he was done—until we got to the castle hall outside the entrance to our apartments. His face held an expression of serious thought when he spoke again, "Dad, I have another question."

I smiled. "I should have suspected as much."

"Why does Mom get angry at you?"

Startled, I looked down and found myself caught by his deeply curious blue eyes. My first instinct was to deflect his question, either by questioning his perception or trying to change the subject, but the honesty in his face disarmed me. My face softened as I replied, "Love—she gets angry because she loves us."

His face registered confusion.

Stopping I gave him my full attention. "Think about it this way. Why do you get angry?"

Putting his hand on his chin my son assumed a thoughtful pose. *I wonder where he learned that gesture. Do I do that?* I wondered, but without an objective third person I couldn't be sure. Then he replied, "I got mad yesterday when Moira kicked me."

"When did she do that? Never mind, that's a good example," I told him. "You were angry because she hurt you, right?"

He gave an affirmative nod.

"Your mother gets upset with me, or you, for the same reason, because we hurt her, or because we might hurt her.

The trick is figuring out *how*. Have you ever tried to hurt your mother on purpose?" I asked him.

"No," he replied shaking his head vigorously. *Damn, he's cute,* I thought.

"Have you ever seen me hurt her?"

He gave another negative head shake.

"So what do you think we might do that hurts your mother?"

Matthew thought for a while before eventually shrugging in defeat. "I don't know Dad. It's a mystery to me."

The adult phrasing sounded so odd, yet serious coming from his lips that I almost burst out laughing. *He definitely spends time around someone who has an interesting way of using words.* I had to force my thoughts back on track. "Well, it is often a mystery to me as well, but through careful thought and a lot of experience, I think I have figured out a large part of it. Would you like to know what I think?"

That got a very strong nod; I had his curiosity fully engaged now.

"She loves us so much, that when we get hurt, or when she just *thinks* we might get hurt—it hurts her. The same thing holds true if you do something mean to your sister, or she does something mean to you. Does that make sense?" I asked.

Matthew's eyes had widened a bit as my explanation sank into his mind. He was still thinking however, and after a long pause he spoke up again. "I think so, but I don't understand one thing."

"What's that?" *Somehow I knew it wouldn't be as simple as one explanation.* Matthew always had 'one more' question.

"Is this like your sword, except instead of something good, it's something bad?" he managed to say with some effort.

I stared at him for a long minute before I had the gist of what he was asking. Then I realized he was talking about the story of the sword my father had made for me. I touched the hilt and asked, "You mean the sword your Grandpa Royce made for me?" The sword was plainly made, without much ornamentation. Royce had made it from the weapon of one of the assassins who had killed my parents, and he had given it to me when I had come of age. The lesson he had taught me with it was that good things can rise from the ashes of bad things.

Matthew's answer was a simple, "Yes."

I was frankly surprised he had remembered the story. I hadn't thought he was listening very well when I told him and his sister about it. I thought carefully as I answered, "That's a very clever way of thinking about it Matthew, but this is different. This isn't actually something bad coming from something good, at least not always, because your mother's anger isn't a bad thing. Quite often it's a good thing."

He frowned, waiting for a better explanation.

"It's like pain," I said continuing. "It helps warn you, so you don't hurt yourself more. A mother's pain comes from the fear that we might be hurt, and because of that, she gets angry with us, but that anger serves the same purpose. It often keeps us from doing something stupid and hurting ourselves."

"Oh," he said, and his expression made it clear he felt the conversation had come to a satisfying conclusion.

Personally I was a bit let down. I had been rather pleased with my explanations, so it was a bit of an anti-climax to get nothing more than a simple 'oh' at the end of it. We continued down the hallways, and we were almost to our destination when he spoke again.

"Why do you get angry with Mom sometimes? Is it the same thing?"

Caught off guard I answered honestly, "No, I get mad at her because she's stubborn, mule-headed, and occasionally just plain wrong." I stopped as my mind replayed my words back to me. "Forget I said that," I hastily amended.

"Why?" my son asked me without a trace of guile. I had to wonder if he was pretending to ignorance.

"You know why. Just leave that part out when you repeat all this to your brother and sister later," I told him.

"But I can tell Mom, right?" The little monster was smiling openly.

I glared at him. *I can't believe I've sired a banker— or perhaps a bandit.* "I'll bring you something sweet from the kitchen later," I said without explanation.

Matthew grinned, "I like the berry tarts best."

"We have a deal then," I replied, tousling his hair with one hand. He gave me a spontaneous hug, and then we started walking again.

I could feel him looking up at me as we walked, but I didn't turn my head. "I wouldn't really have told on you," he said.

"I know," I answered.

⊰•—◦—•⊱

After leaving the boys with Lady Rose, Dorian and I walked together for a ways. He was heading for the barracks to double check the men before King Nicholas arrived later in the day. I had several other things to do, last of which would be going to collect said king and his entourage.

"Dorian," I said, using a tone that signaled I had something serious to talk about.

My friend was a consummate worrier, and his face wrinkled up immediately. "Uh oh," he said.

"Penny had a dream last night," I began, "the sort we don't like, if you take my meaning."

"Go on," he urged me.

"The shining gods—and Mal'goroth as well, have crossed into our world."

"You said that wasn't possible," Dorian noted in a deeply worried voice.

I stopped walking and turned toward him. "Normally it isn't possible, unless they have help from a wizard on this side."

"But all the wizards we know of are here, with us."

"Somehow, they created the bridge without any aid from this side." I held up a hand to forestall his next question. "I don't know how, but I think the more important question at this point, is why."

Dorian looked at me as though I had gone mad. "That should be obvious, Mort! They're here to exact vengeance upon you and the rest of us as well. This is what we've been expecting ever since the day you turned Celior into a pretty stone."

I shook my head. "That's what I thought seven years ago, but a lot of time has passed since then. I had all but given up on the notion that they would seek revenge. In fact, I think perhaps they were afraid to face me."

"Then why now?"

"I think they're desperate. Mal'goroth is much stronger than they are. I think they're afraid of him," I explained.

Dorian was disbelieving, "How could you know their relative strengths? Did you convince them to come in so you could measure their 'Celiors'?"

I was impressed that he had used my new unit of measure, though his question annoyed me. "No, I simply felt it. Last night while Penny was having her vision, I had a dream of my own. I sensed each of them, and the difference between them was like the difference between a mountain and a foothill. They have good cause to fear Mal'goroth. Worse, I believe I'm the one that helped give him that power."

"Now I know you're crazy," Dorian observed.

"When we fought the army of Gododdin, he told me that the deaths of his soldiers would only make him stronger. He also told me that his cultists would sacrifice the families of every soldier that didn't survive. I wiped out over thirty thousand men at the end of that war—and his priests damn near succeeded in killing all of their families. That's what finally sparked the revolt that put Nicholas back in power," I said firmly. "Think how much power Mal'goroth must have gained from all those lives. He can't draw power from human prayers like the shining gods can, but he gains a considerable amount from each life taken in his service. I helped to give him that power, whether I intended to or not."

"This sounds a lot like you throwing a pity party for yourself again. Stop trying to take responsibility for everything that happens," my burly friend growled at me. "What's more important is how we respond—what we do."

I couldn't argue with that point. "You're right. Though in my defense, I didn't want pity. I just wanted to explain my theory on his gain in strength."

Dorian snorted, "Sure, fine. We need to call the men back. Cyhan needs to return. If the gods plan to attack us, we'll need every one of our knights."

We had begun planning for a situation similar to this years ago. "That doesn't match our third contingency plan," I told him. The third plan dealt with our response if all three of the shining gods came against us together. "Having them here only makes evacuation more problematic."

"Just because they all crossed over doesn't mean they will all come here. They still might send only one or two. Do you have any idea how much time we will have?" he asked.

"Something on the order of a week, possibly more," I replied.

"You have to call the other men back. We cannot assume that the worst scenario will play out," Dorian advised me again. "What will you tell King Nicholas tonight?"

That hadn't even crossed my mind yet, so it took me a moment to decide. "Nothing, other than the fact that we've got some sort of training planned, and that the patrol will be delayed. Anything more would just put him ill at ease over something he can't control. We'll let him return home. He should be safer there."

Dorian grimaced. "I don't like lying. We should cancel his stay and call everyone together to refresh them all on the plans. The celebration this week should be canceled as well."

He was referring to the annual holiday to honor our defeat of the army of Gododdin. The same event I had argued with King Nicholas about. Although I truly loathed the reminder of what I considered one of my darkest decisions, I felt canceling it would be a mistake. "No— it won't interfere with our preparations. We are already prepared as well as can be, and as far as lying goes, just keep your mouth shut and I'll lie for both of us."

"But you can't…," he started.

I interrupted him before he could get too worked up, "I've made up my mind, Dorian, let it go."

He closed his mouth for a moment and then opened it again, "People need to be reminded about their duties when the alarm goes out. When will we start drills?"

"Tomorrow," I answered, "As soon as Nicholas is on his way and out of our hair."

Dorian's hands were clenching and unclenching unconsciously, a sign of his agitation. "It isn't right to let the man go without a warning."

"I've already saved his kingdom and his life, on two separate occasions. We send men to protect his people twice yearly. I'll be damned if I let you saddle me with more guilt!" I said, raising my voice harshly. I hadn't realized how tightly wound the tension inside me had become. Taking a deep breath, I tried to calm down before continuing, "Forgive me Dorian, you deserve better than that. We disagree, but you'll have to accept my decision. Nicholas would refuse to leave if I tell him, and I already have enough people here to protect without adding a head of state."

"What will you tell James," Dorian asked calmly, "and when?"

"I will tell him everything, as soon as I can see him privately. Hopefully that will be in just an hour or two, before I return here with King Nicholas," I answered.

"Very well, I'll return to getting the men ready for his visit," said Dorian stiffly. I could tell he was still angry with me. "If I may take my leave?" he added formally.

That was a sure sign I had upset him. He'd just have to deal with it though. "You're excused," I told him. The words left a cold feeling in the pit of my stomach.

Later, in Albamarl I found Adam, who was now the chamberlain for King James. Given my familiarity with the various staff, and the allowances that James had made for me over the years, I could have easily gotten in to see him without seeing Adam for a formal audience, but then a formal audience wasn't what I needed. Adam was well aware of that fact too, and his eyebrow twitched, hinting at well-disguised curiosity. "How may I assist you, Your Excellency?"

I didn't bother to hide my smirk. "I'm sure you're aware that I'm here to transport the King of Gododdin and his entourage to Cameron. What I need to know is whether James is alone at the moment. I need to see him privately before you announce me."

Adam gave a polite bow. "I'm sure you have your reasons. I will check and return presently." As he left I found myself missing the days when my rank and station had been less certain. Adam had been much cheekier then. These days he was so respectful it was hardly any fun.

A good ten minutes later he returned. "If you will follow me," he said, and proceeded to lead me toward one of the inner palace courtyards. Once there, he left me at a bench near a bush that was furiously in bloom. I was at a loss to remember the name of it, but I didn't have long to wonder. Within a moment I sensed James approaching along the small garden path.

He smiled as he walked into view. "You must have something serious to talk about. It's been a while since you wanted an impromptu and private meeting."

I responded with a rather tense smile, "I would that I had different news James. I hope Adam wasn't forced to give any strange excuses to pardon your sudden leave."

"You picked a lucky moment," James chuckled, "I was alone when Adam found me. So what do you want to inform me of?"

There wasn't much point in beating around the bush, so I got right to the point, "The gods have crossed into our world."

The King of Lothion's face grew a shade paler, "Gods? Which gods?"

"All of the remaining shining gods, as well as the dark god, Mal'goroth," I said with little enthusiasm.

His face grew puzzled, "Are they working together?"

I shook my head, "I am unsure, but I believe the three shining gods are. Mal'goroth may have simply taken advantage of the opportunity when they managed to create a path to our world."

"Any idea what their purpose may be, vengeance, rescue, or war with each other?"

"I truly have no way of knowing yet, nor do I know when to expect them. All I know with any degree of certainty is that we have at least a week before anything happens," I responded.

"Another of Penelope's visions?"

I nodded, "I don't intend to alarm Nicholas, for I fear he will insist on staying if I do. I'd rather he return home quietly. I think he'll be safer there."

James frowned. "That's a large gamble you're making on his behalf, and without giving him any choice in the matter."

I met his eyes evenly. "Do you disagree?"

"No, you're probably right. In fact, faced with a problem of this size, I find myself wondering if there's anything any of us can do," he admitted.

I put my hand on his shoulder. "Survive. These are powers beyond any of us, but you can survive. If they come here, they must not find you. There is nothing you can do to stop them, but so long as you survive to rally our people, we can rebuild."

"It doesn't feel right, Mordecai, that I should hide while my people face the wrath of the gods. Is that what a true king should do?" His face registered an honest doubt that I had never seen on Edward's face while he was king.

My chest felt tight, seeing my friend's father, always so sure in the past, wavering with uncertainty. I answered with a certainty that I myself did not truly feel, "You know the answer to that. The stories tell of kings and their glories, but the truth is darker. A king makes choices no man should bear and must constantly question his own motives. In this you must trust me, James, this nation needs you. Do not fault yourself for hiding from a foe you cannot possibly face. Folly is not bravery."

"Your logic only holds true if we assume that you find victory against not one, but four deities," he observed.

"It may not come to that," I replied. "You remember where the entrance is?" I was referring to the hidden bolt hole we had created for the King of Lothion some five years past. Using enchantments, similar to the ones that hid Moira's stone and the enchanting room in the Illeniel house, I had crafted a hidden room within the palace. With just a moment's warning James could hide himself within, it and even the gods would be unable to find him.

"Of course," he replied a bit snappishly, "I'm not in my dotage yet."

"That secret is but one of many. I have not been idle these seven years, and the World Road has not been my only work. We still have hope, though I cannot guarantee safety to any but a few, and you are one of them."

"What of my family? What of Genevieve and my children?" he asked suddenly.

"Keep them close at hand until this is over, so that they can hide with you," I told him simply, though I feared his next question.

"What of Marcus?"

My stomach felt as though it held a lead weight, but I kept my features calm. "He lives his own life, James. If it helps any, he told me that he plans to move to Agraden with his wife. If his preparations are still on schedule, he may have already left the city. He may be safer than any of us," I told him. *Except that he is leaving to die in another city,* I reminded myself. It tore at my heart to keep the knowledge from James, but I had promised Marc. *How many secrets can one heart hold, before it destroys itself?*

CHAPTER 13

I brought King Nicholas and his bodyguard, Sir Barnabas, to Castle Cameron after first transporting the rest of his entourage. It was actually a relief to be done with the good-byes. The parting of ways between the two kings had taken an exorbitant amount of time. As usual the excessive and lengthy ceremonies reminded me of one of the main reasons I had set James in place as king, rather than take the throne for myself; aside from the fact that I thought he was the best man for the job.

"It should be fascinating seeing the home of the great wizard of Lothion," commented King Nicholas as we stepped away from the teleportation circle. For a moment I suspected him of sarcasm, but after a second's pause, I realized he was speaking in sincerity. He must have seen the pensive look on my face though, for he followed his remark with a preemptive apology, "Please, do not look for hidden meanings in my words. I feel terrible for my foolish words at the feast. Yet again I am in debt to you and your valiant wife."

I couldn't help but chuckle at his words, "She really is something isn't she?"

He smiled, "I have never met her equal."

I laughed, "You may well be correct, but then you've never seen our Queen Genevieve when she gets really cross either."

"If all of the women of Lothion are as frightful in battle, your nation will never need fear another invader," he added.

My lady wife, the Countess di'Cameron, made her appearance at that moment, greeting us as we stepped out of the building that housed my teleportation circles. "You honor us with your presence, Your Majesty," she said with a formal curtsey.

"Raise your head Countess!" he responded immediately, while stepping forward to take her hand and lift her. He held onto her hand long enough to lean forward and kiss the back of it. Meanwhile, Sir Barnabas went to one knee beside him, facing her.

"I owe you my life Countess," said Nicholas. "It is I who should be showing deference."

I could tell Penny was profoundly uncomfortable receiving such attention from a king, but she covered her surprise well. "Please, Your Majesty, you do me too much honor. Call me Penelope; there is no need to address me with titles here."

"Then you too must address me as Nicholas, for otherwise I will feel ill at ease with your hospitality," he answered. I noted he still held her hand. He was perhaps a bit too forward with Penny for my comfort.

She withdrew her hand carefully, without making a show of it, though to my eyes it seemed that the King of Gododdin let his fingers linger too long upon hers. *Surely the man isn't trying to woo my wife right in front of me?* I supposed I shouldn't underestimate the boldness of royalty. If the man were a womanizer, he might be used to husbands turning a blind eye to his indiscretions. Perhaps I was overthinking it though—it was impossible to guess.

"I will gladly call you thus, Nicholas, but only if you tell me what mention you just made of invaders in Lothion, but a moment past," Penny replied.

With that the conversation returned to lighter banter and I found myself admiring Penny's skillful handling of the overly friendly king. My thoughts were interrupted before we reached the entrance to the main keep. A man in grey wool stood before the door. His stance was unremarkable, but his positioning was not, for he blocked our path. Every man, woman and child in the keep knew better than to interrupt me with our royal visitor, yet this man—a stranger I noted quickly, stood plainly in our way.

We stopped and the two guards flanking us moved forward to stand between us and the bold outsider. At the same time the two door guards came toward us and took positions behind the man, warily encircling him. Dorian had been very thorough in his security preparations. I also noted that two of the four guards were actually Knights of Stone, Sir Daniel and Sir Jeffery.

The stranger was the first to speak, throwing back his hood and staring at us with wild eyes. "I come bearing a warning for the dark wizard, Mordecai Illeniel."

I had already extended my shield to cover Penelope and King Nicholas when the latter spoke in return, "Cheeky devil! How dare you address the rightful lord of this place in such a tone?!"

It was rather amusing, considering I had the King of Gododdin addressing the challenger as though he were my chamberlain. Setting my hand upon his arm I spoke quickly, "Please, Nicholas let me deal with this."

He nodded quickly, "Very well, this is your house," and then stepped back.

"You do well to listen to your master, puppet-king of Gododdin," the stranger taunted him. Nicholas' face turned a new shade of red, while Sir Barnabas surged forward, intent on punishing the man for the affront to his king. I kept the boundary of my shield fixed, and he fell back when he struck it, surprised at finding an invisible wall in front of him.

"Offend my guests again, and your god will need to send a new messenger," I said to the stranger, while ignoring Barnabas as he rose from where he had fallen.

The messenger smirked before replying, "What makes you think I need messengers, Mordecai?"

The words, combined with a flare of power around the man, signaled his complete possession by whichever of the gods he served. I nodded to Sir Daniel, and he and Sir Jeffery moved with lightning speed and precision. Their swords came out more quickly than eyes could follow, and I saw little more than a flash of light from the enchanted steel before the stranger's body fell apart in a shocking display of violence. His head tumbled away in one direction, while his torso and two dismembered legs collapsed where he had been standing. Blood was everywhere.

The suddenness of his death appeared to unnerve even the already enraged Sir Barnabas, but his eyes grew wider still, when the disembodied head's eyes focused on me again and words issued from its lips, "That was rather rude." The eyes then moved to gaze at King Nicholas, "Perhaps you see now why I referred to him as the 'dark' wizard."

I glared at the impudent face, "Finish your message before we discover whether you can function with nothing more than ash to carry out your will." I illustrated my point by waving a hand at the rest of the now dismembered body while softly vocalizing, *"Pyrren."* Flames rapidly consumed the flesh in a flash of intense heat that left nothing behind but a foul smoke and white ash.

"It matters not to me what you do with this vessel. As you are aware, we no longer need your kind to serve as our conduits here. This is merely a courtesy call," the bodiless head told me.

"You haven't the faintest idea what courtesy is. For your kind, it is nothing more than another empty word to be used in manipulating your cattle. You'll also have to pardon me, for since you didn't bother introducing yourself, I have not the faintest idea which of the remaining petty gods you are," I responded acridly.

The eyes narrowed as the still animated head stared upward at me. "Mellicenth was right; there is no bargaining with you. I am Karenth, called the Just, and I am here to offer you one chance: release Celior, and we will ignore your past insults. Otherwise, we will wipe the earth clean of you and all your kith and kin. Nothing will remain when we are done, and not one soul will be left that remembers your name, even if we must purge all of Lothion to accomplish the task."

I laughed, "You are the worst beggar I have ever met. You're desperate or you'd never deign to make such an offer. I will be happy to show you my brand of courtesy if you decide to come here personally and make good upon your threat. You would make an excellent addition to my collection, Karenth." I was goading him deliberately, for I couldn't afford to show any weakness. The only thing that might give them pause was the fear that I might be able to do the same to them that I had done to Celior.

Rage lit his eyes. "I will not come alone. I do not understand how you defeated my brother, but I will not make his mistake. When we come, there will be no place for you to hide and no hope for anything but a slow death— after you have watched us torture your worthless spawn."

In my younger days such a threat might have overwhelmed my better sense, but I knew the game Karenth was playing. I could also tell he had not the faintest clue about the subtleties of the human mind. I paused for a moment before answering thoughtfully, "You may have a point, but I am not yet ready to concede. I will consider your offer. How long will you give me to think before you make good upon your threat?"

Now it was Karenth's turn to pause. Clearly he had not expected such a rational response from me. A few seconds passed, and then the head's mouth opened, "I will give you two weeks. Be prepared to answer us, or suffer the consequences fourteen days hence."

I smiled. "Excellent, I'll look forward to seeing you then. Now if you will excuse me I need to tidy up a bit." With another word and a gesture, I incinerated the head, just as I had the rest of the body. With my magesight I could see a flash as the energy that represented Karenth dissipated, and then we were alone.

Looking around, I noticed everyone's eyes were on me; in particular, King Nicholas seemed both shocked and appalled by my actions. "Was that truly Karenth?" he asked.

"We only have his word on it, but it was one of them," I answered. "Most likely he was telling the truth." I wondered how Nicholas would react to the knowledge, that the man who had just insulted him was actually the god that he had worshipped for most of his life—and a very desperate and angry god at that.

Dorian appeared then, his nose wrinkling in disgust at the lingering smell of burnt flesh. "What happened?"

Sir Jeffery gently escorted Nicholas and Sir Barnabas into the main hall, while I stayed behind to describe to my friend, what had occurred. As quickly as things had happened, it still took several minutes to explain it all to him. When I had finished, Dorian looked at me questioningly, "Why did you tell him you would consider it?" He knew very well I had no intention of attempting to barter with the gods.

"Time," I answered. "It's a lot easier to plan for something when you know 'when' as well as 'where'. Now I have the answer to both of those questions, whereas before I couldn't be sure of either."

Dorian rubbed his freshly shaved cheek, "Only you would think to take advantage of an angry god. Do you think they intend to make good on their threat?"

"Of course," I said, "the real question is, why now? They've had seven years to plot their revenge but done nothing. Now they appear suddenly and seem to be acting hastily. If they truly cared to punish me for Celior's imprisonment, they would have done something long before now. That they didn't, tells me that they are more afraid of me than they care about their lost brother."

"Then what forced their hand?"

I was worried that I might already know the answer. "I think there's someone they fear more than me."

The dinner and other festivities were a bit more somber than Penny had planned, mostly because of our unfortunate encounter with Karenth. Nicholas seemed deep in thought, responding to most questions with short answers and barely laughing at my occasional jokes. We wound up calling it a night a bit earlier than anticipated, much to everyone's relief I think.

The next morning Penny and I met Nicholas for breakfast and afterward we wished him well on his journey home. Contrary to my initial fear, that he might stay and insist on being involved once he knew of our imminent problem, the King of Gododdin seemed only too glad to be leaving. As he said his final private goodbyes to us, he paused and looked at me apologetically.

"Mordecai," he said after a moment, "I want you to know that you have my respect and gratitude for everything that you and your wife have done for us, but…"

I interrupted, "You don't have to explain. I understand, Nicholas."

"No, no! I do. I owe you so much, yet I cannot bring myself to go against the mandate of my god. I fear I have damned myself already by befriending you, and yet I cannot help but think there should be some way to resolve this. You are a good man, Mordecai, and my god is a good god. Perhaps if you accede to his wishes and ask forgiveness—the two of you could work together to stop Mal'goroth and the shiggreth as well."

Over the course of my time with Nicholas I had come to like the man, but he obviously had blinders on; or perhaps it was because of the difference in our personal experiences. "A good god would not threaten the lives of innocents because of my actions, right or wrong. A true 'god' would not need to bargain with me, nor could one be imprisoned. These are not gods we are dealing with Nicholas—not of the sort we were taught of as children. These are overgrown and monstrous supernatural bullies. The only difference separating them from a human tyrant is the magnitude of their power. If there is such a thing as a true god, and he is good, then Karenth and the others should be afraid, for they will be the first on his list of wrong-doers to punish."

The King of Gododdin gave me an incredulous look. "Every time we speak, new blasphemies fall from your lips as easily as fish breathe water. How could there be a god above the gods? If such a god existed, would you advise him as he sat in judgment of gods and men? What hubris is that?"

"Call it hubris if you will, but if he didn't have Mellicenth at the top of his list, then the term 'good' couldn't be applied to him. Either that or good and evil themselves are nothing but relative moral terms applied by those in power to justify their actions," I told him firmly.

Nicholas looked away, "You are mad, and yet I will pray for mercy on your behalf." Sir Barnabas opened the door for him, but before the King of Gododdin exited he looked back at me. "Farewell Mordecai, it has been interesting getting to know you."

"Farewell Nicholas, I wish you good fortune and shelter in the coming storm," I replied and then he stepped out. That was the last chance we had to speak privately, for after that our goodbyes were said in the presence of all the residents of Castle Cameron and Washbrook. Needless to say, it was a large crowd that had gathered to wish Nicholas well on his trip home. It wasn't often that we hosted a king within our walls.

Once things had quieted down later in the day, I retreated to my study to write the letter I should have sent the day before. *Too many things happening at once*, I told myself mentally. With pen in hand I began the letter:

Cyhan,

We are under threat of imminent attack here at Castle Cameron, therefore I must order you to reverse your steps and return at once. Make all haste to return within the week if possible. I will explain the events that led to this once you return. For now I will simply say, the gods have returned and are anxiously looking forward to a reunion with their lost brother.

Mordecai

I reviewed the words twice before folding the letter and placing it within the box that would transport it to Cyhan as he traveled to Gododdin. He had already been on the road for a number of days, and it would probably take an equal amount of time for him to return. I did a mental calculation, *five days,* I decided at last. He had left with the patrol four and a half days past, so logically it should take him approximately five days to return.

According to Karenth's reply to my question, we should have thirteen days before the excitement started. That would give me plenty of time to evacuate most of the people and review the plans Dorian and I had created years before to cover the various situations we thought might occur when the gods finally came to have their due.

CHAPTER 14

The next morning I found myself up early. Well, to say 'I found myself' is a bit misleading, the truth was that Penny threatened me with a bucket of cold water. "I'm up dammit!" I shouted as I stumbled from the bed in a panic. She hadn't reacted well to finding me napping again after the first warning.

The room swam about me as I tried to catch my balance. Penny was kind enough to set her bucket down and catch me by the arm before I stumbled into the side table. The word 'groggy', was a bit of an understatement. "How late were you up?" she asked curiously. Her voice was devoid of the malice that had lain behind her warnings of a moment ago; instead it now conveyed only curiosity and perhaps innocent concern. I was never quite sure how she managed to switch from naughty to nice so quickly.

I had been working until nearly dawn, making sure that the enchantments I had laid years before were still in perfect shape. I had gone over them with painstaking care, making sure there were no mistakes, no flaws. Any imperfection would mean not only my own death, but could potentially cost me the lives of my family, along with everyone else who depended upon me. Last night wasn't the first time I had checked and rechecked them—I had done so at least yearly for the past five years.

Penny got my attention again by snapping her fingers in front of me, "Hello? Did you hear me?"

I struggled for a witty answer and eventually came up with, "Huh?"

"I asked how late you were up," she repeated patiently.

"M'not sure, two or three perhaps," I hedged. "Do you have any tea?"

"Liar," she rebuked me, "I woke up close to dawn, and you weren't in bed yet. Lilly will be up with the tea in a moment. What were you doing?"

"Working on the defenses," I said, using a half-truth. "Why am I awake so early?" I was hoping the question would deflect her attention.

She handed me a wet towel to wash my face. "You know very well why you're awake. Dorian wants to start the meeting bright and early. Don't try to distract me. When are you going to share the details?"

I should have known better than to expect I'd get away easily. This was a conversation we had had on a number of occasions in the past. "I have told you the details, those that I can share."

"Not good enough," she argued, "We have our children at risk, and now we know they are coming for sure. I want to know what you've kept hidden."

"No," I answered simply.

"Why?"

I sighed, "We've been over this before. The time may come when you are unable to conceal the information. That would effectively nullify my plan."

"You don't trust me?" she said, changing tactics.

I gave her a hard stare, "You know better than that. They might take the information straight out of your mind."

Penny drew out the amulet I had given her and held it in her hand. It shielded her mind from magical influences. Years ago I had created similar necklaces for every man, woman, and child of Washbrook and Cameron Castle.

"That might not be strong enough," I told her, "and if you are captured they could easily remove it."

"If you are captured there is no one left that knows how to put your plan into operation," she countered.

It was a valid point. "If I am captured, and they learn the plan then it won't matter. No trap will work when your enemy knows the nature of it. Besides, only a mage could set this in motion."

My wife's face did not reflect happiness. "You've grown too comfortable with secrets Mordecai," she cautioned.

"Maybe," I admitted. "I don't like it either, but I'll do whatever it takes to keep you and the children safe."

She turned away and busied herself with dressing. "Whatever you *think* it takes," she muttered quietly to herself, and in the interest of peace I pretended that I hadn't heard.

⊷━━━⊶

Dorian stood at the head of the table in our council room. "I think you all understand why we are gathered. Yesterday's 'messenger' was a reminder that we have powerful enemies, enemies that will soon be coming to pay us a visit."

I couldn't help but admire my friend's poise. Over the years he had developed a strong confidence when it came to leading the men. Looking over the crowd, I could see that he had the rapt attention of every man and woman in the room, and there were a lot of them. Today's meeting included not only the usual members of the Knights of Stone, but also Penny, Peter Tucker, Chad Grayson, Walter and Elaine Prathion, and of course myself. Peter was representing the castle staff, while Chad was my chief huntsman and consequently was in charge of the men I would be using to maintain a watch in and around the castle and its surrounds.

"Consequently," Dorian continued, "we will maintain a position of high alert until after the current threat has passed." Looking down the table, Dorian pointed at Peter, who had quietly raised his hand, "You have a question?"

"Yes mi'lord. I realize this may seem trivial, but will the yearly celebration still be held at week's end?" he asked. He was referring to the yearly feast that commemorated our victory over the army of Gododdin.

Dorian nodded, looking toward me, "I would prefer to skip it this year but I will defer that question to our lord. Your Excellency…?"

My first instinct was to agree with him but as I started to rise I felt Penny's hand upon my arm. I leaned closer and she whispered into my ear, "Morale will suffer greatly if you skip it. We have another week after that still."

"The celebration will go forward as usual," I told them. "It shouldn't interfere, although I feel badly for your men, Chad," I said, referring to the master huntsman. "Many of them will miss it to maintain watch. Also I will have to ask that everyone refrain from drinking overmuch."

The man I had taken on as my huntsman a few years ago was young, close to my own age, but he was a man of few words. I had hired him away from the Lancaster's on their huntsman, William Doyle's, recommendation. Since then I had rarely been disappointed in his ability to find game. I would be counting on him and the other huntsmen to act as advance warning in the week to come.

"Don't fret on our behalf, yer lordship," he replied immediately. His courtly graces were lacking, but then that wasn't what mattered in his line of work.

Sir Harold spoke next, "Given the fact that we have a good idea of when they will arrive, will we be altering our responses?" A big man, Harold had grown out of his boyish looks, and his short golden beard made him seem somewhat lion-like.

I was grateful for the question, for it led us directly to the heart of the matter. "Yes," I answered, "it will alter our planning, although the basics will stay the same. Primarily, it will enable us to evacuate many people prior to the day we expect the gods to arrive. Dorian, would you mind going over the three basic plans for everyone? Just to make sure everyone remembers…"

"Certainly," said Dorian before he drew a deep breath. He showed nothing of the nervousness he had once had difficulty with, but looking around the room, I could tell everyone was inwardly groaning at the thought of hearing the outlines of our emergency plans again. This was something we went over yearly; including a drill to make sure people knew what to do.

"As I am sure most of you know, we have been anticipating something like this for many years now, ever since our good count brought the 'God-Stone' back to Castle Cameron for safekeeping," Dorian began carefully. "In the event of an attack or other emergency, there are three evacuations plans which we have designated with the colors blue, yellow, and red. The most optimistic plan is blue; although none of the three should be mistaken for a good situation."

Dorian's eyes roved across the room, making sure everyone's attention was on him. "Blue means that we intend to stay and fight. The only people to be evacuated are those without assigned roles in the defense of the keep, primarily women, children and the elderly. From the yearly drills, the townsfolk and castle inhabitants should know to gather at the building housing the teleportation circles in the castle yard. All guardsmen, knights, and of course our few wizards, will report to their assigned locations. George and Elaine Prathion are responsible for making sure that those to be evacuated are taken by 'circle' to Albamarl."

"Condition blue was created as a response to an attack by *one* of the shining gods, and the presumption is that our lord, the Count di'Cameron, will be able to handle one, preferably outside the castle environs, while the good Baron, Lord Prathion, will maintain the defensive barrier around Castle Cameron." That was actually a bit of an oversimplification. The defensive barrier was an enchantment I had devised and built that would harness power from the God-Stone. The enchantment didn't actually require much besides a mage to activate and deactivate it when desired.

"The next color, yellow," Dorian said, continuing, "indicates a more serious state. The thought here is that we will use this color if we think that two of the gods are attacking in concert. The count has made it clear that in the event two of them attack at once, it will be impossible to achieve victory in a head to head confrontation. Everyone will be evacuated in this case, except for the knights and the Count himself. In addition the escape points will be different. Those in Washbrook will make directly for the Muddy Pig."

The 'Muddy Pig' was the name Joe McDaniel had chosen for his tavern. The name was also a direct reference to my first meeting with the previous Baron of Arundel, when I had covered myself with mud before our introductions. That notable had been less than amused, but luckily the current baron, Walter, had a much better sense of humor. If the circumstances sound implausible— well, I had my reasons. Honestly.

I had created a safe haven beneath the cellars of the tavern, a large room that was magically concealed. The idea being that if we didn't have time to evacuate the townsfolk, they could hide there until the 'storm' had passed. It also held a circle that led to Lancaster.

"Those within Castle Cameron will make for the great hall, while those manning the walls or in the yard, will make for the building where we house the circles. Elaine Prathion will be responsible for moving people there, while George Prathion will be responsible for transporting those that take haven at the Muddy Pig. The Baron will handle those that gather in the great hall." Dorian paused for a moment, for Sir Ian had caught his eye. "You have a question?" he asked.

Sir Ian was a dark haired man with deep brown eyes. People meeting him for the first time often described his looks as 'fierce' or 'intimidating'. Later they would realize he was actually one of the mildest mannered men amongst the knights; his looks were in contrast to his true personality. He addressed Dorian hesitantly, "No disrespect Lord Dorian, but we've been over this at least once a year and I still have one concern." It was a statement that begged the question.

"What is your concern?" said Dorian.

"There is no mention in any of the plans regarding how the Count and his family will be evacuated. Is this an oversight or a deliberate omission?" asked Sir Ian.

Dorian glanced in my direction, for he knew this dealt with matters I would rather not discuss openly. I raised a hand to let him know I would handle it and stood to face the questioner. "Your question has two answers Sir Ian," I told him, giving the man an honest stare, "neither of which you will like. One, I will not be part of the evacuation in any of the three scenarios we have planned. In most cases I will be handling matters that will likely prevent me from joining the exodus. I will provide for my own exit, if possible. Second, my family will either evacuate at one of the previously mentioned points, or via another route that we have kept private. In each case the final decision will rest with my lady wife, depending upon circumstances."

There were a few mutters around the room, but I stared at them until silence returned. Once they had gone quiet I asked Sir Ian, "Is that answer sufficient for you?"

"Yes, my lord," he responded promptly.

I nodded at Dorian and he resumed his explanation. "The last plan is designated red, and is quite similar to blue. The main difference is that there is no provision for any resistance. In blue, the Knights of Stone and our Count remain in order to defend and delay. Red will be used if we think that all three of the remaining gods have come against us at once. In this case we activate the barrier defense immediately, and everyone within the keep is to report to the meeting points to evacuate without delay. Those unfortunate enough to be outside the castle walls when this happens, will have the option of trying to make it to the Muddy Pig to hide or simply striking out into the wilderness."

Peter spoke up then, "If we don't hope to win in a 'yellow' emergency, why don't we simply evacuate everyone immediately. I'm not sure I see the need for a separate red and yellow plan." Several of the knights gave him scornful looks. It was a question any of them might have been wondering, but given Peter's position as my chamberlain and a non-combatant, they considered the topic outside of his purview.

Before any of them could speak up, I stood and answered him directly, "The difference is one of time and urgency. In red we take everyone we can and leave immediately, leaving behind some unfortunate enough to be unable to get within the walls in time. In yellow we control our departure, and the knights remain until I give them the order to depart."

I thought that would be enough to quiet him but Peter's curiosity wasn't quenched yet, "Begging your pardon, my lord, but how will you be able to provide the time? If you can handle but one, then any number beyond that will be the same, will it not?"

I had cultivated a certain freedom of speech amongst those that served me, but Peter constantly surprised me. There were grumbles in the room at his presumptuous questions, but I held up a hand to forestall their complaints. "The barrier enchantment around the castle should be strong enough to keep any one god from breaking it quickly. Two will probably be able to accomplish the task easily, but it will take them some time; hopefully as much as half an hour or possibly more. Three combined would probably shatter it within minutes, and that is the main reason for the difference in the evacuation plans," I finished. I left unsaid my other reason, for it involved a great deal of personal risk, and that was never a popular topic among the Knights of Stone. They were fine with risking their own lives, but never mine. "Any further questions?" I asked him, to make sure he was done.

Peter bowed his head deferentially, "No my lord, thank you for your patience with my inexperience in these matters."

"If that's out of the way then, we can proceed to current matters. I've given the broad outlines of our emergency action plans," said Dorian, "but now I would like to move on to two particulars of pertinence in the present. First, the disposition of Master Grayson's hunter's this week, as well as any changes he would like to make before the anticipated arrival of the gods in less than two weeks' time. After that we'll go over the advance evacuation schedule that is to begin at the end of next week. We need to make sure everyone that isn't absolutely needed, is out two days prior to Karenth's return."

Dorian went on for some time before calling Chad forward to discuss the positioning of his scouts. *No matter how many of these I attend, they never get any less boring,* I thought while stifling a yawn. It wouldn't do to let the men see me showing signs of disinterest.

Late that afternoon I checked the message boxes and found Cyhan's reply waiting for me. Opening the box, I saw a neatly folded piece of paper. Unfolding it I saw his distinctively bad penmanship. His handwriting was on a par with Penny's, in fact it might even be worse.

My Lord,

Your message is received and understood. Currently it is still morning as I write this. Will make haste and should return within five days. Look for us on the morning of the fifth day hence. That will be the morning of the festival.

Your Servant,
Cyhan

"Five days!" I muttered to myself. That meant he'd be force marching the men. I considered writing another letter to try and make him slow down rather than tire them out, but in the end I decided it would be pointless. That was the sort of order he'd ignore. *He always was a damn overachiever.*

Instead, I simply drew a deep breath and penned a quick acknowledgement. At least they would get to enjoy the festivities. Checking the rest of the boxes, I found another message, this one from Marc.

Mort,

I hope this letter finds you well.

The journey to Agraden has been noteworthy only for its boredom. We should arrive in another day, and Marissa's uncle assured us that he will have room for us until we can find a place of our own. Despite my true reason for moving here, I find I am somewhat looking forward to seeing new things, and the search for whatever remains of the Gaelyn family library might also prove interesting.

I will write again once I have some definite news, or at least something interesting to tell.

Marcus

I read through his short note twice and found that despite my original opposition to his move, I now felt relieved to know that he was well away from all the excitement in Lothion. I considered my reply carefully before setting pen to paper again.

Dear Marc,

I'm glad to hear that your journey is almost done. I do hope that it wasn't a hardship for Marissa. Don't forget that if the house costs more money than we anticipated, I will write a letter of credit for you. The bankers in Albamarl assure me that they have a stable arrangement with the moneylenders in Agraden, so that shouldn't be a problem.

Things are busy around here, what with the festival preparations at this time of year. There always seems to be something. Perhaps if you get well settled, I can make the journey to visit next year some time. One visit and I'll be able to set up a circle, which will make any future trips trivial.

Write soon.

Mordecai

I felt a bit dishonest for not mentioning any of my recent problems, but given the distance, the only thing my friend could have done about them would be to worry needlessly. Pushing those thoughts aside, I rose and went to find Walter. I wanted to meet with him and make sure he remembered the specifics of how to raise and control the barrier enchantment around the castle. As I walked, I decided we should include Elaine this time. She was older now, and there was always the possibility that neither he nor I would be around to activate it when needed.

CHAPTER 15

Walter and his daughter stood beside me in a small room not far from the great hall. The room itself had originally been designed as a small waiting room, but I had repurposed it as a central place to control the enchantments that protected Castle Cameron. The walls were unobtrusively marked with runes that effectively hid the room from magical sight, while the door would only open to the touch of a few specially designated people—both of whom were standing next to me.

This was the first time Elaine had been inside, and I had just finished adding her to the short list of people that the enchantment would allow to open the door. She looked about the room with observant eyes. "So this is the room that controls the keystone for the barrier enchantment?" she asked carefully.

I nodded.

"It's a rather unassuming room. Somehow I always imagined it would be more impressive," she said with a half-smile.

"Since very few people will ever see it, I felt ornamentation was unnecessary," I responded dryly before gesturing to the stone pedestal that stood in the center of the room. "Everything is controlled from there."

The object I was indicating was four foot in height, made of plain grey granite. The top was smooth except for a number of symbols lightly engraved in the hard stone. The wall directly in front of it was adorned with twelve pieces of flat, clear glass, each one twelve inches on a side. In fact the glass had originally been made to be window panes. Such things were expensive, even in the city, where they were most frequently used, but I had bought them with a new purpose in mind.

I pointed at the symbols across the top of the stone pedestal. "Each of these corresponds to one of the glass panes you see on the wall, and each of those panes corresponds with another pane located at various points around the castle. There are two mounted high on the outer faces of each of the four main corner towers, approximately twenty feet from the ground. Those account for the first eight panes you see there. You activate each one simply by applying a small amount of aythar, here...," as I said that, I activated the first symbol.

The top leftmost pane of glass abruptly changed. Where before it had shown nothing but the grey stone it was mounted against, it now appeared to be letting in the afternoon sunlight from outside. An empty field could be seen beyond it, with trees a hundred or so yards in the distance. A few small buildings were visible in the field of view, buildings that had been built there against my advice. I had warned the people of Washbrook that I could not protect anything built beyond the stone walls of the town.

Walter remained silent. He had seen most of this before, but Elaine was amazed. "Is that the western side of town? Beyond the wall?" she asked in a tone of wonderment.

"Yes."

"How? Is it some sort of illusion? Are you passing the light with the same sort of magical spell that we use for our invisibility?"

Walter coughed.

"No," I answered. "We tried that originally, and although your father managed to make it work for short periods of time, we were unable to design an effective enchantment that could maintain the effect."

"How else would you do it then?" she said in puzzlement.

Walter spoke up then, "Mordecai and I created a type of portal enchantment between each of the matching panes of glass. When it is active, the glass is actually serving as a real window between here and the location of the other piece of glass."

Elaine's eyes narrowed, "What if an enemy discovered the connection? Could they enter the keep through the portal?"

"No," her father replied smugly, "The enchantment, the portal lies within the glass itself, so only light may pass. If anything else were to physically try to pass, it would break the glass and destroy the portal simultaneously."

"In addition, the portal is only open when the enchantment is activated here," I explained. Passing my hand along the top of the stone, I 'turned on' the rest of the windows, and soon we could see out from many vantage points. "The first eight, as you can see, look out from the tower walls, showing us the land around Washbrook. The last four look out from the towers around the outer wall of Cameron Castle; from those you can see the town itself."

Elaine studied the stone, and I let her try her hand with the symbols. She was easily able to turn them on and off. "What are these for?" she asked, pointing to the symbols along the bottom row, "Do these activate the barrier?"

"Those light the warning beacons," I explained quickly. Each of the towers, both those of Castle Cameron and those of the town walls, had a large glass sphere mounted atop their tower roofs. "This one turns the signal on and makes the color a bright blue," I said pointing to the left most of the bottom three symbols. "The middle one sets it to yellow and the one on the right is for barrier around the entire town and the castle. The next one down just sets it around the castle proper and it's more powerful in that configuration—less area to cover."

"What are those two?" she asked, pointing to the two I hadn't mentioned yet.

"Those open the barrier in one of two places, either the city gate or the castle courtyard gate, without removing the main portion of the barrier," I answered. "That way you can…"

"…let in refugees without dropping the defenses entirely," Elaine finished for me. Although she was bright, and a quick learner; her tendency to jump ahead was occasionally annoying. "How will you know if something tries to slip in with them?" she added.

"Here," I told her, pointing to another rune. "This one activates the window near the city gate, and this other one does the same near the castle gate." I turned them on to illustrate the point.

"But they are so small, how would you—oh!" she remarked, cutting off her statement abruptly.

"Were you about to ask how we would see well through such a small window?" I said with a faint smile.

She nodded. "Yes but I can see now, when the portal windows are open, more than just light passes. I can sense everything beyond the glass, just as though I were standing behind a regular window."

Walter spoke then, "That's right, and so long as the glass remains intact, it will function that way, but remember that magic will pass both ways. If you open it and you sense something powerful, such as one of the gods, you must close it immediately, as well as the barrier; otherwise you risk yourself along with our defenses."

"Yes, of course Father," Elaine replied demurely, though I could tell the advice annoyed her. If she had been a teenager, she might have rolled her eyes—fortunately she was older than that.

"Needless to say," I said, breaking the tension, "you are only to use this room if I am away and your father isn't present. You already know the rules for determining whether we will use the red, yellow, or blue signal, but in my absence it is quite simple. If any of the gods show up while I am away, it should be red—immediate evacuation. If it is only one and you think the barrier will hold for a while you might use yellow to allow more time for an orderly evacuation but if there is any doubt don't risk it."

"I understand," she replied smoothly, her attitude with me was much more deferential. I wondered if I would have similar problems someday with my own daughters. Imagining Moira's sweet smile and eager to please demeanor, I couldn't believe it. *Surely not,* I told myself.

"From here I think the only things we need to worry about are the preparations for the festival. We've done as much as we can to prepare for the worst, and we should have almost a week after the festival before they arrive," I told them both.

"I don't know if I'll be able to enjoy myself with a sword hanging over our necks," commented Walter.

"You can manage! I for one intend to enjoy the dancing," Elaine said with enthusiasm. "No sense in worrying over things we can't change."

Inwardly I agreed with her, but I had a feeling I would still have the same problem as Walter.

⊰─────⊱

The next few days went by uneventfully, and despite my fears I could find little else to do to prepare. I had been preparing for years already. Instead, I used some of the time to work on the glass mirror that Gram and Matthew had inadvertently broken.

It was still two days from the festival as I stared at the glass fragments I had spread out upon the worktable in front of me. I was a bit frustrated already, for I had been staring at them for some time. My first effort had been to organize the pieces by shape and size, and somehow begin fusing them back together. That hadn't worked at all.

While I could easily fuse any two pieces together, they weren't necessarily the 'right' two pieces. They were so small and so many that I had little hope of fitting them back together as they had been originally. "I might as well just melt all the glass down and create an entirely new mirror from it then," I said aloud to myself. I didn't really want to do that though; my intention was to restore the mirror to its former state, complete with any flaws or imperfections that had made it a keepsake.

I took a deep breath and tried to relax. No good would come from beating my head against the wall. After a time I let my mind wander a bit, and I realized that I could hear the tiny voices of the pieces of glass. Now that it was shattered, each shard had its own unique voice. Focusing on them was merely a matter of patience and practice. Compared to their tiny songs, the beat of the earth was like a massive drum and the sky outside sounded like a rushing river.

Of course none of these were true 'sounds', but that is the only way I can describe them. Along with those, I could also hear the faintly disturbing melody of what I had come to think of as 'death' underlying the others, much like a counterpoint to the song of the rest of the world. *Why couldn't I hear it before?* I wondered. It was only since rescuing Walter's spirit from the void that I had begun to hear it running alongside all the other voices of the world.

Turning away from that topic, I focused again on the tiny shards of glass that lay before me, concentrating on their small harmonies. At first they were all separate, but as I let my attention drift, they began to come into focus as pieces of a more elaborate harmony. *Perhaps I could 'convince' them to resume their former condition...*

That was a dangerous thought, especially since I had once again given Elaine the day off. I wasn't supposed to exercise my abilities as an archmage without someone keeping an eye on me. Still, this couldn't hurt much. *I won't go far,* I assured myself.

With that, I opened myself to the wider influence of the crystalline melodies that lay across the surface of my work table. Keeping myself tightly anchored, I joined the tiny glass songs to my own and slowly began coaxing them into returning to their former state. The effort, though small, took intense concentration, and my sense of time rapidly faded while my consciousness grew ever more ordered.

An observer watching me would have seen the fragments slowly rearranging themselves, moving and locking into place with each other. That same observer would probably have become bored, for while I had lost my perception of time, hours slipped by unnoticed as Penny's mirror gradually reformed.

Eventually, I was almost done, but I was having trouble remembering what the word meant precisely. For that matter, I was no longer sure exactly why I was doing what I was... I frowned and a memory appeared; that of a woman's face. I forced myself to focus upon the memory, for I felt instinctively that it held the clue to my reason for being there.

The woman's eyes were dark brown, and her hair fell around her in heavy brown curls. In appearance she was much like Penny. *Penny?* For a moment I struggled to remember the significance of that name. *Penny! That's her mother—I must have dredged up a memory of her from our childhood.* With the memories I found it easier to withdraw from the work at hand, but not before finishing; and as I coaxed the last few pieces into place a stroke of inspiration hit me.

Making subtle adjustments, I altered the now complete mirror, working as quickly as I could before the vividness of my memory was gone. Stepping back, I studied what I had done, pleased with the result. *I hope she likes it, if not this might upset her even more.*

CHAPTER 16

Though I had anticipated Cyhan's arrival the day of the festival, he managed to outdo himself and arrive very late the evening before that. Coincidentally, it also led to a lot of work on the part of those at the castle who were responsible for feeding and welcoming our soldiers back. No one complained though, at least not aloud. Well, perhaps that wasn't true after all, I have little idea what may have been said in places out of my earshot.

What the servants didn't know, however, is that I wouldn't have punished them for their negative sentiments. In fact I was a bit irritated myself, though I knew it was irrational. They had returned because I had commanded it, and they returned at the time they did because they had pushed themselves to the limit to return as soon as humanly possible.

Rationality can go fling itself into a fire! I told myself silently, in response to those more reasonable thoughts. "They could have taken their damn sweet time and gotten here a day or two later!" I opined in a loud and entirely unsavory voice, as I dressed hastily.

"Quit complaining and go, before you wake up the children," Penny hissed at me in the dark.

"If the damn pounding on the door a minute ago didn't waken them, my swearing won't do it!" I responded at a somewhat quieter volume.

Penny didn't respond to that remark, but with my magesight I could see her glaring at me in the dark.

Sometimes my gift is less of a blessing and more of a curse. My better sense finally got the upper hand, and I shut up and left the room to make my way to the hall that joined our house to the apartment in Cameron Castle. Along the way I managed to get my trousers up far enough that I wasn't in danger of exposing myself.

Reaching the door I flung it open. "Give me a damn moment to get dressed, and I'll be right along!" I said without preamble. I was surprised to find Elaine standing next to the footman that guarded my outer door. Her eyes widened at the sight of me, and her cheeks flushed. I was too many years beyond puberty to be embarrassed. "Never seen a man without a shirt on before?" I barked in annoyance, "I thought you had a brother at home."

She put her hand up over her mouth to hide her amusement. "You are 'not' my brother...," she replied, belatedly adding, "...Your Excellency."

I stared at her for a moment, before shutting the door a bit abruptly. *I'm far too old for this sort of silliness,* I thought, as I tromped back to finish dressing myself. A second thought followed quickly after it, *No you aren't.* "And that is exactly the sort of stupidity that will get you in trouble," I responded aloud to my inner-renegade.

"What sort of stupidity?" asked Penny mildly from the direction of the bed.

"I was just chiding myself for being too angry," I said quickly. *Someday I will learn to keep my mouth closed until my better sense catches up with me.*

Pulling a large over-tunic on, I left the room before I could say anything else stupid in my sleep-addled state. Elaine and a second footman followed me from my door and down to meet our returning soldiers. As we walked, a thought occurred to me, "Why do you happen to be up at this hour Elaine? I wouldn't expect you to be dressed and ready to greet anyone this late at night." She was still wearing the same dress she had had on at dinner, several hours earlier.

She paused for a moment, obviously uncertain how to reply, "I went to the room you and Father showed me. I was experimenting with the viewing windows, to make sure I would remember where everything was if the need arose later. I saw them arriving at the city gate before the news reached the castle."

That explained a half an hour perhaps, but it wouldn't have kept her up this late. "Studying the enchantments we used to create the window portals?" I said, guessing. Her reaction was all the answer I needed to know I had hit the mark.

She nodded.

"I'll be happy to teach the pattern to you, and your father already knows it as well," I offered. "There's no reason to be embarrassed about it."

"Thank you," she said quietly, but it was still obvious that she wasn't revealing what was really on her mind.

We kept walking, and after a moment I spoke again, "Why don't you just spit out whatever it is that you're thinking."

"How do you do it?" she blurted out suddenly, "How do you keep creating these enchantments?"

I sighed, "I had some advantages. I found a book detailing enchantments used by wizards in the past. I know I've told you this before…"

"No," she interrupted, "Father said you figured out the basics before you found the book."

"Those were very crude enchantments, and I was lucky that I didn't kill myself experimenting. Most of what I learned came from the book I found," I said, hoping to put her off.

"One of your early enchantments was the rune channel you put on your staff," she said, pointing at the pouch that I stored my staff and other cumbersome tools in—a pouch that was also the result of a clever enchantment. "Yet despite what you learned in that book, you saw no need to improve or replace it."

I had actually decided that my design was slightly better than the example of a rune channel found in the book, for mine included the adaptability of being able to store a temporary spell, such as a light, within the enchantment. "It was a good design," I answered, "sometimes even fools get lucky." Elaine stopped walking and her brow furrowed. Was she angry? She rarely showed that side of her personality to me, unlike her poor father.

"I've studied every enchantment you showed me. I've looked at that book that you claim taught you," she began, speaking slowly, "and I barely understand the designs, even after you explain them to me. Every day you seem to come up with some new innovation. You're a better enchanter than whoever wrote that book you keep pointing to for explanations."

I gave her my best roguish grin, "I won't deny that I may have a natural talent." Her serious expression told me she wasn't buying my story.

"Where is it coming from?" she asked suddenly, "Moira Centyr? Is she still hiding in the shadows, whispering the secrets of the ages in your ear?"

A cold sensation passed over me, for I *knew*, without a doubt, where the knowledge originated. *"You are the heir of Illeniel's Doom. The sin of our progenitor has passed to you, along with the betrayal of his heir. Illeniel's Promise remains unfulfilled and must remain so, my son. We share the same burden; the guilt of generations, still refusing to pay our debt, for the cost is too high."*

I could hear Jaryd Illeniel's voice in my mind, remembering his words as clearly as if he had spoken them just a day before, yet I was sure he had died at least a generation before Balinthor threatened to destroy all of humankind. With that memory, came the realization that I also remembered the man who had first taught him those words, Dalyn Illeniel, Jaryd's father. The memory, and the words, stretched back within me, through a line of fathers and sons, unbroken until it reached the source— the first Illeniel.

"The man who destroyed my people and who set me on the path that has led me now to you, his great grandson many times removed. Did you think you descended from some noble line? The man was a murderer a thousand times over." Mal'goroth's words echoed in my head, as I remembered our meeting shortly before I finished massacring the army of Gododdin.

"Are you listening?" said Elaine, her voice interrupting the cascade of dark thoughts that had almost overwhelmed me.

My eyes narrowed as they focused on Elaine's. Pushing aside the confusion of memories threatening my sanity, I drew upon anger to hide my weakness. "Are you accusing me of something, Elaine?" I responded, in a tone that radiated chilly animosity.

She hesitated then, as my sudden anger had caused her some uncertainty. Glancing toward the footman, as if seeking reassurance, she answered, "Perhaps we should talk about this another time—for the sake of discretion."

"You require privacy?" I asked, and without waiting for an answer, I created dark grey shields around the two of us. They were opaque, blocking all sight, and the sudden hush around us gave testament to their sound deadening qualities. "You may speak freely now, no one will see or hear us."

Unsettled, Elaine looked around before straightening her back and squaring her shoulders. "I want to know where your knowledge comes from," she said with sudden boldness, even daring to step closer to me, as if to show that my angry demeanor had not frightened her.

"I have many secrets," I admitted, "but I have hidden nothing concerning my knowledge of magic from you." *A half-truth is still a lie.*

Elaine stared unwaveringly into my eyes and parted her lips as if to speak, but she closed them again without saying anything. There was defiance in her gaze.

"Spit it out, no one can hear us," I said.

"I may speak freely?" she asked.

As she spoke I noted the dilation of her eyes and the increase in her breathing. She was afraid of me, either that or—I pushed the thought away. "I already told you that. Speak what is on your mind," I told her.

"You're lying," she said abruptly.

"What?" I said, shocked at her brazenness. Absently I also noted that her cheeks were flushed. *And she smells uncommonly good,* observed the voice in the back of my head.

"You heard me. I called you a liar," she said, stepping even closer and looking up into my eyes. Our faces were too close; she had invaded my personal space. Usually it made me uncomfortable, but despite my anger, or perhaps because of it, I did not step back.

"I've been watching you for years now," she continued, "and I've learned to read your expressions. You've become an excellent liar. You lie to everyone; to Dorian, to my father, to your wife, and to me. I know you do it for good reason. You want to protect us, but it doesn't have to be that way."

Rather than dodge the accusation, I accepted it at face value. "That is my decision to make," I stated calmly, though my temper was rising.

"You have other options, Mordecai. Everyone needs a confidant, someone they trust, someone to share their secrets. I want to help you," she said, pressing even closer, her hand on my chest.

Her hand was hot, or so it seemed, for it seemed to burn where she had laid it against my chest. Such a casual gesture, and yet my senses told me that her heart was beating rapidly. Even worse, her perception would have already betrayed my own quickening heart rate. I took a deep breath, "Elaine, you've made a mistake, an understandable one, given the situation, but a mistake nonetheless. You don't really want what you think you want. If..."

"No," she interrupted, "you do need me." For just a second her eyes darted downward.

Wicked girl! I knew then that she held no illusions about the nature of her actions. This was no innocent. *She's only four years younger than I am,* my inner commentator reminded me. *I have thought of her as a child since I first met her, but she's a woman of twenty three now.*

Her features softened as she looked up at me with sky blue eyes, eyes that were full of sorrow. "I've watched you, learned from you, studied you..., and loved you, Mordecai, since the day you saved me from Celior's cruel grip. I know you have obligations, but I would give anything to help you. I am not a child."

For a second I wavered as I looked at her. It would have been easy after all, and I need have no guilt over her innocence, for she had just proclaimed her clear intention.

Of course, it would be a betrayal of my family, my wife, and her father, who trusted me. My hormones didn't really give a damn about any of that though. The doorway that had opened in my mind held glimpses of similar situations: other men's moments of weakness or strength, and in those memories I saw that many otherwise good men had made bad decisions. Better men than I had made this mistake, often with few consequences.

Some of them had tragic results, my inner monitor reminded me, but my lower regions were shouting something entirely different at me. I closed my eyes for a moment while, with my magesight, I saw Elaine leaning in, her arms rising to circle my waist. Her own senses had surely alerted her to my body's physical reaction, so she had little reason to doubt how I would answer her.

Her face registered shock for a moment. I had caught her wrists in my hands to prevent her embrace. "No," I said softly, looking down at her with what I hoped were firm and compassionate eyes.

"What?"

"No," I repeated. "This is never going to happen."

"I don't understand," she began, a look of confusion in her features, "I can *feel* your true response. Why are you...?"

"This would do nothing but bring harm to both of us. I love my wife, and your father is my friend. I have many flaws, and I have made plenty of mistakes, but I will not add this to them," I explained carefully.

Elaine frowned, "That isn't what you want." Again her eyes flashed downward, in a not so subtle hint.

My temper returned quickly. "You think *that* is an indicator of a man's true desires?" I rebuked her, "That it's a sign of love perhaps?"

Her cheeks flushed red with embarrassment, and she stepped back from me, providing me with some welcome space. "I never thought you would love me," she replied, "I am not a fool. I was simply offering my confidence, my trust, and *any* comfort that you might want of me, but I already knew I could not claim your heart. Is that so wrong of me?"

I had to give her credit. She made adultery sound almost noble. Even worse, I was pretty sure she truly meant what she said. She was willing to give me whatever I wanted, and she expected nothing in return. It was a tortured form of love. It was also self-deceit.

I ignored her question and answered with one of my own, "Do you know what separates humans from the beasts?" The question was rhetorical, and after a brief pause I went on, "The distinction between love and lust, the ability to occasionally overcome our impulses for self-gratification, and instead do what is best for our loved ones. We frequently fail at this, but once in a while we succeed."

She flinched as though I had slapped her. Opening her mouth to reply, no words came out, while instead tears were already falling from her cheeks. My remarks had definitely produced the intended result. *Now if I can calm her down. Getting on a moral soapbox may not have been the best method. She's not likely to be very rational for a while,* I observed mentally.

Whirling about she ran headlong into the grey shield I had put around us. "Let me out!" she cried at me through her tears.

"Not yet," I answered calmly. "I have a few things to tell you first."

She met my gaze for a moment, and I was shocked at the transformation. In less than a minute, she had gone from lovely young woman to puffy-eyed, snotty-nosed, and thoroughly disheveled. She also seemed to be acutely aware of it, for she hid her face. "Just let me go, I don't want to be here anymore. Please!" she sobbed.

My anger had already dissipated, to be replaced by pity and empathy. "I know you're hurt and embarrassed, which is understandable. I refuse, however, to lose a promising student over something so profoundly normal. After I remove the shield, you may return to your room, but you are not to leave. You may have tomorrow off, but I expect you back at your duties the day after that."

"I can't face anyone after this…" she moaned.

"Use your invisibility. No one need see you as you return. I will explain your sudden absence to the guards," I told her sternly.

"But tomorrow…" she began.

"This was between us. It's settled now and I for one see no need to shame you for what are perfectly human feelings. I will speak to no one regarding this conversation. Do you understand?"

She nodded mutely and after a moment she became invisible to normal sight. I took the shields down and faced the guards, who had been patiently waiting for many minutes now.

"Is everything alright, my lord?" asked one of the men.

"Where is Elaine?" the other inquired promptly.

"I sent her on a different errand," I informed them brusquely.

"But…"

I held up my hand. "It does not concern you. Now, let us continue. I am anxious to see Sir Cyhan."

⟢———⟣

Cyhan and the rest of the men were already settling into the main hall when I got there. Servants, sleepy eyed and occasionally yawning, were moving to and fro to bring the men bread and small beer. By their appearance, I could tell they had been pushed hard to reach the castle so quickly.

"My lord," said Cyhan as I approached the table.

He had already half risen before I could gesture for him to stay seated. "Sit! Rest!" I admonished him, while looking around the room. The rest of the men were standing as well, so I motioned for them to relax, "You have traveled long roads at a fast pace, take your ease men." Glancing back at Cyhan, I told him, "Eat and we will talk in the morning."

The look that crossed his face spoke volumes. Cyhan would rather have gotten the exchange of news taken care of immediately. Opening his mouth, he hesitated for a second as he read my face, "Very well my liege," he said at last.

After that I took the next few minutes to walk among the men and check on their general condition. Once I was sure they were well taken care of I retired, for I could still hear the call of my bed. As I walked back to my family suite, I thought again of my conversation with Elaine. *Nothing good comes of waking up in the middle of the night,* I said to myself.

CHAPTER 17

Morning arrived with a thump, as the wind was driven from my chest by a heavy blow to my abdomen. Since I had been dead asleep, the air rushed from my half open mouth with a 'whoop', followed by a choking gasp as I sought to fill my lungs again. The blow had been precisely aimed however, and my diaphragm was refusing to assist me in the effort. It had taken the day off in protest at the abuse I suppose.

"Daddy!" Conall yelled exuberantly from his perch atop me.

He had my full attention, as I struggled to breathe. One thing I had learned early on in fatherhood was the importance of calmness. I did my best not to alarm him with any excessive grimaces or gasps. Sitting up I tried to relax so I could draw a shallow breath, while at the same time, I gave my three year old son a feeble smile.

My small son gave me a serious stare. "You look funny, Daddy."

"The joke's on you, when you grow up to look like me then," I managed to get out with a wheeze. As usual, my fine sense of sarcasm was wasted upon him, and my senses quickly told me that Penny was no longer in the bed. *Never anyone around to appreciate my fine sense of humor,* I thought to myself. Reaching out I pulled Conall in for a hug and a cuddle while my diaphragm recovered. On general principle, I tickled the squirming monster as he tried to escape me.

"No, no, no!" Conall shouted, laughing all the while.

"You woke the dragon, you reap the consequences!" I told him.

"No! Mommy told me to do it! Go reap her!" he yelled back, as I finally let him slip free.

There was no point in replying to such a hilarious remark. I filed the thought away though, for future reference. *Sowing and reaping is how I wound up with three of my four children,* I thought with a smirk. *Perhaps Penny will consider some reaping and pillaging later.* Even as the thought occurred to me, I knew I had mixed my metaphors, but then, if you can't butcher the language in your own head, where can you?

I rose from the bed with a growling roar that sent Conall shrieking out of the room in delight. Cold air made me regret throwing the covers back almost immediately. "You'd think I could figure out something as simple as how to keep a room at a comfortable temperature," I mused aloud.

I had in fact made a few attempts in years past, but in every case, the enchantment gradually turned the room into an oven. It didn't seem to matter how gentle or small it was, the constant addition of heat, made all but the draftiest of rooms swelteringly hot. What I really needed was some method for the enchantment to recognize when the appropriate temperature had been reached, so it could stop—but I had yet to figure out how. It had to be possible, for the house I had inherited in Albamarl had something similar at work, along with many other, even more complex enchantments. I just hadn't found it yet.

Penny had risen early to get started with the day's preparations. Tomorrow would be the celebration marking the eighth anniversary of our triumphant defeat of the army of Gododdin, so she had a long list of things to accomplish. For my own part, I still wasn't keen on the joyous remembrance of my act of mass murder, which was the way I recalled the event. Penny, Dorian, Marcus, Rose and pretty well everyone else close to me, had counseled me to keep my personal opinions to myself, and let the people enjoy a reason to celebrate. Never let it be said that I didn't listen to advice—but I still didn't like it.

I looked for Cyhan in the main hall while I had something to eat. I ate breakfast there, since Penny had started her day early. He was nowhere to be seen. I discovered him in the barracks with Dorian, going over the preparations for the Knights and soldiers.

"I agree," the older warrior replied to something Dorian had just said. "I've told the others to limit themselves to no more than two drinks over the course of the day. They're also to remain in their armor."

"That seems excessive," I commented as I walked in.

"Good morning," Dorian answered, without any sign of hesitation. "Don't worry about this end of things, Mordecai, Cyhan and I have it well in hand."

"You're planning to keep the Knights of Stone in full armor all day, and limit their drinking? We didn't even expect to have Cyhan and his group. Why not let them split the day? There's no need for them to all be miserable," I said, offering my advice to an unreceptive audience.

Dorian gave me a glare that spoke volumes. "Why don't you…," he began, but Cyhan interrupted him.

"Sir Dorian," he interjected, "please allow me to answer this one." The two men shared a short knowing glance before Dorian nodded and Cyhan turned to address me. Years before I had wondered if the two of them could work together but my doubts had been unfounded. The two of them were almost always in complete agreement.

"My liege," Cyhan continued, "I will take your suggestions under advisement. Sir Dorian and I will see if we can allow the men breaks in which to dress more casually and enjoy themselves tomorrow."

Cyhan's quick acceptance was unusual, but then I had rarely been able to read the man's intentions, either before or after he had taken service with me. I glanced at Dorian to see his reaction to his subordinate's quick acceptance.

My friend was too honest to attempt deception, so he didn't bother. "I think it's a stupid idea," he grumbled. "Tomorrow would be the best day to attack us. We should be on full alert." He paused and glared at me for a long moment. "But if you and Sir Cyhan both agree, then I will let him see about arranging the breaks you think are so damned important."

Something odd flickered across Dorian's face, as if he had just had a humorous thought, but Cyhan spoke again before I could ask him about it, "It shall be as you say, Grandmaster."

Grandmaster was Dorian's nominal title as the head of the Knights of Stone. "Don't you two ever relax? You're worse than the men you command," I noted. After a moment I added, "There's no need for such formality, when it's just the three of us."

"As you wish, Your Excellency," Cyhan responded with a bow. I thought I could see a hint of a smile on his face.

I looked at Dorian, hoping for some understanding, but instead he grinned, while adopting a pose of attention. "My lord, shall I have Knight-Captain Cyhan punished for his insolence?"

Glancing back and forth between the two of them, I realized they had me completely outflanked. "You're both impossible. I'm going to go find someone with some sanity left to talk to." Turning around I left the barracks. *This is why I like children,* I mused. *They're not nearly as unaccommodating as these so-called grown-ups.*

⸺◆⸺

I had decided to escape the preparations and try to get some work done in my workshop, but I was intercepted on my way there by a large, and very nearly bald, man. His name was Claude, and I had retained him several years before to run the kitchens at Castle Cameron. Overall he was an excellent head cook and I rarely had cause for complaint.

"My lord!" he called as he hurried toward me.

For a moment a childish urge took me, and I briefly considered pretending I hadn't heard him and finding some way to turn a corner and disappear before he reached me. I had never mastered the invisibility that the Prathions used so effortlessly, but I was pretty sure I could have managed something. Instead I stopped and gave him my attention, "Yes? Do you need something, Claude?"

The cook seemed a bit out of breath. At a guess I'd say he had been looking for me for a while. "Yes, my lord, it's about the meat we have set aside for tomorrow's feasts. I had not realized that Sir Cyhan and his men would be returning so soon. That's two hundred men's stomachs I hadn't planned on filling."

Several flippant and unproductive remarks passed through my mind. I ignored the idle thoughts and asked instead, "Why aren't you taking this up with my lady wife?" She had generally turned the celebration into her personal project, which suited me just fine.

A look of embarrassment passed across the cook's face, "She sent me to you, Your Excellency."

Translation; she's too busy. "Slaughter another cow," I suggested.

Claude looked down nervously, "Well I had considered that, Your Lordship, but the problem isn't really beef."

Now I was confused, "You just said the problem was meat."

The man's face flushed as he opened his mouth to reply. "Well—more the variety of meat. People expect a wide selection of game and wild meats to complement the beef and other domestic meats."

"You are honestly telling me that you think people will be disappointed if there isn't enough wild fowl, venison, and small game at the feast tomorrow. Are you serious?" It was occasionally difficult to wrap my head around the importance of what I thought of, as trivial concerns. Dealing with kings and fighting gods had changed my perspective on such things.

Claude nodded his head affirmatively without saying anything else. I gave him a long stare before taking a deep breath. "Have you mentioned this to Chad Grayson?" I suggested. Technically it was his job to provide game for these events, along with managing my forests.

"I did, Your Excellency. He told me that his men would be engaged in extensive patrols for the next week or two and that he wouldn't have any men free to hunt until the current crisis was past."

Of course he did, I thought to myself. "I'll talk to him, though I'm not sure what he can do in half a day's time."

"Thank you, Your Excellency," Claude answered gratefully.

"Don't thank me yet, he may be unable to catch anything quickly enough for you."

"That may be true, but I also wanted to thank you for tomorrow, for the reason for our celebration. This holiday is mostly a day of thanks for what you did, my lord." Claude was looking at me with an expression of heartfelt sincerity.

His words sent a surge of anger through me, and my stomach felt as though it held a lump of iron. My eyes hardened even as I fought to keep my tongue still. *He doesn't understand. I mustn't take it out on him,* I reminded myself. "That day was not…" I started to say, but then I changed my mind. "Thank you for that, Claude, though I don't feel I deserve praise for it," I said reluctantly, then I turned and without waiting for a reply I left him there.

My face was a mask as I strode away, but behind it I felt lost. *The only things I will be remembered for will be my butchery.* The World Road itself was perhaps only a way of distracting me from that, or an attempt to make a lasting and more positive impression upon the world. The only other positive thing I had done was to set James Lancaster upon the throne, and my role as kingmaker would never be known. All that the world would remember were the battles—and all the men I had slaughtered.

Kill thirty thousand men and they give you a holiday. Slay a god and make a king and they will never know, much less appreciate it. That wasn't fair really. Some knew, most of them either Celior's clergy, or men of power and station. As a rule those people either feared or reviled me for what I had done.

⟫━━━⟪

My master huntsman was a stubborn man. "My foresters are currently occupied making certain that no one slips onto your lands unnoticed," he told me again.

"Tell them to take the day off and go hunting," I replied.

His brown eyes were unyielding. "My lord, you told me that we face an imminent attack, and that my men were to ensure the safety of your people, or at least provide early warning. Has this become less of a priority for you?" The words were phrased with a tone of rebuke; not something I was used to hearing anymore, at least not from those that served me.

"Master Grayson, are you arguing with me?" I asked curiously.

"Frankly, yes."

"The attack won't take place for another week," I informed him. "If I thought setting your men to providing game would endanger us I wouldn't ask this of you."

"That's as may be, but only a fool would assume that his enemy might not attempt a surprise attack," he responded evenly.

My eyes narrowed. "Are you calling me a fool, Master Grayson?"

"If you act like a damn fool, I'll call you one," he replied without flinching.

"You neglected to add the honorific," I noted.

Chad nodded before repeating, "If you act like a damn fool, I'll call you one..." After a short pause he added, "...my lord."

We stared at each other for a long tense moment before I broke down and started laughing. It was a good laugh, the deep sort that comes from the belly. I credited James Lancaster for teaching me the value of such laughter, as I had seen him use it to great effect, but today I laughed simply because I couldn't help myself.

The huntsman watched me seriously for a bit before he eventually began to chuckle himself. After a moment he relaxed, and we laughed together. When we calmed down I spoke first, "You're right of course."

He smiled confidently, "I knew that already, Your Lordship."

"Forget the honorifics," I told him. "From now on I don't want to hear any more 'Lords' and 'Excellency's' from you—unless it's a public occasion. Understood, Master Grayson?"

"Fine, then you'll have to call me Chad. I can't have you addressing me properly if I'm not allowed to do the same," he answered.

I readily agreed to that with a nod. "Alright then, Chad it is. Now, will you send your huntsmen out to get extra game for tomorrow?"

"No," he answered bluntly. "I'm not some foolish whore you can buy with a smile and a laugh. You asked me to protect your lands, and if I pull the men away from that, I'd be neglecting that duty."

My eyes went wide with shock. This man really wasn't overly impressed with titles and nobility. After years of people bowing and scraping it was refreshing to find someone able to speak honestly, even if he was a rude ass. I thought carefully for a moment before replying, "Tell you what, send a token number—say five men, out to hunt game, and you can keep the rest on watch."

He watched my expression carefully. "And if I refuse?"

"I'll have you whipped for insubordination and replace you. We may be friends, but I can't allow my men to ignore my orders," I answered plainly.

Chad smiled, "They'll be a' hunting before another hour passes."

"Excellent," I answered. "Have you eaten lunch yet?"

"No."

"Come eat with me, everyone else is busy today, and I prefer to eat with a friend," I told him.

"Don't mealtimes count as formal occasions?" he suggested. He was indirectly reminding me that the Master Huntsman didn't ordinarily eat at the high table.

I snorted, "Not today they don't. There will be more than enough formality tomorrow." I clapped him on the shoulder, and we headed for the main hall.

CHAPTER 18

Islept late the next morning, until Penny forced me out of bed for breakfast. Even then she had delayed it until nine, which was rather late for us. Breakfast was a sort of sacred ritual for our family. Being an important nobleman had put all sorts of strains and obligations upon me, that tended to limit my ability to spend time with my wife and children, but breakfast had been the place that Penny had drawn the line.

Lunch and dinner were usually eaten in the great hall, and even if we didn't have any special guests, it still put us in front of the people. It was never about simply eating. We were a symbol. Breakfast was different though. It was just for us. Penny cooked and the children and I ate together in our quiet mountain cottage. It was a short time each day, but during it, we could pretend we were just a normal family, eating and sometimes laughing together. Well, in my case, mornings being as early as they are, it was frequently eating and growling.

That morning was no exception. I was in an unusually good mood, probably because I had found a genuine friend in Chad Grayson the day before. He and I had hit it off quite well, despite our rough start. I found myself smiling and making silly faces, to amuse the children as we ate.

"You seem very happy this morning," Penny observed.

My cheeks were stuffed, with one boiled egg in each, so it was a bit difficult to answer. "Ish that sho'? You do ash well m'dear!" I replied. My garbled speech had Conall and the twins laughing hysterically.

Penny smiled. "In years past this has been the one day I could almost guarantee you would be in a bad mood. It's good to see you finally relaxing."

I spit one egg out and quickly ate the other. Don't judge me on my table manners; I was forced to behave with decorum and dignity for most of every day. Once my mouth was free I answered her, "I could say the same for you. Normally you're as anxious as a mother hen when we have feast days."

My lovely wife looked thoughtful for a second before replying, "You're right. I think perhaps the looming attack next week has put the minor anxieties of today in perspective. I'm determined to enjoy this."

"You don't think that *that* has anything to do with it?" I asked, pointing at her sword. She kept it close by her at all times now, and currently it was hanging on a peg near the oven.

"That may have a part in it as well. I have missed it, since we dissolved the bond," she said honestly. We weren't really talking about the sword, so much as the power she had given up, when we dissolved the bond between us years ago. She had continued to practice with the weapon on a regular basis, but without the strength and speed provided by the bond, she had always felt like a shadow of her former self. The earth bond had changed all that.

"What does Momma miss?" Moira asked suddenly. As usual she had been following the conversation carefully. The boys, Conall and Matthew, were more interested in seeing if they could imitate my feat with the two boiled eggs.

"Nothing honey," I answered immediately, trying to quell her question out of pure habit.

Penny apparently felt like fielding the question though. "My strength, dear heart... Your father has given me back the strength I used to have, when I was his body guard," she answered. We had told the children stories of our years before they were born, many times over.

"Like Uncle Dorian?!" interjected Matthew excitedly. Obviously he had been paying more attention than I had realized.

Moira was a bit put out with his presumptuous idea. "No, she couldn't be that strong, Uncle Dorian is the strongest man in the world."

"Well, in this case, I bet she comes pretty close...," I started, but they were in full swing now.

Conall piped up, "I thought Daddy was the strongest man in the world."

"With magic," Matthew informed him very matter-of-factly, "but physically, Uncle Dorian is probably the strongest."

"If Mommy and Daddy fought who do you think would win?" Conall asked immediately. Trust a child to ask the most embarrassing question possible. I gave Penny a sheepish grin.

Matthew thought the question over seriously for a second, "Probably Dad, there isn't much you can do about magic. He could set her on fire or something before she ever got close to him."

"Hmmph! Shows how little you know!" Moira said jumping in. "Mommies have a secret weapon. It doesn't matter how powerful Daddy is, she can always beat him." Penelope was looking at me now with questions in her eyes. Clearly she was wondering if I had put any strange ideas into our daughter's head. I immediately shook my head, 'no'.

Matthew was curious now, "What secret weapon?"

His sister looked down her nose at him, perfecting her imperious gaze, "I heard the maids talking about it the other day, when they didn't think I was listening. Ladies have something that their husbands can't live without."

"What?" asked Conall.

"I'm not sure what it is, but it's called a p—mmmph!?" Moira's words were cut off suddenly, as Penny's hand covered her mouth.

"That's enough for now, children. Boys help your father clear away the dishes. Moira come with me—we need to talk a bit," Penny said with brisk efficiency. Rising from the table, she led her daughter away by the hand.

I couldn't help but grin as they left, which of course put Matthew's curiosity on high alert. He knew well that something had been left unsaid. "What's wrong with them?" he asked me.

I picked up the egg I had put aside earlier and ate it carefully while considering my son's question. After a moment I answered, "I'll explain later."

"But Dad…!" he whined.

"Don't complain or you'll be clearing dishes by yourself," I told him. He shut up after that.

⟡—⟡

The day passed quickly, and for much of it I had little to do, other than look good and be seen. Over the years I had practiced my smile for many such occasions, and now it seemed almost as genuine as my real smile, although I was sure my close friends could still tell the difference.

One small thing I noticed was that all of the Knights of Stone seemed to be dressed in their full armor, with weapons at the ready, and the sober looks of men who hadn't had a drop to drink. Generally this wouldn't have been something I'd have noticed, but given my discussion with Dorian and Cyhan the day before, I'd been paying close attention. None of my knights were particularly prone to drunkenness, but on a holiday you could expect that some would be partaking of the copious amounts of wine and ale that were flowing.

I made mention of the fact at the first opportunity, which happened to be late in the afternoon. Both Dorian and Cyhan had been carefully avoiding me. I caught up with Cyhan in the hall, after having deliberately tracked him down. It's rather hard to avoid a man who can pinpoint your location within a mile or two. "I notice all the knights seem to be exceedingly sober," I said, as I approached him from behind.

He gave no sign of being startled, but calmly turned to face me, "As are you, my lord."

"I prefer to wait until dinner before I begin drinking."

"It seems the men are inclined to follow your example," he responded adroitly.

I had to admire his reserve, but I wasn't about to give him the satisfaction. "Don't give me that horse-shit. Not a one of them has neglected to don armor and bear arms today."

The veteran warrior's face showed nothing. "The armor you crafted for your knights is exceeding comfortable, my lord, indeed I find it more comfortable than fancy garb and binding velvet doublets. I am not surprised that my brother knights deem it so as well."

I leaned in close to stare him directly in the eye. "You ignored my explicit orders and kept them all on duty today."

Cyhan stared unflinchingly back, though he remained silent.

"Answer me!" I barked. I had been irritated before, but I was downright cross now, after dealing with his taciturn manner.

"You didn't ask a question, my lord."

I could almost see the twinkle in his eye as he replied. *The bastard is enjoying this!* I realized immediately. "You deliberately ignored my orders regarding the men and today's holiday—didn't you?"

"Yes I did, Your Excellency," he said with alacrity.

"Why?"

"I did not wish to violate my oath."

I exhaled explosively, "What?! What oath?"

Squaring his shoulders and standing a bit straighter, Cyhan responded, "When you took me into your service, my lord. You made me swear to you, that if ever my conscience conflicted with my other oaths of service, I was to use my own judgment."

That took me aback for a moment. I had indeed insisted on exactly that when I had taken his oath of service. Taking a deep breath, I thought for a moment before responding, "How long have you been in my service Cyhan?"

"A bit over seven years now."

"And yet I've known you even longer than that. You even attempted to kill me once," I said slowly.

"Yes, Your Excellency," he agreed, before adding, "I'd have succeeded too, if it hadn't been for Sir Dorian."

I ignored the blunt admission of his killing intent, and went on, "In all that time, I don't think I've ever been quite as angry with you as I am right now," I stated, with a calmness that belied my inner agitation.

The older warrior thought carefully before replying, "I think perhaps you've forgotten the day that you buried me up to my neck in the earth, for trying to force you to take a longer road." He was dead serious as he relayed the information.

The man was incorrigible, and I couldn't maintain my angry façade any longer. It just wasn't possible. It would have been easier, and probably more productive, to have been angry with a stone wall. "I'm beginning to see why you've never been married," I said acerbically. Sarcasm had ever been my refuge when there was nothing better to be said or done. "I expect to see you raising a glass during the toast this evening, at the very least."

He bowed respectfully. "As you wish, my lord."

I resisted the urge to use my power to knock him down as I walked away. Such antics were beneath my station. *Like hell they are!* I thought impulsively. *I just need something more subtle.* I amused myself by thinking of the possibilities as I walked. Unfortunately nothing appropriate and suitably untraceable came to mind.

"Why am I surrounded by so many insubordinate retainers?" I wondered aloud.

Walter Prathion appeared without warning, just a few feet away. "Perhaps because you encourage independence and initiative among your vassals, and even among your servants," he said, in answer to my question.

My shields doubled in strength almost without thought, and I fought the reflex to pin my fellow wizard to the wall as well. "Son of a bitch!" I exclaimed loudly, "What are you doing, Walter? I might've killed you, you startled me so!"

The older wizard looked down a bit sheepishly, "I don't really like the crowds on holidays. I went invisible to avoid having to deal with a crowd of enthusiastic well-wishers just a bit ago, and you sort of happened by shortly thereafter."

"Bull," I said immediately. "You made yourself invisible to magesight as well."

"I felt you coming, and decided that rather than reveal myself, it would be easier to completely shield myself and wait for you to leave," he explained.

If it had been anyone else, I might have doubted him, but Walter had a bit of shyness in him that I had learned to accept over the years. "I think my heart would be in better shape if you had stuck to your original plan, and waited for me to leave."

The mild mannered wizard smiled at me, "Your conversation was too interesting to avoid commenting. I also felt a bit guilty for overhearing it without your knowledge. I thought privately letting you know I had been listening, might be the best course. I hope you will accept my apologies, my liege."

I had run out of energy to spend on being annoyed with people, not to mention I still felt bad about my last conversation with his daughter. I had been painfully blunt. "Forget about it," I advised him. "How is Elaine? I haven't seen her in a day or so."

Walter grimaced, "She's been extremely out of sorts for the past few days. I've never seen her quite so temperamental before."

"I'm sure she'll get better," I reassured him, with a confidence I didn't truly feel. I felt a twinge of guilt for not telling him about our conversation, but I had promised Elaine that the matter would remain between the two of us. She might come to terms with her embarrassment if I didn't create any additional humiliation for her. That was my hope anyway.

The other wizard sighed, "Perhaps—until she gets upset again. Women are a chaotic mystery, especially at her age."

I thought about my own daughters. Moira seemed like an utter angel at her current age. Surely the same wouldn't happen to her? *Surely not,* I thought to myself, but I felt a bit of doubt on that account.

CHAPTER 19

That evening arrived after a day that had gone on too long. Though I had started the day with every intention of trying to enjoy the festive atmosphere, the underlying reason for the celebration still bothered my conscience. I was looking forward to the wine that would come with the feast. Once we were past the toast itself, I could relax and try to pretend that it was simply another holiday. The alcohol would be a welcome way to take the edge off of my nerves.

The hall itself was full to bursting with people. When we had restored the castle, I had had it built with what seemed to be more than enough room, but on days such as this one, it felt cramped. Penny often told me that this was not such a bad thing. If it were large enough for everyone on big holidays, then it would seem overlarge the rest of the year. She also subscribed to the notion that not being 'quite' big enough to hold everyone, made a holiday feel more special. Something about the feeling of being elbow to elbow with everyone.

I was pretty sure she was just plain wrong. The damn place needed to be a bit bigger. *As soon as you enlarge it more people will show up and it will be too small again,* I thought to myself pessimistically.

The walls were bedecked with flowers and garlands, and the stone floors had been swept and fresh straw and fragrant grasses scattered, to give the hall a pleasant smell. Everything seemed bright and beautiful, which seemed an ironic contrast to the fact that we were, in fact, celebrating an epic slaughter. *It's a good thing I chose the spring to do my butchery. We didn't have a good holiday for this time of year before that,* I thought bitterly to myself.

A hand on my arm broke me from my reverie. Glancing over I saw Penny's eyes on me. She knew my moods better than anyone. Without a word, her touch and knowing look communicated her sympathy to me, along with a gentle message to 'snap out of it'. Her empathy had limits; if I continued to sulk she'd give me hell later.

I gave her my best smile and rose from my seat, doing my best to project warmth and cheer to all whose eyes were now fixed firmly upon me. "I would like to thank you all for your efforts to make this a happy occasion," I said loudly, addressing the entire room. "As you know we have more to worry about this year than we have in years past, but I am confident that if we continue to work together, we will come through this crisis just as we did the event that led to this celebration. Before we begin the feasting and drinking, we will have our traditional first toast, to be given this year by our good Lady Rose, at her request. If the servers will bring in the wine, we can begin!"

The kitchen doors opened, and the staff began circulating through the room, bearing ewers of wine, filling each cup. As they did Penny touched Moira on the shoulder, and my daughter hurried from the room. Matthew watched her go enviously, while Conall hadn't a clue what was occurring. Little Irene was being kept in the nursery. I glanced at Penny, a question in my eyes.

"She's fetching your cup for the feast," she said in answer to my unspoken query.

"Ahh," I said in sudden understanding. Idly I watched Moira's progress with my magesight while half listening to Rose's introductory speech. My daughter was met in the kitchen by Peter, who handed her a small silver tray bearing a bottle of wine and two silver goblets. I could tell by her posture that she was excited by the responsibility, and Peter patted her on the head after carefully passing her the tray. After she left him, I noticed that she stopped behind the door for a moment. *That little scamp, she just stole a drink from my cup!* I couldn't help but smile. What child doesn't want to know what their parent's drink tastes like? I could sense her face crinkling in disgust after her sip.

As Moira emerged from the kitchen and approached the table, Rose motioned toward her, "As a gesture of peace and goodwill, even as we remember that bloody day, King Nicholas was gracious enough to gift us with a bottle of Dalensan Instritas, one of the finest, and since the war, rarest, vintages from Gododdin. While there isn't enough for all of us, our good Count and Countess will be using it for the toast tonight in acknowledgement of the peace that now exists between our two nations."

I had to hand it to her—Rose knew how to manage a crowd. Her skillful speech had put a thoughtful face on most of the crowd, although I did hear one person in the back muttering about 'damned Gododdin wine'. Moira approached me with a look of serious concentration, determined not to spill the wine on the tray before her.

"I brought your wine, Father," she said as she set the tray down on the table. With a flourish that must have been rehearsed, she picked up the first cup and handed it to me. "This one is for you, Father—and this one for you, Mother," she announced as she passed each goblet to us. After we had taken them, she curtsied and moved back to stand in her place beside Penny. My heart swelled with pride to see her so graceful in front of the crowd.

Rose's voice rose majestically as she spoke, emphasizing her movement as she lifted her goblet, "Raise your cups, for peace and remembrance—for those that sacrificed that we might be here today, for the blood that was shed for us, and the lives that were lost! Raise your cups that we might never forget the price of the peace we now enjoy! Raise your cups for the man that defends us still, and drink in the certain knowledge that we will defend him and his honor to the last! Drink to our most noble lord, the Count di'Cameron, Mordecai Illeniel!"

As her speech rose to a crescendo, her eyes met mine, and I was surprised to see tears in them. Looking past her to Dorian, I noticed his own eyes were wet as well. I felt unworthy to see such devotion in their gazes, but everywhere I turned I saw it echoed—even in my own family's faces. A deafening roar drowned even my jaded self-doubt, as every man and woman in the hall shouted out their agreement.

A wave of love and affection from the people I had striven so hard to preserve and protect washed over me, and I found myself moved to tears even as I returned their gesture. Turning my cup up, I downed it in one long draught before setting it aside to stare at the noisy crowd of people, *my people.* "I don't deserve this, but from my heart I thank you all," I answered them; though it was doubtful that any beyond the closest could hear me. My throat had become choked with emotion.

Returning to my seat, I waved for everyone to sit down. I studiously ignored the smiles of my friends, as I wiped away my tears and pretended to look for the food. My task was made more difficult, as first Penny and then each of my children insisted upon kissing me on the cheeks. *And people wonder why I hate this damn holiday.*

Rose leaned across the table to whisper close to my ear, "I meant every word, lest you think I was putting on a show, but I still think you're an ass for making my husband continue his patrols."

My eyebrows shot up in surprise at her remark, and for a moment my heart relaxed. For some reason, while all the praise and adulation had made me more anxious, her honest complaint eased my tension. I gave her my most genuine smile of the evening, "That is an unfortunate consequence of the responsibility I have taken as the Count di'Cameron."

She nodded in understanding. Lady Rose Thornbear might not agree with my decision, but she did understand the position I was in as liege lord. She had been born to such authority after all; she knew it as well as any.

"I think that was the best toast we've had since we began these holidays," Penny told me from where she sat beside me. "Rose certainly has a way with words."

My lips quirked into a half smile. "When she knows she can use them to embarrass someone, she will go to any length to accomplish that goal," I replied.

My lovely wife laughed, "I told you she'd find a way to punish you."

I nodded in agreement, "At least the worst is over. Now we can relax and enjoy some wine. My nerves could certainly use another cup."

Penny reached for the bottle, and began to fill my goblet, but as I reached for it a wave of mild dizziness washed over me. Placing my hand against the side of the table in an attempt to steady myself, I put my other hand against the side of my head, "Whoa…"

My wife's brows furrowed, "Are you alright? Do you sense something?"

I waved my hands at her, "No, I'm fine. Just felt dizzy for a moment. That wine may be more potent that I realized." I took a sip from the goblet in my hand. It didn't taste particularly strong, but then the best wines generally didn't.

"You never have been able to hold your drink," Dorian teased from where he sat beside Rose.

Opening my eyes wide, I responded gleefully, "Oh really? You are going to lecture me on drinking? Perhaps the ladies here would like to hear about your first time with a full tankard of ale in your belly."

Dorian's face pinked in a subtle blush. He knew I had him at a disadvantage. "Well now let's not get ahead of ourselves my friend. There's no need to go delving into ancient history now."

Rose had lifted one eyebrow in interest even as Penny chimed in first, "I for one would *love* to hear this story." Lady Rose nodded her head in agreement.

"I think we were—what was it Dorian, fourteen perhaps?" I said to my friend, while he tried to look busy refilling his own cup.

"Fifteen," he corrected.

"So we were," I agreed happily. "We snuck into the ducal wine cellar. Marc had stolen the keys from the cellar-master, and while we were down there we found a freshly tapped keg of spring ale. For some reason it hadn't been finished, and they decided to lock it up rather than leave it out."

"Probably to keep the teenagers from getting into it…" grumbled Dorian.

"In any case," I continued, "Marc and I concluded that it would ruin if it was left too long, so we convinced Dorian to have some with us. None of us were particularly keen on wine back then, so we were rather glad to be able to drink ale instead."

"No need to make it sound as if we were regular drinkers."

I laughed, "Indeed, *we* were not. While Marc and I had stolen a bit of wine a few times before, our friend, Dorian the Pure, had never tasted a drop of alcohol before that day."

"What happened?" said Rose, leaning in closely. The story had her complete attention. Dorian groaned.

"We found three large tankards and filled them to the brim," I explained. "To be honest, they really were large. Each one would hold a full yard of ale, but after we had each drunk ours down, Dorian here was overwhelmed by emotion." I grinned at my childhood friend.

Rose let out a small laugh, while Penny asked me, "What sort of emotion?"

Looking at the ceiling I sighed dramatically, "The noblest of emotions, love—that is what spoke to Dorian's sloppy drunken heart that day!"

"You don't have to be so damned poetic about it," complained Dorian.

"Marc and I tried to cover the fact that we'd had a bit to drink, but it was no use with Dorian beside us. After we left the cellar, we tried to sneak into the kitchen to steal some of the left over bread. When the cook caught us, he could barely scold us for all of Dorian's professions of love and affection. From there he forced us to stop every time we met someone so that he could tell them how much he loved them," I laughed as I recounted the tale, and the lights in the room seemed to dim.

"It wasn't as bad as all that," said Dorian sourly.

For some reason it had gotten really quiet, so much so that it made Dorian's voice seem louder than normal, but when I listened I still heard the same background noise as usual. In fact the room was quite loud with people's voices. *Strange.* Shaking my head I responded to my friend's remark, "Oh, it was bad! You told Benchley that you loved him as well." Benchley was the valet and chamberlain for James Lancaster, and a figure of stern authority throughout our boyhoods.

"I forgot about that part," Dorian admitted.

"Hah!" I said in a voice that sounded too loud to my own ears. "You threw up on…," I paused as the room grew dim. The light was fading rapidly, but no one else seemed to have noticed. An oppressive silence grew around me at the same time.

A feeling of panic gripped my heart, and I stood up suddenly. My friends watched cautiously, unsure if my strange expression was meant to be part of my tale, or something to be concerned about. I felt Penny's hand on mine as she studied my face. "Is something wrong, Mordecai?"

I was smothered in a darkness so profound, even my magesight could not pierce it, while at the same time my ears seemed to have stopped working. Looking at my wife's face I spoke, "I've gone blind."

She stared at me curiously. "Don't be silly, you're looking directly into my eyes."

That made no sense, yet she was correct. I could still see her, and everyone else for that matter. The sensation was similar to the first time I had experienced seeing with my magesight alone, an occasion in which I had been in a pitch black room without realizing that there was no light. "Wait, that isn't right," I said agreeing with her, as comprehension of my situation dawned upon me. "I can still see—it's my magesight that's gone."

"Now who's drunk on one cup of wine, eh?" commented Dorian.

I ignored him and stared wildly around me. My sensation, my 'feeling' for everything around me was completely absent. Though my eyes still worked, everything looked flat and two dimensional, as if the world had lost all depth and much of its color as well. I couldn't hear anything either.

It wasn't ordinary mundane sounds of people talking around me, or the sound of plates and cups as people ate. No—the sounds I was missing were the voices that had been my constant companions for many years now. It had been something so pervasive, so omnipresent I hardly noticed it anymore; the tiny songs and melodies of people's bodies, of furniture, or the gentle susurrating music of the wind—the deep drum beat of the earth's heart below. It was all gone, as though the universe itself had gone still, holding its breath in anticipation of some important event.

"He's not joking, Dorian," said Rose to her husband, "Something is wrong with Mordecai."

"What's wrong with Daddy?" asked Moira, tugging on Penny's dress.

"Nothing darling, I think he just had too much wine," said Penny immediately.

I had broken out in a cold sweat, and a faint feeling of nausea swept over me. "I think perhaps I should retire for the evening," I told them uncertainly.

Penny didn't waste any time. Reaching out she caught the nearest server by the arm as he was passing by with a tray of meat, "Tell Peter that the Count isn't feeling well and has decided to retire for the evening."

The poor fellow was startled and almost attempted to bow with the platter in his hands. "Yes, mi'lady." Turning he started to continue down the table with his tray.

The countess' voice caught him before he had gone two steps, "Set the tray down, it can wait. Inform Master Tucker immediately."

I was already on my feet, so I began heading toward the exit without waiting. Dorian caught up with me in time to prevent me from walking into the door frame; I had looked back to see if Penny had the children in tow. I wasn't used to navigating without my magesight. Before I could pass through the doorway, a collective gasp echoed through the hall, and looking back I knew immediately why—one of the large enchanted lights in the center of the great hall had turned a vivid blue color.

Complete silence fell over the crowd for a moment that seemed to stretch into eternity, until it was broken by the sounds of the bell tower beginning to ring. We were under attack.

CHAPTER 20

I was numb with shock as I stared at the blue light. *Not blue*, I thought to myself, *it should be red*. *I can't fight without magic!* Panic overwhelmed me for a moment, as all my well made plans crumbled around me, falling apart like a house of cards. Everything had hinged upon my magic, without it I couldn't face the gods, without it I couldn't use the enchantments that I had prepared.

Black despair devoured my courage as I realized that everything I had worked for was about to be destroyed. Everything I had ever done would be wiped out. *After they kill me, they'll undo everything I've ever done. It was all for naught...* The urge to vomit sent me to my knees. "They shouldn't be here yet," I said quietly.

Looking up I realized that every eye in the room was upon me. I was their hope, and most of them had no idea that something was seriously wrong with me yet. *Run!* I wanted to scream at them. *There is no hope.* Once they discovered that my magic was gone, they would surely panic anyway.

A small voice cut through the madness in my head, "Dad? What's happening?" Matthew's small hand was on my arm, and then I saw his blue eyes, looking to me for reassurance.

I spit, trying to clear my mouth and stop my urge to retch. "I'm a little sick. I think I ate something bad, but I'll be alright." *I've been poisoned*, came the thought as I said that. "The blue light means that we are under attack, and that the castle defenses have been activated." Taking a deep breath, I stood and stroked his hair. The gesture was to calm myself as much as it was for him.

Dorian's gaze bored into me. "Your orders, my lord?" We had stood together through worse before this.

"This should be a red condition," I told him without explaining.

His eyes widened slightly, "It's too late for that, the plan is too different. Yellow is the best we can manage if people are already heading for the blue meeting points."

He was right of course; it was a flaw in my plans that there was no easy way to switch from blue or yellow to red. It was also something I should have realized before now. "Give the men orders for yellow then. I'll find Walter and have him change the color immediately."

My friend nodded and turned to his fellow knights, "You heard our Lord! Pass the word and get to your stations. Encourage everyone to pick up their pace! We need everyone to head for the teleportation circles in the courtyard immediately."

Penny stood next to me now, with a hand on my arm to steady me. "What's wrong with you, Mort?" she said quietly.

I wanted to lie to her. I needed to lie. If I didn't she might not leave me to do what must be done, but as I looked into her brown eyes I felt my will falter. "I think I've been poisoned."

"Then you'll come with me," she answered immediately. "You can't fight like that." Her part in every one of the plans was to take our children and retreat to our hidden mountain cottage.

"No," I said firmly. "There are things that must be done."

"You said your magesight was gone. What of your magic?" she asked pointedly.

I already knew the answer to that question. Whatever else the poison might have done to me, it had completely snuffed out my power. "I will have to find Walter and instruct him on what to do."

Penelope's cheek twitched as she clenched her jaw. We both knew I was likely condemning myself, and Walter as well, to death. In years gone by, she would never have cooperated with such a plan, and her eyes showed me clearly how she felt about it, but she was a mother now. Instead of arguing she kissed me quickly before whispering, "You're a good father and a stupid husband. I love you."

"I love you too," I managed to reply before she turned away. Tears were starting in her eyes.

Penny began issuing orders immediately, "Rose, you will accompany me. Is Gram in the nursery? We have to stop there first anyway, to collect Irene."

Before Rose could respond, I spotted Elaine and her brother George heading for the door. "Elaine!" I said loudly, to get her attention.

She stopped and walked toward us instead. Elaine had been avoiding me since our 'conversation', and something in her step now told me that she'd rather not have to deal directly with me, even now. "Yes, my lord?" she asked.

"Where were you going?"

"To the building in the yard, to begin transporting people to Albamarl, that is my assigned task if the blue beacons are lit," she replied calmly, though she had an edge about her.

"I'm changing it to yellow once I reach the central chamber," I informed her, "for now I want you to escort Rose and Penny." I put a hand on George's shoulder, "I want you to handle the teleportation circles. Go now."

Walter's only son straightened a bit, and with a mute nod left. His sister seemed confused, however. "You don't trust me to handle my task?" asked Elaine.

"No, it's because I trust you that I'm sending you with my family. They will likely need a wizard with them in the days to come, and I won't be there," I told her.

Her gaze went to the floor, "You should send my father instead."

"He'll be staying with me, and you'll likely curse me for it later. I've chosen you for this, Elaine." I commanded, and without looking back I began walking. I needed to get to Walter, and I didn't have much time. Without my magesight, I couldn't be sure, but at a guess their eyes were on my back. The urge to look back, to see Penny and the children one last time, was almost overpowering, but I knew that if I did so, I wouldn't be able to continue.

My eyes were burning, and my steps were a bit unsteady, but I made it out of the room without stumbling. The anger helped. People were everywhere in the halls, rushing back and forth, gathering their children and essential items, but they gave way before me, so I had little trouble reaching the entrance to the keystone room.

The wall was unmarked, and few even knew it was there, since I had had it hidden with masonry and enchantment. Even if I had had my magesight I couldn't have found it; the runes hid it from even magical sight. *I hope the door still opens for me*, I thought to myself. It didn't require magic, but I worried that without my magic, it might no longer recognize me. Placing my hand in the proper spot, I was relieved when the door opened silently before me.

Walter looked up in relief as I entered, "I put up the barrier as soon as I sensed him."

I tried to project a calm I didn't feel. "Where did they appear, and which one is it?" I asked.

"I'm not sure," Walter replied, "I haven't actually sensed one of *them*. One of Master Grayson's foresters spotted a large group of foreign men moving through the woods a few miles off."

A sense of relief flooded through me, if it wasn't one of the gods we would be fine, assuming I could survive whatever had poisoned me. A question leaped to the forefront of my mind, "Wait—why did you light the blue beacon then?" An attack by a mundane army wouldn't be enough to justify evacuating the entire town.

"Our scout was undetected as far as he knows, and he spotted them several miles off, but by the time he reached the town gates, he realized that they were close behind him," Walter explained. "He barely had time to signal the guard to close the gate before they reached it. He said they were moving impossibly fast."

"What does that mean?"

"They were running as fast as horses," said Walter, "…even though they wore armor. When they reached the gates, they began pounding upon them with the heavy iron maces that they were armed with."

His description suggested that they were supernaturally enhanced, much like the Knights of Stone, but there were no such troops that I knew of. "What happened then?"

"By the time the runner alerted me, they had nearly demolished the town gate and some had scaled the wall itself," replied Walter. "The guards managed to knock several off the walls with poles, but one reached the top and got inside. He killed over twenty guardsmen, and nearly managed to open the gate itself, before Master Grayson brought him down with a lucky shot through the eye."

Luck has little to do with that man's aim, I noted silently. "How did they scale the walls so quickly? Did they have hooks?"

"I am told they simply drove steel spikes into the walls and pulled themselves upward, withdrawing the spikes as they went and driving them in higher up."

"Using hammers, that would take too long, they should have been full of arrows by then," I observed.

"They didn't use hammers. They were driving the spikes in bare-handed and pulling them out the same way. A rough count indicates that nearly two hundred of these men are outside the walls now. Should I have used the blue beacon, or simply put up the barrier enchantment?" asked Walter uncertainly.

"Two hundred!?" I said incredulously. There were only twenty Knights of Stone, and I was the only man capable of creating such bonds. The gods had to be involved, of that I could be certain. "You chose rightly," I reassured Walter. "I'm assuming the barrier enchantment put an end to their attempts to enter." As I spoke, I leaned against the wall and slid carefully down to the floor. There were no chairs in the room, and I was still feeling very unstable.

"Yes," he said, nodding. "When it went up, those still climbing were flung from the wall itself. Those battering at the gates haven't been able to do any more damage at all. Are you alright? You don't look well."

"As a matter of fact I don't think I am," I said honestly, "I think I may have been poisoned." To further emphasize my point, I leaned over and emptied my stomach onto the floor. I've never been very good at vomiting, and frankly, it wasn't the sort of thing I really hoped to acquire skill at. They always tell you, you'll feel better afterward, but in my experience that was generally untrue. Once my belly was empty, the retching simply became more painful.

Walter went pale and covered his own mouth with his hand. Evidently he wasn't the sort of fellow with a strong stomach for such things. He managed to keep from joining me, though. After a few minutes I had regained control of myself, and I moved away from the mess I had made. Idly I wished that Walter was good enough at healing to block my nausea. That had been a useful trick I had learned during Penny's pregnancies, but it required a certain degree of sensitivity and a lot of confidence to accomplish. Though I trusted Walter with my life, I didn't trust him enough as a healer to ask him to muck around with my brain like that.

"It looks worse than it is," I told him eventually, as I tried to regain my dignity.

"And it smells worse than it looks," he answered acerbically. Walter occasionally showed signs of dry wit.

"Thanks for your sympathy," I responded, with a crooked smile.

"Don't we have a healer who can help?"

I shook my head negatively. "No, just you and me, and I'm afraid I won't be doing any healing for a while."

"I know nothing about treating poisons," said the older wizard.

"Neither do I, and the only person that I know of who does, is in Lancaster," I told him.

"Who?"

"Lady Thornbear—don't you remember how she kept you drugged until I could question you?" I reminded him. Many years before, Walter had been forced to aid in the kidnapping of my wife. He had been captured and Dorian's mother had kept him drugged and insensible for days, before I was able to talk to him.

He shuddered at the memory, "I was sick for days after that. I think I'd rather die than take any remedy she offered."

"Heh…," I uttered, giving a half-hearted chuckle, "I can't say I blame you. I'd probably feel the same if I'd been in your position."

"You should let me take you to Lancaster. Perhaps there's something she can do for you," he suggested before adding, "How serious do you think this poison is?"

"I thought it was bad, but now that a few minutes have passed, my symptoms seem to be improving," I replied.

"Why would anyone bother poisoning you with something non-fatal? Your enemies aren't known for their mercy," Walter argued. A moment later he clarified, "Not that I'm hoping it's a fatal poison, you understand."

I waved my hand to indicate that I wasn't upset. Just moments before I had been convinced of the same thing, but the more I thought about it, the more I realized that the poison's purpose had probably just been to render me unable to fight, and if that were the case, then it probably wasn't something lethal that I had been given. Ultimately the goal would still be to kill me, but my death would probably come as a result of the assault on the castle, rather than because of whatever had been put in my drink or food.

I explained my reasoning to Walter, as well as describing the primary effect the poison was having, namely the complete suppression of my magical abilities. As I spoke his face grew pale, and rather than finding reassurance, my friend seemed to be becoming more anxious. Finally I stopped talking and just stared at him. "What?" I asked.

"It's magebane," he replied simply, as if that one word was enough.

"You'll have to explain. I'm afraid I've not heard the term before," I told him, but even as I said it, the word tickled the back of my mind, stirring one of my 'other' memories, a memory of a classroom from a time well over a thousand years past. In my mind's eye I saw a thin, balding man pacing in front of his students while discussing what had seemed at the time to be an interesting, but useless bit of trivia. *The plant we call 'magebane' today, was originally called 'glintel's flower', and supposedly was one of the few things known to be highly poisonous to the She'Har. It was renamed later when it was discovered that, while it had been thought to be harmless to humans, it is in fact deadly when given to those with any degree of magical ability.*

"I know only what my father taught me," said Walter, "According to him, it was a deadly poison manufactured to kill wizards. It was used by some assassins not long after the Sundering. Though it can't be proven, it was thought that the secret of making it was held by one of the four churches."

"Did he happen to tell you how it might be countered?" I asked without much hope.

"No. He said no one knew what the poison was made from, and neither did they know of an antidote. It completely suppresses magical ability in the short term, and most victims die a painful death a few days later," Walter's voice was apologetic as he finished.

"This is still better than I expected," I told him with a wan smile.

"What?"

I laughed sardonically. "When I came in here, I was expecting you to tell me that we were under attack by one of the gods, in person. Without my power, I figured the two of us would die trying to tr...," I paused as I realized

I had been about to give away one of my closest secrets. "…trying to keep them from getting the stone," I amended.

"How would you fight them without your magic?" asked the other wizard.

"The barrier enchantment still works, though my own strength is gone," I told him by way of example. "I've spent years preparing for this. I have other surprises waiting, though I'll still need your help, since I can no longer sense magic."

"So you planned on volunteering me to assist you in your last stand?"

"It was either you or one of your children," I said with a shrug.

Walter flinched at the thought, "Point taken."

"I'm a father too. I figured you'd agree with my reasoning."

"I still don't see how this is better than what you expected," he replied.

"If it's just high-powered warriors assaulting us, we can win easily, which means you don't have to die as well," I explained.

"Better still, I'll take you to Lancaster. If there's any chance that Lady Thornbear can help, then you should take it. I can return and help the knights repel these invaders," Walter suggested.

As he spoke, I couldn't help but remember the man I had first met, a man so gentle and unused to violence, that he cried when he thought he had killed one of his enemies—a man afraid to face the shiggreth with me. Then I remembered the stories of what had happened when he went to rescue his wife and children, only to be told that they had been killed. He didn't find out until almost a day later that his family was still whole, but that was too late for the men that had held them prisoner. Walter had hunted the survivors mercilessly through the wilderness.

It made me a bit sad to think that such a kind soul had become acclimated to violence, just as I had. I pushed the thought aside; what was done was done. "You are probably right, but I will at least wait until the evacuation is done," I replied.

He shook his head in resignation, "Your stubbornness will be the death of you, Mordecai."

"Stupid never dies," I said in rebuttal, but Walter didn't laugh. *If Marcus had said that, it would have been funny,* I thought to myself sourly.

A faint vibration passed through the ground, and a small bit of dust sifted down from the ceiling. Walter's eyes widened in shock, "What the hell was that?"

"A bit of dry wit," I shot back, "no need to act so surprised." I knew very well that he was referring to something else, but I couldn't pass up the opportunity.

"Something powerful just struck the barrier," said Walter, ignoring my second attempt at humor.

And that would be one of the gods, accompanying his enhanced warriors, I thought with a sinking stomach; *so much for seeking an antidote.* My heart sank, as my short lived bit of hope died a quick death, but rather than panic I took refuge in sarcasm, "Could you at least pretend to laugh at one of my jokes?" I said petulantly. "Dying wouldn't be half so miserable if you'd just let me think I was funny."

Walter gave me a look I had seen many times, the 'is he serious or just crazy?' look. After a moment he gave up and went to the stone pedestal that controlled the barrier enchantment and the magical windows we had crafted. As he activated the various 'windows' one by one I was annoyed to realize that without my magesight, I could see very little through the tiny glass panes. That hadn't really seemed like a problem before, when all I needed was a small opening to sense everything beyond it.

When he got to the window that looked out from the town gate, Walter visibly stiffened, and his hands gripped the stone pedestal, as if he needed it to remain standing. Without my senses, I was effectively blind to what he was experiencing, but the memories of my battle with Celior were still with me, and I could guess that he must have opened a window close to where one of the gods was standing. *He's being overwhelmed by the oppressive aura they have around them,* I realized.

I had barely withstood the same thing by armoring my mind with every bit of strength I had possessed, and even then I had been unable to move. I'd had to draw upon the power of the earth to completely resist the effect. That's how powerful they were. Walter wasn't an archmage, and his power as a mage was probably less than half of my own. He didn't have a chance in hell, unless I could close the windows—and I needed magic to activate the controls, even if it was just a tiny bit.

Frustrated, I watched him struggle, as the god slowly crushed his mind. He had gone pale now, and his knees buckled, which caused him to sag slowly downward beside the pedestal. Only his hands, which were tightly gripping the sides, kept him from falling. Rising as quickly as I could, I tried to hold him up, though I knew it was a futile gesture. It didn't really matter if I kept him standing, if an immensely powerful, supernatural creature destroyed his mind—or worse, possessed him. "Damnitt!" I cursed helplessly.

Just as I thought he was lost, Walter stood up again. His body had relaxed, and his hands released the stone pedestal. "It's alright," he reassured me, and reaching out he touched the runes and deactivated the window portals.

I watched him suspiciously. *He couldn't have resisted something like that. It's taken his mind,* I thought, but I held my tongue. "What happened?" I asked instead.

He gave me a tired smile. "I don't have your strength, Mordecai, but I have other ways. I was overwhelmed at first, but then I made myself invisible to magic."

His words confused me for a moment before I realized what he meant. In the past we had learned that just as making yourself invisible to normal light made you blind, so making yourself invisible to magesight made you unable to sense magic. He hadn't stood up to the god's mental assault directly; he had made himself unable to 'feel' it. "That was damned clever!" I said clapping him upon the shoulder.

"They're inside Washbrook," he said, ignoring my compliment. "The barrier around the town is broken already." His face was downcast.

"Is the gate between the castle and the town still open?" I asked.

He nodded, "No, I closed it just now."

"There are probably still townsfolk trying to get into the castle. You have to check that gate," I told him.

Fear was written on his face. "If I open the window and that god is there, I don't know if I will be able to escape his grasp again."

"So it was either Doron or Karenth?" I questioned.

"I'm not sure, but I got the impression it was masculine," Walter answered.

I filed that away mentally before continuing, "The castle gate is on the opposite side of Washbrook from the town gate, they probably haven't gotten that far yet, but I'd bet my arm there are townsfolk trying to get through."

"If you're wrong…," said Walter carefully, letting the sentence trail away without finishing it.

We both knew the risk. "Do it," I told him.

Reaching out, he touched the stone pedestal again and another of the glass squares lit up as light began passing through it. Knowing that I'd have difficulty seeing, I had positioned myself close to it to get a better view, wishing again that I still had my magesight. Even as poor as my view was, I could see that a crowd of people were beating against the invisible wall of force that my barrier enchantment had created. Guards stood on the inside. They had opened the physical gate, but were helpless to allow anyone through the magical barrier. People were screaming to be let in, and the guards were frantic to help them.

"Open the barrier for them!" I shouted.

"He's close, Mordecai! I can feel him already, and his warriors are at the outskirts of the crowd!" Walter replied desperately, indecision warred within him.

My own decision seemed crystal clear, "Open the gods-damned gate! The Knights can deal with those of the enemy who slip through! Now!"

Walter opened the gate, and the people flooded through, spilling into the courtyard while the soldiers and two of the Knights of Stone stood back to let them pass. It took what seemed like an eternity for the crowd to push through, and even after the initial press there was still a steady stream of stragglers coming through. Some of the enemy's fighter's came through as well.

Ignoring the people, they raced through on feet that seemed to have sprouted wings. Their movements were such that they had slipped through the crowd and past the castle defenders before they could be stopped. At least eleven or twelve of them came through the crowd in a rush.

Not all of them made it past the guards, however. One quick young soldier managed to tangle the legs of one of the foreigners, sending him into a sprawling roll. Two other guards stepped forward, and thrust their spears through his midsection before he could regain his feet, but the man ignored the wounds and stood anyway. His lips split wide in a bloody grin as he ran up the spear one of the guards held, and brought his heavy iron mace down upon the startled man's head. Blood and brains flew in all directions.

The soldiers of Cameron Castle looked on in dismay and disbelief, fear taking root in their hearts. For a moment the battlefield seemed to freeze, as the soldiers morale wavered, then Sir Ian's two handed sword took the man's head and upper torso off in a clean sweep. "They're berserkers, but they can still die!" he shouted to the defenders, and as quickly as that, the spell was broken. The defenders took heart and renewed their attacks on those of the enemy that remained within reach.

It broke my heart to watch them fight through the tiny window, but I had no way to help them. Walter's voice caught my attention, "He's here!" The light from the window was replaced by a view of the cold stone that lay behind the glass, as he shut off our view and closed the barrier's gate. My last sight was of a woman and her child running for the gate. They, and many others, didn't reach it in time. *All my plans and preparations, and yet I still failed to protect them,* I realized. *My own pride and cleverness blinded me to the possibility that they might just be cunning enough to do something like this.*

I slid back down against the wall. Nausea, brought on by the poison combined with my own remorse, and I felt hot tears leave burning tracks down my cheeks.

Before I could get far in my self-recriminations, Walter interrupted me, "What's next?"

Taking a deep breath I wiped my face and looked up. "Now we wait, until whichever god it is breaks the barrier."

"That's it?!" said Walter in a voice that had an edge of hysteria in it. "I thought there was a plan?"

"There is," I explained, "but it begins after the people are evacuated, and the barrier comes down. After that we begin a deadly game of cat and mouse."

"Which part do we play?"

I laughed wryly, "Without my power? We play the mouse."

CHAPTER 21

Penelope Illeniel, the Countess di'Cameron, strode briskly through the corridors, while the two women with her hurried to keep up. She carried her sheathed longsword in one hand and struggled to keep her pace slow enough for Rose and Elaine to stay with her. That wasn't much of a problem for Elaine, but given Rose's condition, she was having more difficulty. She was slightly over seven months pregnant, and her swelling belly presented a significant obstacle to moving at anything beyond a normal walk.

"Penny—please, I can't run," reminded Rose.

Penny looked back and again tried to hide her impatience. She had borne three children herself and knew well the stresses her friend was under, yet she couldn't help but push her. They were heading for the nursery to collect Irene, as well as Rose's son Gram, who hadn't been allowed to attend that evening's feast.

A tug on her skirt drew her attention to Moira. "Momma I don't feel very good," said her adopted daughter. The seven year old's face was pale; despite the quick pace at which they had been moving.

"I'm sorry sweetheart," Penny told her, before glancing again at Rose, "I'll slow down. We should have plenty of time to reach the nursery and then get to our apartments." According to what Mort had told her previously, the barrier enchantment should last at least fifteen minutes or so, and quite possibly much longer. That and the fact that they wouldn't be using the teleportation circles meant that they should have more than enough time. Penny still wished they could run.

People were everywhere as they went, rushing back and forth along the corridors. Because of their slow pace, it took them almost ten minutes to reach the nursery and gather up their children. Lilly was still there watching them, so Penny ordered her to come along with them as well. Lilly wasn't a part of the plan for the Illeniel family escape, but Penny was sure she would need the other woman's help in the days to come.

"What about Peter?" asked Lilly, as they headed for the stairs that would lead up to the 'rooms' that the Illeniel family supposedly occupied. She was referring of course to her brother, Peter Tucker, the chamberlain for Castle Cameron. "He's expecting me to take the circle to Albamarl with everyone else. He'll be worried sick."

Lady Rose patted the younger woman's shoulder, "I'm sure we'll find some way to contact him once the dust settles."

"My husband keeps several private message boxes in our home. We can send a message to King James, and he can send a messenger to let your brother know you are with us," said Penny quickly. "Let's go. We may not have as much time as we think," she continued. In the distance she could hear yelling and the sounds of fighting in the castle courtyard. *Things shouldn't have progressed that far yet,* she told herself silently, but there was no denying the evidence of her ears.

They made a motley assortment as they traveled the corridor; four women, three young children, one toddler, and an infant. Lilly carried the baby, Irene, allowing Penny to keep her hands free on the slim chance she might need to use her sword. Rose held little Conall's hand, making sure that he wasn't separated from them, while the twins and Gram were allowed to follow closely on their own. Elaine stayed in the rear of their group, to make sure that none of the children fell behind.

Only one corridor separated them from the stairs that would lead upward to their refuge, but as they started down the long hall, Elaine finally spoke, "There's fighting just beyond that door; a lot of our soldiers and five of the enemy, I believe." She pointed to a door midway down the corridor, a door that led to the front entry hall.

"Let's keep moving," urged Rose, "The stairs are close."

Penny nodded and unsheathed her sword, staying in the lead as they went. Roughly a quarter of the way down the hall, just as they had passed one of the servant's doors leading to the kitchen, the door ahead burst inward. The sturdy wooden door hadn't been opened; it had simply disintegrated under the blow of a heavy iron mace. Adrenaline had already slowed her perception of time, and Penny idly noted that the head of the mace was far too large for someone to use easily. *They must have brought those for breaking down doors.*

A heavily muscled man followed the large weapon through the shattered door. He was armored in a leather coat with steel plates sewn across the chest and back, though his forearms were bare, covered only with tattoos. The iron hammer of Doron, the Iron God was prominent among the designs, indicating that the man was probably a temple guard.

Even as Penny noted those things, another man, one of the castle guards, followed the stranger through the door, thrusting at him with a spear. With an almost beautiful grace, the foreigner sidestepped the spear thrust, and reaching out with his right hand, he caught the guard, gripping the top of his breastplate. Twisting, he easily lifted and threw the guardsman into the wall, tossing him as though he weighed no more than a ragdoll. The castle defender slumped to the floor limply, though Penny couldn't be sure if he were dead or merely unconscious.

The guard's helm fell from his head and then she recognized his face. His name was Alan, and while he was an unassuming and quiet man, he was frequently selected to guard the door of the Illeniel family suite. He was no one of importance, but Penny knew the man would have died before allowing an enemy to hurt them—in fact he might just have done so. Enraged, she leapt forward, her sword eager to repay the intruder for his rude treatment of one of *her* people. "Keep the children back," she shouted, hoping her companions would understand. *And cover their eyes,* she thought belatedly. She knew that what was about to happen wouldn't be something she would want her children to see.

Racing toward her opponent, she was surprised at the speed with which he reacted. The massive iron mace he was wielding came up far more quickly than should have been possible, even for a man of his size. She was forced to dodge to the side to avoid it, but even so, she wasn't worried. No matter how strong her enemy was, her sword would be far faster than such an unwieldy weapon. Twisting her torso as she dodged, she brought her sword neatly around to sweep above the head of his weapon, as she launched herself upward.

Or rather, as she attempted to launch herself upward— the formal dress that she had worn for the celebration, caught upon something at the last moment, tangling her legs and sending her unceremoniously to the ground at her enemy's feet. Unable to check her fall quickly enough, her head struck the stone floor hard enough to make her see stars, while her sword went skittering away from her hand.

"Looks like your dress got caught on something, bitch," said the man, with a ghastly smile on his face.

Dazed, Penny struggled to roll away, but her body was still sluggish from the shock of the blow to her head. Looking down, she discovered the reason she had fallen, the man was standing on the hem of her dress. It was an effective tactic, and one she had used many times herself, one she probably wouldn't have time to recover from.

Before she could move any further, she was struck in the belly by a heavy boot, driving the wind from her lungs. Leaning over her, the grinning bastard laughed, as he began ripping the skirts from her dress. "Let me help you Countess," he said while she lay on the floor, choking and gasping for air. The strength in his hands was incredible, and he shredded the fabric simply by pulling, as though her dress was made of tissue rather than sturdy linen. "Your husband should have taught you better. If you're going to fight, you shouldn't be wearing a dress."

Her eyes locked on his as she realized that the stranger knew exactly who she was. She struggled to get enough air into her lungs, if for nothing better than to curse him, when a glimpse past the man's legs showed her Lady Rose running frantically toward them.

Rose had her dress pulled up to keep her legs free, and she ran on bare feet, to keep from alerting the man looming over Penny. Unfortunately, her hands were also empty of anything resembling a weapon.

"After you're dead I'll make sure that what's left of your mangled corpse, will send a proper message to your dying husband," said the man, as he finished ripping away the last of her skirts. His eyes followed hers and looking over his shoulder, he spotted Rose. "Guess I'll have to kill this one first," he said with a shrug, lifting his mace easily with one hand.

Penny had finally gotten a half breath of air ,and her hand caught the man's where it gripped the handle of his mace. "No," she wheezed. *You're not killing my friend.*

The stranger ignored her, though she had his hand locked in an iron grip around the weapon. Instead he stood and dragged her upright along with the mace. His strength was such, that it seemed as if he might happily attempt to swing her along with the heavy iron club.

Having used his help to stand, Penny threw a poorly aimed jab at the warrior with her free hand. Predictably, given the lack of force, he caught her fist in his own. Once both their arms were locked together however, she pulled backward using all the strength she could summon and simultaneously drove her knee into the man's sternum.

She felt a crack as her knee connected, and she knew that whatever had broken, her opponent would be helpless and unable to breath. Depending on how badly she had hurt him, he might even die.

It appeared that someone had failed to explain that to the stranger though, for he still held her in an iron grip. Instead of collapsing, as any normal man would have, he straightened and pushed forward, driving her smaller mass against the stone wall. "It will take more than that to stop the will of Doron, bitch!"

Penny lost her focus as she hit the hard stone. This time at least, she managed to keep from striking her head, but now he had his hands around her neck. She struggled with him, trying to pull his hands away from her throat, but despite her own strength she was unable to do more than achieve a stalemate—one that she was slowly losing.

A spasm went through the man, and his arms went limp. Pushing his heavy form back Penny saw Rose standing behind him, and as he slowly collapsed, she glimpsed the hilt of a long dagger protruding from his neck. She had driven the blade into his spine. "He wasn't easy to kill," commented Rose. That was when Penny noticed the second wound. Apparently Rose had put the blade through his kidney once before switching targets. "He didn't even flinch at the first wound," Rose added.

"Where are the children?" asked Penny, as she sought to steady herself. Neither they, nor Elaine, were anywhere to be seen.

"Right here," answered Elaine, becoming visible not twenty feet away. Lilly stood beside her, holding onto Irene, while the rest of the children gripped Elaine's dress.

Relief shot through Penny once she was sure that everyone was alright, but Matthew immediately began peppering her with questions. "What happened to you, Momma? We couldn't see! Did you kill that man?" Although he seemed calm, Penny could feel the undercurrent of fear in his voice.

"Momma, you're naked," added Moira, observing that the bottom half of Penny's dress had been ripped free, exposing her long legs.

Penny sighed, "It's just my legs, dear-heart. I'll explain later. We don't have time to talk now." She started to ask why they had been unable to see when she realized that Elaine had kept them invisible the entire time. Mort had explained previously that, when invisible, the person hidden could no longer see, because the light was being diverted around their body. *That was a blessing in disguise,* she thought to herself. After a second she began chuckling at the inherent pun in her thought. *Mort must be rubbing off on me—wait till I tell him.* That thought triggered a whole host of unwelcome emotions, so she quickly shuttered them away. *There will be time for that later.*

Before they could move Elaine interrupted them, "There are more coming!" Throwing her hands up, the younger woman spoke an unintelligible word and gestured toward the open doorway. The guardsmen on the other side were all dead now, and four of the strange warriors were heading towards them, with deadly intent on their faces. The first of them ran head first into the invisible barrier that the young wizardess had erected to block the shattered door, bouncing back as though he had struck stone.

"Lilly! Rose! Take the children up the stairs! Don't wait!" ordered Penny, as she recovered her sword.

"You can't handle that many if they break through," protested Rose.

Penny straightened her back and let her anger show openly on her face. "Damnitt Rose! I don't have time to argue. Elaine, stay with them. If you meet any more of the enemy hide them all," commanded the Countess di'Cameron, before adding, "Rose will be able to open the door to my rooms—make sure she opens the door first. Do you understand?"

Rose stared at her without showing any emotion before nodding her acceptance, but Elaine's face was tormented by unexplained sadness. A tear rolled down her cheek as she answered, "I'm so sorry," before turning away to obey Penny's command. With Lilly carrying Irene, and the other children close beside them, the three women hurried to the staircase and the hope of refuge.

"I'm not dead yet," replied Penny without understanding the underlying reason for Elaine's apology. "If I can't manage them, I'll try to draw them in the other direction," she added, heading back toward the doorway blocked by Elaine's magic.

Standing about ten feet from the invisible barrier, she couldn't help but imagine what a ridiculous sight she must have been for the four men standing on the other side. She wore no armor; that was still in her bedroom upstairs. Instead, she was clothed only in the upper portion of what had recently been a beautiful formal gown. The skirt had been ripped completely off, leaving her bare legs fully displayed. Her only consolation was, that she had worn soft leather soled slippers under her dress, rather than the awkward thick soled shoes that many women preferred, to give them the illusion of greater height.

One of the men drew back with his heavy mace and swung it against the magical barrier. The weapon bounced back, and the barrier held. Growling he began to swing again.

Meanwhile, Penny drove her own sword into the stone floor in front of her, to free her hands for a moment. Reaching across, she ripped the sleeve from her left arm, a task that would have been difficult but for her enhanced strength. Never taking her eyes from the doorway and the men pounding at it with their iron clubs, she used the torn sleeve to tie her long hair back. It had been elaborately coiffed not long ago, but her recent fight had caused it to fall loose.

Once she had finished, she pulled her sword from the floor and assumed a relaxed pose, waiting for her opponents. They had been battering the invisible wall for two or three minutes now, which led her to doubt her decision. *If I'd known it would take them this long, I would have stayed with the others.* She toyed with the idea of following them then, but she knew if she did, her enemy would see the direction she went. *Better to kill them here,* she decided. She closed her mind against the possibility that she might not survive.

Then the barrier vanished, and one of the intruders stumbled forward as his heavy weapon failed to meet the expected resistance. Penny was waiting for him. Despite her calm pose, her body was thrumming with adrenaline. As the brute's body came through, her sword flicked out, faster than thought and neatly sliced through his throat, before whipping back and severing the tendons of his weapon arm near the wrist.

Blood sprayed from her enemy's throat and arm, and a thrill ran down Penny's spine, erasing the doubt that her previous near failure had left her with. Banishing all thought, Penny leapt forward, sidestepping the dying man and thrusting her sword at his comrade standing beside him. As she went, she noted the quick reactions of the two others standing further back, both had their weapons up and whistling through the air almost as quickly as she had advanced, whipping the heavy iron maces through the air, as though they were as light as willow switches. One came in high while the other would strike her at the waist, either would likely kill or maim her with a single blow.

Ordinarily she would have dodged backward, turning her thrust into a feint, but the man behind her, the one whose throat she had cut, was reaching for her with his good arm. She might have wondered at his continued ability to fight, but she was in a place far beyond conscious thought, where time ran slowly, and hesitation led only to death.

Never take your feet off the ground, Cyhan had taught her long ago. He had punctuated his lessons with painful reminders every time she had used her strength to attempt a high flying jump. *As soon as you jump like that, you lose the power to control your direction until you touch the ground again. A skilled opponent will take advantage of this,* he had told her.

Penny sprang upward, twisting into a sideways roll as she went over the heads of the two men at the rear, the ones swinging the maces. Their weapons had too much momentum to change direction, even for men possessed of such inhuman strength as they were. Instead one of them reached for her with his free hand, seeking to arrest her flight and send her disastrously to the ground. It was exactly what Cyhan would have done.

Her sword removed his arm from the elbow down, the enchanted steel slicing through bones as easily as flesh. Finishing her arc, she landed behind them and let her momentum take her all the way to the floor. Her opponents' weapons continued to sweep in a full circle, as their wielders followed through in an attempt to strike her as she landed. Her mid-air twist became a spin, as her legs folded into a crouch, and she took the left leg of the man she had just wounded, off at the knee. Off balance, his weapon went wide, giving her just enough room to slip beneath his companion's mace.

From that point, the fight became simple slaughter, as she systematically dismembered the four men. She had already discovered that shock and loss of blood had little effect upon them. The only thing that stopped them was removing their limbs, and the only thing that killed them seemed to be decapitation. Fortunately, the magical sword she used was perfect for that task. Their speed and strength was as great as her own, possibly greater, but their combat experience was definitely more limited. If they had been better trained, or had possessed lighter weapons she would have been unable to prevail against so many.

Those maces are better suited for use against heavily armored opponents... she thought to herself, as she retreated from the bloody scene, heading for the stairs ... *like the Knights of Stone*, the unwelcome thought finished itself in her mind. "Damnitt!" she swore.

⊷——⊶

Meanwhile—upstairs from where Penny was fighting, Elaine, Rose, and Lilly led the children away from the stairs and down the long corridor leading to the Illeniel family's rooms. Elaine already knew they weren't going to make it unopposed however, her magesight told her that three waited at the door that led to safety, dead guards at their feet. Two more were entering through a small window at the opposite end of the hallway, their hands ripping stones from the wall to make the opening large enough for them to pass. Within moments she and the others would be trapped between them.

How can they be so strong?, she wondered silently. In her magesight, they glowed brilliantly with an intensity to their auras that she hadn't seen since—her mind balked at the thought. *That isn't possible*, she thought. *Celior's aura was stronger still, and his presence made it difficult to even think. Besides, there are too many of them.*

"There are three ahead of us, and two more will soon be approaching from behind," she told the others.

"There's nowhere to hide!" said Lilly, in a voice tinged with incipient panic.

Rose put a hand on Lilly's shoulder, trying to calm her, "Take a deep breath. Elaine can always make us invisible again."

Gram tugged on his mother's arm, "Where's Dad? How did they get in here?"

"I'm sure your father is still fighting below. Once he's finished there, he will come and get rid of these as well, never fear," Rose answered calmly, hiding her own fear that something must have gone terribly wrong with the defense of Cameron Castle. "For now we have to take care of ourselves until he can get here. Do you understand?"

Gram nodded, and Matthew and Moira nodded along with him. They were all listening closely with a seriousness that made it clear that they understood the gravity of the situation.

"When a Prathion doesn't want to be found, a Prathion isn't found," said Elaine softly to herself, repeating one of her father's old sayings. Raising her voice, she spoke to the others, "Everyone move up against the wall. I'm going to shield you from all sight, magical and otherwise, just to be safe."

"Will we be blind again?" asked Lilly worriedly.

"Yes, there's no way around that, but you'll still be able to hear—and be heard, so stay as quiet as possible," Elaine explained carefully.

Rose was already lining the children up against the wall. Glancing over her shoulder, she said, "You sound as if you don't intend to be with us. Don't we have to be in physical contact for you to make us invisible?"

"Not as long as you stay in one place," answered Elaine, "This spell will be stationary; if you move more than a foot in any direction, you will become visible again."

"What will you do?" prodded Rose.

"Teach them why it is never wise to hunt wizards, or their friends," Elaine replied, with a show of bravado that she hoped she could live up to. *That's probably something like what Mordecai would have said,* she told herself. She intended to make her mentor proud.

Only a minute later the two men who had climbed through the window made their approach from the southern end of the corridor, spotting her as soon as they rounded the corner. They stopped some fifty feet away and smiled at the lone woman standing there before them. A moment later, the three that had been in front of the Illeniel family rooms appeared at the northern end of the corridor.

They're coordinating somehow, noted Elaine mentally, as the five began to approach from both ends of the corridor. "Stop," she told them calmly.

"Where are the children?" The words came from all five of them simultaneously. Eerily, they spoke in utter synchrony.

That answers one question, thought Elaine. *They're being controlled by one entity.* "Here is my answer," she replied and followed it with the words, *"Bradek Tyrestrin!"* The hallway erupted with lightning; flashing from her hands, it forked and split multiple times to arc in both directions. Unlike natural lightning however, it did not vanish quickly; instead it remained for long seconds, forming a giant web of small bolts that engulfed and transfixed the five trespassers.

After what seemed an eternity, the lightning abruptly vanished, leaving a dark silence in its wake. The five men were still standing, though their bodies twitched and smoked. Black marks covered them where the electricity had burned holes in their skins. As one, they smiled at the woman standing between them, "You'll have to do better than that."

Four of them charged at her, two from either direction, while the fifth turned and swung his massive iron weapon at a nondescript and otherwise empty section of wall. There was no visible reason for his action, other than the fact that that area was guarded by a shield of magic. Like most such shields this one was not visible—not unless one possessed the ability to see magic.

"No!" shouted Elaine, as the iron struck her shield with incredible force. She gasped in pain as the shield collapsed under the impact of the blow, and the wall sent forth a shower of stone shards as it was struck. As she reeled from the shock of her shield failing, the warriors around her attacked. Her arms went up instinctively to protect her head from the lethal violence of their swings.

Elaine's illusory double vanished, and their weapons found nothing where she had been only moments before. She reappeared forty feet further down the hall. *Clearly they can see magic, since they easily spotted my shield decoy. They also won't be easy to kill, and if I try to shield myself from the force of those weapons, I might go unconscious from the strength of the blow.* Speaking again, she tried one of the simplest of spells, *"Shibal."*

There was no visible effect.

"I expected better," said the five men as one. Three of them headed for her new location, while two began systematically working their way along the walls, their hands feeling for things unseen.

Three more copies of the young wizardess appeared at various places along the hall. "I'll make it more interesting for you then," Elaine replied, her voice emanating from all four mouths, making it impossible to tell which was really her. Reaching into her sleeve, she withdrew a pair of identically engraved wooden wands, taking one in each hand. Each wand was made of willow and painstakingly carved with runes. Mordecai had favored using a larger staff to channel power when he needed it, but Elaine had always preferred the smaller wands. They suited her better in terms of precision and style. *Plus, two is usually better than one,* she added mentally.

The two searching the walls ignored her, while the three advancing upon her each separated to attack a different image, in the hope that one would be the real one. There was no hesitation or discussion among her opponents; they continued to move in unspoken coordination.

"Pyrren sills thylen," said Elaine, and fire snaked out from the ends of each of her wands, forming long ropy

lines five foot in length. Each of her images mirrored her actions, as she lifted her arms and began swinging the fiery whips into blurring arcs of flame around her.

"Flame will do you no good against the iron will of Doron!" shouted the fighters, as three of them brought their terrible iron mauls to bear on separate images of the slender woman.

Two of them met no resistance as their illusory opponents vanished. The third met a far different fate, as lines of incandescent fire cut through his weapon, his arms, and finally his chest. In seconds, the blazing whips sliced him into neatly cauterized pieces of smoking flesh, as first his arms, and then his head and torso fell in different directions.

Having discovered her true position, the other two attacked without hesitation, coming at her from two directions. Without flinching she stood between them and spread her arms wide, swinging her whips in brilliant arcs, to intercept each of them, but she could not focus her attention perfectly on both sides.

With inhuman speed and perfect, selfless coordination, the one to her right threw himself bodily at her, allowing her magical whip to bisect him from one shoulder to his waist. Even so, the momentum of his lunge made it impossible for her to avoid being struck by the upper portion of his body, knocking her off balance, as his companion to her left dove under her fiery attack on that side.

Stumbling Elaine was engulfed in blinding agony, as her left leg was struck by an iron mace. As she collapsed, she knew without looking, that her femur had been shattered, while her thigh was probably a red nightmare of bloody flesh. Unable to see from the pain of her injury, she heard a scream of terror as one of the enemy's searching hands touched an invisible child.

Her right hand still gripped one of her wands, the other she had lost in the fall. Blinking, she was unable to clear the tears of pain that blurred her vision, but her magesight was more than sufficient. Above, her closest assailant raised his iron weapon for a blow that would certainly finish her. She had no time to think, raising the wand, she pointed it past her immediate opponent and uttered her last words, *"Borok Ingak."* The head of the man, who had just found the children broke like an overripe melon, as the force of her spell slammed him against the stone wall. She had no time to repeat her spell, before a heavy weight crushed her to the floor painfully, and a warm and welcome darkness swept her away from the agony that engulfed her consciousness. She had no time, even for regret, as oblivion took her.

CHAPTER 22

Sir Dorian had gone first to the barracks, to ensure that all the men were heading to their assigned stations, which primarily meant defensive positions along the castle walls, as well as reinforcing the guard at all gates and assisting the citizenry to reach the gathering point in the southern courtyard. As he went he gathered up two of the Knights of Stone, Sir Grant and Sir Daniel, along with a reserve group of ten soldiers that had somehow been left without an advance assignment.

From there he proceeded to the northern courtyard, which also contained the main gate that led into Washbrook. His first impression wasn't good. The walls seemed empty of men, and where he had expected to see a small regiment of men under Sir Ian's command guarding the open gate, he saw none. Perhaps it would be better to say that he saw none 'standing'.

The gate itself was wide open and several men stood just beyond it. *The gate barrier enchantment must be closed*, thought Dorian. He could already tell by their postures and warlike garb that the men were not townsfolk. *If they're still trapped out there, how did they kill my men?*

He reached the castle gate and found the remains of a bloody slaughter. Well over fifty bodies lay strewn about, and at a glance it appeared that almost all of them were his men. Mixed in with them were a few of the townspeople and even one or two children. He recognized each and every one of them, with the exception of two strangers.

One of those strangers had been cloven into two grisly pieces, while the other looked to have been wounded a multitude of times, mostly by spears. The second one still held two of the guardsmen by the throat, having apparently choked them to death, even as he himself bled to death.

None of the defenders were still living, and among them Dorian immediately spotted one of his own brother knights, Sir Ian. Kneeling down he examined the body of the young warrior he had trained and fought beside for the past five years. His death had been gruesome. The armor that the Knights of Stone wore was nigh on impregnable, but Sir Ian's opponents hadn't bothered trying to pierce it. Instead his arms had been ripped off.

It was the sort of injury one would expect if someone had been tied between two large draft horses—not the kind of wound people received on a battlefield. "What in the hell did this?" Dorian wondered aloud.

Beside him Sir Grant touched his elbow, "I can hear sounds of fighting toward the postern side. I think the battle has moved."

Sir Dorian, Grandmaster of the Knights of Stone, was no stranger to making quick decisions. "Close the gate," he told the soldiers that had come with him. "Sir Grant, go back to the keep and check the men guarding the entrances. Make sure none of the invaders entered. Afterward report to Sir Cyhan, he should be somewhere within the castle still, making sure all the servants have gone to the rally point."

"As you will, my lord," answered Sir Grant promptly, before turning to head for the main entrance to the keep.

Turning back, Dorian watched as some of the men began lowering the heavy iron portcullis using the winches, while others pushed the heavy wooden gates shut. Some thirty yards from where he stood, a tall regal figure stood in the center of the path leading to the gate. The figure's clothes appeared to be made from grey linen and were heavily embroidered with gold thread.

Dorian walked toward the man, until he stood just ten feet from him, as close as he could get with the barrier enchantment blocking his way. *Grey hair, grey eyes, grey clothes, and the balance of justice,* he noted mentally, taking stock of the stranger's appearance. The fellow's sleeves were each embroidered with golden scales, the favored symbol of Karenth the Just.

Once upon a time, Dorian would have knelt in the presence of the god of justice and wise governance. Now he merely felt sorrow, a deep sadness that probably stemmed from the loss of his innocence. "I believed in you once," he said quietly. "My family was devoted to your sister, the Lady of the Evening Star."

Karenth the Just smiled at him, "It is not too late for you, Dorian, son of Gram. Lower this magical barrier and I will show you and your family mercy."

"And if I don't?"

The god opened his mouth, showing perfect teeth in a menacing grin before he answered, "Then you shall suffer the same judgment as the rest. Every man, woman, and child serving under Mordecai Illeniel shall die, including those that seek to escape."

"You're too late, many are already gone," Dorian replied.

"I know you, Dorian Thornbear, I know your wife Rose, and I know your son, who you named after your departed father. It does not matter if they have fled. I will find them. No one escapes my justice."

"Justice?" said Dorian. "Don't dirty the word with your liar's tongue. I said I believed in you *once*. I don't know what the hell you are, but I do know that you are no god. Power does not make you just, nor does it make you divine." As he spoke, the wooden gates drew closed in front of him. Before his view was entirely eclipsed, he spit upon the ground, making certain that Karenth knew exactly how he felt.

Gesturing to the soldiers that had just closed the gate, he spoke again, "Come with me to the circle building. We need to make sure that everyone there is being transported, and then you need to join them."

"What about the gate, Your Lordship?" asked one of the men. "Shouldn't we be manning it?"

Dorian grunted, "Closing it was more symbolic than anything else. If the barrier comes down, it won't last more than a moment." Turning away he began jogging toward the wall that divided the northern and southern castle courtyards.

A minute later and he had passed through the arch leading into the southern courtyard, which these days was largely dominated by the building that housed the teleportation circles. The building itself was crowded, and the space around it was filled with people for almost thirty yards in every direction.

Transporting nearly a thousand people, in groups of thirty at a time, was time consuming. Mordecai had originally calculated the time required to be, at or slightly over, thirty minutes, assuming that the wizard charged with that duty could move at least one group every minute. With good organization, discipline, and order it might be possible to do it more quickly, but the wizard given the task might exhaust themselves.

Given the size of the crowd, Dorian guessed that things had been proceeding according to plan, although the people outside the building seemed to be agitated. As he drew closer he could see the reason why—there were numerous bodies scattered about. Sir Harold, who was in charge of organizing the orderly evacuation had already spotted him approaching and met him outside the building.

"My lord, the defense has been breached," Harold said without preamble. "We were beset by four outsiders."

"Four?" Dorian replied incredulously, "Four men did this?"

"Yes Sir. Sir Lionel was gravely wounded as well," continued Harold.

"What? Explain."

Harold drew a deep breath, "I was inside the building, trying to keep order. Lionel was outside, overseeing the guardsmen organizing the townsfolk. From what I am told, the men approached and waded into the mob, slaying any who got in their path."

"And none of the guards noticed their approach?" said Dorian with a severe tone.

"Begging your pardon Sir, but we have had a steady stream of people. It has been utter chaos, but with the barrier still up we believed that there would not be any enemies among them. The guards tried to intervene as soon as the cry went up among the people. They were unable to stop them until Sir Lionel reached them," explained Harold.

"And how did Lionel get wounded?" asked Dorian. It was a simple question, but it bore a heavy weight. The armor that Mordecai had crafted for the Knights of Stone was so effective that it had become almost legendary. In the seven years since the order had been founded, none of the Knights wearing it had ever been seriously wounded. The worst injuries had been one concussion (from a training accident) and a variety of mild sprains and muscle injuries that no armor could prevent. *With the new exception of whatever it was that pulled Sir Ian apart like that,* Dorian noted silently.

Harold coughed. "I wasn't aware of the attack until after it happened, but witnesses among the crowd tell me that one of the men struck him with a massive iron maul. Each of the four of them was armed with one. Sir Lionel cut two of them down before the third caught him from behind, with a blow to his head. He has not regained consciousness yet, and I fear he might die before he does."

"How did the third get behind him?"

"He leapt over them, Sir. According to the crowd he jumped almost fifteen feet into the air while Sir Lionel was fighting the other two."

"How did it end?"

"I finished the third man before he could reach the building. The fourth entered the crowd from a separate direction and reached the interior of the building by smashing a hole in the side wall. I caught him inside and slew him there. My guess is that he hoped to use the distraction to get inside and kill our wizard before we could stop him," answered Harold.

"The men guarding the town gate are dead, including Sir Ian," said Dorian without waiting. "It appears our enemy is as strong as we are."

Harold was shocked. "Ian is dead?"

"Along with every guard there and quite a few townsfolk," replied Dorian. "It looked as though they caught him by his arms and pulled him apart." Now that he understood the strength of their foes, Ian's death made perfect sense.

Harold grimaced, and Dorian spent the next minute describing what he had found at the gate. When he finished, Harold commented, "At least they don't have our armor. We have one advantage at least."

"Those iron maces are devastating. Sir Lionel's armor didn't fail, but he's still half dead. They also have us greatly outnumbered. I saw well over a hundred men similarly armed beyond the wall, along with a man that appeared to be Karenth. How many of the knights in Washbrook returned after the outer barrier went down?" asked Dorian.

"None have made it here, though some may have reported to Cyhan in the castle," said Harold.

"I doubt it," replied Dorian. "They were to head for this rally point after leaving those positions. We have to assume they are either dead or trapped outside." Dorian mentally tallied the numbers; *six knights were stationed at the gates in Washbrook, including Sir Daniel commanding them, Sir Ian is dead, and Sir Lionel wounded—that leaves nine knights still active, twelve if I include myself, Cyhan, and Harold.*

Twelve Knights of Stone, facing something over a hundred foes with similar strength and speed, foes that did not flinch at wounds or stop for anything less than death or dismemberment. "At least we don't have to deal with Karenth," muttered Dorian under his breath. "He's all Mort's; assuming he isn't too sick from whatever he ate." Glancing about, he wondered if Castle Cameron would be half destroyed by the battle, as the royal palace in Albamarl had been after Mordecai's struggle against Celior. "How long before we have all the townsfolk and servants out of here?" he asked, as he returned his thoughts to the present.

"At least fifteen minutes and probably more like twenty, and then we still need to transport the guardsmen after that," said Harold.

"If the barrier lasts that long—the outer one came down sooner than we had planned. Send a runner in to inform Cyhan of the status out here," instructed Dorian.

"You and I will stay until the barrier comes down, and then we'll take whoever is left and join him in the castle itself. Let us hope George can get most of them to Albamarl before that happens."

"Where is the Count?"

"Inside, with Walter—the two of them are preparing something to deal with Karenth," assured Dorian. As he said it though, he thought of how ill Mort had seemed before he had left him. He couldn't help but wonder if his friend would be able to live up to his own plan.

CHAPTER 23

What's happening?" I asked Walter again, as I had every minute or so for the last quarter of an hour. I didn't enjoy nagging him anymore than he enjoyed me constantly asking, but without my magesight I had no idea what was occurring in the castle, or more importantly what state the barrier enchantment was in.

"He's still trying to bring it down. Every ten seconds or so he strikes again; it makes the whole thing vibrate when he does," replied Walter patiently.

"How is the evacuation going?" I added.

"They were attacked by some of the ones that got through the gate, but it appears to be over now. Some of the people there are dead, but George is still transporting the rest," he told me.

I ground my teeth in frustration. Those deaths were my fault as well. I had kept the gate open to save some, and others had paid the price. "Can you tell how much longer it will be before they finish?"

Walter shook his head negatively. "I think roughly half of them are gone, but there are too many to count. I can't be sure." After a long pause he added, "There are men fighting in the great hall now. I think they're trying to find you."

"Dammit!" I cursed. "Where are Penny and the children? Have they reached the apartments upstairs?"

Walter frowned as he focused upon the many people moving within the castle, trying to identify them. "They're close to the fighting. No—wait, the Countess *is* fighting."

The next few minutes were some of the worst of my life, as Walter quietly relayed the events unfolding. My heart was in my throat as he told me of Penny's fall, and her subsequent close call with death. When he began describing the events with Elaine and the children upstairs, we both grew tense.

"I can't sense the children any longer, she's hidden them with a stationary invisibility illusion—and she's created an empty shield, probably as a decoy. Clever girl!" said Walter with pride. "They can't tell where she is hiding. She's managing multiple illusions now, and maintaining the invisibility around Rose and the children. When did she grow so skilled? I doubt I could manage all that at once."

"Where's Penny?" I said tersely.

"She's coming up the stairs now. Oh my! Fire whips? Where did she get that idea? Did you teach her that?" asked Walter.

"Entirely her idea," I responded.

"She's facing them down now, but..." Walter's voice trailed away as he trained all of his attention on the fight between his only daughter and the warriors trying to find my wife and children. "No!" he shouted suddenly, and my heart leapt into my throat.

"What?!"

"She's down! One of them got to her!" cried Walter. The man was already on his feet and heading for the door. I was right behind him. The rest of the world could go to hell, if it meant my family would suffer for it.

He stopped before opening the door, concentrating, and then he relaxed. "She's alive!" he said as I looked at him with concern.

"And the others?" I said worriedly.

"Safe, your wife took the last two of the enemy from behind, but Elaine is badly wounded. She seems to be unconscious. The last of them fell over her after your wife cut the top half of his head off—when did she get so strong? She fought like a demon!" said Walter, with some surprise.

"I'll explain that later. Tell me what's happening," I told him impatiently.

"My daughter is definitely unconscious, they've dragged her out and it appears that Lady Rose is tying her leg up—it's a terrible mess. I think she's made a tourniquet. Your wife doesn't have much of a dress left, they used one of her sleeves for it," he explained.

That brought a smile to my lips for a moment. *If only I were there to give her some encouragement,* I thought. "Such a wanton...," I said quietly. I didn't bother saying it loudly enough for Walter; he wouldn't have gotten the joke. "Are there any more of the enemy near them?" I asked.

"No," replied the older wizard. "They're almost to the door now. The countess is carrying Elaine. Her leg looks to be a mess. I don't think I can heal something like that," he admitted. "She might not walk again unless..." he looked at me before looking away.

Unspoken was the fact that if it required a complex act of healing, I was probably the only wizard alive that could manage it. "We have to survive this before we can think about anything else," I told him.

"If we don't..." he began and then paused for a moment before continuing, "Her wound is bad. I'm not sure she'll survive for long without some sort of healing."

"They can send word to George, if we don't survive," I said to reassure him. "And if by some miracle we do, then you can help her, maybe." I slid back down to rest on the floor. The cold stone felt good. It helped distract me from the nausea. "How is the barrier holding up?"

"No real change," said Walter in a quiet voice.

"I'm sorry," I told him. "I never meant to put this sort of burden on you. I always intended to do this alone."

"Don't apologize to me," Walter replied in an angry tone. "You always do that. It isn't fair."

"Do what?" I was curious. Walter rarely showed his irritation.

"Take responsibility for everyone else, and then apologize when you can't do it all by yourself. How do you think that makes the rest of us feel? I'm a grown man. I may not be able to move mountains and bring gods to heel, but I can damn well do my best to protect friends and family—so don't apologize to me for not being able to do everything for me!" he snapped back.

I lowered my head, "You're right. I'm sorry, Walter."

"What did I just tell you?" he barked back, but as I looked up his eyes held a glint of amusement.

I laughed, "Alright, I don't know how to answer that, but you have a point. How is the barrier now?"

"Why do you keep asking that? You do realize I will tell you the second it breaks don't you?" he answered.

"I should have been clearer. If possible, I want to open the barrier before it breaks. That's why I keep asking. If you detect a weakness in it, we should turn it off then," I explained.

"Even if the people aren't finished evacuating?"

"Yes."

Walter frowned. "I thought the idea was to buy as much time as possible. Why would you give up even a half a minute to them?"

"Because if it fails, the feedback might destroy more than the barrier enchantment, it might undo the enchantment that keeps Celior contained within the gem," I replied. "That could make our situation significantly worse."

My friend put a hand over his eyes. "You really should tell me these things sooner."

"I don't really know for sure," I said. "It's just a worry I have."

The older wizard's eyes lit with understanding for a moment, "Ah ha!"

"What?"

"Now I understand the 'Ironheart Chamber' a bit better. All that iron never made sense to me. You didn't need it for the concealing enchantment, you needed it to help contain Celior if the gem failed," Walter declared.

I had been watching him carefully from the moment he mentioned the Ironheart Chamber. It probably didn't matter at this point if he knew the purpose, but I still relaxed once I heard his theory. For a moment, I almost corrected him, but I held my tongue. *If one of the gods gets another crack at his mind, it might spoil our last chance,* I thought.

That led me to another uncomfortable realization; without my power, how could I protect my own mind? Ignoring Walter's sudden 'insight', I asked him a question instead, "What do I look like to you?"

"How do you mean exactly?"

"My aura, my mood—I can't shield my mind. Can you read my emotions? Do I still look like a wizard?" I said, clarifying my question. Normally, if I wasn't careful to shield myself, not only would another person with magesight be able to sense my emotions but they could also get a relative feel for the strength of my power.

Walter's look was one of sympathy, or perhaps pity, "I'm sorry Mordecai. I don't sense anything around you, other than a very faint aura, just enough that I can tell you're still alive. Your power is gone— not just your sight."

His description was disheartening. I had half-hoped that perhaps my problem was simply being unable to sense or 'feel' my own aythar, as well as the aythar around me. Still, there might be one bright side to my problem. "When you say 'faint', how faint?" I asked.

"Like Dorian," he said bluntly.

Dorian Thornbear was what the wizards of old had called a 'stoic', meaning that he was completely dead to magic. He could neither manipulate it, nor sense it, and likewise he could not be affected by it, except in a purely physical sense. "Try to put me to sleep," I suggested.

"Huh?" said Walter with a confused look.

"When you were fighting the influence of that god a few minutes ago, I couldn't feel a thing. I think, for all intents and purposes, I may be like a stoic now. Put me to sleep, or paralyze me, anything—see if you can touch my mind," I explained.

We experimented for several minutes before coming to the conclusion that I was indeed, essentially a stoic now. "Congratulations," Walter told me. "Your theory was correct and you are completely powerless. I fail to see why you are even slightly happy about it."

"Sometimes it's the little things that matter," I replied. "I may not have my power, but at least I don't have to worry about them picking information out of my head, or fighting against their overwhelming compulsions once he—or they, do get in here."

"They—do you think it's more than one?"

"I hope not."

Walter snorted, "It doesn't really matter. I'm no match for one, two would just be overkill."

"We still have some hope—if it is just one," I suggested.

"I really wish you would tell me what you have planned. It would be a lot easier to help you," retorted Walter.

"You can be my hands, but if you want my secrets, you'll have to pry them from my mind," I said tapping my head.

"Hmmph," grunted Walter, "Not even your wife can get through that dense skull of yours."

"Exactly, my friend. Exactly!" I crowed.

"You seem to be feeling better at least," observed the other wizard.

The nausea had in fact faded to some degree. "I think you're right. Perhaps I'm not dying after all?" I suggested hopefully.

He shook his head sadly, "From what I learned, you don't start the bad part for a few days. You'll turn yellow first before going slowly mad with pain and hallucinations."

"Yellow?" I said incredulously. "You didn't mention anything about odd color changes before. That hardly seems realistic."

"Not bright yellow," Walter corrected, "I think it's more like the color some old drunks turn before they get really sick."

"Jaundiced?" I asked.

"I couldn't think of the word, but that's it," agreed the older wizard.

I was beginning to wish I had paid more attention to some of the things I had read in the past, regarding illnesses and the physician's art. *No I don't,* I thought suddenly, *as it stands now, any knowledge I might have learned, would probably just have frightened me more.* "Let's talk about something else for a while," I suggested. "Like our impending struggle—how is the evacuation progressing?"

Walter's eyes unfocused for a moment, as he concentrated on things beyond our physical sight. After a few seconds he answered me, "They're getting close to finishing. Most of the people have been moved. I think soon they'll be able to start on the soldiers." He cocked his head to the side a bit, as though he were listening to something before continuing, "The barrier feels different now. The 'pitch' of the vibration seems higher when it's struck."

"That's not good," I told him. "It's getting close to breaking."

"What do we do now?"

"Can you project an image where Harold is? He's supposed to be in charge of the evacuation at the circle building," I asked.

"Easily," said Walter. "I am a Prathion after all."

The Prathions were known for their facility with illusions, as well as their ability to become invisible. I could sense things almost two miles distant—well, I had been able to, but projecting an image was much more difficult, because of the level of control and finesse required. Before my poisoning, I could have sent an image that far, but I had never tested Walter to see his own limit. I had just assumed it would be a shorter distance than my own range.

"Good, place it close to Harold and tell him that the barrier is coming down in one minute. Your son should take his last group and remain in Albamarl," I instructed.

"Dorian is there. Should I direct the message to him instead?"

"Sure, just make sure he knows they only have a minute to get those who are left inside the keep," I said.

A long moment passed before Walter responded again, "Alright, I think they understood. They seem to be moving everyone left toward the keep now. What's next?"

"Shhh," I said abruptly, as I counted under my breath.

"Huh?"

I waved my hands at him, "I'm counting."

"Oh!" he said in sudden understanding.

I tried to keep my pace slow, as I mentally worked my way up to a count of one hundred. I'd have just counted to sixty, but I was afraid that nervousness and adrenaline might have affected my sense of time already. Once I reached my mark, I asked the question, "Where are they?"

"It's a mess," replied Walter, "Most of them are in the courtyard trying to get into the castle. They don't have enough time. There are probably three hundred people or more out there, between the soldiers and what's left of the townsfolk."

"And the Knights?"

"Cyhan and the others have the main entry doors open, as they try to usher everyone inside. Dorian and Harold are out in the yard, trying to keep the soldiers from pushing past the few remaining citizens," answered the other wizard; his face was drawn with anxiety.

"Can you cover them with an illusion?" I was desperate to find a way to protect them.

Walter shook his head, "Not from here, not that many people."

An idea struck me then, "Can you project an image of me on the wall, near the gate? I may be able to delay them." I had never tried to project an image of someone besides myself over such a distance, so I was unsure if Walter would be able to make the illusion believable. I had disguised myself *as* other people before, and I had projected images of myself on occasion, to deliver messages, but I had never tried to do something quite that complex before.

To my surprise, Walter responded positively, "I can project your appearance and voice there, but I won't be able to imitate your aythar at this distance, nor do I have any way of hearing their responses from here."

"Really?" I said with all the wit I could manage. "You could imitate my aythar?" That was an aspect of illusion that I hadn't really considered before. In times past, Walter had shown that he was able to make himself invisible to magic, just as he could to visible light, but it had never occurred to me that one might make an illusion that encompassed magesight to create such an effect.

"I am a Prathion after all," he said somewhat proudly, "but even I have limits when it comes to illusions."

I stared at him mutely for a moment. "Could you project an image of me that would fool even *them*?" I asked.

He nodded, "I think so, but not at this range and I wouldn't be able to duplicate the strength of your aythar."

"As far as the present situation, I don't think it matters. They won't be able to sense it through the barrier—but if they were here now, you could create an illusion that would seem as though I hadn't lost my magic?" I said, hoping for clarification.

"It wouldn't have the same apparent strength or brightness that you usually possess," he reiterated.

That might not matter, I thought silently, *to one of them, even my normal strength is feeble in comparison. They might not notice the difference.* "Let's focus on the present," I announced. "If you can, have an image of me walk out onto the top of the wall and stare down at them. Once we have their attention, tell them this…"

Atop the wall, between the two towers that guarded the castle gate, a man appeared. Dressed in fine clothes of grey velvet and soft furs, there could be little doubt as to his identity. Mordecai Illeniel, the Count di'Cameron, stood looking down upon those who had come to assault his home. He did not look pleased.

"Would you mind explaining to me what you think you are doing?!" he shouted down in an imperious tone.

Karenth, known as the Just, paused in his efforts to break the magical barrier that protected the castle. "The time for discussion has passed, mortal. You well know the reason I am here. Lower this shield and I will make your passing swift, though I cannot promise it will be gentle," answered the shining god, showing perfect teeth in a feral grin as he spoke.

Mordecai leaned forward, cupping one hand behind his ear, as though he were having trouble hearing. "You aren't supposed to be here for another week!" he shouted, as though the distance between them was too great for a normal tone of voice to carry. "I haven't finished making my decision yet!"

"Do not play coy with me, human. I was not taken in by your ruse, and you only insult your dignity, by pretending that you actually believed your own lie," said the shining god calmly, though his voice held hints of a great anger barely held in check. "Soon I will be inside, and you and your people will pay in blood and suffering for imprisoning my brother Celior."

The Count di'Cameron's face held a look of confusion while he turned his head from side to side, as though trying each ear in an effort to hear better. Finally he gave up and shouted down, "What?!"

Karenth's anger skyrocketed, as he realized his foe had not heard him at all. Shouting in a thunderous voice, he repeated himself, "Once I am inside, you and your people shall pay in pain and unimaginable torment! You will beg for death, before I see fit to allow you to die! All this will be your punishment for imprisoning my brother!" The sound of the god's voice was so loud that it sent vibrations through the ground and even those within the castle could hear him, though his words weren't intelligible at that distance.

Mordecai squinted down at him. "I'm sorry! It must be this damned barrier spell! I think it is blocking sounds as well. Perhaps if you spoke a bit louder—I could almost hear you."

Karenth uttered a scream of pure rage and frustration, which shook the walls and put the birds of the forest for miles around into sudden flight.

Before his scream was done, the Count put his hands up, waving them apologetically at the apoplectic god below. His mouth was moving as well, and Karenth cut off his own primal scream so that he could hear the wizard's response.

"I really can't hear a damned thing!" shouted Mordecai. "Give me a moment. I'm going to go inside and lower the barrier so I can hear you, then maybe we can talk properly, without all this silly shouting! I'll be right back!" The wizard went back inside one of the towers and disappeared from view, leaving Karenth below, staring upward in complete amazement.

"Surely he does not truly mean to open the barrier for me?" said the god to himself. "Even he cannot be so foolish." Still, he withheld his attacks against the barrier for a moment on the odd chance that the mortal might be as stupid as his words indicated.

Minutes passed with no sign of the wizard, and Karenth grew bored. It might have been just as well to say he grew angry, but he hadn't really stopped being angry at any point in the recent past. At last he decided that the Count was making a fool of him. Clenching his will, he began assaulting the barrier again.

After half a minute, Mordecai reappeared atop the wall and shouted down, "Will you be patient a moment! Undoing this enchantment isn't as easy as you might think, and it certainly doesn't get any easier with you pounding upon it!" Disgruntled, he went back inside.

The god of justice paused again, staring up at the empty space where the wizard had recently stood. "He is mad…" he muttered to himself. "Can he truly not realize I am here to kill him?"

A few seconds later, the wizard reappeared, grinning widely. "I bet you were wondering if I had gone mad. The truth is I just wanted to see how stupid you could be. Did you really think I would open this barrier for a big, blustering buffoon like yourself?! Ha!" Turning around, the wizard lowered his trousers and presented his naked posterior toward the god, before standing back up and giving the deity a stern gesture with his left hand.

Karenth was stunned. In over a thousand years of dealing with human beings, he had never been so directly and crudely insulted, not even by those that had defied his priests. He stared blankly at the human as he continued waving his hands and making odd gestures. "Now he's sticking his tongue out at me," he noted aloud, with a sense of complete astonishment. "No one has ever—ever done that before."

Before the god could gather his anger to renew his attack, Mordecai stopped and looked at him carefully. "Now that you know how I feel, I will go and lower this barrier. I hope you are brave enough to enter once I do, because I have a lot of interesting plans for you. Your brother will enjoy having some company." The human went back inside the tower.

Karenth's rage reached new heights, as the wizard's words echoed in his mind. Drawing his strength to him, he prepared to assault the barrier once more, when something truly astonishing happened.

The magical barrier vanished.

Karenth looked about, staring at the warriors around him, each of them housing a portion of his brother Doron, the Iron God.

Each of them returned his look of utter amazement. That meant little however, for Doron was not known for his intelligence, even among his own kind. A chill went through Karenth, a sensation he was unfamiliar with. If he had been mortal, he might have had a better name for it. Fear.

CHAPTER 24

Ooh! He's really upset now!" I said to Walter, as the echoes of Karenth's rage faded away. I couldn't quite understand the words from where we were inside the keep, but his meaning was clear and it caused me to giggle a bit.

Walter stared at me as if I'd gone mad. "You realize he's going to take us apart when he gets in here, don't you? Like a child playing with bugs...," he muttered.

"He was planning to do that anyway. If we are going to be squashed like bugs, at least we can thumb our nose at the hand that does it. Right?" I retorted. "Put my hands up, like this," I said, demonstrating the motion in front of him. "Then cock my head to the side, as if I can't hear him."

Walter did as I asked. "He seems to have stopped for a moment." An unearthly howl cut through the air at that point before Walter spoke again, "No, forget I said that. He seems to be losing it now. I think you've driven him insane."

"Tell him this," I said, dictating carefully, "...I really can't hear a damned thing. Give me a moment. I'm going to go inside and lower the barrier so I can hear you, then maybe we can talk properly, without all this silly shouting. I'll be right back."

"You aren't serious are you, about lowering the barrier?" asked Walter concernedly.

"No, I'm just teasing him for now," I reassured the other wizard. After a moment the howling noise from outside the castle stopped. "What's happening now?"

"The attacks on the barrier have stopped," reported Walter.

I grinned back at him, "How are the people in the courtyard faring?"

"It's still a confused jumble, but they should all be inside within another couple of minutes, I think," answered Walter.

"Let's see how long our guest is willing to wait," I replied.

Minutes passed before the attacks resumed. Frankly, I was surprised at how patient the shining god had been. "Is everyone inside?" I asked.

"Not quite."

"Send my image back out and tell him this, 'Will you be patient a moment?'" I said, as I began to dictate another message to our irritated foe. The attacks ceased again. "What do you think?"

Walter blew out a lungful of air to release his tension. "I think, that whichever god that is out there, must think you are a madman. It also appears that everyone is inside now."

"Time for one last message then," I said, rubbing my hands together. Then I began explaining to Walter what I wanted him to say, describing the visual aids and gestures I wanted to accompany my monologue.

The older wizard seemed to have caught a bit of my madness, because he began to chuckle. Perhaps the stress of our situation was beginning to get to him. Still, I approved of his change in demeanor. Humor is generally a better way to face adversity, in my opinion.

After a moment Walter spoke up, "I think I delivered your message with the appropriate artistic style."

"What do you mean?"

"I embellished it a bit," said Walter, "not the words, just the gestures."

"How so?" I asked. I thought my directions had been fairly inspired, so I was curious as to what my fellow wizard thought could have improved upon them.

"I mooned him," said Walter, with a sudden laugh. "Or perhaps I should say, 'you mooned him'."

I groaned, "I hope none of the townsfolk saw that."

"If you're worried about your reputation, it's a bit late for that," said Walter. "You gave your true nature away back when you covered yourself in mud to greet the previous Baron of Arundel, all those years ago."

"True enough," I responded. "Now let's make good on our promise and lower the barrier for him."

"Are you really sure about that?" asked my friend.

"Yes," I lied. "Now be quick. It will make him think twice, if you do it before he begins his attack again."

Walter stared at me for a long moment, holding his breath, before at last reaching out and touching the appropriate rune on the stone pedestal. Given my current state, I couldn't sense or see any change, but I could guess from the way that he expelled the air from his lungs, that Walter had finally lowered the barrier.

We waited—and then waited some more.

"What's happening?!" I asked in exasperation.

"Nothing," said my friend frowning. "They seem to be just standing there. I can sense them a lot more easily, now that the barrier is down."

"He's scared," I announced suddenly.

"What?"

"We did the last thing he expected. First, we insulted him, and then, after having mocked and teased him about it already, we did the unthinkable. We lowered the barrier and dared him to come in. He's wondering if it's a trap," I explained.

"Is it?" said Walter hopefully.

I gave Walter a long appraising look. "Can you feel the pressure of the god's mind yet?" I asked.

He blinked at my sudden change of topic. "It's like an ominous thundercloud on the horizon at this distance. Is it a trap, Mordecai?"

I let the air out of my lungs dejectedly. "No, not without my strength; currently it's the furthest thing from a trap. Our only hope is to guide him away and hope that he doesn't get any hint of the Ironheart Chamber from our minds."

"You mean my mind, don't you? Yours is currently unreadable," corrected Walter.

"Yes," I agreed. "Currently the only people that know of its existence are the two of us, and the Knights of Stone."

"Aren't you worried he'll get the information from them?"

I laughed, "You haven't tried to peer into any of their heads, have you?"

"I'm not generally an intrusive sort of man," he answered a bit huffily.

"The bond between them and the earth interferes with any attempt to reach into their minds, much like the old bond between a mage and his Anath'Meridum did," I explained. "I doubt even one of the shining gods could see into their hearts."

"That's some comfort then, though we still have to worry about me," said Walter, tapping on his skull to illustrate. "Perhaps I should cloak us both magically, so that he can't find me," suggested Walter, referring to the trick he had used earlier to escape the god's oppressive influence.

"No," I said immediately. "I need you to help me distract him with more of those wonderfully realistic illusions." A pang of guilt shot through me, as I realized how coldly and cruelly I was about to use my old friend, but I quickly pushed the thought aside. I'd have time for remorse later. *No you won't,* said my inner spectator, *you'll be dead too. Either the god will get you, or the poison will.* I put a little more effort into shutting my inner voice down, he was depressing—as well as annoying.

Walter's face changed, and his posture became tense. "They are entering now. The fighters are running forward, toward the keep, while the god is following behind them more cautiously," he informed me.

"Show me from the top of the keep, making sure I appear to have some magic. Try waving at them," I told him.

"I'll be sure to add your most foolish grin as well," replied the other mage.

"That's the spirit!" I agreed. My nausea was all but gone now; though a sudden vibration in my feet made me wonder if I was developing new symptoms. It was followed by a loud crack, as though lightning had struck close by. A shiver in the stone walls told me that something unprecedented had just occurred. "What was that?"

"He just blew the top of the wall and part of one tower away!" reported Walter.

The keep itself consisted of four large corner towers, enclosing a large square stone structure. Between the four towers there were merlons and battlements to protect defenders that might be positioned there. After a short discussion, the other wizard explained that the invading deity had destroyed part of the top of the keep, along with the uppermost part of one tower.

"When you say destroyed…" I said again.

"I mean he damned well reduced it to dust. It simply isn't there anymore, other than as a pile of rubble. He threw this massive purplish bolt of power at it!" said Walter, as he described what he had sensed. "It was the spot where your illusion was located," he added.

"He seems a bit irritated," I noted drolly.

Beads of sweat were forming on Walter's forehead. "Do you think so?!"

I chuckled, "Come along, we need to start moving. He'll be inside soon."

Walter was squinting now. "I think you should let me hide us."

"Is the pressure getting worse?" I replied, referring to the god's increasing proximity.

"Much."

"Alright," I said. "Just until we get below, then I'll need you to create another illusion."

At my agreement, Walter immediately acted and his face relaxed. We could still see one another, so I could only assume that he had just made us invisible to magic. "That's a lot better," he announced. "I can't sense anything now, but at least I can breathe without feeling like I have a giant standing on my chest."

From my own encounter with Celior, I knew exactly how he felt. Clapping him upon the shoulder, I began leading him out the door. I kept my hand on him too, just in case I suffered anymore sudden bouts of vertigo.

"What did you mean, below?" asked Walter.

"We're heading for the cellars," I told him.

His face was a picture of puzzlement. "Won't that put us closer to what we are trying to hide?"

Don't ask questions, and I won't have to lie to you, I thought silently. "He won't think to look near where he finds us. He should be expecting us to lead him away from the God-Stone, not toward it."

"Makes no sense to me either way," declared Walter with a shake of his head.

I smiled, "Just make sure I don't stumble and fall. I still feel a bit unsteady." Leaning carefully upon him, the two of us made our way out into the corridor and toward the door that led into the cellars.

CHAPTER 25

Dorian Thornbear looked out from the keep's main entrance and breathed a sigh of relief, as the last of the soldiers passed inside. A light touch on his shoulder drew his attention to the man standing beside him. He gave a simple nod to indicate his readiness to listen.

"Sir Dorian, what instructions would you have me give my men?" asked Carl, the most senior of the soldiers and their primary leader, when both Dorian and Cyhan were absent.

"Captain, I'd like you to have the men take up defensive positions throughout the keep. Put bowmen in the windows and embrasures, and make sure there are spearmen close by in case they manage to reach the top of the walls," Dorian told him.

"How many would you have remain here, at the entrance?"

"None, the Knights will secure the main door here," replied Dorian firmly.

Carl gave a quick bow as he acknowledged the orders, "Very good sir," and then he was gone.

Harold had been listening and stepped up beside Dorian. "Are you sure? There are only twelve of us here to guard the door."

"From what you told me, I don't think I want our men anywhere near the enemy. I'd rather they keep them at range if possible, or at worst, spear's length," answered Dorian.

"The ones that got inside were fast," said Cyhan, coming up behind Harold. "They slaughtered the door guard and made it through quite a few of the halls before we caught the last of them."

"I found five bodies upstairs near the Count's apartments," offered up Sir Aaron. "They looked much like the ones you fought down here. They were already dead though, with burns and marks all over them. We aren't sure who dispatched them."

After a brief exchange of descriptions, Cyhan offered his opinion, "Sounds like Mordecai, and perhaps Penny or some of the soldiers stopped them."

"Where are they now?" asked Harold.

Dorian took up the question, "The Count had his own plans for evacuating his family. Wherever he has taken them, I sincerely doubt we need to worry about it at this point."

"I hate to ask the question then," said Sir Thomas, in a quiet voice, "but what is our purpose here then? There are none left to guard but soldiers and perhaps twenty or thirty of the townsfolk."

All the knights looked at him then, and the Grandmaster of the Knights of Stone squared his shoulders as he stared back at them. Dorian waited until he was sure everyone was listening before he spoke and he made sure his voice was loud and strong when he did, "We are here, to be last. We remained so that others could escape. We were not given our strength to save ourselves, but to protect our fellow man."

"There's almost no one left to protect," said Sir Edward from across the room.

"Then we've already won the best part of this fight, but so long as there is even one man, woman, or child remaining, our fight is not done. Do any of you feel differently?" questioned Dorian bluntly.

Sir Edward had always been a bit rough around the edges but he was a solid knight through and through. "Nah, you know better than that, Your Lordship. I just thought Sir Thomas had a good point. We aren't really fighting to protect very many people, now that most are gone."

"And what if all of them were gone?" asked Cyhan suddenly.

Sir Edward smiled, "Then I'd fight just to be stubborn. I didn't take the oath to die old and in my bed." A chorus of laughs and words of agreement went up among the knights at that remark.

"They're on the move. I see men running toward us now, from the courtyard gate," announced Sir William from the doorway.

"Close the door," commanded Sir Dorian, preparing to order them into defensive positions. His command was interrupted by a deafening noise, followed by stone and dust falling to the ground outside.

The sound was so unexpected that everyone stood still for a second, unable to comprehend the source of the cacophony. Harold was quickest to recover, but his speed was almost his undoing. Leaning out, he looked up to find the source of the sound. Only Cyhan's good sense saved his life, for he hauled the younger knight back just as a colossal piece of stone masonry passed through the area where Harold's uncovered head had been but a second before. It crashed to the ground sending shards and splinters of stone flying in all directions.

"Son of a bitch!" yelped Harold, in a voice that was half curse and half startled cry.

"How did they get siege weapons this close so quickly?" said Cyhan, ignoring Harold's yell.

Dorian grunted, running his hand over his short beard, "I don't think it was a siege weapon. I'd put my bets on Karenth. He's following behind his boys there." He pointed to indicate the well-dressed man following the charging invaders. "Not much point in barring the door, leave it open," he added. Raising his voice, he began barking orders, "Step away from the doors! Weapons out! One of the gods is with 'em, so it's time to die—anyone need to take a piss first?!"

Only tense laughter answered him as they moved back from the entrance, a nearly ten foot wide opening framed by solid stone walls. The hallway that led into the castle was over thirty feet in length, before reaching the doorway that led into the great hall, where meals and most large events were held. Two doorways on either side of the entry hall led into other parts of the castle. The first two doors, a few feet in on the right and left sides led to small rooms; the one on the left being the chamberlain, Peter Tucker's office. The one on the right led to a foyer that had been repurposed as a cloak room. The next two doors led into hallways that ran on either side of the great hall, connecting it to various servants' quarters, the kitchens, guard rooms, and the corner tower stairs.

They had only scant seconds before the enemy would be upon them, as Dorian bellowed out positions, "Cyhan, Jeffrey, take the chamberlain's office to the left, Harold and Brian, take the cloak room! Grant, Egan, you'll be in the left hall, Edward and Phillip, the right—everyone else with me!" That left Dorian standing with Sir William, Sir Thomas and Sir Aaron just inside the great hall doors, directly opposite the main outer entrance. The other eight men were located in two's behind each of the other doors leading into the entry hall. "Wait until we have them piled up in the entry before you open those doors—if you're unsure just wait till you hear me call for flames!"

As quick as the Knights of Stone were, they barely reached their places before the first of the enemy leaped through the open entryway. Fearless, the man seemed to have no caution or instinct to preserve his own life as he ran toward the entrance to the great hall, where Dorian and three of his fellow knights stood waiting. As he approached, his eyes darted left to right, noting the lack of visible defenders to his sides, before he threw himself bodily toward the four men blocking his path.

Sir Thomas took a single step forward, lowering himself as he did to slip beneath the high swing of the attacker. His great sword came up in a reverse swing that might have lacked the power to cut, if wielded by a normal man. Sir Thomas was not however, a normal man, and neither was the enchanted blade he carried. The blade's mystically sharp edge was driven by his enhanced strength, and its edge took the invader from groin to shoulder, cleaving bone and muscle with equal ease. The warrior was already dead, as his momentum and the upward swing of Thomas' blade sent his bisected body over their heads— to land with a sickening thump behind them.

"You certainly haven't lost your enthusiasm for your work," commented Sir William, who stood beside him.

Sir Aaron felt a bit differently though, "Damnitt Thomas! Every time! Every damn time! Look at me!"

Dorian had already noticed what the other man was complaining about. While Thomas' cut had sent blood flying in all directions, Sir Aaron had been covered in gore and the unspeakable contents of the man's stomach, as he had flown over his head.

Thomas apologized quickly; a soft spoken man despite his deadly prowess, but Sir William had begun giggling with what some might have termed combat induced hysteria. Not for the first time, Dorian wondered if the effects of the violence they had seen over the years, had finally unhinged the man. "Don't be so damned prissy!" chided Dorian with a half-laugh, to distract Aaron from his predicament, "We'll all be covered in that and worse before this is over."

"At least these are fresh," noted Sir Aaron as he wiped some of the gore from his breastplate. "They don't stink near so much as the shiggreth do." Although they all agreed with that sentiment, they had no time to respond, as the main body of the attackers began to pour through the entrance.

Those that followed the first, entered without even glancing to the sides, moving in perfect coordination, they assaulted the four armored knights guarding the great hall entrance. The ones in the front attacked in pairs, lunging forward two at a time at each of the defenders and making little, if any effort, to protect themselves from the deadly blades wielded by Dorian's brother knights. In that first rush, the knights were nearly overcome, as their foes abandoned their lives to tangle and bind the sword arms of the armored defenders.

It was immediately apparent to Dorian that their attackers fought not as men, but as parts of something more, something that didn't fear to lose those parts, so long as the goal of crushing their enemy was attained. Their long great swords cut through the first and second ranks rapidly, while they began backpedaling to avoid being caught by their suicidal attackers. *They fight with no concern for themselves, like the shiggreth do,* noted Dorian mentally, *and they work in perfect coordination, as though they were controlled by a single mind.*

Fortunately the Knights had had extensive experience fighting foes that did not fear their own deaths—backing through the doorway behind them, they used it to shield themselves from the weight of the crowd pressing inward. William and Aaron stepped slightly to the sides, where they could cut down any that crossed the threshold, while Dorian and Thomas blocked the enemy's advance several feet back from the entry. Together they were able to render any foe foolish enough to enter their deadly circle into numerous pieces, and the stone floor before them soon looked like some grotesque abattoir.

Those penned in the entry hall began pulling at the side doors, attempting to find other means of ingress into the castle proper. They were met by the blades of the Knights guarding each door, but the fighting was desperate. Those unable to reach the defenders began using their large iron mauls to widen the doorframes; smashing masonry and stone blocks aside with a strength and ferocity that was difficult to believe. Dorian knew if their efforts persisted for more than a minute, they would soon be able to come at the defenders from all sides—and the fight would not likely last long after that.

"Flames!" commanded Dorian, in a voice that cut through the din, and the Knights prepared to use their swords in the manner that had caused the people of Gododdin to name their enchanted blades 'Sun-Swords'.

As one, the Knights of Stone lowered their blades to point at their foes as if they were spears, and each of them uttered the command words that would unleash the power fettered within their magical seals. Incandescent flames rushed forth from their weapons, blazing with a white-hot heat that sent the temperature in the room quickly soaring. Each sword sent forth a radiant fan of flames that reached out almost five feet in front of its wielder, and the strange warriors attacking Castle Cameron began to burn, as the flames flowed over them from multiple directions.

The area rapidly filled with rancid, black smoke, as the ravenous flames consumed human flesh and rendered those caught into little more than burning fat and black resinous ash. Mordecai had designed the enchantment on the Knight's swords with the express purpose of incinerating the bodies of the shiggreth, since that was the only way known to permanently dispose of them. The enchantment channeled power from the God-Stone and produced temperatures so great that almost anything the fire touched would be quickly reduced to its most basic elements.

The Knights kept up their incendiary assault for long seconds, letting the flames do their work. Experience had shown them time and again how long it took to render a corpse completely to ash and habit guided their hands. Almost a full minute passed before they relented and allowed the flames to die out, leaving a burnt silence filled with little more than the crack and pop of embers. Aside from the Knights, not a living soul stood in the ruined entry hall, and the remaining enemy had given up their attempts to enter.

"Damn that stinks!" yelled Sir Egan from the side hall he had been guarding. "I'll never get used to that smell."

"It isn't that much worse than your armor after a week on the road," joked Sir William. "I wouldn't think it would be that hard for you to get used to it." Several of the Knights chortled in appreciation of his joke, even as they all began to choke from the smoke that filled the room.

Dorian had little time for humor though; he knew how dangerous the smoke could be, especially given the enclosed space they were in. "Harold, Cyhan, Brian, and Jeffrey—move to my position in the great hall!" he barked out, and even before he had finished uttering the words he saw their forms emerging from the smoke, seeking clear air. "Grant, Egan, Phillip, and Edward—back up down those hallways as far as you need, but stay vigilant! You're all that's keeping them from entering and encircling us."

Several long slow minutes passed while the smoke cleared, and the Knights of Stone waited patiently. Eventually Cyhan had enough of waiting and spoke up, "They aren't coming back. They've got something else planned. I'm going to look." Without waiting for confirmation of his decision, Cyhan stepped out, and picking his way through the smoldering ashes cautiously looked out the entrance to see where their opponents had gone. He visibly stiffened as he saw the figure approaching the door.

"What are they doing?" asked Harold from his position.

Cyhan didn't answer; instead he seemed to be fighting to raise his sword, as though it had suddenly become immensely heavy. "You may not—enter—here," he gasped out, as if even his breathing had become labored.

The shadow of a tall man fell across the threshold as Karenth the Just stepped into the hall. He merely smiled, as he watched Cyhan struggling to raise his blade. "Your will is strong o' guardian, but it is nothing before my judgment—and I find you lacking." Raising his hand the god prepared to unleash his might against the man daring to defy him.

"Wait Brother!" came a dozen voices from the castle yard. "Do not seek to spoil my fun."

Karenth closed his hand into a fist and relaxed his arm, letting it fall to his side. "You dirty yourself playing with these creatures Doron, but if that is your wish." Turning aside, Karenth continued walking forward, ignoring the Knights standing on either side of the entrance to the great hall. All of them were struggling to reach him, as if they were fighting against a powerful gale, the sheer force of his presence kept them at bay.

Only one of them stood unbowed. Dorian Thornbear watched Karenth's approach calmly, as if the deity was simply another intruder. His sword rose lightly to point directly at the god's chest as he drew close, "You will not enter this house," he said simply.

Karenth was amused and his lip curled into a sneer as he glanced down at the blade leveled at him. "You are remarkably resilient, perhaps you are simply too stupid to intimidate. Will you try your flame upon me, Sir Knight?"

Dorian's cheek twitched for a moment in annoyance. "I am unable to use a Sun-Sword," he admitted with his typical honesty.

"Does not your impotence make you unsuited to lead these men?" asked Karenth.

"Power comes in many forms," answered Dorian immediately, "and none of them grant the wisdom necessary to lead." As he spoke, his sword snapped to the side and back again in a lightning-quick strike. So fast was his stroke, that even the shining god was caught unprepared, and the blade struck him cleanly in the neck with such force that he should have been decapitated. Unfortunately, the deity was not so easily slain. The blade stuck after passing no more than a half an inch through his skin; blood, the color of liquid gold, oozed from the wound.

Angry now, Karenth swatted the sword away with his left hand, sending the weapon flying from Dorian's hands. At the same time, Karenth stepped forward, driving his right fist at Dorian's armored chest.

Dorian was no stranger to hand to hand combat, however. Before the god's blow could land, he side stepped, and moving too quickly for an observer's eyes to see, he caught Karenth's wrist as he swung. Twisting and using his other hand to drive the deity off-balance, he used his opponent's momentum to throw him bodily across the room. Karenth slammed into the wall with such force that the stones cracked. His eyes opened wide with shock at the sudden reversal.

But Dorian hadn't wasted time gloating. Even before his foe had struck the wall, he had launched himself into motion, charging at the shining god. Before the god could recover, he had closed the distance and his armored fists began hammering into Karenth's head and stomach. Inside his armor, the son of Gram Thornbear howled his rage, even as he drove his powerful punches home, each one striking with the force of a battering ram.

The stone blocks of the wall behind Karenth shifted, and dust fell from above, as Dorian pounded mercilessly at the shining god's body. However, his blows had little effect upon the god himself, and eventually he could hear the god laughing, even as his body was driven against the hard stone again and again. Enraged, Dorian refused to relent, for he knew his foe would recover within seconds if he stopped.

He had underestimated the power of the shining god however, and after a time Karenth grew bored. "I think you've had enough fun," said the deity, and with nothing more than a thought he sent Dorian flying across the room, as though he had been struck by a giant, invisible fist.

Dorian had been thrown in a similar fashion once before, during his brief and disastrous confrontation with Celior, and this time he was better prepared. Twisting in the air, he managed to get his feet under him, and while he still struck with enough force to break stone, he was able to keep from being stunned by the blow. Instead, he launched himself from the wall, using it as if it were a springboard, to propel himself back at his divine enemy.

"You really are too stupid to know when you're beaten," said Karenth, and with another exercise of his will, he caught Dorian in mid-air with a blast of pure force, sending him flying again into the wall. This time the Knight of Stone was unable to save himself from a bad landing. He struck the hard wall sideways, at an awkward angle, before crashing to the floor. He began struggling to rise almost immediately. The god of justice raised his hand again, and a dark purple light began to glow around it, as he prepared an attack that would put an end to Dorian's resistance.

Dorian glared at Karenth through the visor of his helm and somehow found the strength to stand again. "Maybe I am," he replied, through lips that felt dry and sandy. His voice had grown deep, almost guttural, "I'd rather be dead than admit defeat at your hands."

CHAPTER 26

think perhaps your fight is with me, rather than my friend here," I said from the far end of the hall.

More quickly than a snake, Karenth switched targets and leveled a scorching bolt of searing purple energy in my direction. I had expected that of course, but it still nearly caught me as I dodged to one side. The high table, a large portion of the wall behind it, and one of the rooms beyond that, were destroyed. Fragments of rock, wood, and other debris flew in all directions, and part of the ceiling above that area sagged downward as it lost support.

"Perhaps you should introduce yourself before trying to kill me!" I shouted once the noise had faded.

The shining god snarled and sent a hasty bolt of pure energy at me. This one was much weaker, but his aim was impeccable, and my reflexes were nowhere near quick enough for me to dodge in time—not that I had planned to dodge; but Dorian didn't know that. He had been moving since my surprise appearance, and with a burst of speed, he managed to intercept Karenth's second attack. It was an action of pure altruism. "Run Mort!" he screamed at me, and then the energy struck him.

Whatever the nature of Karenth's purple bolts of energy truly was, it wasn't pleasant. It had already destroyed part of the roof and some of the interior of the castle, not so much with physical force, but with a type of ravenous purple fire that seemed to consume whatever it touched. Dorian was close when he intercepted the beam, which allowed him to block the entire thing, before it had spread much. It ran over his armor like a beast trying to devour him, even as the blast itself flung him across the room to land beside the spot where I stood.

A second blast engulfed my body, and in an instant I was gone.

***

Walter jerked for a second before glancing at me again.

"What?" I asked, "Did he take the bait?"

"Dorian intervened, he took the blow meant for the illusion," said Walter in a tone of utter shock.

"No!" I shouted back at him. "We were going to draw him away! Is he alive?"

"I'm not sure," said Walter, concentrating. "His armor appears to be gone, but I think his body is intact. There's something strange about him. Karenth is approaching him now, looking for your remains I think."

My mind raced, and I silently cursed my inability to use my own magesight. It would have been far simpler if I could have seen what was occurring for myself. "Create another illusion of me, place it further back, outside the hall in the area he destroyed. He might think I avoided it somehow. If he follows after, create a fog to obscure things and then drop the illusion and create another one close to the stairs."

"You still think we can lure him?" said Walter uncertainly.

"Just do it! Don't waste time," I commanded.

A tense minute passed while I waited for Walter to tell me the result of our latest ruse. I could only hope that the disappearance and reappearance of Walter's exceedingly realistic illusions would convince Karenth that I was teleporting myself somehow. Not that I was capable of such a thing. While it might be possible for the gods, it took far too much calculation for a human wizard to teleport without a lot of extensive preparation—that's why we generally used circles. I could only hope that Karenth's opinion of my abilities was overinflated.

Sweat was beading on Walter's brow when he finally spoke again, "He's coming for the second illusion now. He's too close, Mort. He can sense me!"

I watched the older wizard struggling to maintain his composure under the ominous pressure that Karenth was creating and felt another pang for misusing my friend in such a manner. *Our sacrifice is the only way to save them now,* I told myself, hoping to ease my feelings of guilt. *If you knew the truth, you'd probably tell me to do it this way.* Of course, if he knew the truth it couldn't possibly work.

We were standing in a corridor running through the cellars and storerooms beneath Castle Cameron. One more turn and another short corridor would put us next to the hidden entrance to the Ironheart Chamber. "You have to draw him closer Walter. One more illusion and you'll be done. Once that's done, you can drop the spell hiding me."

"But—he'll find you then!" said my friend.

I shrugged, in what I hoped was a nonchalant and heroic fashion, even as I flinched inwardly at my deception. "Just do it! I'll be hiding inside the chamber in a moment anyway. He won't be able to touch me."

"You're going inside? That makes no sense!" he protested.

The time had come to reveal the rest; I only hoped it wasn't too soon. Squaring my shoulders, I faced him. "I've kept some secrets Walter. The Ironheart Chamber isn't meant purely for protecting the God-Stone, it's also a weapon, and one that I think can stop Karenth dead in his tracks."

"But…," Walter began before I interrupted him.

"Hurry up! I'll explain the rest in a moment, after you do the next illusion. There isn't much time," I insisted.

The older wizard closed his mouth and gave me an irritated look, before closing his eyes to concentrate. His lips moved as he quietly whispered the words to give power to his illusions, and his forehead creased in an expression of pain, as the shining god grew ever closer. I watched him closely, with eyes that seemed woefully inadequate without my magesight. After a moment he began to twitch ever so slightly, and the veins on the side of his head bulged; I doubted he could hold out much longer.

Suddenly his eyes went wide in fear and pain, while his mouth gaped, as if he were a fish dying for lack of water. His entire body went tense before it relaxed, and he fell forward into my arms. "Walter, are you alright?!" I asked worriedly. "Talk to me, did he find us?"

A few seconds passed before the other wizard got himself under control. "Sorry, I almost couldn't shield myself in time," he explained.

My eyes were locked on his face, reading every expression, searching for hidden signs. "Thank goodness you did. I'm going to leave you now. The hidden door is down that way," I said pointing in the direction I would be heading. "I'll use it to enter the Ironheart Chamber, while you make your escape. I don't think he will be able to find you if you make yourself fully invisible. Just try to get as far away as possible."

He grabbed my arm, "Wait. You never told me what the chamber does. You owe me that much at least."

I sighed, "Fine, but make sure you are completely invisible to magic first, otherwise he might glean the secret from you." I waited a moment while he complied and then continued, "The Ironheart Chamber is actually a gigantic enchantment I designed, to allow the user to fully absorb the power of the God-Stone. It will give whoever uses it, full control of Celior's power."

Walter's eyes were wide with disbelief, "Is that possible? Why haven't you used it before?"

I grimaced, "I wasn't willing to take the risk. I'm not certain what it will do to a human being, to undergo that sort of transformation. It might kill me, or I might be overwhelmed by whatever remains of Celior's mind. It's only now that the risk is worth taking. It's all or nothing."

Walter nodded, "I'm glad you never told me before, Mort."

"Why's that?"

"I might have been tempted to use it for myself if I had known," he admitted.

I clapped him on the shoulder, "Now you understand my secrecy. Go ahead and hide yourself, I'll go the rest of the way alone." Turning away I left him there, walking confidently down the empty hall. Inwardly, I feared that I might never make it to my destination. If I had miscalculated, I might be struck down at any moment.

Rounding the final corner, I made my way to the spot that hid the secret door. The enchantment was such, that it was invisible to magesight, as well as mundane vision. Because of that, I had memorized the location I had to touch to open the door. The enchantment should recognize me even without my magic, just as the one guarding the Keystone room had earlier.

I placed my hand upon the correct area and watched the door slide open, but before I could step forward a voice sent a chill of fear down my spine. "Did you really think you could make a fool of me and get away with it?" said the icy voice of Karenth the Just.

"You never know if you don't try," I answered, keeping my voice light, though my heart had leapt into my throat at his sudden appearance.

"Kneel!" grated Karenth, in a tone that would brook no disobedience. Under normal circumstances it would have taken all of my power simply to resist his compulsion, and that would have been using every bit of my aythar. It had taken that and the strength of the earth to enable me to truly defy Celior. I had neither of those things now—and it hardly mattered, my mind was just as dead to his commands, as it was to magic.

I kept my face passive. "You really should listen to yourself. You've been playing at being a god for so long, that you're starting to believe yourself. You really did capture the essence of 'authority' there." I made no attempt to genuflect before him.

Karenth stared at me for a moment, "The magebane has made you resistant to certain things I see, as well as destroying your ability to use magic—how unfortunate." Reaching out, his hand caught me by the shoulder and my world dissolved into pain as his power coursed through me. It seemed to last for an eternity, and through it I could hear nothing beyond the sound of my own screams. He did not relent until I had run out of air and I had begun to think I might die before I could draw breath again. When his hand let go of my shoulder, I collapsed bonelessly to the floor.

Staring down he smiled, "Good thing the old standbys still work just fine. Pain is such an excellent teacher. It is almost a shame you won't have very long to learn your lessons." Turning, he looked over his shoulder at Walter, who had appeared quietly behind him. "Why did you ever serve this man?"

Walter's jaw clenched as he attempted to answer, but his lips would not move.

Waving his hand, Karenth said dismissively, "Speak your mind slave, I would hear the truth from your lips," and the tension in the older wizard's face relaxed.

"Because I believed in him," said Walter in a dry voice, "because he saved me, saved my family—he gave me hope." His words echoed with empty resignation, the tone of a man who knew his death was near, yet hoped it would not be too painful. "Forgive me Mordecai, I couldn't stop him! His will was too strong for me…"

"How touching," commented the shining god, with mock sympathy. "Your tragedy is so poignant I can hardly bring myself to cut it short. But then I suppose I hardly need to do so—the poison will kill you slowly over a course of days." He looked down upon me in pity.

"How did you poison me?" I asked in sudden curiosity.

"It was the wine, of course," he replied succinctly, "I'm surprised your pet wizard didn't drink it as well."

I frowned, "How did you get it into my cup—what of the tasters?"

The god of justice smiled beatifically at me, "You think too small. It was in all the wine given to you by the King of Gododdin. It's harmless to your tasters and other humans. Only those with the forbidden gifts of wizardry need fear its taste upon their lips. Frankly I'm surprised you waited till this celebration to drink it. Millicenth even thought you would sample some before today. Your patience is admirable, and it certainly made for a most dramatic day."

My lip curled, "He betrayed us?"

Karenth laughed, and the music of his laughter echoed down the halls, until I thought it might drive me mad. "Fool! The men that attacked your king were a ruse, to draw attention from those that were tampering with the wine. Your petty kinglet is of no use to me. I have spies enough amongst your people. Now if you will excuse me, I have my brother's mantle to claim." The god moved to enter the Ironheart Chamber.

"It's a trap," I told him. "You'll never leave that room if you enter."

"Such a pathetic attempt," replied Karenth, staring down at me. "You've told too many lies wizard. I've already drawn the information out of your servant's mind, and honestly, I don't care. If your enchantment works—wonderful! If it doesn't—well at least Celior will be free again." Without waiting for my answer, he stepped inside and drew the door closed behind him. The heavy iron door shut with a massive 'click' that carried a sense of finality.

Lying on the cold floor, barely able to move from the recent magical torture, I still smiled as the Ironheart Chamber door sealed itself. "Can't say I didn't warn you," I said quietly, fighting to control a giggle that probably would have been more frightening than reassuring. "You were the only one I told the truth to," I added with some satisfaction.

Once the door had finished closing, Walter collapsed, much like a puppet with its strings cut. Shuddering, he looked over at me where I lay not far off. "I'm sorry, he was too strong," he apologized, "I couldn't fight him."

"I should be apologizing to you," I said, returning the sentiment. "I used you badly."

"What do you mean?" Walter asked, but I couldn't answer immediately, for that was when Karenth realized that the God-Stone wasn't within the Ironheart Chamber.

"What trickery is this?" came his booming voice, clearly audible, even through the massive iron walls. It was followed shortly after, by a deep note, as if someone had struck a giant bell. My guess, was that he had just attempted to exit after discovering that the magical stone within, was merely a decoy.

"So it was a trap all along?" asked Walter with some confusion, as his mind hurried to fit the pieces together, "Then where is the God-Stone?"

I tested my muscles to see if I could lever myself up to a sitting position. Karenth's torture spell had left me feeling as though I had been thoroughly beaten and bruised, though I didn't have a mark on me. Successful, I leaned against the wall and replied to Walter's question, "That's one secret I'm keeping under my hat. I'm sure you understand after what we've been through today." A louder noise issued from the Ironheart Chamber—Karenth was probably beginning to test the strength of his new prison.

The sound made Walter visibly nervous, "Can he get out of there? Should we be attempting to escape now?"

I laughed, "There is a possibility. After all, I've never tested it before. I'll wait until I'm sure, before I tell you what I think might work for him."

"Why?" questioned the other wizard, as he began to bite his lip nervously.

I lowered my voice conspiratorially, "Because I'm not sure how good his hearing is—let's wait until it's too late, before we give away the secret." The noises from within were becoming louder and more consistent and they were joined by a scream of pure rage. "Can your magesight see anything?" I added curiously.

"No, the concealing enchantment hides everything from my view," he answered.

I nodded, "I forgot about that. Well, if that wasn't in the way, you'd probably be noticing the interior enchantment beginning to glow as it warms up. As the process continues, it will get more and more intense, until…" I let my words trail off.

"Until what?!"

I shrugged, "Well until Karenth runs out of aythar, or his power overloads the capacity of the iron vessel."

"Overloads…," repeated my friend as his eyebrows went up.

"Boom," I said with an evil grin.

"Let me help you up," Walter answered, with newfound urgency.

It hurt to laugh but I did anyway. "Don't worry, there's enough iron there to hold everything he's got to give and then some. I did a lot of quantifying to see how much power Celior had. Assuming Karenth isn't more than twice as powerful as his brother, that chamber should be able to manage him." The ground shook faintly, and a roar came from within. The noises from the chamber had settled into a regular rhythm, as the shining god struggled to batter his way free.

Walter started to ask me another question, but I shushed him as the sounds from inside grew louder still. Keeping a finger to my lips to signify silence, we waited long minutes as the power and volume of the god's attempts to escape increased. After what might have been a quarter of an hour, possibly more, the volume and frequency of the sounds began to decrease. "I think we're past the breakpoint now," I said, restarting our conversation. "Now the easy part of our job is done. The difficult part comes next."

"Breakpoint? Difficult?" said Walter, with an expression that clearly said, 'I want to go home now'. Unfortunately for him, we were already home.

"Breakpoint—the chamber is absorbing the power he uses. The more he throws against, it the more powerful the enchantment becomes. The dangerous part was at the beginning, when the enchantment was relatively weak. If he had used all of his strength then, he might have cracked it before it could hold him," I explained, before adding in a much louder voice, "but the so-called *God* of Justice was far too cautious for that!" The last part was meant for Karenth's ears, and he responded with an inchoate scream. The pounding however only grew weaker.

"So what is the difficult part?"

I grimaced. "His brother Doron is still up there. We have one more god to deal with."

"Please, Mordecai!" came the voice of Karenth through the iron wall. "We can negotiate. I can see now that I was wrong to want to punish you."

"Negotiating is generally done before invading someone's castle and attempting to murder everyone within," I answered loudly.

The god's voice was desperate, "I can help you. There is an antidote for the poison. It could save your life."

I had been afraid he would say something like that. It was the most tempting thing he could possibly offer; a new hope of life for a dying man. If he was telling the truth, he held my life in his hands, just as I did his, trapped within the Ironheart chamber. It was effectively a stalemate. Even worse, without my power, I had no hope of controlling him or forcing compliance if I agreed to release him. If I let him out, he would undoubtedly renege on the deal, and all of my work would be for naught. Even if he kept his word, he would still be free to return at a later date. If my goal was to rid mankind of its spiritual parasites, I would be throwing it away for the sake of my own life.

In the end, it really wasn't a choice. "You can go straight to hell."

The god's voice sounded tired now, "There is no hell mortal, but your life could be spent in paradise if you release me."

I could feel my anger rising again as I answered, "There's a hell alright. You're staring at it, an iron prison and nothing but your own conversation for eternity—or however long you last; and the best part, is that you put yourself in there."

"There must be something you want."

I ignored his plea and leaned on Walter, indicating it was time to start back up the hall toward the stairway. "Have fun," I said, over my shoulder. I won't bother to relate his response. It was ugly enough to make even me blush. It did put a smile on my face though.

CHAPTER 27

We climbed the stairs slowly. My nausea had almost completely passed, but either the poison or Karenth's attack had left me feeling shaky, so my footing was unsure. Walter let me keep a hand on his shoulder, and as we neared the top he opened the conversation again, "So—about the 'difficult' part, I'm hoping you have a plan for this part as well, preferably one that doesn't require using me as bait."

"Don't worry," I replied brightly, "I don't have any plans involving you at all."

He stared at me suspiciously, "Somehow that doesn't reassure me."

"Actually, I didn't expect to live this long. I figured Karenth would kill one or both of us before he finally entered the chamber," I elaborated with a shrug of my shoulders. I probably wouldn't have been so flippant if I had been alone, but since I had an audience in Walter, I felt I should make the most of my limited time before the poison finished me off.

Walter stopped, forcing me to come to a halt as well. "Earlier you said you had a plan."

I gave him an apologetic look, "Well, originally the Ironheart Chamber was the backup plan, in case two of them came at the same time. I figured I had a good chance of handling, one if I could just trap the other one. Obviously that isn't possible now."

The other wizard gave me a serious stare for a moment before taking my arm firmly over his shoulder and changing direction. He didn't bother uttering a word of explanation.

"Where are you going?" I asked.

He kept going, dragging me along without offering me a choice.

I wasn't in the best shape, but I had enough strength to fight him to a standstill. "Dammit! Will you stop!?" I protested, "I'm not going anywhere till you explain yourself."

"You just admitted you can't fight, and you don't have a plan. It's time to leave and seek aid. There is still a chance Lady Thornbear knows of an antidote," he answered stubbornly.

"No!" I argued, "If Doron finds his brother, he'll free him and we won't have accomplished anything."

"If he finds you, he won't leave enough behind to have a proper funeral, then he'll search out his brother, and we will be even worse off without you to help when they come back to finish us next time," returned Walter. Even I had to admit his reasoning was fairly sound.

"Damn you! Stop making sense," I said, conceding his point. "Let me think for a moment. I have something in the back of my head."

"Two minutes," he said crossly. "Then I'm going to haul your obstinate ass out of here, even if I have to bind your arms and legs with magic and levitate you behind me."

"I'm your liege. That would be an act of treason," I threatened.

Walter was truly irritated. He spit on the ground in a most un-Walter-like fashion. "You can have me hanged afterward if you wish. You have a minute and a half left now."

My mouth opened in protest, but I could see the conviction in his eyes. He meant it. Instead of debating, I focused on the problem at hand and ran through the possibilities in my mind. Try as I might, I could see nothing. Holding my hands up, I stared at them, their emptiness seemed to symbolize what I had left to use against Doron; absolutely nothing. With Karenth, I had had the advantage of an elaborate, enchanted trap and many carefully crafted lies. The biggest irony being that I had lied to everyone *but* the shining god. I had known he wouldn't believe me. Instead, I had put the information I wanted him to believe, in the mind of someone he would have expected me to trust.

Of course, Karenth had been fairly intelligent. According to the rumors I had heard, his brother Doron was much simpler. A complex ruse would probably fail to work if the opponent was incapable of understanding the information presented to them.

"Your time is up? Have you produced a miracle?" said Walter sardonically.

I frowned, "No." It felt like I had something tickling the back of my head.

Walter gestured and said a few words. My arms and legs were drawn to my sides, held there by an invisible force. Another word and I was lifted from the ground. Motioning with his hand, my body floated upright beside him, and the older wizard began walking in the direction that would lead us to the main entrance.

"Stop it! You're taking us to the entrance anyway— they're still fighting there. We will be spotted for sure," I argued.

Walter laughed, "I'm a Prathion. No one spots me unless I choose it."

And just like that, it all fell into place in my mind. "I've got it," I announced.

My jailer ignored me and kept walking.

"Let me go Walter. I have an idea."

He snorted, "I've heard that before."

"Then just leave me here, this won't require your help," I suggested.

"Not a chance. How long do you think I'd live once the Countess discovered I'd left you behind?" he replied.

"Did I ever tell you the story of my chess match with Devon Tremont?" I said, changing the subject abruptly.

"Several times—are you planning to challenge Doron to a game of chess? Somehow I doubt he is a big fan of the game," retorted Walter wryly.

I nodded, "You are probably correct, but as my father used to say, 'there's more than one way to skin a cat.'"

He ignored my clever allegory and continued walking. I floated behind him, drawn along as if by some invisible string.

"You know how much I enjoy games," I continued.

"A selfish pleasure, since you usually win," replied Walter, "But Doron isn't going to take you up in a game of skill or strategy. He's far more likely to crush your skull and make pudding out of your brains."

"There's one type of game that I sometimes lose, especially when I play Marcus," I hinted.

"I'm not particularly interested in tossing dice and casting our lives away on a game of pure chance," said Walter, "nor do I think Doron will consent to giving up his advantage. He has us at his mercy already."

"Not dice, more like cards…," I corrected, "…and perhaps the advantage is ours. Perhaps the god of iron should be seeking mercy from us instead."

Walter stopped. "I know I will regret this. Go ahead and explain what you're thinking."

I explained my plan intently while he listened. Once I had finished, he removed the spell binding my arms and legs and let me walk on my own feet again. I gave him one of my confident smiles, to let him know he had made the right choice.

"Don't grin at me like that," he groused.

"Why not?"

"Because your idea is one of the stupidest things I've ever heard. There is almost no way it will work, and when it fails, you and I will both suffer long and painful deaths," he complained.

I ignored his pessimism, "Hah! You said 'almost'. So you agree there's a chance?"

He peered at his feet, "No, not really."

"So why are you going along with me?" I asked, somewhat surprised.

Glancing up, Walter's visage held an expression of sincerity. "Because of the way you said it," he admitted.

That seemed a bit odd to me. "That's a rather silly way of deciding something," I told him.

He muttered something under his breath. I didn't hear it clearly, but it sounded as if he said 'you can't fix stupid,' one of my favorite mottos. I dismissed the thought. The phrase was utterly un-Walter-like.

"You have no idea what you're like, do you?" Walter said questioningly. "Most of the time, you are completely oblivious to your effect on the people around you."

"I have wondered," I admitted, "but being a nobleman, I've just assumed I will never get an honest answer regarding people's opinions of me."

"That isn't really what I'm talking about, Mordecai. I mean the look you get, when you're intent upon something," said Walter.

I could tell he was about to drift into embarrassing territory, so I tried to divert him, "Are you referring to me sticking my tongue out of the side of my mouth when I concentrate?" I demonstrated what I meant.

In point of fact, Penny had often told me it was an endearing expression.

He let out an impatient sigh, "No, I'm talking about your absolute confidence. Many times now, we've been in, what I thought, were hopeless situations, and whenever it happens, you always come up with something. It usually sounds implausible, and I frequently think it's a bad idea, but I go along with it anyway."

"You have to," I interrupted, "I'm your liege. Obedience is mandated."

"Don't interrupt," he grumbled, and then he snapped his fingers and vanished in front of me. His disembodied voice continued, "I don't have to do a damned thing. I'm a Prathion, and one of the few living wizards that remain. If I wanted, I and my family would return to quiet obscurity somewhere far from anyone that knew us."

"Point taken," I agreed.

Walter reappeared as suddenly as he had vanished. "The reason I keep following you into dark caves," he said, referring to the first time he had faced the shiggreth with me, "is because of your absolute conviction. It's the look in your eyes and the tone of your voice. It tells me, and everyone else around you, that you are certain of your course of action. Even though you're betting your life, and frequently the lives of many other people around you— you don't waver or hesitate. You should though—any *sane* man would suffer some self-doubts or indecisiveness, but if you did, I imagine people wouldn't follow you."

I swallowed; my throat dry after listening to his revelation. *I doubt myself constantly. Do I really seem so sure to others?*

"That's why I released you from the spell. That's why I'm here, when every instinct in my body is screaming at me to get as far away as possible. I can hear it in your voice and see it on your face when you find your answer, and no matter how stupid it sounds to me, I can't help but believe in you," Walter finished.

There was nothing to say to that, so I put my arms out and embraced him. "One of these days you'll get yourself killed following me around," I stated somberly.

"You saved my life not long ago, and I probably owed you several for helping my family even before that. I'll still be coming out ahead on the bargain, even if I die today," answered the older wizard.

We didn't talk for a bit after that, just walked, heading ever closer to the area that Walter indicated still had quite a bit of fighting. It wasn't long however, before my friend held up his hand, gesturing to me that we should stop. "We're close. There are at least twenty men ahead, fighting just past that door," he pointed at a door that led into the scullery.

That room itself was of modest size, but it connected to the much larger main kitchen area. "How many of them are ours?" I asked.

"Only a few, Harold and two others, wear your armor. One of the enemy is fighting alongside them—no, wait— that's Dorian!" stated Walter at last.

That puzzled me. "How could you confuse him for one of the enemy?" I questioned.

"He's fighting naked," said the other wizard. He didn't bother to elaborate further, for I could easily understand the confusion that might cause him.

"That blast of Karenth's must have completely destroyed it," I postulated, remembering the moment earlier when he had intercepted the attack meant for my illusory self. "If we survive this day, he will never live this down," I added. Dorian had always been easily embarrassed.

CHAPTER 28

Walter had suggested using invisibility until we could get to a safe place to make our 'entry', but I dismissed the thought. There really weren't any safe places, and being fully invisible would also mean we would be blind, since in order to hide from Doron we would have to cloak ourselves from magic as well as visible light.

Instead, I asked him to put a shield around the two of us until I could get the situation under control, though I wanted him to remove it once I got started.

"That's reckless," he insisted, "Why do you want to be unprotected?"

"Your shield wouldn't stop Doron if he's serious, and it might hurt your chances of escaping if the feedback stuns you when it breaks. I just want to make sure we don't get killed by flying debris or a wild swing before I can get his attention," I explained.

"That doesn't sound like a…," began Walter, but his words ended quickly as I opened the door and stepped through, leaving him little choice but to follow.

The scullery itself seemed almost untouched. A basket of turnips had been overturned, and a few dishes had been knocked to the floor, but if it hadn't been for the raucous noises coming from the larger main kitchen area, we might never have known a battle had passed through it. I stepped through the open archway leading into the kitchen and had to blink as a wooden stool passed through the air near my head.

The preparation tables had been reduced to kindling, while pots and pans had been tossed willy-nilly about the room. Backed into one corner, Cyhan and Sir Thomas were struggling to avoid being overwhelmed, using the ovens to guard their backs while they faced seven of the intruders. Thomas still held his sun-sword but somewhere along the way Cyhan's had been broken, which was not an easy feat. The veteran warrior held the remaining foot of the blade and hilt in one hand and used a large butcher knife with his left hand.

No one had taken notice of us, entering as quietly as we had into such a noisy scene and as I looked on, the fight continued. Those facing Cyhan and Thomas were using the same tactics as before, coordinating their movements and occasionally attempting to entangle one of the knights by sacrificing themselves. Fighting someone that doesn't mind being wounded or maimed is a difficult thing, especially when he has a friend next to him ready to crack your skull like a ripe melon the moment you are unable to fend off his blows.

Cyhan and Thomas however, had something that none of Doron's possessed warriors had—experience. Next to them, the berserk warriors seemed like amateurs, despite their advantage of numbers. It was a deadly game though, one that would punish the first mistake on their part with a swift death. The iron-headed maces were unforgiving, and their wielders would be quick to follow up on any misstep.

Cyhan fell backward, stepping awkwardly upon a piece of broken furniture and drawing his enemies' swings down low, to crush him where he fell. His fall turned out to be a ruse however, and as he slipped downward he pushed off on the oven behind him and went into a slide that sent him between and behind his attackers. Meanwhile, Thomas' great sword caught the two who had sought to take advantage of his comrade, cutting both arms from the closest one at the elbow, while removing the second's hand at the wrist.

His attack had drawn his defense out of line, and one of the others facing Thomas stepped forward to make certain he couldn't recover, or he would have, but for the fact that Cyhan held him by the ankle.

Standing rapidly, Cyhan jerked the berserker's feet out from under him, causing him to flip forward to slam face first into the stone floor. Meanwhile, Thomas' backswing caught the man's companion in the side, neatly bisecting the god-ridden foe, and sending a wash of blood and gore down onto his senior knight commander.

Not that the older warrior particularly cared; Cyhan was already covered in blood and he had never been squeamish. He pushed himself upward, clutching one of the maces that the invaders had dropped, and moved to drive their mutual enemy back from where they were pressing in to flank Thomas. As he stood, he was caught squarely in the back by a heavy iron-headed weapon that had been thrown from across the room. The force of the blow drove him forward to smash into the great brick oven, and while the backplate of his armor protected his spine, the shock of it rendered him senseless for a moment.

Thomas was forced to swing wildly as he attempted to cover both his fallen commander and himself. Under normal circumstances that would have been sufficient, but against these men, it merely delayed the inevitable by a few seconds. Several of those who had already been maimed, threw themselves at him, and even as his sword cut them down, their bodies put him off balance, and he fell under the weight of them while still others grappled his arms and legs.

Only one was left free and able to wield his iron mace, but one was more than enough. Bringing the weapon down in a crushing blow, the berserker struck at Thomas, heedless of his comrades who were pinning the knight. The iron head destroyed the spine of one of the wild warriors, and yet still had enough force behind it to rattle Thomas inside his armor. The second blow was better aimed, and the stalwart Knight of Stone felt something break as it drove him down against the stone floor. The armor he wore was nigh invincible, but the flesh and bone beneath it could only take so much.

During their struggle, Dorian had been valiantly battling against three others and his fight had gone better, despite the fact that he had begun unarmed and stark naked. Without his armor he could not afford to be struck, but it also made him even faster and more nimble. Ducking and dodging, he had managed to get his enemy to do much of his work for him, their maces striking one another as they sought to match his speed.

Using his hand like a claw, Dorian had caught one of the wounded warriors by the nape and clenching powerfully, he crushed the man's neck. Without pause, he spun and twisted to avoid an attack from his second adversary and as he moved, he deftly caught his opponent's wrist. Sidestepping and pulling his foe into an awkward stance, he broke the man's arm before he could recover.

I saw him catch his enemy's weapon as it fell and use it to block a strike from his third opponent. The two maces met squarely, and the poorly tempered steel exploded at the sudden impact of the metal heads. One razor sharp shard of metal lodged itself in Dorian's chest, as bits of steel flew in all directions, but if the Grandmaster of the Knights of Stone noticed, he gave no sign. His heart thundered in his chest as he drove the shattered wooden haft forward into the other man's abdomen.

As he fought, Dorian saw Thomas' plight unfolding. Unable to reach his fellow knight to stop the awful battering he was enduring, he used the only weapon available to him—his legs bent as he crouched and levered upward on the haft of the broken mace, using it as handle to send the man impaled upon it flying across the room, to slam into the back of Thomas' opponent.

Before he could recover, his second opponent, the one he had disarmed and left with a broken limb, caught him squarely with a powerful punch that sent him reeling backward. Another blow followed before he could recover his wits, and Dorian stumbled, trying to protect his head and body. The one armed berserker pummeled him, but despite his enhanced strength he was unable to land a solid strike, for Dorian kept rolling with the blows as he struggled to regain his balance.

As I watched, Dorian seemed to wilt for a moment, and then as his opponent's next swing came, he straightened and caught the man at the wrist and shoulder before whipping him around to slam into one of the few remaining oaken tables. The heavy wood survived the impact, but my friend wasn't done—before his foe recovered he lifted the man with both hands and drove him down onto the table again, this time with the force and weight of his own body behind it. The table shattered, and while I couldn't see what happened to Dorian's enemy, he did not rise from where he lay.

All of this took place in the span of less than a minute. Without my magic I was unable to intervene, and Walter was slow to react. The fight ended as Dorian finished off what remained of Cyhan and Thomas' opponents—by first hurling the remains of the table he had broken and then wading in with a broken board to make sure that their enemies progressed from 'injured' to 'dead'.

Understandably, it wasn't easy to get his attention. "Don't kill them all!" I shouted, "I need one to talk to!" My words went unheeded, as he used the end of his impromptu club to crush another of the still moving berserker's skulls.

My childhood friend looked nothing like I remembered him. Gone was his beard, eyebrows, and sometimes sheepish grin, they were replaced by bare skin marked with blood and scorch marks. I had yet to hear him utter an intelligible word. The only sounds emanating from him were deep growling noises, so low as to almost be beneath the threshold of hearing. They were audible though, and the feral sounds sent a chill down my spine.

I moved closer, careful to keep outside of the radius of his makeshift weapon. "Dorian! Are you alright!?" I said loudly, and he finally took notice of me.

The board in his hand twitched as his eyes locked onto me, leaving me to wonder how close I had come to receiving another of his death blows, but it did not move further than an inch. He had frozen, staring at me with a look that bespoke confusion. A noise started in his throat, but only a wordless grunt emerged.

I smiled at him and stepped into his reach, opening my arms in a friendly gesture, "It's me, Mordecai. You can relax my friend. Do you recognize me, Dorian?"

His lips parted for a second as he attempted to smile, and I caught a glimpse of granite teeth. It was a sight that worried me, for it meant that he had drawn far too heavily upon his bond. Over the past few years I had had to release two of my knights from their bond because of similar changes. One of them had only had the bond for a few months before he began changing, while the other had lasted a couple of years. I still didn't understand why some turned so quickly, while others showed few signs yet, but the process was dangerous.

My ancestral home in Albamarl contained a living reminder of the fate of men who used the earth-bond too much. The golem Magnus guarded the house and he was but a rocky shell of the man who had once been Moira Centyr's bodyguard. I had always feared that such a fate might someday happen to one of my knights, and Dorian was the last one I wanted to lose. *I can't release him without my magic—nor can I help restore him to full humanity,* I thought silently to myself.

Dorian seemed to have calmed a bit, so I reached out and put my hand on his shoulder in a familiar gesture. "You look terrible," I noted honestly.

Something seemed to crumble within him then, and his face softened. "Mort? You're alive?" His big arms caught me up in a bear hug, and I felt his body shaking. Without my magesight I couldn't tell, but I knew without evidence, that tears ran down his cheeks.

"I'm fine," I reassured him, while thumping his back with my hands. It didn't feel quite right. The skin was rough, and whatever lay beneath the surface was too hard to be normal flesh and bone. "I'm more worried about you."

Stepping back I held him at arm's length while I inspected him. The piece of metal embedded in his chest looked ugly where it protruded from his left pectoral, but if he noticed any pain from it he gave no sign. Indeed, there was virtually no blood oozing from the wound either, which worried me in an entirely different way.

"After you disappeared—I wasn't sure what had happened," began Dorian in a gravelly voice. "I thought you were slain, and more of them kept appearing." He gestured to the dead berserkers that lay scattered about the kitchen in grotesque positions. "Where have you been?"

I smiled at him, even as my eyes saw one of the corpse's eyes glance in our direction. It was the body of the man whose neck Dorian had broken. Apparently even though the body was paralyzed it still retained enough life for Doron to animate it. Raising my voice I answered my friend's question, "I was dealing with Karenth. Now that I'm finished with him, I need to find Doron. It's a shame you killed all of them."

"Doron?" asked Dorian.

I nodded, "Yes, the god you've been fighting. He appears to have split himself into a multitude of his worshippers, imbuing them with strength and speed. Are there any left? It would simplify things greatly if I could talk to him."

Dorian looked around him before giving me an apologetic look. "I'm sorry. I didn't think of saving any of them. Until just now, it seemed as though we'd never run out of them."

Cyhan groaned as he eased himself up from the floor. "I don't think there can be very many left. We fought them by the dozens throughout the halls."

"What happened to you?" I asked, for I had lost track of him after the mace had hit him from behind.

"I was just recovering from the mace that hit me, when I caught a table full in the chest," he answered, giving Dorian a hard glare.

"I didn't see you," replied Dorian.

Cyhan coughed and twisted to the side in an attempt to unkink his back, when he grimaced suddenly and stopped. "I must have broken something," he explained. Glancing at Dorian, he continued their conversation as though a broken bone wasn't a matter of great concern for him. "I'm not surprised you didn't see me. After the god back there blasted the armor off of you, you seemed to go bat-shit crazy. You were wilder than they were," he said pointing at one of the bodies.

The eyes were still following me, but I gave no indication that I had noticed while I helped the two knights pull Thomas free of the pile of dead men. It was hard to tell how badly wounded he might be inside his armor, but at least the younger knight was still breathing, though he seemed to be unconscious.

"Where are the rest of the men?" I asked them.

The expression on Cyhan's face was discouraging, not that he was known for his sunny disposition. "We were scattered in the fighting. A good number of the enemy scaled the walls and came down the stairs. I believe the men on top were killed. I saw some of the remaining knights fall in various fights around the keep. Some of them may still be alive, but I doubt many of them are still able to fight."

"The two of you should see how many are left. Some of them may be in need of help," I suggested.

The two knight's stared at me for a moment before Dorian spoke, saying what was on both of their minds, "We shouldn't leave you undefended. There may be more of them running loose near here."

I dismissed their concern immediately, "If I can handle the God of Justice without breaking a sweat, I don't think Doron's little flunkies will be a problem for me. Do as I have asked. I will wait here for your return."

Their eyes moved from me, to Walter, and back again, before they both rose and made their way toward the door that would take them toward the main hall. I didn't bother wondering what silent communication they had shared, as long as they followed my orders, I was satisfied. They collected a few weapons as they went, and a stray thought popped into my mind as they stepped out.

"Dorian!" I called out, to get my friend's attention. He turned back to look at me as I continued, "You do realize you're naked, right? You should at least try to find some trousers while you're out there."

His face passed through several shades of color before settling on a deep red, as his mind processed my statement. Closing his mouth Dorian hurried away and I could hear Walter chuckling beside me.

"This will make a wonderful story later," noted the older wizard.

"It will indeed," I agreed, "once we get rid of our unwelcome guest." Moving forward, I stared down at the face that had been tracking my movements. "Isn't that right, Doron?"

The mouth of the paralyzed warrior opened, but without control of his diaphragm he was unable to reply. Instead he gaped and worked his tongue to no avail, attempting to speak.

"You need to stop your game and face me. You have already seen that you are not the equal of my knights. Stop playing the coward and assume your true form; my patience grows thin," I said, addressing the immobile warrior.

The face went slack as the force animating it disappeared, and a moment later I saw an outline appear in the air above the fallen body. It grew quickly from an insubstantial haze to a solid form, as Doron's power consolidated in one place. If I had still retained my magesight, I imagine it would have been blindingly bright as the god's aythar gathered into one distinct place, but as things were I didn't have to worry about being distracted by the shining god's power.

Walter vanished as Doron gained solidity. Taking on his true form would concentrate the deity's power here, and without being able to shield himself, Walter would again be at risk of succumbing to the overwhelming presence of the Iron God. The elder Prathion would be rendering himself invisible to both magic and light to protect his mind. Walter's disappearance was fine with me, for in this case I had nothing to gain from his presence, quite the opposite actually. The other wizard knew exactly what cards I would be playing, and that knowledge would be our undoing if Doron were to pluck it from his head.

Being invisible to magic as well as light, would also render Walter completely blind. He would still be able to hear, but he would be unable to render any sort of aid, without removing the invisibility that protected him.

"Your friends have abandoned you," came the deep bass voice of Doron. It was an attractive voice, as all the gods' voices were, but without the added influence of his aythar, it was merely a voice to my ears.

"At least I still have friends," I returned, "unlike you."

The Iron God stood before me with his arms crossed. Muscles seemed to bulge excessively in every direction, and his lightly oiled, bronze skin only enhanced the effect. The form he had taken was large, probably close to seven foot in height and broad-shouldered. I had always been tall compared to my peers, but Doron's height made it easy for him to look down upon me, a deliberate attempt to intimidate me.

He relies upon his physical strength to impress others, I thought silently, *and he would rather possess his followers and fight, than use his divine power directly.* So far the Iron God was living up to my assumptions about his nature. "Since you have seen fit to talk to me face to face, I will offer you a chance," I added.

The god's chest seemed to swell and his entire demeanor radiated menace. Overall it reminded me of a cat hissing and trying to look bigger as its hair stood on end. "You offer *me* a chance, a chance for what? Do not make me laugh human. You have no power and no hope."

As he spoke he reached out toward me with one massive hand. He could kill me with a touch or a simple exercise of his power. His reaching hand was a test. *He is a physical creature,* I thought, *he will attempt to put his hand on me to confirm my presence and demonstrate his superiority.* Once he had me, he would kill or torture me, and all of my bravado would be for naught. No words would dissuade him.

I did not flinch, instead I looked calmly up at him as his hand came down, and just before it reached me I flashed my teeth in a defiant smile. He stopped then, his palm hovering an inch above my shoulder. Inwardly, I felt my fear diminish and my confidence soared. *I've got you now, you bastard. You've already lost this game.* I made no attempt to keep my triumph from my features.

"So close," I said suddenly, "yet you hesitate. Perhaps you have more wisdom than your brother."

The hand withdrew as Doron's brows knitted themselves in an expression of concern. Clearly the Iron God was not adept at hiding his emotions. "What do you mean?" he asked.

"I'm sure you've noticed Karenth's absence," I stated calmly. "You must have wondered if he had abandoned you to face me alone, but I am afraid the truth is much worse than that."

"You have no power. You cannot fool my eyes," he declared, but his face was uncertain.

There was steel in my voice as I replied, "You are welcome to test that notion, but I must warn you, the moment you put your hand on me, our parley is over. I will offer you no second chance."

Being completely unable to sense my mood or read my emotions had to be driving Doron to distraction. I had already determined that he was not the brightest candle in the bunch, so to speak, but without being able to read my mental state, he was lost. I almost felt sorry for him. Almost.

"What is it that you are offering me? I have everything already, including you," blustered Doron.

"A chance to avoid your brother's fate. I suspect it was Karenth's idea to come here, so I will consider allowing you to leave unmolested—unless you would prefer to wind up like Celior," I told him plainly.

"You have no magic. Your threats are empty," growled the Iron God.

I smiled again, "Why don't you ask Karenth then?"

"Where is my brother?"

My eyes never left Doron's. "I could show you, but I don't think you'd like my methods."

"If you have such power why are you negotiating with me? You offer to let me leave? Why not simply make good on your threat?!" The shining god gloated at his sudden insight, "Your words betray your weakness!"

I kept my voice calm and level, "I never said I would 'let' you leave. I offered you a chance. You will give me something of value, or I will crush you into a mindless vessel of power, subservient to my will. I am beginning to suspect you have nothing worth bargaining for, however." My words dripped with malice.

"I am Doron the Breaker and I have riches beyond your imagining, mortal," said the indignant god. His posture told me all I needed to know though, he had shifted, and now he would seek to impress me with his value. Without admitting it aloud, he had already surrendered the advantage to me.

I scoffed at him, "I could care less for your wealth. There is only one thing of value to me…" I let the words trail off without finishing.

"What is that?" said Doron leaning forward as he took the bait. He was firmly in my grasp now.

"Information."

I could see the thoughts flickering across the child-like god's face as he realized he might escape for the price of nothing more than a few words. Unlike his brother, Doron had no real grasp of the importance of knowledge. "What would you ask of me?" he said after a moment.

"Why did you, your brother, and Millicenth leave your home? How did you cross between the worlds?" I asked immediately.

"Mal'goroth," answered Doron. "He has grown powerful beyond imagining, from the sacrifices you fed him. He devoured his brethren and grew more powerful still. He opened the way."

"The shining gods have allied themselves with him?" I said, shocked.

The god's face flinched at the thought. "No. We seek to avoid him. Karenth sought to release Celior that we might have the power to face him again."

It was a polite way of saying they were on the run, but I had to make sure. "Why did he open the way between the worlds for you then, and for that matter, who helped him?"

"No one helped him. After consuming the power of the remaining dark gods, he no longer needs assistance from the other side. He tore a breach between the worlds that he might cross at will. We merely took advantage of the rift to escape before he could capture us as well," admitted Doron.

I couldn't imagine Mal'goroth being so clumsy as to make a gateway and then allow his enemies to cross through it. There had to be more to the story. "How did you manage that, and where is Millicenth?"

Doron frowned, "She engineered the distraction that allowed us to use the rift, but she was unlucky. My brother thought Mal'goroth had caught her before she could follow us."

"And now you are all alone," I observed.

The Iron God grew angry. "Do not mock me with your false pity mortal."

I dismissed his protest with a wave of my hand, "Very well, I accept your information in payment for the damage you have done to my home and my servants."

"Your impertinence will be your undoing," growled Doron.

"It will be yours first. Do you wish to renege on our bargain?" I said icily.

He paused for a long moment before replying, "No."

"Then you may leave…," I started, and the shining god had grown wings in preparation for his flight almost before I could finish. "…but, you need to be aware of something."

Doron paused impatiently, "What?"

"I will give you a few minutes to be clear of my lands. If I find you within them again, or if I sense you near my vassals, my king, or my family, I will show no mercy. Make certain that we do not meet once more, or it will be the end of you. Have I made myself clear?" I declared with a venom in my words that required no acting on my part. Power or no power I meant it.

The Iron God glared at me in hatred and frustration before answering with an ear-shattering scream of rage as he leapt skyward, smashing through the roof of the kitchen and several floors of the keep, before he emerged above the castle. Seconds later, and he was gone, while I dodged to avoid the falling masonry and broken timbers that he left in his wake. I waited, staring upward for long minutes before I decided he must surely be gone.

"I think it's over, Walter," I said tiredly, as fatigue washed over me in waves. The adrenaline that had kept me standing firm was fading now, leaving me weak and trembling.

The other wizard reappeared, standing near the back wall, and moved to stand beside me. "What you did defies my ability to describe in a credible manner. Even if I try to tell this story to the bards, no one will believe it," he said wonderingly.

"They will believe that and more," I insisted. "Stories grow larger with every telling. By the time my grandchildren are grown, they will be saying I challenged him to an arm wrestling competition and bested him at it, or something equally silly."

Walter shook his head, "No, the truth was even more amazing than that." Then his eyes grew worried as he saw how pale I had become. "Are you alright?"

The light was dimming, and my head felt light as I sank downward. I might have fallen but for Walter's intervention. "I don't feel so good," I told him. "Perhaps I should find my bed for a while."

"You need help," said Walter. "What would you have me do?"

"Find Penny, she always knows how to make me feel better," I suggested. "I think I'd like to see her again, before the world is done with me. I'll sleep well if I can make sure she and the children are still alright."

"Dramatic speeches don't suit you," said Walter looking down on me. There were tears in his eyes. "You aren't dead yet. You still have a few days ahead if the stories are true. How do we find your family?"

"Just take me to my room and knock on the door. If it isn't too late, I'm sure she'll let us in," I said blearily. "She doesn't like it if I come home too late," I added softly, closing my eyes.

"She's in your apartments? That doesn't make sense, Mordecai. They should have evacuated. Where would they go in an emergency? Mordecai! Can you hear me? Wake up! Where would she have gone?" he said urgently.

I could barely hear his words however, and I was tired—so very tired. "Take me home," I managed, before slipping away into the soft gray silence that surrounded me.

As I faded away, I thought I could hear someone yelling, "Dorian! I need your help!"

CHAPTER 29

I'm not an expert in these matters but it doesn't look good for her," said Lady Rose from somewhere close by. Consciousness had come upon me gradually and I hadn't stirred yet, preferring to enjoy the warmth of my bed.

Penny responded then and her voice sounded closer still, "It just isn't fair. She fought so hard to protect you and the children. Isn't there something her father can do?"

Elaine, I realized, *they must be discussing Elaine.* I kept still and remained silent. My awakening would change the conversation, and I wanted to hear about my student's condition before they started fussing over me.

"He's spent the last few hours with her," answered Rose, "but he says there is only so much he can do. His skill in healing is very limited. He told me that he has fixed the bone and sealed her skin, but the muscle and soft tissues are a mess underneath. Even if infection doesn't take her and she somehow recovers, she'll never walk again."

"*He* could do it. If this hadn't happened," said Penny and I knew she was referring to me. Her voice broke when she spoke again, "He can't be dying. Walter must be wrong about this poison."

The air in the room stirred, and I imagined Rose must have moved closer to my wife, probably to put an arm around her. "We can't know for sure, but he was very sure of what his father taught him about it. I cannot think that there would be many poisons like that in the world. You have to prepare yourself, in case the worst does happen."

"This is my fault, Rose! I chose to take the earth-bond knowing it would blind me to the future. This was my gamble, and now it has cost me my husband, and possibly my child! How can I prepare myself for that!? There is no strength in the world that could help me to face it. How do I tell my husband that my arrogance has doomed our daughter as well as him?" insisted Penny in a voice thick with tears.

I longed to comfort her, but her words had frozen my heart in sudden shock. *Our daughter?* I knew she couldn't mean Irene; therefore it had to be Moira. How? Then I remembered and cold fear replaced the blood in my veins.

"I'm sure she's just sick, Penny. She never had a chance to eat or drink anything at the table," said Rose reassuringly.

"It was in the wine," I said slowly, opening my eyes. "She snuck a drink from the cup when she was bringing it to me."

Penny looked down upon me, beautiful despite tears and puffy eyes. "Are you sure?" she asked fearfully.

I nodded. "I still had my magesight then—I was watching her as she took the tray from Peter."

"Peter Tucker!" exclaimed Rose, in a moment of sudden insight. "After all these years I never suspected the snake still had venom in him!" she added with growing anger.

"Shhh!" admonished Penny. "His sister is in the next room," she reminded, referring to Lilly.

"Wait a bit before you call out the guard," I suggested quietly. "The wine was poisoned back in Albamarl, when those men tried to assassinate King Nicholas. Peter had nothing to do with it." I quickly filled them in on what Karenth had told me.

"How do you know he had nothing to do with it? You already know of his prior reason to kill you," said Rose firmly.

"In seven years, neither he, nor his sister, has ever given me cause to doubt them, even though I do not doubt that he once hoped to get his vengeance. I will not listen to slander against the man unless someone can show me real proof. Besides, if Peter ever decides to take his revenge he will do it with sharp steel, not poisoned wine," I replied in a tone that implied I would brook no further argument.

Rose had never met an argument she couldn't further, and she wasn't about to stop now. "How could you possibly know that?" she asked.

Because he keeps an enchanted dagger close against his heart at all times, I thought to myself, but I declined to reveal that bit of information. It would only further incriminate the man I was certain had nothing to do with my poisoning. Peter Tucker might still harbor a secret grudge against me, but I had known him for too long to suspect his character. He was a good man, through and through. If and when he decided to seek his due, he would do it with his own hands, not by poison.

"It's a feeling," I told her instead. "I trust him and from what I learned from Karenth, his only connection to the whole thing was doing his job, which happened to put him in that place at that time."

"Let it go, Rose," urged Penny. "I trust him as well, and before I took the earth bond, my intuition was something worth paying heed. My heart always told me he would never hurt us."

Rose looked back and forth between the two of us before letting out a long sigh, "I'm not used to losing arguments, and it never happened before I met both of you. I can never win when you both argue against me." She said it petulantly, but her voice was masking a smile.

I knew for a fact that *that* was a lie, even with Penny and me on the same side Rose rarely took a position in an argument that she couldn't win. I let her comment slide though, for a wave of nausea was sweeping over me and I hadn't the heart to start bantering. I tried to ignore the queasiness and change the subject instead, "How long have I been asleep?"

"No more than five or six hours," answered Penny, "We are into the small hours of the morning now."

"Where is Moira?" I asked then.

"Asleep in her room."

"Would you bring her to me? She can sleep here," I suggested.

Penny gave me a look, "Right now?"

"We can be sick together," I told her. "Later we might be too ill to appreciate it."

Her eyes softened. "Matthew will want to come too. He's been anxious to see you ever since Dorian carried you in."

"That's fine," I acknowledged. "At least until it gets too bad. I don't want him to see me if I get really ill. It might be too much for a child to see."

Penny rose and started to leave, but I caught her hand, "I need to talk to Walter before you bring them though."

"He won't want to leave his daughter's side," Rose interjected. "Why not wait until morning?"

"It cannot wait," I replied. "If he argues tell him I have that 'look' again. He'll come."

The two women nodded and left, but in the hall I could hear them talking. "What did he mean by that 'look'?" wondered Rose aloud.

Penny's fading voice answered as they walked away, "Probably that stupid vapid expression he gets when he thinks he's being clever."

Even as I'm dying she makes jokes at my expense, I thought quietly. *I knew I picked the right girl.* I smiled and closed my eyes while I waited for Walter.

He took longer to appear than I expected, and I fell asleep again while I waited. A soft touch on my shoulder woke me after he arrived. Dorian was leaning over me, looking anxious, while Walter stood a few feet away.

Dorian spoke first, "Mort, you look terrible."

I caught a glimpse of his teeth and was surprised to see they were once again white, with no hint of the grey granite I had seen earlier. *That's unusual.* I pushed the thought aside; whatever was going on there could wait for deeper reflection later. "You say the kindest things," I replied sarcastically.

His eyes were rounded with concern, "I mean it. Your eyes look odd, and your skin is sallow."

"At least I'm wearing pants," I remarked wryly.

My friend blushed, "I have on clothes!"

"Now you do," I replied, "but I'm afraid my image of you will never be the same again."

"Get over it. We used to swim together as kids," he said gruffly.

"As children!" I emphasized, "You weren't all—hairy and ape-like back then."

Dorian was beet-red now. "Well what do you expect? I'm a grown man!"

"What has been seen cannot be unseen," I said in mock-seriousness while putting a hand over my eyes, as if to ward off an evil vision.

Walter interrupted then, "At least now we know what Lady Rose sees in him."

I stared at Walter in shock and even Dorian turned to look at him, mouth agape. I had often despaired of the other wizard developing a decent sense of humor, but his latest remark was even worthy of a comic genius such as Marcus. "Wow!" I said after a moment.

"What?" asked Walter, "I thought it was funny."

"It was!" I said to reassure him. "It was damned hilarious. I just didn't expect it from you. Well done my friend."

"Now you're being condescending," grumped Walter. "While we're at it, *he* carried you back, sans trousers."

"Ugh," I said immediately. "I really didn't need to know that."

"What was so important that you wanted me to come right away? You should be resting," continued Walter.

"I need you to fetch Dorian's mother, tonight," I said plainly.

"Tonight is almost over," replied Walter.

Dorian frowned, "You think Mother will be able to help?"

"She's probably my last chance," I replied. What I didn't voice was my suspicion that his mother had been much more than a simple healer and herbalist. She had named herself a 'poisoner' back when I had questioned her about drugging Walter into unconsciousness for days. I now believed there might be more to it than simple knowledge passed from mother to daughter, as she had claimed.

"How do you want me to get there?" asked the other wizard.

"Just walk out the door," I answered. "I'm sure you've figured out the secret of my portal door by now. Once you're back in the castle, you can just make your way to the circle building."

Dorian spoke up, "The castle side is buried under stone rubble. Some of it had collapsed already. We cleared a bit to get to the door, but the rest fell as we entered. I don't think it's passable."

Probably a direct result of Doron's theatrical exit, I mused. "Can't you just clear it?" I asked, looking at Walter.

He nodded, "Certainly, but it will take time. I am not as strong as you were."

Were. His use of the past tense stung a bit, but I ignored it. "Make a circle then," I said, changing tacks.

"I don't know the circle keys for Lancaster," said Walter gruffly, "and even if I did, I don't have my book of diagrams handy to guide me in constructing a circle anyway."

He was forgetting that I probably had my books stored nearby. We were in my home after all, but it was a moot point either way. "We don't need any books. Just get me a sheet of parchment and some charcoal. I'll draw it out for you."

His eyebrows shot up, "You've memorized the keys and the circle design?"

I had yet to forget any of them, not just Lancaster, but I didn't feel like gloating, so I just said, "Yes," instead.

A few minutes later, I had created a passable depiction of the circle and given Walter my stylus to use in creating it. I handed it over to the other wizard. "I was a little hasty sketching it out. Can you read all of the symbols?" I asked.

Walter nodded and studied it carefully for a few minutes before commenting, "I have no idea how you remember things with such intricate detail, but this is certainly clear enough. My hand is not as steady as yours but I'm sure I can produce a workable circle using this; shouldn't take more than thirty minutes or so if you have a suitable spot. I do have a question though, why don't you have any circles here?"

"Paranoia," I replied. "I put this house in the most remote, and inaccessible place I could find. Making a circle that could reach it, would just be like giving away the keys to my treasure box. I decided to only use the portal to get in and out. I figured I could always make circles later if I needed to for some reason."

Walter seemed to accept my reasoning, but he had another question, "This design will take me to the circle in Lancaster, but I'll need to create another circle that leads back to this one if I am to return with Lady Thornbear…," he let his words trail off.

"So make one—we can always destroy it later to prevent anyone else from finding my home," I replied, completely misunderstanding his hesitation.

"I don't know the formulae to calculate the return keys for this circle," admitted Walter finally. "I'll need to borrow your books so I can work it out in advance."

I couldn't fault him for that. The formulae for calculating the return key for the other end was complicated, although solving it wasn't particularly difficult if you remembered all the steps. "Here, let me add that, it won't take me but a moment," I said, waving for him to hand the parchment back.

I ran through the process in my mind before jotting the rune keys down, and then I took the additional step of drawing the rest of the other circle out around them. That part probably wasn't necessary, since it was identical to the previous circle, but it only took a few minutes and it couldn't hurt to be sure. I hadn't realized how much Walter relied upon his references before this. Possibly, it was due to the late point in his life at which he had been exposed to it.

"Thank you," said Walter, with visible relief as I handed the sheet back to him.

"There's a stone patio on the side of the house facing the mountain, it would probably be the best place to set it up. Take Dorian with you. He'll be able to explain things to her more quickly," I told him.

"Yes, my liege," Walter answered rather formally, completing the phrase with a quick bow. He and Dorian turned and left the room.

I grimaced at the extra formality and shouted after him, "You'd best hope I die soon if you intend to keep using honorifics in private!"

Easing into a more comfortable position, I closed my eyes. My head felt foggy and considering the recent sleep I had had, it probably was due more to the effects of the poison than to anything else. *At least the painful part he told me about hasn't started yet,* I thought.

Penny woke me up as she laid Moira down beside me, and a bleary-eyed Matthew crawled into the bed on the other side. "You asked for children," she told me, with a wan smile.

My wife had never looked more beautiful in my eyes, sitting on the edge of the bed; the candlelight behind her set glowing highlights in her soft brown hair. The thought of dying didn't bother me as much as the thought of losing her. I glanced down at the little girl I held snugly in front of me. *Losing them,* I mentally corrected. "How are Irene and Conall?" I asked.

"Sleeping," Penny replied softly, "as they should be at this hour."

I nodded. "But they're alright?" I prodded. "They weren't hurt or badly frightened by all the fighting?"

She shook her head to indicate that they were unharmed. "Irene was hardly aware and little Conall was more disappointed that he didn't get to see me battling the bad men," she added with a slight laugh.

"He couldn't see?" I said questioningly before I realized. "Oh, Elaine hid them!"

"She kept everyone invisible," agreed Penny.

"How is she?" I asked.

My wife's face took on a pensive expression. "It isn't good. Rose was being optimistic earlier. You know—she almost took a second, fatal blow," observed Penny.

"What do you mean?"

"I had just come from the stairs, but I saw what happened. She was already down and there was one of them standing over her. She had her wand in her hand, and she could have killed him before he struck, but she attacked a different one instead," said Penny, describing the scene for me. "I didn't understand why at first, until I realized afterward, that the one she slew had just found Rose and the children."

"What happened then?" I asked. Walter had relayed the story to me at the time, but Penny's description was much more detailed.

"I threw my sword. I didn't have time to reach him otherwise. It didn't kill him, but it bought me enough time to get there," explained Penny.

"You fought the last two barehanded?"

"I was very cross at that point," she said, without elaborating.

"Makes me almost feel sorry for them," I commented wryly.

Penny's tone changed, turning sad, "I feel terrible for Elaine. She was a hero, Mort. She sacrificed herself for our children. If I had just been there a minute sooner, I might have prevented what happened to her."

I reached out to stroke her hair. "Don't talk like that. We all did the best we could. Whatever comes—comes. We did our best."

She nodded and smiled for me, but it was obvious that she was covering her feelings. I could only imagine how she must feel; her daughter and husband poisoned and probably dying, another friend that could be healed—if I were able to use magic again. Add to that the fact that we still had two or possibly three deities with a serious grudge against me, and my family, by extension. Despite my planning and efforts, I couldn't see much light in her future if I didn't find a way to survive.

Penny sat with me while I drifted back to sleep with a child on either side of me. Despite the excessive warmth they generated, it wasn't long before I was out.

CHAPTER 30

A hand shaking my shoulder roused me after what felt like only a few minutes. Elise Thornbear, Dorian's mother, was sitting at the bedside. Her son was sitting in a chair across the room. Other than the two of them, and Moira, who still slept beside me, the room was empty.

"Drink this," commanded Lady Thornbear, holding a small cup toward me.

I sat up and struggled to collect my wits. The bed was empty on my left-hand side. "Where is Matthew?" I asked.

"He wasn't poisoned, so I asked Penny to take him out," she replied, still holding the cup out.

I took it from her at last and smelled it. "What on earth?" I exclaimed, "This smells like some sort of spirits."

"It isn't just some 'sort of spirits' it's the purest distilled alcohol I had," she corrected me.

"And you want me to drink this?" I asked before continuing dryly, "Is my fate so bleak, you've decided I'll be happier drunk before I die?"

She gave me a sour look, while over her shoulder I could see Dorian shrugging helplessly, as if to say he had no idea what her plan was. "Drink that and I'll answer your question," Lady Thornbear replied.

I stared at her stoically as I threw the entire cup back, finishing it in one long draught. My manful feat was ruined by the fit of coughing that ensued afterward though. My belly felt as if it had caught fire, and my throat seemed to be attempting to repay me for the insult by choking me to death. "Damn it all!" I gasped at last. "What was that?" It hadn't been like any alcohol I had ever tasted before.

Elise smiled for the first time since I had awakened. "Next time pay attention. It was pure alcohol, or as close as I could distill it." She handed me another cup, "Try to get her to drink this."

I could only assume she meant Moira, but there was no way in hell I would put my daughter through such misery. "She's only seven!" I protested. "You can't expect me to give that to a child."

"Taste it," replied Dorian's mother in a voice that indicated I had said something foolish. She never failed to make me feel as though I hadn't managed to grow up completely. I sniffed the cup before trying a small sip. I found it to be sweet and much more pleasant. It tasted as though she had mixed her spirits with milk and honey.

My first thought however was indignation, "Why did you mix it so sweetly for her yet you forced me to drink liquid fire!?"

Elise Thornbear seemed exasperated. "How long has it been since you were poisoned?" she asked, ignoring my own question.

Of course I had no idea how long I had slept, so I simply stared at her in frustration for a moment before gesturing to Dorian. "Well? You should know better than I do right now. How long?"

My friend looked uncomfortable at my dragging him into the tense discussion with his mother, but after a few anxious seconds he managed to tally up the hours. "I believe it's about seven or so now, so probably around ten hours," he answered.

"The poison in your system primarily affects your liver. It has already compromised its functioning, and sometime between twelve and twenty-four hours after ingestion your liver will begin to die. At that point there is nothing anyone can do to save you. If you want your daughter to live, you'll give her that cup first and we can discuss my reasons afterward," explained Lady Thornbear.

As Penny will tell you, I am sometimes rather thick, but when it comes to my family, I tend to sort my priorities out quickly. I woke Moira and coaxed her into drinking the sweet mixture. My daughter was none too happy about it though. She still felt nauseous, and the taste of the alcohol in the drink wasn't pleasant for her.

"Do I have to drink this Daddy?" she said, after finishing the first half.

Stroking her cheek, I smiled at her, "I know it tastes bad, but you have to drink it if you want to feel better." I continued encouraging her until she managed to finish the entire cup. Once she had finished I turned my attention back to Dorian's mother, "Now if you wouldn't mind explaining why I'm trying to force feed a bit of tipple to my daughter. Is it some sort of antidote?"

Lady Thornbear graced me with a smile before answering, "Not exactly. Something in the poison you imbibed affects the liver in a negative and very permanent manner. At some point though, it was discovered that alcohol seems to prevent the damage it does to the liver. It doesn't negate any of the drug's other effects though, it simply preserves the liver until your body can eliminate the poison on its own."

"What about the damage it has already done?" I said anxiously. I was worried more for Moira's sake than my own. She was only seven. Starting life with a badly damaged liver didn't seem like a good beginning to me.

"Your power should return once the poison has worked its way out of your system," said Elise, trying to reassure me.

I shook my head, "That's not what I mean. What about her liver?"

"It will recover. Of all the organs in your body, the liver is one of the few that can regenerate—given half a chance," she replied.

A warm feeling washed over me, and my cheeks felt flushed. The potent spirits that Elise had given me were already starting to take effect. "So you really think drinking will keep us alive?" I asked.

"Yes," she answered. "The theory is that your liver, which normally filters and removes toxins from your blood, damages itself when it tries to break down the active principle in magebane. As you may also know, the liver is primarily involved in destroying alcohol in your body as well. There really isn't any way for us to be sure, but the most likely possibility is that keeping your liver busy with an overabundance of alcohol, prevents it from damaging itself by interacting with the magebane."

My thoughts were fuzzy now, but I was still following the conversation easily enough. My early studies in physiology hadn't been nearly as in depth as whatever Dorian's mother had learned, but they enabled me to keep up at least. "If the liver filters and removes toxins, and the alcohol prevents it from removing the magebane—how does it work itself out of my system over time?" I asked, somewhat astutely I thought.

Lady Thornbear's features softened, "You were always bright as a child, Mordecai. The kidneys also remove waste products from the blood. Given enough time, they will remove many things, even if the liver hasn't done its job on them."

"Momma says Daddy is the smartest man in Lothion," piped Moira suddenly. Proof that she paid more attention to adult conversations than I usually credited her with.

I blushed even more, "I really doubt that's the case, sweetheart." *She never says that in front of me,* I noted with an inward smile.

"Your mother is a very sharp woman, dear one," said Elise, putting a hand on Moira's cheek. "She had her eye on your father long before he realized it, back when he was just a lad. Now I need you to drink another cup for me. Can you do that?"

Moira made a face but nodded her agreement.

"How much do you intend to give her?" I asked worriedly.

Lady Thornbear frowned. "Too much, I'm afraid. No one is really sure how much is necessary. Given the high stakes, I plan to push the limit. I will have to make sure you are as drunk as you can possibly manage, without endangering your life. The hangover afterward will probably be quite memorable."

I gulped. "For how long?"

"One day might be enough, but two days to be sure. You will hate me by the time this is over, Mordecai," she replied as she poured another measure of liquid torture into my cup.

I forced myself to drink the terrible stuff before finally broaching the topic that had been on my mind, "Years ago, Genevieve told me that you learned your herbal lore from your mother, but that isn't really true is it?"

Elise flinched, almost as if she had been struck, and then her features hardened. "Dorian, take little Moira for a walk for a few minutes."

He balked at that, "I don't think she should be walking right now, Mother."

"Then carry her, dolt! I didn't mean she should have to walk herself!" snapped his mother suddenly.

Dorian gathered my daughter into his large arms and carried her out. His manner told me that his mother's words had stung his pride, but he wouldn't argue with her. Dorian's father, Gram, had been very strict about obedience and respect in their family.

After he had gone, Elise sighed. "Honestly, he's just like his father, a good man, but his mind follows a very direct course." She paused then, as if to see if I would prompt her, but I waited silently for her to begin again. "You are right. While I did learn some rudimentary lessons from my mother she is not the one who taught me most of what I know on the subject."

I nodded.

Whatever she had to say was obviously painful, that was easy enough to see from her expression as she continued, "When I was fourteen my parents sent me to study at the church in Albamarl. I was born to a low ranking knight in the service of Duke Tremont. I was the youngest of three children and since my father couldn't afford to provide a good dowry, for me they decided I should seek my vocation in the service of the Lady of the Evening Star."

"What my parents did not know, but which you have probably realized, through your dealings with Father Tonnsdale, is that the Church of Millicenth specialized in a number of secret and illegal practices. Though at the time I was hardly more than a child, I shudder now to remember some of the shameful things I was taught to do then."

Father Tonnsdale was the priest of Millicenth who had poisoned my parents and nearly poisoned the Lancaster family years ago, shortly after I had first discovered my abilities. He was also, as she had surmised, the first clue that had led me to wonder about her knowledge of poisons. "It isn't my place to judge your past, Elise," I reassured her, "You were always kind to me, almost a second mother, but life has taught me a number of hard lessons as well. I simply want to learn as much as I can."

Her eyes held mine for a moment, and then she forged ahead, "Initially I was given mostly drudge work, along with the standard classes they put most of the girls in, but as time passed, and my body filled out, I was sent to work in the brothels. My instructors also noticed my excellent memory and aptitude for learning, so I was given more advanced instruction in healing as well as herbal lore."

The look on my face was probably incredulous, despite my attempts to keep my features smooth. *Dorian's mother was a prostitute!?*

Elise looked downward, "There's no need to make that face, Mordecai. I'm sure you never expected to learn that Gram Thornbear's widow was a paid pleasure girl, but the facts are rarely what we would wish them to be. At the time, I was not proud of my work, though I did at times take some pleasure in it myself. I will not lie about that. It was distasteful, but it was not entirely as terrible as some may think. I was well-fed, and my treatment as a prostitute was many times better than as a common drudge for the church."

It was probably a toss-up to decide who was more embarrassed at the revelation of her prior work as a lady of the evening. In fact, looking upon the term, I began to realize that perhaps that was why they were called 'ladies of the evening', though I had never realized that the church venerating the 'Lady of the Evening Star' had operated brothels. It was yet another glaring reminder that I was more naïve than I thought I was. *Marcus would probably laugh to know that I hadn't been aware of the reason they were called ladies of the evening.*

Elise watched my face carefully, "You seem deep in thought. Does it shock you to learn of my shameful past?"

I almost stumbled over my words, as I struggled to correct her misimpression, "No! Uh, well a bit, yes. But truly, my biggest shock was learning that the church dabbled in prostitution."

"So you're saying you always expected I had been a wanton?" she asked with a raised eyebrow.

"No, of course not!" I said immediately, but I was wise enough to know she was merely teasing me now, probably to ease her own tension at revealing such a shocking secret. I turned the tables on her by responding with complete sincerity, "Elise, I have always held you in high regard. I never knew your past, but the woman that raised Dorian, that loved Gram, and that looked kindly upon me as a common child playing amongst his betters, that woman is still in front of me. Nothing in what you have told me so far has changed that in the slightest."

Her eyes filled with tears, but just as Rose would have, she looked away to hide her face, "You speak well, Mordecai, but wait until I have finished my tale before you grant me such kindness. Your opinion may change."

I started to protest, but she held up her hand. "Let me continue," she said. "In spite of your ignorance, which probably speaks well of you, it is common knowledge that many of the brothels, particularly in Albamarl, are operated by the Church of Millicenth, or rather they were. Your ban upon the churches in the capital has probably had some effect there. I would be surprised if they did not still have some interest in the remaining brothels still operating in the capital."

"But why?" I interjected, "I gave up my illusions about the righteous nature of the religions of the shining gods years ago, but it seems to me that prostitution runs counter to their 'public' image. Why would the church deliberately tarnish its image in such a way?"

"Your illusion was based upon childhood teachings. I assure you, adult society always knew and accepted their other 'doings'. The brothels were considered, at least publicly, to be a service to the suffering of unmarried or unhappy men. Privately, they were centers for gathering information. The pillow talk collected by the whores in those dens of pleasure was carefully sifted and refined, for use by the church elders. That information was a resource more valuable than gold, and it could be used to control and maneuver, to blackmail and inform."

"By the time I was sixteen, I was one of the more accomplished and sought after whores in service to the church, but my talents extended far beyond the simple pleasures of the body. It had been determined that I had the wit and talent necessary to be taught additional skills. I was trained in the hidden secrets of the church. They taught me the art of gathering information, the techniques of assassination, and the lore of poisons. The devotees of the Lady had been studying the poisoner's arts since their inception before the Sundering, and I was perhaps their most able student."

She had finally reached the heart of what I had suspected, though I still wasn't comfortable with the way she had said 'assassination'. "How did..." I said slowly, letting my words trail off.

"How did I wind up with Dorian's father?" she said with a laugh, "That part is simple enough, I was assigned first to gather information from him, and later I was tasked with his assassination."

My head was swimming already from the alcohol, so I doubted my ears for a moment, "Wait, what?"

"You heard me," she said, before repeating herself, "I was tasked with assassinating Gram Thornbear."

At some point my mouth had fallen open. Once I noticed, I closed it quickly, my teeth clicking audibly.

Elise smiled, "Andrew Tremont, the Duke, wanted a spy in the Lancaster household. He paid the church a large sum to acquire such a person, and since my superiors knew already of Gram's patronage at the brothel, I was the obvious choice."

"His patronage?"

"Gram was more worldly than our son. As a young man, he came to the place that I worked, and I caught his eye right away. He had been seeing me regularly for several months before the request came for me to try and use him to the Duke's advantage," she explained quietly.

"So they wanted you to shpy on him?" I said, slurring a bit despite myself.

"I had already used him for information. They wanted something more involved. I was supposed to compromise his integrity, force him into situations that would cause him to commit small deceits; things that would seem harmless but which he would know ran counter to his lord's wishes. In general, the method involves requesting small favors that, over time put him at a serious disadvantage. Eventually, the agent will drop the charade and threaten to expose their target. At that point, the relationship becomes an ugly one of cold blackmail and exploitation, essentially forcing the target into the service of whoever is paying the agent," she explained.

"Sho how did it go from that to ashashination?" I cringed inwardly at my pronunciation, but I knew there was no hope for it; the alcohol had permeated my brain, and even now I was growing more numb.

She sighed, "The problem arose when he refused my requests. He was infuriatingly unaccommodating when it came to my little 'favors'. He steadfastly refused to do anything that went against Lancaster's wishes. The whole thing was exasperating, and was made even more so by the fact that he always brought me flowers."

"Flowersh?"

"The first time he came to see me, he brought daisies," she said with a faint smile. "Almost no one brings flowers to a whore, although it isn't unheard of, but he brought them every time he came. Make no mistake, he knew what his coin was purchasing, and he made good on his claim, but he always behaved as though he were courting me. For a girl who had been raised as gentry, then turned into a prostitute, it was a bittersweet thing. It reminded me of my life before, of my hopes and dreams for a normal life."

"After a few months, I began to grow angry. I was sure he had played me for a fool. He had to have guessed at my game by then, he had already refused so many of my requests. Yet he continued to bring flowers; wildflowers, lilacs, gardenias, roses, whatever he could find, whatever was in season. Even worse, he paid double whatever I asked, always saying, 'this is for you, and this is for whoever claims your fee later'. He knew they took most of what we earned, so he paid twice, so I could keep it and give the mistress her share as well. I couldn't understand him, or what his motivations were, and it drove me mad."

As she spoke, I could almost see Dorian doing something similar, if he had ever been so bold as to frequent such a place. Clearly his father had been a hopeless romantic as well, though he had obviously been very earthly in his desires.

Lady Thornbear went on, "My masters were growing impatient with my lack of progress, so at last I decided to try something more direct. During his next visit I admitted my duplicity and threatened to reveal his secret visits to the brothel. While that wouldn't have been much of a scandal, I had convinced myself that his rigorous sense of honor must be based on pride, a pride that would not bear to see itself shamed. I was sure that rather than taint his name even slightly, he would turn traitor."

I laughed, "You really didn't undershtand him at all did you?"

She shook her head ruefully, "No, I did not. You must understand, at that time my own soul had been so blackened by my circumstances and my actions that I truly could not believe anyone would act unselfishly. The shadow in my heart had convinced me that his honor was just a sham, something one puts on like a coat when you go outdoors."

"What happened?"

"He laughed at me. 'Go ahead and tell people whatever you want,' he told me. He was not at all worried about the 'appearance' of honor, just the substance of it, and he knew he had not failed in that. He even bragged that once people had seen me, they would understand his reasons for visiting me so frequently. It didn't embarrass him in the least."

Elise frowned, "His flippant attitude made me furious, and I threw him out. Afterward I reported what had happened, and my superiors decided it would be best to eliminate him. They were worried that if he repeated what I had told him, that someone might guess at my ultimate employer. There was already considerable tension between Lancaster and Tremont, and it would have cast a dishonorable shadow across Tremont, although it would have been impossible to prove anything."

"He returned a week later, and I received him in a far different manner than I had the time before. The poison I had prepared days before; a slow acting poison much like the one I gave you when Dorian was abducted. I slipped it into his cup so skillfully he never had a chance, but then…," her voice trailed away for a moment.

Her story had created such a dramatic tension I became agitated, "Then what?!"

Lady Thornbear's cheek had a fine track of tears on it now, "It was his smile I think, that undid me—or perhaps it was his trusting eyes. As he lifted the cup to his lips, they pierced my heart, and I couldn't bear to watch him drink it. I caught his hand and confessed what I had done. I still didn't realize my own true feelings. I just couldn't let him come to harm. When he didn't become angry with me for what I had done, I became angry with him instead. I had already told him to leave for his own sake, but he wouldn't listen. He was ever so stubborn."

"When I asked him why, he said something I have never forgotten. He had always been unfailingly polite, but that day his patience had finally grown thin. 'Elise, you are the dumbest woman I have ever known, for you do not know your own heart. You claim the world is full of darkness, and that everyone acts only for their own gain, yet you ignore the evidence of your own heart. You love me as keenly as any woman ever loved a man, and I have loved you since the first day I came here. In this chest of mine beats two hearts, yours and mine both. That's why you couldn't let me drink that cup. Deep down you knew that the poison would kill us both.'"

"At that I became even angrier," continued Lady Thornbear. "I called him a fool for loving a whore that would never return his affection. I mocked his feelings and made light of the flowers he had brought. I said every wicked thing I could think of to drive him away, and all the while my heart cried within," she paused for a second and stared into my eyes. "Do you know what he did then?!"

I shook my head in a vigorous 'no', making the room spin around me.

"He picked the cup back up, and in the space of a heartbeat, he gulped the contents down, saying, 'If what you say is true, then this world is no place for me, and I will not live in it.' That was when my heart finally broke, and everything turned upside down. I knew then that he was not merely pretending to be an honorable man, rather he was exactly what he had presented himself as, an honorable man, too stubborn and half-witted to survive in the cruel world we existed within." Lady Thornbear stopped then and dabbed at her eyes with her sleeve.

For my part, I was already crying and too drunk to care. "That shounds jusht like him!" I exclaimed, in a voice now thick with both tears and drink. She still didn't continue immediately, waiting instead for me to recover my own equilibrium.

Once both our eyes were dry, she resumed her story, "After that, he refused my aid until I confessed my love to him, which I did, crying and babbling in a way that I had thought forgotten with my childhood. That was the day I rediscovered my heart. It was the first and greatest gift that he ever gave me."

"What happened then?" I asked blearily.

"I put my fingers down his throat until he had vomited up everything in that bottomless pit he used for a stomach," she said bluntly. "Then he took me away. There was no discussion, he told me to gather my things, and that was that. While I did, he went downstairs and arranged to purchase my contract from the mistress of the house. I didn't get to see that conversation, but I discovered later that she did not react kindly to his offer. It was only after he threatened to kill her and burn the entire establishment to the ground that she reconsidered."

That surprised me a bit. "They jusht let you go—ash easy ash that?"

"Officially, yes, she signed away their rights to me and I was free to go. In reality though, it was never that simple. Because of my knowledge and training, the church could never release me, and because of the circumstances, I had the potential to create a terrible political problem for two of the most powerful houses in the land, as well as the church itself," she said with a sigh, "But Gram would listen to none of it. He asked for my hand, and I agreed to his proposal. I determined that if he would not listen to sense then we would be happy for as long as we could, until they 'removed' the problem."

The further her tale went, the more amazed I was at the complexity and tragedy of her life. My old notions of Dorian's mother were completely incompatible with the scarred, flawed, strong, and beautiful woman I was learning about now. At the same time, I was a little sad that Dorian had never been given the chance to hear this story as well. If anyone deserved to know, it was him.

"You were waiting for their assassins to kill you?" I asked, to clarify her statement.

"Both of us," she corrected. "They could not afford to leave either of us alive. I waited, fearful of every shadow until Father Tonnsdale arrived and took the position at Cameron Castle. He soon visited the Lancasters, and I knew that he would seek me out. When he did, he surprised me with an offer that allowed everyone to have what they wanted most."

I felt an inner tension building when she mentioned the name of the priest that had poisoned my parents. Her posture had changed subtly too, stiffening as if she were remembering something unpleasant. "And that was…?"

"I remained in the service of the church, acting as a spy and an informant for them from within the Lancaster household. In return, I and my husband were allowed to live peacefully, free from interference or threat. The church really didn't want to kill us both, for it would have created other problems for them. They knew that Duke Lancaster would blame them, and the political cost might have been severe," she explained.

I was shocked, "You betrayed them?"

Elise Thornbear frowned sharply at me, "Watch your tongue, Mordecai. I have committed many sins, and you may well hate me for some of them, but my story is not done yet. When I have finished, you may decide whether to brand me a traitor or not."

"I'm shorry," I said quickly. It was already apparent that the strong drink had gone to my head and my emotions were shifting rapidly from one extreme to another.

"Don't be too quick to apologize either," she added sadly. "Just wait until I am done. After the priest and I made our arrangement, I went to Gram and confessed to him. I expected him to punish me, or have me put aside, but instead he took me before his lord, James, the Duke of Lancaster. He explained what I had told him, and together they hatched a plot to use me to Lancaster's advantage. Well, I say 'they', but in reality it was James' idea," she stopped and looked directly at me. "When you decided to play kingmaker you made a good choice in him. If there was any man in this kingdom able to step into Edward Carenval's shoes and hold our country together, it was him."

"In any case, I digress," she said, before returning to her story. "From that point on, my life changed dramatically. I was free from fear, and the shadow of the church hanging over me, no longer seemed so dreadful. I sent occasional reports to Father Tonnsdale regarding the doings at Lancaster Castle, after letting Genevieve review them first. She would discuss them with her husband, and if they felt anything shouldn't be told, I would remove it from my report, or alter it to suit them. Ironically, it was this interaction that initially drew her and me together as fast friends over the years."

"I was also called upon occasionally to share my knowledge of poisons. I did this in various ways, mostly benign. I helped heal the sick and treat the wounded on occasion at Lancaster. I also shared my knowledge with Father Tonnsdale. His interest seemed primarily to be about healing herbs, but I was also asked to teach him the recipes for several of the church's more deadly poisons. This didn't concern me overmuch at the time, and Genevieve felt that if I refused to share the knowledge with him, it might send a signal to the church authorities that I was no longer a loyal servant. In any case, he would have been able to learn the information he sought from other sources within the church headquarters at Albamarl. I was merely much more accessible." Lady Thornbear stopped and looked down.

My mind had gone numb. *She taught Father Tonnsdale.* My tongue seemed to cleave to the roof of my mouth, while I struggled to formulate the question in my heart; but I already knew the answer. Elise looked up and our eyes met, and in them I could see her guilt, her sorrow, and her final shame.

"Yes, Mordecai," she said simply, to answer my unspoken question. "I taught him the poison he used to kill everyone at Castle Cameron, the same poison he tried to use against the Lancasters. Penny did the world a great favor when she stove in that evil man's skull."

Even in the midst of my emotional shock, I was surprised at that revelation. As far as I knew, no one beyond Penny and myself knew she had murdered the priest. My eyebrows went up for a moment, "You knew aboutsh that?"

She nodded, "Genevieve figured it out quickly enough. She also hid the knowledge that she had seen Penny that day."

Somehow I managed to focus my sluggish thoughts. I had already suffered a series of shocks during her story, but there was one matter that cried for my attention, one thing that I needed to know. "You had to know he was the poisoner," I said, referring to Father Tonnsdale, "Why didn't you reveal his crime?"

"I have only excuses, Mordecai, and none of them are sufficient to expunge my guilt. None of them will bring your parents back," answered Elise Thornbear. "It had been years since I taught him the recipe. I was pregnant and almost ready to deliver Dorian at the time of the fire, and I wasn't able to examine the bodies of the dead, so I couldn't be sure at first what poison had killed them. Naturally I did suspect Father Tonnsdale, but I had no certain proof. I shared my thoughts with Genevieve, and they had him watched, but nothing incriminating was ever discovered. In the end, I did nothing to avenge them, and I was helpless to prove his guilt."

A fire was building in my gut, a ball of futile anger, but I had no good place to direct it. Could I really blame this woman before me, my best friend's mother? For most of my life I had loved her as a kindly authority figure and sometimes as a surrogate for my own mother. Even through my drunken haze, I felt my jaw clenching.

Elise watched me carefully before adding, "It does nothing to assuage my guilt in the tragedy of your early life, but I knew who you were long ago, even before you and Dorian became friends. When your father came to the castle, the news moved quickly, Royce Eldridge had gained a son. He never shared the story of how he found you, but Genevieve told me of her letter from your dying mother, and I knew it had to be you. I did my best to see to it that the timing and circumstances of your arrival at the Eldridge household never reached Tonnsdale, or the ears of the church."

"You're right," I said hoarsely, "It does nothing to assuage your guilt, but…" My bitterness was evident in my voice, and despite the alcohol my anger gave clarity to my words. "…what's done is done and I cannot blame you for the doings of that evil man. Tonnsdale was damned for his own actions." I paused for a moment, swallowing to clear the knot that had formed in my throat. "There is one thing that you are entirely wrong about," I told her.

Elise Thornbear's eyes were red and swollen with tears now, "What?"

I was tired now and my voice began to slur again. "I don't care if you ever share the story of Tonnsdale and the poishon. That ish a matter that lies purely between us now, and I forgive you of it, but your son deserves to hear the tale of how hish father and mother met. You do him an injustice to keep such a shecret from him," I informed her bluntly.

"You know how my son is; he walks a straight and narrow path, with no room for bending. How can I shame him with the knowledge that his mother was a whore? I think it better to leave him with a past he can be proud of than to tell him the truth," she argued.

I shook my head, sending the room into another dizzy spin. "You are wrong there. You shon is very much like hish father. Gram Thornbear saw the truth of your heart, deshpite your self deception. He knew your worth, even before you did. You shon will not be deluded by the circumshtances of your past, and he will love you even more for knowing the truth."

Laying back into the pillows, I determined to let sleep have its way with me. I had had enough shocks for one day. The world swam gently behind my eyelids, and as I drifted into a drunken slumber I could hear Lady Thornbear's quiet sobs.

CHAPTER 31

The next few days really weren't worth remembering, and thankfully the alcohol helped to keep my memories from being too clear. I suffered through a haze of nausea and vomiting, interrupted periodically by Elise Thornbear, as she forced me to drink more of what had already made me sick. I had never been a heavy drinker, but by the second day I felt certain I would never desire even the slightest taste of anything alcoholic ever again. It was all made worse by the fact that I had to witness my young daughter suffering the same treatment I was receiving.

"No more," I told Elise weakly as she entered the room once more. She carried a platter with a large pitcher in the center of it. "I don't care if I die. Just let me die in peace!"

"And what of your daughter?" she asked with an odd expression.

I mulled that thought for a moment. Was it alright to make her suffer for the sake of survival? What if she hated me for it later? "Save the child, but don't tell her it was my decision till after I'm dead," I replied at last.

Elise chuckled and handed me a heavy clay mug, "Drink this. You'll feel better."

"No! I told you, no more! I won't do it," I insisted.

"You will like this cup, it's different," she told me.

I glowered at her, "If I still worshipped the gods I'd call for an exorcism, since you are obviously possessed by an evil spirit."

"It's mint tea," she explained, "It will help settle your stomach and get some fluid back into you. You are dangerously dehydrated."

I kept my eyes on her as I suspiciously sniffed at the cup. It smelled fresh and minty, suggesting she might be telling the truth this time. She had already fooled me a time or two the previous day, when I had begun trying to reject her offerings. Still, my nose detected no hint of alcohol, and I was terribly thirsty. A small sip and I found myself swallowing rapidly. The tea was cool and delicious. I took the pitcher before she could offer, and refilled my cup.

"How do you feel?" she asked, as I gulped it down.

My eyes narrowed, "Like something that has died, been brought back, then slain again, dried out and stretched full length on a bed, with an audience to occasionally visit and comment upon its suffering."

"That sounds positively awful," she remarked. "I am beginning to think you don't like my treatment very much."

"I don't like *you* very much at all," I agreed. "In fact, yesterday, if I had had my power back, I might well have done something permanent and possibly fatal to you for sneaking that cup of honeyed liquor into me."

She laughed before responding, "After listening to your whining the past few days, I have to say that I think you would complain even if you were hung with a new rope."

The observation sounded so much like something my father would have said that it gave me pause. Musing about it for a moment or two, I lost my train of thought and asked her instead, "How is Moira doing?"

"Very well, better than you in fact, but then children usually do recover quickly," said Elise. "Not to change the subject, but you remarked about your power a moment ago, have you had any sign of its return yet?"

"Yes," I admitted, "though I feel weak as a kitten when I try to exercise it. My magesight was back when I awoke today."

"Then I think I shall declare my treatment a success," she announced.

I took another sip of the tea she had brought, finding that it did indeed seem to help ease my nausea, though my headache was another matter entirely. "I'm not used to calling a treatment a 'success' when it leaves the patient feeling worse afterward than they felt in the beginning," I noted dryly.

"It's a matter of perspective," she replied, as she rose and moved to the door. "I'll step out. Dorian has been waiting to talk to you."

"It isn't as if I'm going anywhere soon," I said.

She shrugged, "You spent most of yesterday trying to turn your stomach inside out. He didn't think you were in a mood for conversation then."

"Point taken."

She disappeared and my large friend poked his head in the door. "Still alive?" he asked with a half-smile.

"Barely, but thanks to your mother I mostly wish I had died," I responded. "Any news?" It had been three days since Lady Thornbear had begun liberally dosing me with alcohol, so I was understandably nervous about what might have occurred in the meantime.

Dorian grew somber, "Only seven of the Knights of Stone survived: me, Cyhan, Harold, Thomas, William, Egan, and Edward," he said bluntly.

"We lost so many?"

"Most of the servants, townsfolk, and soldiers survived, except those who didn't get transported in time. We lost over fifty guardsmen and twenty of the townsfolk, including nine children. Most of those casualties occurred in the town, though a few were hiding in the castle before they were discovered by the god-ridden berserkers of Doron's," he said, elaborating.

"Any changes among the Knights that survived?" I asked, knowing that they must have drawn greatly upon their bond during the fighting.

"No, thankfully, since I doubt you are up to releasing anyone at this point."

I stared at Dorian's face, wondering if I had imagined the granite teeth in his mouth a few days ago. He had clearly begun transforming, and while that was to be expected of someone who used a lot of the earth's power, what wasn't expected was for him to spontaneously revert to his normal state. I couldn't even decide whether to ask him directly about it. "Did your mother ever talk to you?" I asked, changing the subject.

Dorian frowned, "No, why?"

For a moment I considered keeping her confidence by misdirecting his question, but for once I was too tired for subtlety. Instead I gave him the most direct answer I could, "You need to ask her that yourself."

He stood, as if ready to do so right then and there, "Perhaps I will then."

"Before you do that, I need some advice," I interjected.

"On what?"

"What do I do now?" I asked.

Dorian looked at me as if I had grown a second head. "You should know the answer to that as well as anyone. We rebuild and we go on. George has already begun moving people back to Washbrook, and we will soon begin repairing the damage to the keep itself. Other than the loss of life, we suffered fairly minor damage to the town and outer walls."

"Not that," I said, waving my hands. "About the gods—I think I've convinced Doron and perhaps even

Millicenth to give us a wide berth, but I'm worried about Mal'goroth. He's become too powerful, even the shining gods fear him now. Worse, he's here, in our world, but I have no idea where, or what he might be up to."

"I told you before; I'll deal with the shiggreth and the foes that can be fought by mortal men—I leave the deities and such in your hands. You and Marcus were always better at strategizing when it came to politics or matters of the gods," he replied.

"Marc!" I said loudly. "You're right, of course. I need to talk to him."

"Good luck. You haven't forgotten he moved to Agraden have you?" reminded Dorian.

I hadn't. "No, but I can still contact him. Have you seen Penny yet today?"

"She's been tending to Elaine. I'm afraid the girl isn't doing well," said Dorian.

"What do you mean?"

"She isn't breathing well," he replied, "though I've never really understood how a leg wound could cause problems with the lungs."

Unlike my friend, I had learned quite a bit over the past few years about how the body responded to wounds. In particular, I had an excellent mental map of how the vasculature carried blood, and his comment set off alarm bells for me. "I need you to do me a favor," I said without preamble.

"Sure."

"Go to my study and open the cabinet to the left of my desk. I keep magical letter boxes in there. Find the one labeled 'Marcus' and bring it to me, along with something to write with," I said, outlining my request.

He didn't waste time and moments later he was gone. As soon as the door had shut, I sat up and put my legs over the side of the bed. The world began spinning and my stomach clenched rebelliously. *I can deal with that,* I thought quietly, *if only my head would stop pounding.* Ignoring my body's warning signs, I stood and started my way across the room. I didn't have to get very far; Elaine was being kept in the guest room across the hall.

By the time I had reached her door, I wondered if I had taken on more than I could handle. I spent several minutes retching as I lost control of my stomach. It was with considerable regret that I surrendered the tea Elise had brought me. *Penny won't be happy about the mess either,* I noted.

Gathering my strength once my internal storm had passed, I opened the door and stepped inside. Both Penny and Walter looked at me in surprise. "What the hell do you think you are doing out of bed?!" said my lovely wife by way of greeting. She looked exceptionally glad to see me.

"Morning dear," I said sweetly.

She gave me an evil glare, "It's afternoon, genius." She rose and moved toward me, clearly meaning to escort me from the room. "You don't need to be in here right now."

"I heard she's having trouble breathing," I replied. Looking over Penny's shoulder, I could see Elaine sitting partially upright in the bed. Her face looked strained and her breath came in rapid shallow gasps, as though she had just run a race and couldn't get her wind back. She was watching me from where she lay, and the panic in her eyes was enough to confirm my fear.

Penny's face broadcast a warning to me. She was trying not to frighten the patient any more than was necessary. Her words were loud and brazen, as though she hoped to distract Elaine from her life and death struggle, "Let me take you back to bed before you infect Elaine with a bad case of 'stupid'. Honestly, you do something like this every time you're ill. I would think you'd learn eventually."

I held my hand up before she got close. "My power has returned, in some measure at least. I need to help her before it is too late." Walter's eyes were watching me throughout the exchange.

"You can worry about that when you're strong enough," said Penny reasonably, "not today."

"She won't live past today if I don't do something now," I answered bluntly. That brought her up short.

Penelope's eyes narrowed as she stared at me in a look meant just for me. There was fear there, hidden in her gaze, fear of losing something she had just regained. "You might not live past today if you do something rash and aren't strong enough to recover from your mistake."

"I have to try," I said, leaning forward to kiss my wife. To her credit, she did not flinch from me, though I surely couldn't have smelled very good. I found myself leaning upon her afterward, for my balance was uncertain.

"Are you certain this is a good idea," asked Walter. His features were sunken from lack of sleep and prolonged stress.

Is it a good idea? No, certainly not, I told myself inwardly, but I knew I had to try. "Put your hand on my shoulder," I said, ignoring his question. "Watch and try to lend me your strength if I seem to be faltering." As I spoke I eased myself into the bed, stretching out beside my hyperventilating student.

Since my first attempts at healing years ago, I had learned to categorize what I did by what level of connection was required. Simple healing was an act of will, requiring only desire and the ability to manipulate aythar; plain wizardry in essence. There was no contact of minds or spirits, and it didn't matter whether the subject cooperated or not. Simple healing could close wounds and mend bones, and it was really as much as Walter had ever mastered.

More skillful wizards could, at some personal risk, connect themselves and send their spirit into the patient. Using such a technique gave the wizard much more control, as they could then use the body's own senses to inform and augment their magical senses. That was what I had done the first time I had used magic, when I possessed the Duke's horse, Star. I had done it again when Penny was dying, after being impaled by a ballista bolt.

The third level of healing was what Moira Centyr had taught me, and how I had actually saved Penny's life when wizardry alone was insufficient. I had listened to her body and made her body a part of myself, using her body's physical memory to restore her to the state of physical well-being. That level of healing required an archmage.

Today I faced several new problems, first being that I wasn't sure my body was well enough to survive the absence of my spirit for any period of time. The second problem was that I was unsure if I could fix her problem with wizardry alone, and my magical senses hadn't returned to the point yet where I could be confident in attempting to 'listen' to her body in that way. In fact I could barely hear even the earth, and it was normally the loudest of the voices in the world around me.

"Elaine, listen to me. In a moment you'll feel me start, and I'll need your help. I'm not very strong right now, so if you resist at all, I may not be able to do what's necessary. You feel as if you're suffocating, so a sensation of panic is entirely natural, but don't push me aside out of reflex," I said soothingly.

She nodded, her eyes watching me as she drew in rapid, shallow breaths. Closing my eyes I began, or I tried to anyway. With my eyes shut, my magesight seemed sharper, but it still wasn't as clear as I remembered. Elaine's body glowed with the force of her aythar, and it was made brighter still by her struggle to survive. Sending my thoughts outward, I tried to enter her body but found myself quickly rebuffed. It was hard enough to force myself out of my own form, but as soon as I came in contact with the raging torrent of her aythar, I snapped back into myself.

Part of the problem might have been that I had never attempted to do such a thing with another wizard, at least not while they were conscious, or still fully inhabiting their body. I needed to be stronger; I simply didn't have the power necessary to push my way inside. *There's a lot of power in the girl,* I thought. *It's a shame I can't use it.*

But perhaps I could, in a sense, if I tried to do what Moira Centyr had done to help me when I was trying to save Penny. Pushing my thoughts outward again, I sought Elaine's mind first this time, as if I were trying to establish a mental link with her. *Help me, draw me in.*

Her response was powerful, and I found myself caught, as her will latched onto me and pulled me inexorably inward. It was a sensation that was frightening, in large part because I had so little control over it. I was within her now, surrounded and engulfed by her power and simultaneously bombarded by the pain radiating from her lower body. There was a tightness in her chest and a feeling of weight, as though a heavy man were sitting upon her, making it difficult to breathe.

I needed to find the source of the problem. Luckily I already knew where to begin. *Follow me and watch,* I told her mentally. Narrowing my focus I delved inward. Using the pain as a starting point, I began following the veins leading from her ruined leg back toward her lungs, until at last I arrived at the obstacle causing her problem. A large clot had partially blocked the pulmonary artery leading from her lungs to her heart. If it had been completely blocked she would have already died, suffocating even as her lungs continued to work, unable to return oxygenated blood to the rest of her body.

Wasting no time, I opened the artery with sharp precision and forced the clot outside; her body could reabsorb it later. I might have broken it apart within the vessel, but I feared that smaller parts of it would block arteries further down or seed the formation of still larger clots. Her body briefly sent blood rushing out the opening I had created, until I had sealed it again. Whole once more, the vessel began sending the proper amount of blood back toward the heart, and I felt her breathing begin to slow as her body no longer had to struggle to keep itself alive.

Thank you, her thoughts came to me, along with a profound sense of warmth and affection.

Not yet, I answered. *There is much more to do.*

I wanted to restore her, completely, as I had with Penny. I didn't have the strength, but I knew how. *Don't panic when you feel the change. You will have a sensation as if you've become someone else; don't reject it. I need to become you.*

What?!

I listened. My own power was small, but she was full of strength, strength I needed if I was to mend her broken body. I couldn't use her power, but she could. Moira Centyr's words echoed through my mind as I remembered our conversation from long ago, 'An *archmage does not wield power, Mordecai. An archmage becomes that which they seek to wield.*'

What I was doing was dangerous. I had never sought to incorporate another sentient, conscious, human being as part of myself. The danger was similar to what I had done before, but the possibility that I might forget my own identity was greater. *Or is it?* I had no way of knowing. Pushing my doubts aside I listened, at first merely to the sound of her heart, beating solidly, more easily now that the clot was removed. Gradually I became aware of a vibration, a song, something bright and feminine. It was vibrant and alive, and as I became aware of it, it in turn became aware of me.

I was in touch now, not with Elaine's conscious mind, but with her very being, the core that gave rise to the thoughts and feelings she experienced. It was a primal thing, not to be lightly tampered with, for it was the source of life, consciousness, and perhaps even free will.

It was me.

And then I knew no more.

CHAPTER 32

I woke gradually, feeling a pleasant tension forming in my shoulders until eventually I was forced to stretch, arching my back. I felt uncommonly good, which was unusual, particularly because it was not an adjective I usually associated with waking up or morning. My body seemed rested and healthy. My memory was a little fuzzy though, and for some reason I thought that perhaps that should not have been the case.

Something told me that I should feel bad, but I wasn't really sure why. The door opened at that point and Penny walked in, her eyes immediately taking in my wakeful state. "You're awake!" she almost shouted.

"So are you!" I shouted back, thinking she deserved the same encouragement.

Then she started crying.

Damnitt! I chided myself inwardly. *I always manage to say the wrong thing, even when I don't know what might be wrong—or right, for that matter.* Seriously, it was a gift. I was the idiot savant of making women cry. You'd think that given complete ignorance of the situation, I'd at least have a fifty-fifty chance of saying something that would make her laugh, but it never seemed to work out that way.

I managed to untangle myself from the sheets quickly enough to catch her before she threw herself into the bed with me. Standing, I caught her in my arms as she ran toward me. It wasn't long before I realized her tears were of the 'happy' sort, which all things considered, is a bit better than the other kind. I considered myself a bit of an expert in diagnosing the different sorts of crying, since I had witnessed plenty of it first-hand.

I spoke soft, comforting words of no particular meaning, while I stroked her hair and held her close, giving her time to wind down. Over the course of my marriage I had learned that frequently tears were a type of stress relief for Penny. Me, I preferred to just go break something or simply ignore my feelings, they usually went away on their own after a while anyway. One of the many differences between us, I supposed.

At some point she gathered her wits together enough to begin a proper conversation, "I don't know whether to be mad at you for taking such risks or glad that you made it back."

I buried my nose in her hair, inhaling the soft fragrance of the woman I loved. "You're such a crybaby," I said affectionately. "I'm not even sure what happened," I added.

She growled into my shoulder, but I held her tight so she couldn't get enough space to take a swing at me. Well, I tried to hold her tight—the earth-bond had given her physical strength far beyond what I could handle. Our embrace turned into a one sided wrestling match, with me laughing as I lost. In the end I wound up flat on my back, in the bed, with her looking down on me. She had my arms crossed and pinned. Tears ran down her nose to land on my chest. I hoped they were tears anyway, the proper definition probably depended upon whether they had exited her eyes and run down the outside—or the inside, of her nose first. I suppressed that squeamish thought quickly.

"You are never to do that again! For anyone, do you hear me? Except for the children maybe, but not even for me!" she declared.

"Do what?" I asked.

"You don't even remember?!" she said, exasperated. "Typical. Elaine was hurt, do you remember that?"

Memories came flooding back then, the assault on the castle, my poisoning, Lady Thornbear's harrowing treatments—and Elaine's terrible wound. I remembered trying to heal her, up to a point, but then my recollection ended in a blank wall. "I don't know what happened," I said uncertainly. "It's all foggy. I started and then, somewhere in the middle I must've passed out."

"Well she certainly remembers enough for both of you!" announced my irritated spouse. "She said you surrendered your life to heal her."

"What?!" I asked, startled.

"You heard me. I didn't really understand it, but from how she described it, you somehow 'became' her, as in— you ceased to be you. She was able to use your gift to restore her body and yours, but she wasn't sure whether you would ever wake up. That was the part that really upset me," said Penny.

As she spoke I noticed that my magesight was back to what I considered its normal acuity, and the voices of the earth and the wind were back to their normal volumes. Whatever had happened, I seemed to be fully recovered. "That does seem foolish of me," I told Penny.

"You're damn right it was! And even worse, after it was all over, she apologized to me," added Penny.

Uh oh, I thought. "Apologized?"

"Yes. She told me she loved me, and that she understood your perspective better now," explained Penny.

"I don't suppose you would mind telling me what the hell that was all about?"

That led to an awkward explanation, but after I had finished Penny seemed to accept it. She even let me have my arms back.

"Next time you need to tell me these things from the beginning," she admonished me before relaxing and snuggling up close against me. "Were you tempted?" she asked then.

A lot, said my inner voice. My inner voice can be pretty stupid sometimes. "I was—a bit," I confessed.

She growled, "I think you need a reminder."

And remind me she did. It was fortunate that I was fully restored beforehand, or I might not have survived.

Later that day I finally got around to looking at the message box that Dorian had kindly brought for me. I had actually intended to look at it, and send a message, but at the time I had merely sought to distract him long enough to escape my room.

The jewel on top of the box was gently flashing, an indicator that it held an unread message.

Mordecai,

Forgive me for the lack of correspondence. Since the move to Agraden, I've been pre-occupied with setting up our new home. Marissa seems to enjoy being close to her family once again, though time and distance has made her a bit of a stranger to them.

I wasted no time looking for the ancestral home of the Gaelyn family, even though as you know that was only my secondary goal. The search was a little anti-climactic in fact, because as soon as I got around to asking questions, I found that its location was common knowledge here. The natives here call the area Drakon Perket, which I have learned means dragon's rest, or dragon's roost.

Given what we already know about Gareth Gaelyn, it seems obvious (at least to me) that he must have spent considerable time here after his transformation, which probably gave rise to the name. There are numerous stories here of people claiming to have seen a large beast. Until recently, they were largely regarded as stories produced by the overactive imaginations of children or unbalanced individuals, but a number of years ago quite a few people claimed to see the creature, rising from the earth. They don't laugh about it anymore.

I would like to make a trip there. It is only a matter of a few miles from here, but my health has begun deteriorating, creating difficulties. If things aren't too busy, you should consider coming to take a look. I know how engrossed you often are with your projects, but I really think that you might find some important bits of information here, and who knows what the Gaelyn family left behind? Apparently the locals here never go there, and those that try invariably wind up wandering without ever getting to the heart of the area. Sounds familiar doesn't it? ...Makes me think of your forgetful day in my father's library.

If you do manage to make the trip, perhaps we could go together—one more adventure, eh? I wouldn't be much use of course, and in my current state you'd probably have to practically carry me, but I'm still good for witty banter. I'd really like to see what's there.

I will close this letter for now. Marissa sends her love, as do I. Kiss the twins for me.

Marcus

Refolding the paper, I felt a familiar twinge of guilt, the guilt of a man who is too busy to keep up with his friends. I hadn't even gotten around to reading the book he had found regarding the Gaelyn family. He had left it for me at the house in Albamarl.

His remarks about his health were particularly troubling, because I knew he would have understated the problem, which meant he was very likely to be much worse. Yet I couldn't afford to leave now. My castle had been invaded. My people were returned, but many things remained to be fixed, and I could hardly leave them defenseless.

I shut my eyes and tried to relax. It was something I had gotten rather good at over the years. Much of my magic required a calm mind, lest my emotions affect my control. My breathing slowed and I began enumerating my problems. One, the two remaining human gods were my enemies, but they might be too afraid to face me directly. Two, the remnants of the shiggreth were still loose in the world, though I couldn't be certain of their numbers or whereabouts. Three, my castle was damaged and my people were fearful, having just survived an assault. Four, Lyralliantha was still locked away, and I couldn't decide whether I dared to release her.

Wait! What did I just list there? I ran the words over again in my mind. I knew they were strange, but frighteningly, they didn't seem so. The name was familiar. *Lyralliantha,* I thought, and an image presented itself within my mind, a young woman with soft silvery hair and vivid blue eyes staring intently at me. She was slender and something in her features made her seem ageless, and then I noticed her ears. They tapered to gentle points, making them slightly longer than would be normal for a human.

The sunlight set her hair to shimmering in the bright summer afternoon. The trees around us were immense, and yet they were spaced far enough apart to create islands of light amidst their shadows. She turned to me and I heard her voice, *"Whatever made you think I was human?"*

I bolted upright from my chair. *Was I sleeping?* Letting my eyes rove the room my heart began to slow to its normal pace. *No, I was awake. How could I forget? Lyralliantha was one of the She'Har.* The thought seemed normal, but I knew it was not. The door in my mind was open and things were spilling through, memories of times and places so far removed they could have no possible bearing on the present, not anymore.

I tried to focus my thoughts on Marc again, but the first thought that came to mind was the day he had handed me a certain wooden box, a box that had held the accord between humankind and the She'Har. *They broke it, it has no meaning anymore. It wasn't my fault.*

"I am losing my damned mind," I said aloud, hoping the sound of my own voice would help to ground me again. "The first thing I need to do is reassure the people. They will want to see that I am alive and still protecting them. Until I do that, I can do nothing else."

Clenching my jaw I shuttered away the unwelcome thoughts and penned a short letter to Marc. I kept it brief, congratulating him on his find and promising that I would try to find the time to visit soon. I deliberately left out the most recent events. It would have taken too long to write them out. That could wait for another day.

After I had finished, I rose and left. It was time and past for me to return to Castle Cameron. The people were back and they needed my reassurance. Taking a deep breath, I kept my steps firm as I walked down the hall. Confidence was the key.

CHAPTER 33

Two days passed relatively uneventfully. I kept Penny and the children hidden away in our private home while I continued to supervise the beginnings of the reconstruction. I still didn't feel that things were safe enough to expose my family, but there was no sign of any return by the gods.

Karenth still moaned and lamented his fate deep below, in the Ironheart Chamber. His power had been drained away and now was stored in the heavy iron surrounding him, forming an impenetrable prison cell. Later I would need to decide how the power should be used. While the structure and shape of his prison was very different than the God-Stone, the functional purpose was the same. It held his power, and if I didn't find a way to make regular use of it, he would eventually overload the capacity of the iron, resulting in an explosion of untold proportions.

My best estimation gave me several years before that was a risk however.

I met with Walter, Elaine and George, assigning George to help with the reconstruction of the damaged parts of the Castle. Walter and Elaine I tasked with taking turns keeping watch over the castle and Washbrook. I wanted someone there at all times, ready to reactivate the barrier if the worst should happen and Doron or Millicenth decided to pay a visit.

As they were leaving Elaine paused and looked back, "May I have a private word with you?"

"Certainly," I agreed, hoping the conversation wouldn't be too awkward.

Once her father and brother had gone, I shut the door and motioned to her to return to her chair. We had been sitting in one of the small meeting rooms of Castle Cameron. Resuming our seats, I waited to see what she would say.

An uncomfortable silence ensued while she gathered her courage. "I wanted to thank you," she said finally, "and to apologize."

I waved my hands as if to deny her words, "No. You have no need to apologize, especially after what you did for my family. Penny saw your acts in the hall. You defended my children as if they were your own."

"That doesn't change the fact that I stepped across boundaries that were not mine to cross. I let my own selfishness blind me to the fact that what I was doing would harm your family," she explained. "After what you did, when you healed me, I understood how wrong I was."

We hadn't actually spoken yet about the events of that day, so I still had many questions regarding what had occurred after I had lost consciousness. "About that," I began, "could you describe what happened for me?"

"You gave me what I had always wanted," she said with a wistful smile.

Myself?

She saw the look on my face and spoke before I could interrupt, "Don't be egotistical. I meant your gift, for a little while I could hear the voices of the world."

"If I went that far—why am I still here? You had everything," I suggested.

Elaine frowned, "Do I seem so shallow, so selfish? I have seen through your eyes now, and I understand better what drives you. I know that my—feelings, may have been wrong, but I am not evil. I cared for Penny, for your family, before—but once I had seen them through your eyes—how could I deny them their father? While you were with me, I didn't just possess your gift. I also saw them, your wife and family, in the light of your love. I had no other choice than to return you, to restore you, as you had done for me."

"I should have thought before I said that," I said, backtracking. "I knew you better than that, or I wouldn't have gone as far as I did."

She looked down, "Don't. Your kindness doesn't help, and that isn't what I came to tell you."

I was puzzled. "So what was it?"

"Before it was over, before I finished, I felt something in your heart, something that was part of you, but was also separate. But when I tried to look at it, to see it more clearly, I could feel it looking back at me, as if it were measuring me," she said. "It frightened me."

The only thing she could be relating was the hidden part of myself, the piece that held the secrets I dared not examine. I had never seen it quite as she described, but I knew it immediately. *You bear Illeniel's Doom.* The words echoed in my mind, though I wasn't sure where I had heard them.

"I asked you about this before, and you wouldn't answer me, but I understand now. That's where your secrets come from, isn't it?" she said without beating about the bush.

"Some things," I agreed. "Not everything, I think, but it's hard for me to know sometimes. I don't think it is quite as separate as you suggest. I think it's just a dark corner of my own mind. I just don't know how it came to know everything that it does."

"It knows," she replied darkly. "It knows how it got there."

I suppressed the urge to shudder. "Did you learn something from it?"

"No!" she said sharply, "It's just a feeling, but I'm certain that it knows."

"You keep saying that as if we were talking about something foreign. I think it's just another part of my 'self'. Some sort of bloodline memory perhaps, passed down from my father, but still a part of 'me'," I explained.

"You may be right," answered Elaine, "but I think you should be wary."

That's all well and good, but how, do you propose that I be wary of myself, I thought wryly. "I'll try," I said placatingly.

⋲──────⋺

That evening I reread Marc's letter. The more I thought about it, the more anxious I was to see him. Things seemed to have stabilized at home, and I began to worry that if I waited very long it would be too late. I sat down in my study to pen a response letter to him.

> *Marcus,*
>
> *My last letter was too short. I omitted most of the recent events here, mostly because I didn't want to worry you about things you couldn't fix. Things have calmed down, and I've decided to make a trip to Agraden. I'll catch you up when I see you. It really is too much to write.*
>
> *Expect me in two or three days.*
>
> *Mordecai*

I folded the small sheet and put it into the box, and then I leaned back and tried to think about how I would explain my reasons to Penny. The more I examined my motives, the more selfish they seemed.

Fifteen minutes later I had given up and I was about to leave my study when I noticed the light flashing on the message box. It was unusual to get such a quick reply. Opening the box I found a small torn piece of parchment, hastily scribbled with a message. It wasn't in Marcus' handwriting.

Dear Mordecai,

Please forgive the condition of this note. I had not the time to find a more suitable medium to write upon. My husband is no longer able to respond. His illness has worsened and he is now confined to his bed. He drifts in and out of consciousness, but I will endeavor to make him understand you are on your way.

Sincerely,
Marissa Lancaster

The room seemed to sway around me, and I could hear my heartbeat pounding in my ears. *This can't be happening.* I stood and stared blankly at the wall as a terrible urgency swept over me, and then my paralysis snapped and I found myself moving. Acting almost without thought, I gathered up the things I thought I might need, my staff, my belt and its special pouches, my stylus—then I stopped.

"I have to tell Penny."

Mercifully I was able to reach her without meeting anyone else, particularly my children. I wasn't sure I could hide the powerful surge of emotions from them just then, and the last thing I wanted to do was frighten them. They'd been through enough recently.

"What?!" she said immediately. I suppose my face had given me away already.

"It's Marc," I began, and over the course of the next ten minutes I explained as much as I could, though of necessity my story was far from complete.

"I don't understand. What did you say is wrong with him?" she interrupted.

Struggling to remain patient, I repeated myself, "It's an illness called the 'grey wasting', an affliction that affects those who have been possessed by one of the gods."

"And how do you know this again?"

I was moving already, heading for the door. "I have to go, dearest," I said as I went.

She saw the look and she already knew there would be no dissuading me. "Let me grab a few things. I'll come with you."

That made me pause for a moment. Penny's face was earnest, and the sincerity in her features reminded me again why I had loved her for so long. Sadly I replied, "You can't."

"The hell I can't..." she started, and then Irene woke from her slumber and began to cry. "Dammit!" she exclaimed and then our eyes met again. Hers were filling with tears as she picked up our daughter and began to rock her gently. She had forgotten for a moment, but reality had reminded her quickly enough, our burdens were not so easily neglected.

I took a moment to kiss my wife and run my fingers across Irene's soft hair, and then I turned away.

"Tell him I love him!" she said urgently as I left. I nodded and after I closed the door I heard her crying gently through the door. Marcus had been her lifelong friend as well, and it wasn't fair that she had to remain behind.

Gritting my teeth to hold back my own tears I headed to the circle that Walter had created, the one that led to Lancaster. There were a few more people I had to tell.

***

My arrival in Lancaster was greeted with no fanfare. No one expected me, and the guard at the circle building knew me well enough that he simply waved me on with a courteous bow and a 'good day'. There had already been considerable traffic between Cameron and Lancaster over the past day or two, as Walter and George traveled back and forth, carrying Lady Thornbear and a variety of news in both directions.

"Where is Roland?" I asked the footman at the door to the main hall. Since James' elevation to the monarchy the day to day business of handling the duchy had fallen into his younger son's hands. Traditionally the elder son, Marcus, would have gotten the job, but he had disavowed his inheritance years before. Marc's sister, Ariadne, was the older of the two remaining children, but tradition meant she would only inherit the title if her younger brother died or was deemed unfit.

Roland was fit enough, though he truly didn't want the job. Over the past several years he and Ariadne had taken it in turns to manage the day to day affairs, allowing each of them long periods to escape the demands of leadership. Naturally this had led to much discussion about who would eventually succeed their father, not just as Duke (or Duchess), but also as monarch.

"I believe His Highness was last seen at the stables, Your Excellency," answered the guard promptly and with perfect etiquette. The Lancasters had taken more effort in training their staff in proper graces. At Castle Cameron many of my retainers were a bit fuzzy on the proper forms of address, nor was it really a priority of mine.

I gave the man a nod and followed his advice. Roland loved horses just as much as his father had, or my father, for that matter. I found him quickly enough, brushing down a lovely white palfrey. As a prince of the realm, or a duke's son, for that matter, he had no need to groom his own horses. He did it simply for the pleasure of the task.

Growing up, Marc's younger brother had been eight years younger than we were, which meant we hadn't really been close playmates. Instead, he had looked up to us while for our part we had probably been a bit cruel in trying to leave him out of our games when we could. Looking at him now, I was amazed at how much he looked like my friend. His hair was a darker shade of brown and his eyes a light blue. He was taller and broader across the shoulders than his older brother. In many ways he was more handsome, though he did not possess quite as much charm as Marc; but then few had that.

"Ho, Roland!" I called out, since he seemed unaware of my approach.

He turned and gave me an easy smile, "Mordecai! How goes it?"

"Well," I answered giving him a quick embrace.

"I did not think to see you out and about again so soon. Lady Thornbear said you were close to death but a few days ago. How is it that you look so hale?" he asked.

"My recovery was speedy thanks to her timely treatment, and Elaine was able to restore me completely once the poison had run its course," I said succinctly, summarizing an hour's conversation in one brief sentence. "Is your sister at home?"

"She is not. Father requested her presence in the city two weeks ago. She has been assisting him with the finances of our fair nation. Some of his other ministers proved to be less than trustworthy," he replied. It was a statement that covered a much larger story I was sure, but I had no time for that either.

I was disappointed, for I had not seen her in almost a year, but I moved on quickly. "I was hoping to catch you both at home, but this simplifies things. I bear ill news of your brother."

Roland set the brush in his hand down and motioned for one of the grooms to take his place. "Perhaps we should walk outside," he suggested.

I followed him out. The early afternoon sunshine seemed a stark contrast to the dark news I had to share. "Your brother is dying," I said, as I embarked upon an intense description of Marc's situation.

Marc had informed his family of his move but not of his health, so my information was a serious shock to Roland. Unfortunately I didn't have the time to allow him to adjust gradually. "I plan to visit him as quickly as possible; do you want to come with me?" I said at the end.

He looked uncomfortable, "Father left me in charge here…"

"Your seneschal can manage for a while. We can be there within three days and the return will be instant once I construct a circle there."

"But…"

"This is it Roland. You won't see him again," I said bluntly.

He straightened and squared his shoulders before nodding, "Let's go."

Taking only the time it required to notify his staff of our departure, we were in Albamarl within half an hour.

CHAPTER 34

You haven't actually said how we are going to travel—have you?" asked Roland uncertainly.

I glanced back at him; we were ascending the stairs that led to the top of Traveler's Pinnacle. "No, I don't believe I did," I agreed.

"The reason I mention it, is because we're taking the stairs 'up', and if you intend to travel by horse, then we should probably be going *down*," he said nervously.

I smiled at him, which did nothing to put him at ease. Of course I knew I was driving him mad with my reticence, but as it often did, dark circumstances brought out an equally dark sense of humor in me. Marc dying was certainly one of the darkest things I could imagine, though I was doing my best not to think about it. Instead I gave myself over to enjoying Roland's unease.

"Unless we're just going up to pick something up— before we leave," he added anxiously. "Is that what we're doing?"

"No," I said.

"No, what?"

"We aren't traveling by horse. It would take a week, assuming we didn't get lost," I replied.

He slipped for a moment on the stairs before catching his balance. "I didn't realize you had already put a circle in Agraden," he commented, clearly hoping that was the case. "Seems like the top of such a tall tower is an odd place to put a circle," he observed.

I laughed, "It certainly would be."

Emerging from the doorway, we found ourselves at the top of Traveler's Pinnacle. As it often did, the view took my breath away for a moment. The wind at this height was fierce and it threatened to make us stumble as we moved into the open. There was no real danger, for we were still ten feet or more from the edge, and there were six foot stone battlements around the edges. Well, the merlons rose to six foot, with crenels four foot in height between them.

Roland looked distinctly pale.

"You don't like heights very much do you?" I noted.

"Not at all," he answered honestly.

He won't like this then, I thought, and reaching into one of my enchanted pouches, I brought out a stone disc heavily marked with arcane symbols. Holding it in front of me I let go, using my power to keep it motionless in the air before me. "We need to step back a few feet," I suggested, using my hand to indicate the direction we should move.

"Why did you ask about my fear of heights?" asked Roland.

I put a finger to my lips, "One moment, I need to concentrate." Extending my staff, I used it to tap the stone disc where it hung six feet in front of us. It broke into twenty-eight separate pieces, which began to move steadily apart, maintaining a pattern relative to each other. They continued expanding even as we stepped further back, until they had formed a circular shape roughly twelve feet across. The edge of the circle was bounded by twelve pieces, while six pieces formed a hexagon three feet above the circle, and another six formed a similar shape below it. Fields of magical force filled the wide spaces between the stones, although they were entirely invisible to normal sight—such as Roland's.

"What is that?" he asked wondrously, forgetting his fear for a moment. He saw only a collection of stones hovering in a strangely rigid formation. My senses showed me something a bit different; a disc-like polyhedron formed of magical planes of force, twelve foot across and four foot thick in the middle.

I hesitated to answer his question, for I knew the truth might cause him to panic. "Are you wearing your necklace?" I asked suddenly.

"Yes."

"Would you let me see it for a moment?" I told him.

Uncertain, he reached into his shirt and pulled it out. I motioned for him to hand it over and waited as he struggled to unclasp it. Once he had placed it in my palm, I took him by the shoulders and said, "It's a flying machine."

"What!?" Roland's expression was priceless.

"Well, it isn't actually a 'flying' machine; it's more of a force structure to protect us from the wind, while I move us through the air. Obviously if we just got inside and pushed it off, it would drop like a stone," I said whimsically.

"Why are you telling me this? I'm not getting in that! I don't need to know," he shouted. His eyes were showing entirely too much white now.

I nodded understandingly. "I had to tell you. It would be unethical for me to take you on a trip like this without telling you how we would be traveling beforehand."

"No need, I've decided to...," he began.

"*Shibal,*" I muttered softly, leaning forward to catch Roland as he slumped toward the stone floor. "What were you saying?" I asked aloud. When he didn't reply, I answered myself, "He seems to have fallen asleep."

Uttering a command word, I caused one of the disc's invisible panels to disappear for a moment, allowing me to drag Roland forward and place him carefully inside. He had quite a bit of muscle on him, so I was forced to use more magic to lift and guide him inside, otherwise it would have been a very awkward struggle. Sitting next to him inside, I closed the panel, sealing us within the strange device.

I hadn't counted on Roland's fear of heights. My bravado had more trouble overwhelming my own good sense when I didn't have an audience. What I hadn't told him, was the fact that I had never actually flown this creation of mine. There had been some discussion with Penny, who had strongly discouraged my flying ambitions. She seemed to feel that flying was firmly the province of birds, and not something to be trifled with by the likes of man. She counseled me that my children needed their father and that if I were to survive a crash of any sort, she would make sure that whatever remained inside my injured body, got its own chance to see the outside world.

She could be very poetic.

In truth however, I probably would have gone ahead with my ideas, if it weren't for the fact that the notion made me nervous as well. My wife's objections merely put the final nail in the coffin. I didn't consider myself afraid of heights per se, but I had a healthy respect for them, and from what I had read in the Illeniel library, many wizards had suffered unexpectedly quick ends to their careers while experimenting with flying.

Perhaps I should run through the basics. Historically, wizards had found a number of different methods to achieve flight, the most basic involved simply using magic to control the air around them, using it to lift and move them. A common variation of this included altering the wizard's mass; making it easier to fly—this involved its own extra problems though.

A few individuals had accomplished the task in a far different manner, primarily by transforming themselves, either wholly, or in part, into various naturally flying creatures. Most of those individuals had been members of the Gaelyn family, whose natural affinity for transformation magics was well known. Gareth Gaelyn for example, was still living, so to speak, albeit as a dragon. His refusal to return to being human was one excellent reason I wasn't particularly interested in that method.

The only other methods all involved a variety of devices, either temporarily enspelled or permanently enchanted to solve some of the problems that went along with flight. Some of the most spectacular deaths had resulted from a few of those ideas, and a number of amazing triumphs as well. Geoffrey Mordan had purportedly created a sort of giant kite that allowed him to glide through the air at great speed, while conserving his magical strength for use in propelling him through the air and controlling the direction of his flight.

In fact, many of the most successful devices were flown by members of the Mordan family, not necessarily because of any particular skill in enchanting, but because of their family gift, which happened to be a sort of intuitive teleportation. Most members of the Mordan line could teleport virtually at will to any location they were able to see. Those with the greatest gifts could also transport themselves to any place they had been before. While teleportation was technically possible for any wizard, only the Mordan family seemed able to manage it without working through a whole slew of mathematical calculations. They seemed to be born with an intuitive ability to handle the calculations subconsciously, while the rest of us were forced to do it by hand.

Because of that ability, they were able to survive many of the mistakes that violently ended other wizards' aspirations for flight.

Another amazing success had been one of my ancestors, Demandred Illeniel, who had built an entire sailing ship that could fly. He had been a skilled enchanter and had invested almost five years of his life into designing and constructing the massive vessel. It had been modeled after a carrack and had supposedly been over a hundred feet in length with three masts for sails. Demandred had suffered a number of setbacks before finally getting his ship 'sailing' per se, largely because flying and sailing were very different endeavors, but he had eventually managed to adapt his design until it was workable. The end result made him famous for a number of years, until he finally set off on an expedition to explore the unknown wilds of the world. He had never returned.

I hadn't been particularly enamored with any of their designs. Geoffrey Mordan's style seemed likely to get me killed, and I had no intention of spending five years building a massive floating ship as Demandred had. There was also the fact that his ship was limited to the speed provided by the wind alone.

My idea had been to create something simple that would enable me to fly in the manner of a wizard who wasn't using any outside devices. What I had created was essentially an aerodynamic shell that would protect me from wind and give me a much larger surface to push against with the wind. I could have done something similar with a temporary spell to create a shield around myself, but this allowed me to keep my attention firmly on controlling our flight and propelling us through the air. It also circumvented the biggest problem Geoffrey Mordan had complained of, which was that at a certain speed the wind buffeting him made it difficult to breathe.

"I hope you're ready," I said to my unconscious passenger, and then I began a spell that would allow me to control the wind around us. I could have done it more easily by speaking with the wind directly, but I didn't intend to use my abilities as an archmage unless my own strength proved to be insufficient.

Quelling the fear that suddenly sent my heart surging into my throat, I used the wind to send my invisible craft rushing up and out over the wide world. My own fears had kept me from doing it before, but desperation had finally provided the impetus I needed.

Holy shit! What have I done!? screamed my inner voice. I might have shouted the words aloud, but my jaw was clenched so tightly I could do nothing to open it. The world beneath us was vivid and bright, as though it had been painted by a giant with a mad passion for color. Blue sky, white clouds, verdant fields, and everywhere the sun reflecting from surfaces that refused to be bound by simple colors. Adrenaline had sent my mind into overdrive, and the world was infused with a clarity that we often talk about but seldom experience.

The sensation of movement, of acceleration, was incredible, and I knew in that moment that I had discovered a new passion. The first minute passed, and my heart rate began to return to something a bit closer to normal as we raced along, driven by a wind that my mind pushed ever harder, giving us a speed unimaginable.

A viewer from the ground would have seen two men, one sitting and the other lying flat, moving rapidly across the sky, if they had noticed us at all. I gained altitude and speed rapidly, putting ever more force into the wind so as not to lose the feeling of acceleration. My face brightened, as I experienced a feeling of pure exhilaration such as I had never known.

The earth below us was moving by lazily, despite our prodigious speed, and I found myself fascinated by the vast distance between us and the ground. *I should get closer and see how fast it appears to move then,* I thought. Adjusting the wind, I applied a small downward pressure on the front of our 'craft' and discovered one of the reasons why so many wizards died trying to fly. Our speed at that point was impossible for me to calculate, but I'm sure it was many times faster than any bird I had ever seen flying, and when I applied my downward pressure at the front it caused my craft to dip suddenly.

The air that had been flowing smoothly over the top now hammered the oblique surface, and some of our forward motion was converted into a chaotic spin. Being only human, I tried to stop it, and my reactions made things worse. In less than a second, we went from flying smoothly at immense speed to dropping like a stone, spiraling and spinning out of control, and the violence of our uncontrolled flight rendered me incapable of knowing which way was 'up'.

I had no way of knowing how much time was left before we struck the ground, but I was certain it would be sooner than I expected and probably with enough force to destroy any protections I might try to use. Even if I managed a shield that was strong enough to protect us, the violence of our stop would probably kill us anyway. I had learned that lesson first hand in treating the wounds of my knights who wore armor that was nigh invulnerable. The human body required gentle treatment.

Giving up my attempts to control our flight or stop the spin, I instead activated the second enchantment built into the stones that made up my nearly invisible craft. I had read the stories and concluded that there was a chance I might wind up in a situation such as this; though once we had started flying I hadn't really believed it was possible. It had seemed so simple, and completely under my control. Thankfully my cautious nature had provided a possible means of survival.

The rapid spinning had thoroughly disoriented me, and I doubted I could have managed even a simple bit of magic at that point, but my enchantment only required the utterance of a single command word, *'lyrtis'*, which was Lycian for 'feather'. The magic reduced our mass to a tenth of what it had previously been, and that meant the overall density of my twelve foot in diameter disc was now very low. We were still falling, but now air resistance was a much larger factor than gravity and inertia. The result was a rapid decline in our downward velocity and slowing of our spin. In no more than a few tens of seconds our spin stopped entirely, and our precipitous fall had become nothing more hazardous than the gentle decline of a leaf drifting in the wind.

As the stark terror receded from my mind, I became aware of a loud shrieking sound; though perhaps screaming would have been a better description. The turbulent brutality of our recent fall had awoken my passenger, who seemed none too happy about our current situation. His voice had already faded, largely owing to the fact that Roland's lungs were empty, and he had thus far been unable to stop yelling long enough to draw a fresh lungful of air.

The younger son of the Lancasters looked to be in terrible condition. His face was marked with blood (probably from striking the walls of our craft while unconscious), and his eyes seemed on the verge of rolling up into his head. *He is never going to forgive me for this,* I told myself, but in reality I was more worried he might relay the tale of our near death to Penny.

"Calm down, everything is alright!" I shouted at him, in a voice that was guaranteed to do nothing more than increase his panic.

The words seemed to help. He stopped screaming long enough to take a long shuddering breath before yelling back at me, "What the fuck is going on?!"

"Don't worry," I told him, more calmly now, "We had a bad turn, but everything is better now."

"How the hell did I get up here?" he shouted, "And what part of this is better? Are you mad?!" And then he threw up.

I'll rephrase that, he didn't *just* throw up. He projectile vomited. I'd almost swear he was aiming for me deliberately (which perhaps was justified). A warm deluge struck me full in the chest, and I fought my own recently abused stomach for control of its contents as well. I had always had a strong stomach though, and it didn't fail me then.

"Dammit!" I cried out. The smell was terrible, and I knew I couldn't fly the rest of the way to Agraden without cleaning myself off. "Now, I'm going to have to land!" I declared.

"Thank the gods!" said Roland, which irritated me even more.

"Go back to sleep," I told him, and then I made certain of it. I knew if I landed, I'd never get him back aboard, so I figured I'd pre-empt his refusal.

Letting the magical craft continue its descent, we landed gently in a small field near a farmer's croft. Roland was dozing comfortably, and thanks to his strong stomach muscles, most of the contents of his belly had landed on me. The rest wound up on the ground when I dismissed the enchantment that created the fields between the stones of my airship. I lowered Roland gently to a nice grassy spot, while the stones moved slowly back together; reforming the small stone disc they had originally been a part of. Once it was complete, I slipped it back into my pouch.

Using magic I cleaned my clothing as well as I could, but somehow the smell lingered. I needed water. I probably could have brought some up from beneath the ground, or created a small downpour, but sometimes simple was the best solution. I left Roland snoozing and walked to the farmer's house.

As I approached I saw an old man in the yard, carrying a heavy bucket toward a pen. At a guess he was taking slop to the pigs. He stopped when he saw me walking up and waved at me. "Hallo, young man!" he said cheerfully, as if I were an old acquaintance rather than a complete stranger.

I smiled back, "Hello, old man!"

"Oh! You're not Sammy," he said abruptly.

"I'm afraid not," I admitted, "I'm just a traveler looking for a bit of water."

"There's a pump over there. You're welcome to help yourself," he replied genially, before lifting his bucket again. The weight of it was a problem, and I could see he had struggled to get it this far.

"Let me get that," I offered, and after a moment's resistance he let me have it.

"I guess it's alright to let you young ones help out now and then," he said, as I carried it over to the pen and emptied the contents into a slop trough for the pigs.

I came back and put the empty bucket near his front door. "It's the least I could do since you're sharing your water with me."

"That's nothing I wouldn't do for anybody, and you smell like you could use some," he answered, wrinkling his nose.

I took a moment to look him over. His hair was mostly gone, leaving his pate bare, and what was left sprouted in gray tufts around the sides of his head. His eyes were a soft brown, but they wandered as he spoke, as though he were having trouble deciding where they should rest. I had no idea of his age, but he appeared to be quite old, possibly into his eighties, which was a very respectable age for someone living such a hard life.

I washed my face and considered removing my shirt so that it could be rinsed, but the prospect of wearing wet clothes wasn't particularly appealing. Perhaps I could dry it afterward using magic.

While I considered my options the old man came closer, "You smell like dog vomit," he said helpfully. "Let me get you another shirt."

His offer was generous. Clothing wasn't cheap, especially for a poor farmer. His age made me suspect his wife was probably already gone, and my senses had already confirmed that we were the only people within a mile or two of his home, aside from Roland. "You don't have to do that," I replied hastily.

"Nonsense, you don't want to keep wearing those things. Do you need some pants as well? I think you might be close to my son's size," he said.

The mention of children made me feel a bit better. "Is he the one you mistook me for?" I asked.

"Yeh, it is. He comes to visit me now and again, just to check on his old dad. He and his wife live about ten miles off—down that way," he said, pointing in a generally westerly direction.

We talked for a few minutes and I eventually accepted his offer, on the condition that he keep my own shirt and trousers in return for his extras. They were of a much higher quality material than his own, so I hoped he would benefit from the trade. The clothes he gave me were rough but clean and they fit well enough, although the pants were a bit short for my long legs.

During the course of our conversation, I determined that his eyesight was severely limited, though his ears and nose were sharp enough. He hadn't noticed the crest sewn into my shirt or the quality of my other belongings. That alone would have tipped off most people regarding my social stature, but I appreciated being treated as a normal person for a change. I couldn't help but wonder if my own father might have been similar in demeanor if he had reached such an age.

After I had changed, I spent a few minutes talking to the old man while I tried to think of some way of repaying his kindness. I could have left a few pieces of gold but he'd probably have had some difficulty spending them without being robbed.

"You're not from around here are you?" he asked, breaking my train of thought.

"No sir, I live in Washbrook, in the county of Cameron. It's way to the north of here, near the border with Gododdin," I answered honestly.

The old man's eyebrows went up, "You really are a far ways from home. Did you travel by that new road the Count is building?"

"The World Road?" I said, surprised.

He nodded, "I think that's what they're calling it. It's supposed to open up the whole world. That wizard, the Count di'Cameron, is building it. Leastwise that's what my Sammy told me last year."

"It isn't open yet," I told him, "but I have heard that it should be soon. What do you think of it?" I was curious now. It was rare that I got the opinions of someone who didn't have good cause to want to please me. As we talked, I quietly focused my attention on his eyes, seeking the cause for his poor vision.

"Thought it was mad at first and my son did as well, but then he don't like the Count much neither," he said.

"Why's that?"

"He's a god fearin' man, was devoted to Celior before the church started having such troubles. He blames the Count; says the wizard killed his god, and that it'll bring doom on all our heads," explained the farmer.

I nodded, "I've heard that. What do you think?"

"Heh! I love me son, but he never was too bright. No way could any man kill a god. I've been around long enough to know how stories is—they get bigger with each tellin'. Whatever's wrong with the church is probably its own fault or mebbe' the fault of our heretic king."

That got my attention, "Heretic king? Are people saying that?"

The old man laughed, "People say all sorts o' stupid things. They say his son was favored by the Lady o' the Evenin' Star and that he turned his back on her. I dunno if that's true, but his father, our king, did toss the churches out o' Albamarl," said the old man, before adding, "That's enough to make him a heretic, if'n you care what the churches think anyhow."

"You don't sound as if you think much of the churches," I observed.

The farmer spit on the ground, "They never put no food on my table, and they wouldn't come when Mary was sick. That's my wife mind you—lost her almost twenty years ago now. She was always a pious woman, but they din't show their heads around here when she was ill. That wizard my son's always goin' on about, least he did something useful."

"What did you say your name was?" I asked.

"I din't, but my friends call me Buck, Buck Shadley," he said amiably. "Anyways, that wizard, he fought off the armies o' Gododdin', an that was accordin' to the old king, who didn't seem to care much for him, so you can bet it was the truth. I dunno if I believe the stories about this road they're buildin', but if it's true, it can't help but be good."

"How's that?"

"If you've ever hauled your harvest to market, you'd understand. A road like that makes it better for everyone and easier to sell food where it's needed, though 'm sure the ones makin' the biggest profits will be the merchants."

"You think it will help you out?"

Buck laughed, "I'm too old to do much or gain much, but it'd be a blessin' for my children who still have a lot of livin' left to do."

I coughed before standing up. "That might be true. It's been a pleasure talking to you, Buck. I don't suppose you'd let me pay you for the clothes? I have to be on my way."

"Nah, I wasn't usin' 'em, and Sam's got his own wife to sew and darn for him. My other kids are too far away to visit. You keep 'em and I'll be happy knowin' they're getting some use," said old Buck. "Sides, I'm too old to spend it."

I handed him a small pouch of coins. "Take this then," I told him.

"I told you I din't need any payment," he protested.

"It's a gift—for Sam," I explained. "Thank you for talking to me." Somehow the old man's words had made me feel much better about things. I might not have a solution for all the world's ills, but at least a few people thought I might be doing something good.

"Hmmph, alright then, though it don't seem right to take a payment for simple hospitality."

I smiled at him, "It was getting too heavy to carry anyway. Take care of yourself, Buck." I picked up my staff and started walking back toward where I had left Roland. I didn't turn back, but my magesight showed me that the old man was watching me until the trees obscured his vision.

I wondered how long it would be before he noticed that his eyesight had improved.

CHAPTER 35

"Good morning," I said, as Roland stirred beside the small campfire. "Did you sleep well?"

He groaned, "My mouth tastes as if something crawled in and died. What did I drink?"

Obviously he hadn't quite remembered the circumstances surrounding his last awakening. I handed him a cup containing watered wine, "Here rinse your mouth out."

"Where are we?" he asked, looking around at the dark and empty landscape.

"The southern desert, a short distance from Agraden," I replied.

Roland frowned. "How did I get here? Oh you bastard!" he said, standing up with a loud exclamation. "You tried to kill me!"

"I wouldn't go that far. I tried to make the trip as pleasant as possible," I protested.

"Pleasant?! Is that what you call it? I woke up being thrown around inside your invisible box and nearly broke my nose, and then I discovered we're miles in the air and falling to our deaths! That's supposed to be pleasant?" he yelled.

I did my best to keep my features calm. Roland was quite upset and it wouldn't do any good to laugh while he was still angry. He had actually been through a traumatic ordeal, especially for someone already deathly afraid of heights. "You're right, but you did repay me a bit for your suffering," I said blandly.

"Repay you?" he said, staring at me blankly. I plucked at my shirt to draw his attention to my clothes; his quick eyes took them in. "Are you wearing a peasant's tunic?" he asked.

I nodded. "I couldn't get the others to stop smelling, so I traded them to a kindly farmer."

"Smelling? Oh! Well it serves you right! What you did was despicable!" he finished, and I could see he was struggling to keep an angry expression on his face, but eventually a smile crept across his lips. "You were covered in it weren't you?"

"Mmm hmm," I said in agreement. "It was hours before I found a place to set down and clean up," I lied. As Marc might have said, 'a little embellishment never hurt anyone,' and in this case it served to make Roland feel a bit better about his inadvertent revenge.

He laughed and I joined him, letting the simple sound ease the tension between us. "How long did it take us to get here?" he asked, once he had finished snickering at me.

"Less than half a day," I told him. I might have been able to manage it in less time, but after our near death experience I had restricted myself to more modest speeds.

Roland let out an appreciative whistle. "As impressive as that is, there is no way I'm letting you put me back in that flying deathtrap of yours," he informed me.

"No need," I replied. "We can walk to Agraden in a half an hour from here, once the sun comes up. I'll make a circle to take us back to Lancaster or Castle Cameron after we…," I paused as the realization of why we were there struck home, "…after we're done," I finished. *Once your brother, my best friend, is dead,* said my inner voice.

I slept fitfully that night, while Roland slept not at all. He had had a very restful day already, thanks to my sleep inducing spells. The next day we started walking early. My companion woke me at the first light of dawn, probably out of spite, but I couldn't complain.

We hadn't brought anything in the way of supplies for camping or traveling, and there was very little food for breakfast. That might sound foolish, but I'd had no intention of making a long trip, and if we had run into serious problems securing food, we always had the option of creating a circle and returning home.

True to my word, I had put us close enough to the desert city that it was a short walk to reach the outer limits within a half an hour. While most of the landscape for many miles in most directions was barren, the city itself was situated in a lush oasis created by a natural system of springs that rose to the surface there.

From what Marc had told me previously, the home he and Marissa had settled into was located near the northern part of the city, in a district that also housed several of her relatives. Much to my confusion though, the city was an elongated elliptical in shape, with the longer distance stretching in an east-west direction. That meant 'northern' encompassed a lot of potential areas.

"I never imagined it would be so big," commented Roland, as we walked down one of the bigger thoroughfares. The buildings on either side of us were constructed of some sort of tan bricks, as almost everything we had seen was. The predominant color was a sandy brown, from the buildings to the road, and it might have been monotonous if not for the large palm trees and lush vegetation surrounding and infusing the city with a sense of vitality.

Remembering my geography lessons I replied, "I have heard that nearly a hundred thousand people live in or near Agraden."

"Do you intend to pay a visit to the Shah?" asked Roland suddenly.

The thought had not occurred to me. As a landed noble of Lothion, it would be considered mildly rude for me not to pay a courtesy visit—for the crown prince, Roland, it would be a diplomatic insult to ignore the Shah. None of that mattered though, if our presence went unreported. "I'm really not dressed for it anymore," I answered, plucking at my shirt. "But we should keep our identities to ourselves for now, just to be safe."

After asking directions several more times we eventually arrived at our destination. The house standing before us was one of the larger ones in the neighborhood, and I could tell from the front that it probably had a large inner courtyard as well as side buildings. *I wonder what I paid for this,* I thought silently. Marcus had used an open letter of credit I had given him to purchase whatever he needed. I wasn't surprised though; he had never been one to do anything by halves.

A servant answered the gate at our knock, and we were ushered into a pleasantly decorated courtyard. Several varieties of small palm decorated the perimeter, along with some broad leafed plants I didn't recognize at all. A large archway led into what I presumed was an area to stable horses, while the other side of the courtyard boasted a highly carved and ornamented set of wooden doors—the main entrance to the house itself. The center of it all was completed by a three tiered fountain, which strengthened the impression that we had arrived at a place of sanctuary and refuge.

Our wait was short. Only moments after the servant left, Marissa appeared, obviously glad to see us. Her features were composed, though her eyes seemed slightly swollen—a sure sign that she had been crying recently. What worried me far more than that was her choice in clothing; she was covered from head to toe in black, the near universal color for mourning.

She embraced Roland first, as was proper, and while I stood watching, I saw her face clench in unspoken grief. The scene was surreal, and it almost felt as if I stood outside of it looking in, watching the drama unfold while not really being a part of it. A moment later her arms were around me, and I embraced her calmly, my mind blank.

The first thing I noticed was the clean smell of her hair, even as her arms gripped me with a strength I would not have expected from her slender frame. Still I felt nothing, but I held onto her nonetheless, afraid for some reason to let go. Her body shook and the sound of loud, ungainly sobs reached my ears. I wanted to cry, yet I was helpless to reach the torrential core of my sorrow.

It was there—twisting my inner-self into an agony of turmoil, but a veneer of numbness seemed to be shielding me from experiencing it directly. I still held Marissa, but finally I found my voice, "When?"

"Early this morning, not long after midnight," she replied, squeezing me tighter.

If we hadn't stopped we probably would have been here, the unbidden thought rose in my mind. We should have continued into the city and gotten directions, even though it had been well past dark when we arrived. I had missed my last chance to say goodbye.

Marissa, now a widow, led us into the house and bade the servants to bring us tea. She offered breakfast as well, but none of us had an appetite. We sat in a silence that was fearful to contemplate.

"Where is he now?" asked Roland.

I had found him already with my magesight, but Marissa answered readily, "He's still in his bed. I've called for the undertaker, but he hasn't arrived to take him away yet. Would you like to see him?"

Roland politely declined, but after a minute or two I was unable to help myself, and I spoke up, "I think I'd like to see him, if that's alright."

"Of course it is," said Marissa, with wet eyes, "You were as much a brother to him as Roland."

I glanced at Roland, and he nodded as well, "I'll wait here, go ahead," he told me.

Entering the bedroom, the first thing I noticed was his color, his skin was unusually pale, almost grey. The muscles in his face had gone slack and he looked gaunt. I gazed on him for only a minute before I looked away. Instead I began taking in the details of his bedroom, not in a desire to pry, but curious about his recent life. Aside from a few books, and a lot of hastily written notes, there was little to see. On his writing desk I found a heavy leather-bound journal entitled, *'On the Nature of Faith and Magic'*. I knew immediately it must contain the primary focus of his scholarly work on magic over the past few years, but reading his papers would be a task for another day.

A chair on one side of the room bore his long coat. He had probably needed it in the evenings, for as I had discovered the night before, the desert could be quite cold at night. I set my hand on it, feeling the texture of the wool, and then I picked it up. Alone and unobserved, I sank into the chair and buried my face in the heavy garment. It smelled familiar and at long last my emotions broke free.

I wept like a child, drawing air in suddenly and releasing it with great, wracking sobs. Self-consciously, I tried to keep from making any sound as I cried, but my attempts only made it worse. My awareness of the world around me had shrunk, and I had become a solitary ball of misery, until I felt a warm hand on my shoulder.

Roland had entered unnoticed, along with Marissa. The two of them had their arms around me, and I found myself surrounded by them in an awkward three way embrace. It was the only comfort any of us found that day.

The rest of the week passed in a whirlwind. After eventually putting myself back together, I created a circle to Albamarl. Informing James of his eldest son's death was one of the hardest things I could remember having to do.

Marcus was buried in Agraden the same day that Roland and I had arrived, but James held a memorial service for him a week later. It was a private affair, attended primarily by the Lancaster family and those of us in Cameron who were close to Marc. I was asked to speak, and I did, but to this day I still can't recall a thing I said.

My second biggest shock came a day after, when Dorian and I had our first chance to talk alone. He had seemed tense ever since receiving the news, but I had attributed this primarily to grief; and not just grief over Marc. He had also lost over half of his knights only a few days prior to our friend's death. All of them had been men he had worked closely with for years. If anyone had reason for mourning, it was Dorian.

"It just doesn't seem possible," I told him, hoping to draw him out. He had been very reticent of late.

"Yeah," said Dorian, his face could have been made of stone.

I put a hand on his shoulder. "It's just the two of us," I reminded him, "You don't have to try and imitate Cyhan."

His eye twitched for a moment. "Alright, I'll spit it out then," he replied, brushing my hand away from his shoulder. His body radiated tension and he seemed angry.

"What?"

"You weren't thinking clearly, and I'll forgive you down the road, but what you did was wrong," said Dorian in a voice that shook with barely suppressed emotion.

I stared at him in shock. *What the hell did I do to him?* I couldn't remember the last time I had truly upset Dorian. It wasn't something I expected.

"When you got word that he was dying, you left without telling me a damn thing. You found Roland, but I didn't merit telling. I had to find out after you had already gone," he bit out.

I held out my hands. "I was in a rush Dorian. I wasn't thinking."

"I know that!" he shouted suddenly. "I found out second hand. You never considered that I might want to be there too."

"We didn't make it in time anyway. It wouldn't have done any good for you…," I began.

"That's not the point, damnitt!" he interrupted me. "You should have told me. You should have given me a choice. You never even considered my feelings. Did you think you were the only one that cared about him? He was my friend too!" Dorian's face was flushed and his cheeks were wet with tears.

That was when it finally sank in. Of course my untested magical flyer was too small for three people, but what my friend had said was essentially true. I had never considered him, not at all. I had gotten the news and left without a word to anyone but Penny.

"And then, you tell me after, that he knew he was dying—before he even moved! You kept that a secret from me as well! What the fuck Mort!? Do you think I'm so unimportant I don't deserve your trust?" he yelled, putting emphasis on each word.

I trust you as much as anyone alive, I thought quietly. "He told me to keep it a secret, Dorian. That wasn't my choice."

"He was an asshole too! Both of you!" The tears were streaming down his face now.

I hugged him. "I'm sorry. You're right."

Even angry, he hugged me back, though for a moment I thought he might break my back, and then he shoved me away. "I'll get over this, but I'd rather not see you for a few days."

CHAPTER 36

The ensuing months were placid and calm; a boring counterpoint to the terror of the gods' attack on Castle Cameron. Marc's death was followed, not with more challenges and obstacles, but with a lack of them, which only increased my anxiety and heightened my depression.

Losing my closest friend had deeply affected my mood, largely in ways that weren't immediately obvious. After the intense grief of the first few weeks, I put it out of my mind as I attempted to focus on living and carrying on with life. The work on the World Road proceeded at an admirable pace, and after nearly a year the day had finally arrived when we would open the gates and connect the far flung corners of Lothion to one another.

I should have been happy, and I tried to appear so, as best I could, but my inner heart felt dead and cold. Penny had noticed my depression of course, despite my best efforts to act normally. She questioned me about it, and while I was honest about my grief initially, once the first month had passed, I began to excuse myself by citing anxiety over the whereabouts of the remaining two shining gods—and Mal'goroth. Let's not forget Mal'goroth.

In truth, I had plenty of reasons to be anxious. The shiggreth had completely disappeared, though I felt certain they were not eradicated. The Knights of Stone had been decimated, and after the attack we had been left with only seven remaining. Dorian had done his best to find suitable replacements, but he was picky in his choices, and I fully supported him in that. I'd rather have been short-handed than give power to men I didn't trust.

Dorian seemed to have gotten over his anger with me, but I still felt a faint coolness from him on occasion, and I knew it would take some time to completely heal the wound I had created in our friendship. We were both content at present to just get through each day and manage the tasks at hand. He had enough on his plate with the recent birth of his second child, little Carissa Thornbear.

In some ways it felt as though we were living under an executioner's axe, constantly waiting for it to drop on our necks. Even so, I knew deep down that my illness wasn't truly because of that. Marc was dead. While few realized how close we had been, to me he had been my closest family. Now the one person who knew me best was gone, and along with him went all the memories he alone had possessed.

Each of us has our own self-image, but what few realize, is that every person around us also possesses an image of us, no less real than our own. Every person close to us has a version of us in their hearts that no one else can replicate or replace. With Marc's death, I had lost not only my dearest friend, but the image of myself that he had shown me in his own life.

Or you could simply be an over-sentimental, over-analytical fool, who merely makes things worse by constantly philosophizing and romanticizing everything to infinity! Life goes on, and so would you if you didn't spend so much time gnawing at problems you can't fix. Move on! The words came to me with Marc's voice, as they often did these days. It said the things he would likely have told me, things that might have helped if he had been alive. Instead the memory of his voice brought tears to my eyes.

"What's wrong, Daddy?" asked Moira.

We were standing on a balcony overlooking the central yard within the keep that protected the World Road. The large gates on either side of the massive open area were open wide and crowds of people stood below, looking up at us. Two more gates within the yard were still closed, the ones that led down to the circular underground highway. King James was positioned in the center of the balcony, addressing the crowd. Penny and I were behind him, with Matthew and Moira on either side of us.

"It's nothing, sweetheart," I told her, "Daddy's just happy."

Penny glanced over at my words, and her eyes appraised me as I wiped away the tears. She knew better than to believe me. I have never been prone to crying when happy, and she was well aware of my depression, despite my claims otherwise. She stayed silent though, for every eye was directed toward us.

The King finished his speech and looked toward me, "Without further delay I present to you, Mordecai Illeniel, the Count di'Cameron, and our nation's most ardent defender—the man responsible for the conception and creation of this marvelous edifice!"

Stepping forward I stood beside him and placed my hands on the stone rail. "People of Lothion," I said, raising my voice, "long have I waited for this day, and at times I feared it would never come! Today we will open the gates and usher in a new era of prosperity. No longer will our traders and merchants need to devote weeks and months to long trips to carry goods from one end of this country to the other. No longer will farmers be forced to trek for days to reach the best markets. This dream, now a reality, will unite people from across our nation in a bond that transcends the distances which once kept us separate. It will transport goods from our ports and bring timbers from our forested lands. In essence it will form a vast artery connecting and transforming our land and our people with a new spirit of unity and optimism."

Taking a breath I paused to look across the crowd, and the look of wonder on their faces almost overwhelmed my reason. *Stick to what you prepared,* I reminded myself, and so I opened my mouth to continue, "It is my hope that someday this road will connect not just the people of our fair country, but the people of every country. There are many places along this road yet unoccupied, places which, if our resolve is strong and our intentions are good, will someday be occupied with gates leading to every nation in this world. The fullest realization of my dream will be when the rest of the world, looking upon our strength and unity, accepts this offer and joins hands with us."

At that point I stopped and waited upon James, who stepped forward again. "What do you think of the Count di Cameron's dream?" he shouted to the crowd. Their response was a deafening roar, one that was nearly impossible to decipher until it began to resolve into a rhythmic chant, 'Open the gates!' they cried. James listened for a moment before speaking directly to me, "The people have spoken, Lord Cameron. Open the gates!"

Reaching into my robe, I withdrew the control rod, a device which was a twin of the rod installed at the center of the Traveler's Pinnacle. The enchantment upon it ensured that whatever actions were taken upon this rod would be replicated upon the original, which actually controlled the gate enchantments themselves. The rod itself was steel, inset with a variety of multihued metal rings that encircled it from top to bottom. Each ring could be twisted from one position to another, which would then cause some action to take place. Many of the rings were set to control the activation of one of the portals, while others were set to open or close one of the many gates that guarded the World Road.

Twisting six rings in quick succession, I activated the portals that led to Verningham, Cantley, Turlington, Malvern, Lancaster, and Arundel. As I did, I felt a massive surge of power, the God-Stone, hidden and protected deep beneath the center of the fortress came to life, pouring aythar into the magical conduits that fed the portal and gate enchantments. There was no audible or visible sign of this, but my arcane senses were very aware of the vast movements of magic beneath us. Once the portals were activated, I turned two more rings, and the gates that would allow people to enter the roads leading down to the great circular World Road itself, opened.

The crowd grew silent for a moment as the massive iron doors opened, and then a cheer went up. The World Road was open, and people from all parts of the nation would soon be traversing it. At each of the six towns, smaller matching keeps protected the other ends of the portals, and the gates there were already open, waiting. Today would be a day that none would forget.

We withdrew from the balcony after that, though my work wasn't done. As momentous as the occasion was, it naturally had to be commemorated with a massive feast. Penny watched me carefully from the sides of her eyes as we went. "Are you alright, Mort?" she asked during a moment when there were no other ears close by.

"Yes, of course," I said promptly, giving my voice a lighter tone than I truly felt. "Why?"

She shook her head, "No reason, you just seem as though you have a shadow hovering over you."

As usual she had seen through my façade. "I'm just a bit pensive, worried about the future of the World Road. Nothing for you to be too concerned about," I replied, hoping to redirect her train of thought.

"If you say so," she said, but her tone implied she knew better.

*

The trees towering over me were massive, larger than anything I had seen before, but for some reason they seemed natural, and I hardly took note of them. Glancing down, I saw another hand in my own, a slender graceful hand, connected to an equally lovely arm. Following the arm to its conclusion, I realized I was walking beside perhaps one of the most beautiful women I had ever seen.

"Lyralliantha," I said softly, as her name sprang to my lips unbidden. *Why did I say that?* I wondered idly; normally I called her by her nickname, 'Lyra'.

"Yes love?" she replied easily.

"Do you think the council will accept our proposal?" I asked.

She frowned, "I do not know. It is still hard for me to accept, and I am in love with you. They will have a difficult time adapting to the notion that your kind are not simple animals, but once they see what you have created, they cannot do otherwise."

"It still isn't true spell-weaving," I told her again.

She nodded, "No, it isn't, but it is something new, something never seen before, and it is akin to spell-weaving, in a way."

A thought crossed my mind and I looked around anxiously, "You don't suppose they can hear us?" I said, indicating the mother-trees on either side of our path.

Lyra laughed, "They are sleeping. They hear nothing unless we awaken them. Do not fear." She leaned closer, and her lips met mine for a pleasant moment. "Perhaps that will distract you," she said, with a twinkle in her eyes.

I kissed her again, and my mind drifted away, the scene fading. When my eyes opened again it was to a different scene. People were screaming, dying, as open wounds appeared spontaneously on their skin. Some writhed on the ground, clawing at themselves even as they bled and died. My magesight showed me the cause of their affliction, but I was powerless to stop it, if I lowered my shields for a moment it would kill me too.

"Save us!" a woman cried, clawing at the shield of power I had extended around myself, but I looked away. I could not meet her terrible, dying eyes. Inside I knew the truth, *this was your fault! You caused this,* my inner voice accused.

Death was everywhere, a tangible thing, and I could smell it, taste it. Worse, I could hear it—a terrible dissonance that played in direct counterpoint to the harmony of the living world. I shut my eyes and clapped my hands to my ears, wishing I could shut out the sensation of it, but this was one voice I could not block out.

Screaming I sat up in bed, clutching my head to shut out the terrible sound of it. Penny was beside me, her arms around me. "Mort, wake up!" it's just a dream.

Desperate, I clutched her to me, burying my head in her neck hoping the sweet scent of her hair would drive away the vivid images that still floated before my eyes. She stroked my head, repeating soft, soothing words while I gradually began to calm down. Slowly I came to realize it had just been a dream, a horrible, terrifying and all too real dream.

No it wasn't, said a voice in the back of my mind. *It happened, and if you aren't careful, it will happen again.* The truth of it sank into me and I began to weep, softly at first, and then more loudly, as if I were a child again. Through it all, I heard the dissonant song of death, just as I had in the dream—only now I was awake.

"Is it Marc?" asked Penny gently, "Did you dream of him?"

"No," I said finally, my voice hoarse and thick. "It was the memories again." I had explained my strange memories to her before, after the visit with Marcus, when he had given me the tablet, but I still didn't understand them very well. Every time I began to examine them deliberately, fear seemed to clutch at my heart until I closed the door and shut the memories away again.

"You're having dreams about them now?" she said, concern on her face.

I nodded. *And I hear the voice of death now,* I added mentally.

"Why haven't you tried to examine them? Maybe they'd be less frightening if you let them see the light of day?" she suggested.

It was a completely rational suggestion, but at that moment I couldn't bear the thought of looking any closer at what lurked in the back of my mind—much like every other moment. Still, I knew I had to eventually face them, otherwise I'd go mad from dreams I barely understood. "You're right," I admitted.

She stared at me for a long minute.

"What, right now?" I said, flabbergasted.

"Is there a better time?"

"Certainly not in the middle of the night," I replied. "I'm still not sure I'll ever sleep soundly again after what I just dreamed about."

"Tell me about that then," she said reasonably. I hated it when she was reasonable.

I spent the next ten minutes describing my dream-memory as well as I could. Unlike an ordinary dream, which would fade upon waking, this one remained crystal clear. When I finished she gave me an odd look.

"I'm not sure how to feel about you dreaming about strange women," she said.

"I don't think it was *my* dream," I answered. "I mean it was my dream, but I think it was really someone *else's* memory. It's just stuck in my head somehow—and Lyra wasn't a woman, exactly."

"Now you're referring to her by her nickname," Penny teased, "but you certainly described her as a woman. You kissed her."

"Someone else kissed her," I protested, "I'm just remembering it, and yes, she's female—sort of, but she isn't human."

Penny's eyes narrowed for a moment, "She didn't happen to look similar to Elaine did she?"

"No," I said, mildly irritated, "she looked nothing like Elaine. She had silver hair, so white it seemed to shimmer, and her eyes were a light blue, like ice."

"That seems a bit unusual."

"No, all the people of her grove had hair and eyes like that," I remarked without thinking, "Their ears tapered to soft points as well."

"Her grove?" asked Penny.

"She was one of the She'Har," I answered, and then I realized that more information was coming out in my replies than I was consciously aware of. Unfortunately, the realization caused my mind to clamp shut in fear and nothing more was forthcoming.

"So who was it that knew her?"

I stared at her for a moment, confused.

Penny sighed. "I mean, whose memory were you reliving? Who was it that she kissed?"

It was the obvious question, but unfortunately I didn't have a good answer. "The problem is that when I'm remembering, I only remember what happened and what they were thinking. Most people don't think about their own names, or other useful details—like what year it was or where they were located, so I'm left guessing," I explained.

"But if you followed the memories far enough, you would probably eventually get those details—wouldn't you?" insisted my lovely wife.

"Most likely," I agreed. "I just haven't been able to force myself to do it. Plus there are so many—I can't be sure, but I get the impression that the memories span thousands of years and hundreds of different people's lifetimes."

"Surely it couldn't all be bad," said Penny.

"You're right, it probably isn't, but there's something really bad in the middle of it all. Every time I try to recall the reason why I have these memories—and I know that that fact is in there—every time I try to get close to it, I find something else," I told her.

"What about other things? Like Illeniel's Promise, or Illeniel's Doom—you mentioned those before, can you get near those memories?" she asked.

"They're all linked together," I said. "I try to stare it in the face, but my inner self instinctively flinches away whenever I get close."

"Well this woman Lyra, if she really is one of the She'Har, then your memories are at least two thousand years old," she noted.

I didn't respond. Closing my eyes I held Penny to me and tried to block out the dark song that seemed to persist around me at all times now. I had begun hearing it shortly after bringing Walter back from the brink of death, but it had only gained in volume since then. It seemed to portend something dark in my future. "I need to find out what these memories mean, but I have a side trip I intend to take first," I said at last.

"Side trip?"

"I need to explore the ruins of the Gaelyn household, near Agraden."

"You've waited almost a year since Marc's death, why now?" said Penny rationally.

I didn't have a good answer though, just a hunch. Whenever I thought about seeking the heart of my memories, or Illeniel's Doom—the dark song grew stronger. I had an intuitive feeling that whatever I found would lead to my ruin, or perhaps even my immediate demise. "It feels safer," I admitted, "And if I can find a way to convince Gareth Gaelyn to help us, it will gain us a mighty ally."

Penny giggled at my choice of words. "A 'mighty ally', eh? I think I'll stick with the one I already have. I'm married to the most powerful archmage in all the world," she teased, "perhaps in all of history." She was attempting to distract me from my dark thoughts.

"I don't think there's any way we can know that…," I said modestly.

Penny leaned in close to kiss me before responding, "Of course there is."

"Oh, really?"

"Definitely," she said, letting her hands roam.

My breath caught in my throat for a moment. "That isn't my staff," I informed her.

"I beg to differ sir…," Penny replied flirtatiously, "…like a mighty oak it grows!"

I snorted with laughter and began to choke, "I can't believe you just said that! Do you know how corny that sounded?"

"You should be grateful for my witty bedroom banter," she answered, before kissing me again.

I was still laughing, "You can't see the forest for the tree."

She snickered into my neck, "And you say my jokes are bad."

We told one another bad jokes for several minutes before we were finally unable to continue, having run out of good, or even bad lines. We had better things to occupy ourselves with anyway.

CHAPTER 37

Explain to me why we're here again?" said Dorian. We stood on a low rise, overlooking the remains of the place that had once been the Gaelyn household. It was a desolate location, dry and rocky. It might have been uninhabitable but for the oasis that was only a few miles distant. The people who had lived there had probably relied upon wells that tapped into the aquifer that rose close to the surface in this region.

"This was the last thing Marc investigated before his death. He thought there might be leftover relics of their magic or even books. The magic protecting this place prevented him from entering before he died. I'm here to find out for certain," I repeated, since my friend had obviously not paid close enough attention before, and then I added sarcastically, "You're here because my wife thinks I need looking after."

Dorian grinned, "You do take a lot of watching."

"Is that what you were doing last night?" I shot back amicably. "It seemed a lot more like you were trying to see if you could induce a hangover." The night before, we had visited Marc together, and honored an old promise to share a drink at his grave. It was something we had decided on as young men when we had had our first stolen taste of beer.

It had been a struggle to take the first drink. My treatment at the hands of Dorian's mother a year before had been brutal, and the memory of that time still made me nauseous. After that I had managed to have a couple more, but I wasn't able to do more. Besides I had had my hands full keeping Dorian from drinking himself into a blind stupor. The grief he found at our friend's grave, combined with his natural inclinations, made it almost impossible for him to moderate himself.

He growled, "Are you going to badger me about that?" It was readily apparent that he was still suffering a few lingering after effects.

"It's what Marc would have wanted," I pronounced solemnly.

"What, the drink at his grave or harassing me about my overindulgence?" asked Dorian irritably.

"Both."

He snorted. "Yeah, you're right about that." Shading his eyes, he looked down at the scattered collection of broken walls and tumbled stones that hinted at what must have once been a large group of buildings. "What do they call this place again?"

"Drakon Perket," I answered, "It means 'Dragon's Nest'."

"Not a very inviting name," he observed.

It probably wasn't meant to be, I thought. I could sense magic hovering in the air around the place, like a diffuse aura, encouraging visitors to stay away—to forget what they had seen. "It must be an enchantment," I muttered to myself, "otherwise it would have faded by now." I started to extend my shield to protect Dorian from its effects before I realized that it probably wouldn't work on him anyway. His mind was utterly impervious to magic of that sort. "Let's go down and see if we can find an entrance," I told him.

"To what?" he asked.

"There's a network of tunnels and cellars beneath the rock and sand. Some of it I can sense, and other parts seem to be shielded," I replied. "Whatever is there, I want to know what it is."

We walked down a gentle slope until we reached the center of what must have once been a large courtyard. Tumbled stone marked places that had once been walls, and a crumbling structure near the center looked as though it might have been a well, although it was full of rubble now. After fifteen minutes of careful searching, we still hadn't found an entry.

"You're sure there are tunnels and rooms down there?" said Dorian.

"Yes."

"Because there's no entrance," he added.

"I think you're right," I responded, wondering where he was heading with this line of thought.

"Doesn't make much sense to build it without an entrance."

"Well the old one might be covered by fallen stone. I can create a new way down if necessary," I replied.

"Oh," said Dorian, "then why are we wasting our time looking around?"

I took a deep breath, "Are you like this at home?"

"Why?"

I had a hunch Rose might regret having him home full time if he completely quit doing patrols, but I decided to keep my opinion to myself. "No reason," I replied, before walking in a new direction.

I found a location directly over one of the closest rooms beneath us. It was only twenty feet down, under an assortment of rock and sand. I briefly considered talking to the earth, to allow us to slip unhindered through the ground, as I once had with Rose. It was a short distance though, and talking to Dorian had left me with a bit of tension, so I decided to use my own power to create a more normal entry. "Step back a bit," I told Dorian, and then I focused my will on the ground in front of me. *"Grabol ni'targoth,"* I said in a commanding voice as I exerted myself. The ground shook as I forced it open, tearing a hole in the earth and reshaping it to form a ten foot wide opening and a steep ramp downward.

My large friend stood next to me with his sword drawn. He looked menacing.

"What's that for?" I asked, pointing to the sword.

"Just in case."

"There's nothing alive down here," I responded. "Nothing close enough for me to sense anyway."

Dorian ignored my wisdom. "You've been wrong before."

Shaking my head, I led the way down. The room that my new entrance led to was full of rotten boxes and dry dust. The smell of mold was overpowering. It appeared to have been a storeroom once, and I'd have guessed that the contents had been food stuffs. Needless to say, they were no longer good.

Dorian started coughing from the foul air, and before I realized it a powerful but subtle wind swept down from above, threading its way through the room and into the tunnels, rapidly replacing the stagnant air with fresh. *Damnitt, watch yourself,* I mentally chided. That was the very reason I was supposed to have a mielte watching me. My abilities as an archmage occasionally manifested without conscious thought.

"Good thinking," said my companion, grateful for the fresh air. Of course he didn't realize that my self-control had slipped.

"You're welcome," I said dryly.

A wooden door that had long ago succumbed to dry rot was all that barred our way out of the storeroom.

Dorian swept it away with his hand, and we began searching the hallway that led from that point onward. Eight similar storerooms and a few smaller closets connected to it, but in each we found nothing more interesting than dust and ruined foodstuffs. Some of the wood was well preserved in the dry air, while in other places it had nearly disintegrated from occasional exposure to moisture.

An hour of careful searching revealed nothing of interest.

"Seems like we've come up empty handed," noted Dorian at last.

I shook my head. "No, there's more—beneath us somewhere."

"Well I'll be damned if I can tell where the entrance is," he answered. "How can you tell?"

"I can feel an empty space beneath us, but it's shielded by magic. It's more than a hundred feet down, so I can only assume that it must connect with this area somehow," I told him.

Dorian grunted, "That doesn't make much sense. How did they get in and out?"

There was the possibility that they had used a teleportation circle, but I had a hunch it was something else. "I think they've used an enchantment to hide the entrance, and some distance beyond," I said as I thought about it. The mistake had been in not hiding the deeper portion of their sanctuary with the same enchantment. "I'll create another way down."

I began using my magic to create another tunnel, but as soon as I started I found that the floor was not what it appeared to be. Beneath a thin veneer of tile lay heavy granite rather than earth or simple bedrock. To my magesight it still appeared to be mixed rock and earth, but now that I had removed the tile, I could see the granite slabs with my normal eyesight.

"That looks an awful lot like a door," said Dorian, pointing at a large square section in the center. He was remarkable in his ability to state the obvious.

Bending down, I could see fine lines traced across the surface of the stone, marking the enchantment that hid the truth from my arcane senses. *Cleverly done,* I commented to myself, noting the pattern that some long dead enchanter had used. "There's something else in this enchantment though—I don't understand why they included these runes," I said aloud. "Give me a few minutes to think. I can probably figure out where the key runes are."

"Key runes?"

"The central nexus of the pattern, the point they would have gone to when opening the door—it may require a specific magical input, or a physical sign. Depending upon how they designed it, I might be able to fool it, or at least figure out what the requirement is for unlocking it," I explained.

Dorian frowned, "I forget that you don't speak the common tongue. How long will doing whatever you were talking about take?"

I ran my hand over my chin, pulling at my beard. "I'm not sure—an hour or two maybe," I answered.

"How about this…," said my friend, "this line appears to be central, and I'd bet the stone is less than a foot thick, if this is truly a door. So there are probably only one or two points here that actually keep it physically in place, behind or within the stone."

I raised an eyebrow, "And?"

"If I can create an opening in the stone, somewhere around here," he said, pointing to the center, "then I might be able to apply enough force to break whatever bar is holding it—assuming that it hinges along the sides there."

"Well yes," I replied, amazed that he thought he would be strong enough to do such a thing. I could have done the same thing with brute magical force, but I had a strong suspicion that the enchantment was tied to something else—something we might want to avoid if possible. I opened my mouth to explain, but I had spent too much time thinking about my answer.

Dorian had already taken my 'yes' as full agreement. Raising his sword, he held it between both hands, with the point facing downward. Exhaling, he drove it into the granite seam. Rock chips flew in several directions and the point bit deeply into the stone. I also felt a surge as the enchantment was disturbed. Something had happened, though I couldn't be sure what.

"Shit," I said bluntly.

"What?"

"You triggered something," I replied.

Dorian was quiet for a moment. "Nothing seems to be happening," he said, and then he drove his sword into the rock again. "How about that time?"

I sighed, "No, whatever it did, has already been done."

He smiled, "No use crying about spilt milk then." In the space of a few minutes, he cut a crude hole through the stone in the middle of our 'door'. It turned out to be no more than six inches thick, and the opening he created was five or six inches in diameter. He stopped to wipe his brow. "This is a lot harder than it looks."

"Swords really aren't meant for cutting stone—or even wood for that matter," I told him wryly. Even enchanted as it was, and with Dorian's considerable strength behind it, cutting holes in granite slabs was a difficult task.

"I think it's enough now," he said, setting his sword aside. Dorian tried to reach inside, but his gauntleted hand proved to be too bulky. Stripping off his armored gloves and removing his helmet, he tried again (I had replaced his armor during the past year). Kneeling down, he slipped his right hand in far enough to grip the inside edge of the stone door.

I watched carefully as he braced himself and began pulling with his right arm, while pushing down against the floor with his left. His face turned red and veins stood out against the side of his head, but the granite didn't move. "You're going to hurt yourself," I warned. "Let me do that. You probably shouldn't be overusing the earth power anyway," I said, remembering what I had seen happen to him after our battle with Karenth and Doron. I still didn't understand what had occurred. In the past, physical changes such as he had undergone were permanent, without immediate removal of the earth bond—and timely intervention of an archmage to help the afflicted warrior recover his humanity. Assuming the process hadn't gone too far.

"No—I can do this," he said stubbornly. Setting himself, he drew a deep breath and began again. This time his face turned red as he exhaled through clenched teeth, but he didn't give up. Groaning, he kept pulling until I began to wonder if he might burst a blood vessel—and then I saw it happen. The tips of his ears changed color, going from red to grey. The color spread slowly across his skin and even his hair changed, from deep black to a dusty white.

Alarmed, I shouted for him to stop, but it was too late. Straightening his legs, he ripped the massive stone slab up from its framework, tearing loose the iron bars that held it in position with a horrific shriek of stressed metal and popping stone. As chance would have it, it actually did hinge along the side he had suggested, and he pushed it back to rest against the floor on that side. Huffing from his exertion, he looked at me with an exultant expression. "See! I told you I could do it," he said in a gravelly voice. "What's wrong?" he asked as he saw the look on my face.

"We've got to release your bond!" I shouted at him, "Now!" All I could see was my friend turning into a golem right in front of me. I didn't want him to wind up like Magnus, but I feared it might already be too late.

"What's wrong with you?" he replied, showing me his hands. The skin on them was still pink and healthy, if a bit callused. Looking up from them, I saw the color returning to his face, even as his hair resumed its glossy black sheen. "I'm fine."

"What the hell?"

"Now you sound like Rose," he said with a chuckle.

I had some trouble imagining her speaking so uncouthly, but then again, she was probably much different in their private life. I was more astonished by the changes in my large friend, even his voice had returned to normal. If I hadn't seen what had occurred, I might not have believed it. *If he hadn't taken off his helmet, I might never have known,* I realized.

"You changed—and then you changed back," I told him. "Did you feel anything?"

"Changed how?" asked Dorian.

I described what I had seen to him before adding, "I thought I might have imagined it last time."

"You saw this before?"

I nodded, "After the battle with the gods—your skin looked different then, and your teeth were granite-like. Things were confusing, and I collapsed afterward so when you seemed normal later I assumed that perhaps I was mistaken. Did you feel different just now?"

"Just the strength of the earth, pounding in my ears like a heartbeat, but it always does that when I exert myself a lot. I didn't think it was unusual. The other knights have described it in a similar manner," he replied.

"But they don't revert to normal after they start showing physical signs—and you were definitely showing signs," I reiterated.

Dorian opened his mouth wide to show his teeth and then pinched his cheek. "Well I'm still flesh and blood."

I thought for a moment before responding, "I wonder if it's because you're a stoic. You must have some innate resistance." As I pondered on it for a moment, I heard a voice in my mind, the voice of a teacher in the distant past, '*When an archmage chooses to make someone a targoth cherek, they must remember that stoics cannot accept the bond, their immutability makes them unable to form bonds with external agencies, elements, or even people.*'

The sudden memory was unexpected, but for once not unwelcome. It surprised me and before I could focus on it, it slipped away. *If that was true, then how did I manage to create a bond between Dorian and the earth?* I wondered.

Dorian shrugged, "Are we going to worry about this all day or stick to business?"

I had been lost in thought for several minutes, and his remark served to bring me back to the present. "Sorry," I answered, "You're right. Let's see what we've found."

Gazing downward, the place the stone door had guarded now revealed a stone staircase, descending into the dark. With the concealing enchantment damaged I could now sense the areas it led to. "This stair goes down for more than fifty feet before stopping in some sort of antechamber filled with chairs and furnishings—and a considerable amount of magic," I said aloud, for Dorian's benefit.

"Anything along the way?" he asked in return.

"Nothing of note," I replied, lighting the head of my staff to give him enough light to see the steps as we descended.

Dorian responded with a grunt and readied his sword. It was a signature grunt that told me immediately that, while he respected my ability to sense things ahead of us, he fully intended to remain alert anyway, which was precisely why Penny had insisted that he come with me.

Leading the way carefully, Dorian tested each step before placing his weight fully upon it; a procedure that I found taxed my patience. My magesight had revealed no hidden traps or pressure plates, and while I knew from experience that it could be fooled, I still disliked spending half a minute for every foot we went down. I knew better than to voice my opinion though, Dorian took his work seriously, and he was almost as stubborn as my wife when he put his heart into something.

After an hour of mind-numbing boredom, we finally reached the antechamber my senses had been exploring the entire time. It made no better sense once I put my physical eyes upon it. In form and appearance it seemed to be nothing more unusual than a sitting room or waiting chamber. The walls were decorated with ancient tapestries which had faded beyond the point of recognition and a collection of book cases covered one wall. There were no books to be seen though, just piles of dust and a few odd metal bookends. A modestly sized table stood in the middle of the room, surrounded by six chairs. Another, smaller table with two chairs sat near one corner, and a plain door exited the other side of the room.

Oh—and every item in the room, from the bookcases, to the tables, and even the chairs, radiated intense magic. Perhaps I should have mentioned that to begin with.

Two lamps suspended by iron chains from the ceiling lit automatically as we entered the room, suffusing the area with a warm natural glow. "Don't move," I cautioned my stalwart friend. "Every item in this room is enchanted."

"For what purpose?" asked Dorian.

It was a sensible question, which irritated me for some unknown reason. "If I knew that, I wouldn't be saying, 'don't move'—now would I?!" I shot back harshly.

"No need to make an ass of yourself," retorted my friend.

I took a moment to breathe before answering, "I'm sorry. I'm just tense. Give me a moment to see if I can figure out what these enchantments do."

I spent close to an hour closely studying the chairs and tables, careful to avoid touching, or even approaching them. Magesight can be handy sometimes. By focusing my perception precisely, I could peer at the individual runes making up the enchantments on each object from almost any angle, though what I saw made little sense and only increased my frustration. My only satisfaction was that I knew that standing still for an hour with nothing to do, and no idea what I was doing, must have driven Dorian to distraction. It was a fair repayment for the laborious descent he had forced me to endure on the stairs.

"How much longer are we going to stand here?" he asked me again, as he had every five to ten minutes for the past three quarters of an hour.

I ground my teeth, "I don't understand these enchantments. The structure is twisted somehow—askew in a way that should make them non-functional."

"Well if they don't work then they should be safe, right?"

I shook my head, "No, if they didn't work they'd have faded by now. These things look just as fresh as the day they were made, which means that the alignment is properly balanced—I just don't understand how."

"So—are we going to stand here all day, or try that door over there? We could take some of these things back if you want to study them later," said Dorian pragmatically.

"Let's just move on. There's something like a vault a short distance past that door. Whatever they were protecting down here is probably in there," I told him. "We should skirt the edges of this room though, just in case—and don't touch *anything*." Double checking my shield, I gave him a pat on the back, indicating he should start moving forward.

Everything went fine, until he reached the side of the room and we began edging toward the far door. A sharp surge of magical energy was my only warning before my eyes were greeted with the improbable sight of a chair grinning at me. That's right, the goddamned thing *grinned* at me. The chair back twisted and changed, revealing two grotesque eyes and a mouth full of what appeared to be razor sharp teeth.

Before I could react, it stood and lunged at me. The back and seat rose, becoming the main body of what appeared to be an oddly shaped wooden stick-man, while the arms stretched out and showed enchanted claws, as if they were cat paws. It struck with breathtaking speed, ripping through my shield and almost reaching my suddenly vulnerable throat. I might have died then, but for the fortuitous presence of Dorian Thornbear.

I hadn't seen him move, so focused was I upon the wooden monstrosity that had attacked me, but his sword struck with blinding speed, cutting through the wooden arms of the chair and sending a rainbow cascade of magical energies flying through the air. I doubted he could see the chaotic and colorful spray of aythar as his sword devastated the magical construct, but it hardly mattered—his sword still did its work.

Things would have been simple if it had just been the chair, for Dorian's second and third cuts rendered it rapidly into antique kindling, but the chair was not alone. It came with a full set of chair friends as well as two brutes that had previously been perfectly civilized tables. As the first chair had already shown, my magical shield was virtually worthless against the enchanted claws and teeth that each former piece of furniture came equipped with, but Dorian's armor was more than sufficient.

Reaching into my pouches, I started to bring forth another stone disk, similar in appearance to the one that served as my magical flying construct, but with a different function. I was interrupted by a massive table leg stabbing toward me with a gleaming spike on its foot. Dodging sideways, I was almost too slow getting out of its path, but fortunately I tripped over the remains of the first chair, and my fall helped me to avoid the deadly attack.

I wish I could say I planned the fall, but I hadn't. I was just clumsy.

Meanwhile, Dorian had gone on a rampage. That's the best way I could think to describe it. The man was an unbreakable, unforgiving, and utterly unstoppable engine of destruction. If other furniture items could see his actions that day, and if that same furniture then had dreams—well they'd have been horrific nightmares of wooden destruction at the hands of a metal clad monster, i.e. Dorian Thornbear.

He moved in a perfect rhythm of violence; graceful and terrible at one and the same time. He had somehow noticed my fall, and he stepped back and to the side to cover me, even as his sword clove through another barbarously deformed chair.

The smaller side table caught his sword as it recovered from the swing and sought to trap his arm. Given Dorian's incredible strength and the nature of his magical blade, it was a futile maneuver—but it kept him off-balance and cost him a precious second as he ripped the blade free of his wooden opponent. During that time the larger table rushed him, slamming into him like an animated battering ram.

I tried to brace him with a hastily erected shield but the enchanted construct's wooden arms tore through it as if it were tissue paper, and Dorian wound up being slammed against the wall, while I served unwittingly as a block to trip his legs as he fell backward. Scrambling forward, I hastily got out of the way, casting about with my senses to find my staff which I had dropped during my initial fall.

The enchantment that powers these things seems to be impervious to normal magic, I noted silently. As I had seen before, magic bound within permanent rune structures was virtually impossible to alter or destroy, unless you used something similar against it. Enchanted swords easily cut through my shields, as had the strangely fluid magic of the shiggreth leader, Timothy. His magic had seemed very similar to an enchantment, even though he created it spontaneously with nothing more than will and words. *Spell-weaving,* came an unbidden memory, *the true difference between a civilized race and animals.* Somehow I knew that the speaker had meant human kind when he had said 'animals'.

Even while these thoughts raced through my mind, my hand reached my staff and I brought it up to bear on the swarming wooden chaos of the room before me. Dorian had recovered from his fall and was now grappling the larger table from his disadvantageous position on the floor. It hardly mattered though, as I watched, his greater strength prevailed, and he began ripping the heavily timbered opponent limb from limb, or leg from tabletop, in this instance.

Focusing my power along the channel of my staff, I burned through the remaining chairs with a white hot beam of pure aythar. Within moments the fight was over, and we were left standing amid the wreckage of the most vicious furniture I had ever encountered. I began chuckling at the thought.

"What are you laughing about?" asked Dorian as he rose from the floor.

"We finished the furnishings," I snickered.

Dorian groaned, "Not again."

That only made me laugh harder, "You smashed the sideboard and broke the buffet while I charred the chairs."

"Alliteration?" said my friend bleakly, "I think I preferred your bad puns."

"Wait," I protested with a grin, "I think I can do better."

"Better is worse," said Dorian.

"You terminated the table's tortuous tumult."

"Even if the gods are false, there has to be a special hell for people like you," he replied.

"A literal hell…," I said before pausing, "…or 'alliteral' hell. Is that what you mean?"

"Goddammit stop!" he cried before adding, "alliteral isn't even a word."

"Well it should be," I said smugly and then I was forced to dodge a wide swing of Dorian's arm. I knew he was only playing though—if he had meant to hit me, I'd never have had time to move.

CHAPTER 38

The door leading from the room we had just wrecked opened into a small hallway with walls faced in smooth marble. The hall ended in a heavy steel door marked with a single inscription in Lycian, 'Shraybet gib Aystrylin'.

"Can you read that?" asked Dorian, pointing up at the strange lettering.

I nodded, "It means 'Repository of Quintessence'."

"And that means?"

"I'm not entirely sure. The word *'aystrylin'* is related to aythar, but it refers to it in a more personal or unique sense. It could be used to mean personality, spirit, or mind, depending upon the context. We only have a short phrase here, so it's hard to guess at the exact meaning," I explained.

Dorian sighed, "Forget I asked. How do we open it?"

"Let me study it for a moment," I told him, knowing that would only irritate him more. I ignored his impatient stance and focused my magesight upon the steel door.

Of course it was enchanted, but this was an enchantment I understood much better. In function it was related to the type of enchantments I used in crafting the armor worn by the Knights of Stone, it hardened and protected the metal that the vault door had been made of. It also included an identity spell, which in this case seemed to be very specific. I got the distinct impression I would never be able to satisfy the requirement that the identity spell was looking for. In all likelihood it was looking for a familial identity, such as being a member of the Gaelyn family.

"I don't think I can open it with anything short of brute force," I told Dorian.

He grinned. "Well I have plenty of that right here," and so saying, he drew his sword again.

"No, wait!" I said quickly.

"What?"

"You might break the sword," I replied.

Dorian looked at me quizzically. "In eight years I've not encountered much that could damage one of your specially crafted blades, or even dull them. Why would this be an obstacle?"

"That door is similarly enchanted, and there's a hell of a lot more of it," I said quickly.

Dorian was dismayed. "So what do we do, if you can't spell it open and it's stronger than me and this blade—we just pack up and go home?"

"You aren't the only brute force we have available," I said wryly. "Go back up topside and wait for me. In fact, move back up the hill a bit. I don't want you too close, just in case."

"Why's that?" said Dorian, confused.

"Because I might forget you're here and kill you by accident," I answered frankly.

"Oh," he replied, and without further argument he left. Before he had gotten beyond earshot he called back, "How will I know when you're done?"

I grinned mischievously, "You'll know."

I kept my magesight trained on him until I was certain that he had reached what I thought should be a safe distance—around a hundred yards or so. Once I no longer had that worry, I focused on the steel door blocking my way. It was almost ten foot tall and a little over twelve foot in width, but it was part of a large steel encased chamber that extended beyond visible sight and into the bedrock. The room it guarded was approximately twenty foot on each side and entirely protected by similarly enchanted steel. I couldn't tell how thick the walls were, but I'd have guessed they were anywhere from six inches to a foot. That's how I'd have made them.

Before I did anything else, I strengthened the shield around myself, making it as strong as possible. Once I began, it probably wouldn't matter, my instincts should protect my physical body, but I could never be entirely sure. The earth wasn't human and its priorities weren't always in line with my own. After that was done, I opened my mind as fully as possible and listened, letting my mind drift downward, deep into the stone below and around me, feeling the heartbeat of the world.

Over the years since my battle with Celior, I had done some experimenting and refined my skills as an archmage, acquiring hard won confidence and quite a bit of finesse. Still there was always risk involved. This time I didn't allow my personal body to change except for slowing its metabolism so that I wouldn't need to breathe—I merely encased it in a protective sphere of solid granite. Claustrophobia might have been a problem if I were still strictly human at that point, but by then my true body had expanded far beyond the small bit of frail flesh surrounded in stone.

The enchanted steel 'box' now seemed like a small thing, enclosed and resting within me. It hadn't been included within my new self-image, and consequently felt something like a foreign body embedded in my flesh. Flexing, I shifted the bedrock surrounding the steel chamber and began moving it upward, toward the sky. The underground halls and tunnels that we had entered through collapsed as the earth heaved and if I had been still in my normal frame of mind I might have been glad that Dorian was no longer within them. As it was, he was merely an afterthought for me now.

As I lifted it, I also applied a downward pressure on one side, attempting to create shear forces strong enough to crack the enchanted room. It resisted at first, but the enormous stress created was too much, and the steel cracked along the seams on one side, releasing a small explosion of magical force, as the enchantment failed. Careful to avoid damaging it further, I shifted the earth and stone above it aside and gently lifted the shattered steel chamber toward the sun.

Once it was there, I brought up the granite sphere that contained my human body, opening the stone to show it to the sky as well. The most difficult part was next, but I managed to remember it, barely. Focusing upon the human resting on the ground above me, I began the difficult task of compressing and reducing myself, trying to become something less than I was. It was uncomfortable, almost painful, and for a moment I almost rebelled at the idea. Deep within though, some small part of me was insisting— *let go, return to what you were.*

And then, as simply as that—I did. Opening my eyes I sat up and blinked at the bright sunlight. Dorian was scrambling toward me, not quite able to run across the broken and uneven terrain.

"Are you alright?" he yelled, in a worried tone.

I nodded. "Yes, things worked out more or less as I intended."

"As you intended?" he said incredulously, and in a voice that was a few decibels louder than I thought was strictly necessary.

"I'm right here. No need to yell."

"You were underground in the middle of a damned earthquake!" he shouted at full volume. "And this is what it sounds like when I'm yelling! Can you tell the difference now?!"

I stood up and gave him my best 'calm down' look. "For a fellow who spends his days hunting undead monsters, you are remarkably prone to overly dramatic expressiveness," I told him.

He opened his mouth for a moment and then shut it again. He then repeated that action a time or two before finally replying, "I've gotten somewhat used to that, but every time we go somewhere you manage to find a way to push the boundaries far beyond my comfort zone."

"Well, I'm sorry," I said at last. "I thought you knew what to expect when I told you to move so far out. I forgot you were mostly unconscious when I fought Celior, weren't you?"

"It wasn't one of my best days," he agreed.

I gave him a sympathetic look before clapping him upon the shoulder, "Let's go see what we've uncovered."

The steel chamber was lying some thirty yards away, shining in the sun. It had cracked open fully along one side, causing one wall to split away, and allowing a large amount of loose dirt to enter the long sealed interior. The enchantment had dissipated once the integrity of the steel structure had been breached. Stepping through the wide opening, I used my magic to clear away loose earth and debris.

It appeared that the room had once contained a number of marble pedestals, but as to what had rested upon them I could find no trace. The floor had been covered in a heavy red rug, though it had been twisted and torn loose by the upheaval. Only one thing stood out in my magesight, glowing with a gentle magical radiance, a small alabaster figurine. It was small enough to fit easily into the palm of my hand, and it had the appearance of a human nobleman. Even as small as it was, the detail and artisanship were incredible, it was an almost perfect sculpture, and I felt as if I could probably recognize the subject if I were to meet him in person. In fact, the face seemed familiar to some degree.

I didn't pick it up immediately, despite its small size, choosing instead to examine it closely first. There was no sign of runes or symbols, and the magic emanating from it had a strange feel to it, giving me the distinct impression that the small statue wasn't enchanted. *Though, for it to still radiate magic after several hundred years without being enchanted, doesn't make sense,* I thought silently. "You must be connected to some other source...," I said aloud, trying to work through the possibilities.

That was when I felt it, the rapid approach of something large, living, and radiant with aythar. It was in the air, rushing toward us at incredible speed and coming from the west.

Dorian was gazing at the miniature statue we had found, his helmet resting on the ground beside him. "Is this all that was in there?" he asked me.

I was staring toward the west. "Put your helmet back on," I told him.

"Why?" he replied, even as he rose to his feet. Despite his question, he was already putting his helmet back in place.

"We're about to find out why they call this place 'Dragon's Nest'," I answered.

"This would be the same dragon you met before?"

I nodded, "I don't think there are any others. This place was his home, once." As I spoke, I used my staff to etch a circle ten foot in diameter around us. Once it was complete, I added a second circle just outside of it and added well placed runes in the space between the two. It was hastily constructed, but it did the job nonetheless. I could create a shield with nothing more than a thought, but it required more energy than if I used words to channel my power—using written symbols made the effort even easier, and added a significant amount of strength.

Dorian had drawn his sword again, but I put my hand upon his arm, "Put it away. I don't want to fight him if we can avoid it."

"He may not give us that option," said my friend. As he spoke, I admired his courage; if he ever thought of running, it never showed in his words or actions.

I shrugged, "If it comes to it, I don't think you'll be able to fight him. If something happens to me and you do—you'll need to cut his head off, he can heal any other wound, given a moment's respite."

There was no more time, for the dragon had arrived, screaming his fury with a rumbling howl that set my teeth on edge and sent cold shivers of fear up my spine. I had intended to hail him, but Gareth Gaelyn, the dragon, spent no time on introductions. Dropping down on us from the sky, he stopped twenty feet above and hovered there, throwing dust and debris in all directions from the thunderous beating of his wings. Opening a mouth full of dagger-like teeth, he sent a raging gout of flame at us.

The heat and intensity of his breath was incredible, and it incinerated everything around us, beyond the edge of my warded circle. The flames continued to come for what seemed an eternity, but in all probability was only a half a minute. Still they made an impression. Gareth was not a happy dragon.

The flames went out and I started to yell at him, but he wasted no time, attacking my shield with claws and teeth. It can be quite hard to make oneself heard over the noise of an angry dragon. Lifting my staff, I pointed the heel toward him like a spear, "Do you really want to do this?" I bellowed, using a touch of magic to increase the volume of my voice. "I thought we might talk first."

He stopped for a moment, staring at me with draconian eyes. "Your magic does not frighten me, human!" he replied suddenly in a snarling voice. My eyes went wide in surprise, when I had spoken to him before, he had taken a humanoid form first; I hadn't known he could speak while in his dragon shape.

"I don't need to frighten you, but if you want, we can find out how well you do with a hole the size of a melon burned through that scaly body of yours," I answered. I couldn't be sure, since I hadn't ever used my magic directly against him, but there weren't many things that didn't develop large holes in them when struck by a channeled line of power from my staff.

"Robber! You break into my home and then have the gall to threaten me?!" bellowed the dragon.

I shrugged my shoulders. "You might have a point there, but I didn't think you had much use for the trappings of your human life anymore."

"Leave!" he roared back.

"Fine," I told him, and reaching down I picked up the small figurine. "We'll just be on our way."

The dragon's eyes had gone wide as I lifted the small statue, his body freezing into stillness. He gazed at the object in my hand with terrible intensity. I paused and then we both stared at one another. After a moment Gareth spoke, "Put that down carefully and leave, and I will forget this insult."

By then I knew I had the upper hand, though I wasn't sure what I had. "You've changed your attitude," I told him. "Are you worried I might break this?" I feigned dropping the small sculptured man.

"No!" shouted the dragon, so loudly that I worried for the sake of my hearing. "You mustn't damage it!"

"Why?"

The only answer I received was a cold reptilian stare.

"Fine," I said at last, "We'll find out the hard way." I set the small figurine on a somewhat flat rock and picked up another in one hand, as if I meant to smash it between the two.

"Stop!" cried the dragon, as he looked on helplessly.

I held my stone wielding arm high and motionless. "I need to hear two things if you don't want me to smash your doll," I said without a hint of humor, "'please', and 'why'." *I should have said 'dolly'*, observed my inner voice, but I doubted I could have kept a straight face if I had.

Gareth stared at me silently for a long half a minute without any indication that he planned to speak. Tired of waiting I shifted and drew back my arm, "Fine, have it your way."

"Please," he said suddenly, in a voice that was soft and desperate compared to before.

"And?" I insisted.

"It's an imprint of my mind—from before," he answered reluctantly.

"What does that mean exactly? Are you still linked to it? Would it kill you if it were destroyed?" I said, asking questions in rapid succession.

"It's a family secret, a means of restoring the humanity of those who lose themselves in transformation magics. Yes and—in a way," he answered.

I had to review my last statement to realize he had answered each of my questions in order. 'Yes' he was linked to it and— I gave him a puzzled look, "What do you mean 'in a way'? That seems like a very simple question to my mind."

"Please, I've told you enough. I'll grant you any favor if you simply return my aystrylin and leave me in peace."

The proud dragon that Gareth Gaelyn had become was practically begging now, and for a moment I felt a twinge of shame at extorting the wild being, but I couldn't look away from the opportunity that lay before me. "Answer the question," I said calmly, "or the toy gets it."

He snarled for a moment as a visible wave of anger rippled through his massive scaled body, but then he calmed and answered my question meekly enough, "If the figurine is destroyed, it will perform its designated function in the crudest way possible. The aystrylin will return to me via the link and it will return me, forcibly, to being who I was over a thousand years ago. My memories, my experience, everything that has happened to me since the day that imprint was taken—all of it will be wiped away."

"From my perspective that isn't all that terrible, you are returned to being your original self and the world gains another benevolent archmage. When was the aystrylin made?" I asked, but even as I spoke I realized my words sounded harsh.

"Several years before Balinthor threatened to destroy the world," answered the dragon, before continuing, "Think how you would feel if someone threatened to erase, not merely the last few years of your life, but the last millennium. What if you were faced with the possibility of being forced to become an entirely different person? I am happy being what I am now, but break that figurine and you will utterly destroy everything that I am."

His words had a certain merit to them, but I still had questions, "You said the 'crudest way possible'—is there another way to use the aystrylin, one that doesn't destroy your memories?"

"That might be the cruelest fate of all," he replied. "If I were to voluntarily activate the aystrylin's magic, it would return me to my prior state, but without destroying my memories. The man I was then would have an entirely different view of the events of the past thousand years. He might not wish to live with such knowledge."

That reminded me of my own demons. I had wiped out the lives of over thirty thousand men at the conclusion of the war with Gododdin, and that had triggered a wave of sacrifices in the nation itself, as the priests of Mal'goroth murdered the men's families. There were still nights that I woke sweating at the thought, but I had somehow managed to go on anyway. Even worse, I seemed to be filled with memories of an event that was quite possibly, more horrifying than that, memories so dark that my mind literally refused to look at them.

Gareth Gaelyn had transformed into a dragon to protect his people from the shiggreth, and instead he had destroyed them along with their enemies. Beyond that, I had no idea what small atrocities he might have committed over the intervening millennium since that day.

Dorian put a hand on my shoulder, "This isn't right, Mort."

"We can't let him stay as he is. How many has he killed already?" I argued.

"None—since the day we met, after your battle with the god, and few before then. I have never had much appetite for men," answered the dragon earnestly.

I waved Dorian away before rising to my feet. I had thrown the stone away, but I held the figurine firmly in my hand. "I don't give a damn, even one is too many. This is my decision: I will keep your aystrylin, until the day you decide of your own will to accept it and return to your humanity."

"Never," interrupted the dragon.

I held up my hand, "Until then you will live by two requirements. You will harm no humans nor damage their livestock, and you will answer my call and obey whatever commands I give you."

"I would gladly give you my word, if you but return the aystrylin to me," said the dragon.

"It will remain in my possession to vouchsafe our bargain," I told him flatly.

Gareth Gaelyn, dragon and archmage, growled menacingly, "You are a thief!"

I held my ground, "Ask me if I give a damn! Now, will you meet my demands, or do I have to destroy this thing?"

.   A long tense moment passed before he finally lowered his head, "I will obey your commands, under duress. The day you lose sight of my aystrylin I will rip out your heart and feed on your liver."

"A finer oath I have rarely heard," I replied dryly. "I do not need your service today, but if I have need of you, how will I call you?"

"Merely touch the aystrylin and speak, I will hear you," he growled.

"Very well then, you are dismissed, but before you go, you should know one thing," I said. "You underestimate the strength of the human mind. Your human self could handle a lot more than you give him credit for."

"I am in a far better position to judge that theory than you are, *master*," he responded with a sneer, and then he leapt from the earth on powerful legs, vaulting into the sky. His wings beat powerfully as he gained altitude, sending a howling storm of air and dirt flying around my shield.

Watching him go, I slipped the figurine into one of my special pouches before muttering, "No—I really don't think you are."

CHAPTER 39

A week had passed since my encounter with Gareth Gaelyn and I found myself still restless. I had gone to explore the Gaelyn ruins in Agradden primarily to assuage my feeling of motionlessness, but I had been fooling myself. The true source of my unease was my continuing avoidance of the darker memories contained inside my head.

I had spent several evenings at the Muddy Pig, after the more formal dinner at the castle was finished. Penny hadn't reproached me on the subject yet, for she usually supported my need for socializing, but I could tell she thought I had spent entirely too many evenings there that week. One or two—that was fine, four or five—and it was apparent I was brooding or possibly depressed.

Even my newfound drinking companion, the huntsman Chad Grayson, had noticed my darker mood. "Are you going to stare into that empty cup all night?" he asked me acerbically. He almost never bothered using the proper honorifics when addressing me, which suited me just fine.

"What else should I do with an empty cup?" I asked, in a half-hearted attempt at wit.

"If you'd let go of it long enough, the barmaid might be persuaded to fill it for you. She keeps watchin' for the chance, but you've not let go of it yet," he replied blandly.

Cyhan was sitting on the other side of me and he chose that moment to interject, "That's your biggest problem half the time." It was the longest sentence he had offered up all evening, a sure sign that he'd had more to drink than usual.

I showed him my grumpy face, "I didn't come down here to have you two catalog my faults."

"Didn't say it was necessarily a fault…," answered the veteran knight, "…just that it was a problem half the time."

"Me hanging onto my cup is a frequent problem?"

Chad spoke then, "Don't be daft, he means your habit of holding onto everything."

Cyhan nodded in agreement.

"Alright, fine!" I said suddenly, "Maybe you two geniuses can find the answer to my problem."

The master huntsman replied, "Better'n you mopin' about it all the damn time." Cyhan merely grunted.

I had already had several cups of wine, or I'd not have been so forthcoming. "I need something, but I can't see it or look at it directly. I know it's there, but I can't grab it with my own two hands."

Cyhan snorted, "Wizard problems," dismissing the conversation.

Chad was not so quick to surrender, "Maybe, but there's often more than one way to skin a cat," he told the bigger man. Focusing on me he said, "Is this some magic thing or something more run of the mill?"

I took a sip of my newly filled cup. "What do you consider run of the mill?"

"Like wantin' to tup the barmaid without the wife catchin' on," he elaborated.

Looking at my words from that angle, I could see how something like that might fit them, so I decided to clarify things for him, "It isn't a woman and it isn't really magic, though it's related to magic in the end—it's information. I know where it lies, but I can't look at it myself. It's like a book sitting on my desk, but I can't read it, whenever I try my eyes close, whether I want them to or not."

"Get someone else to read it for you," said Cyhan, before setting his cup down and resting his head in both hands. He had definitely drunk more than was wise.

The huntsman nodded in agreement but I stopped them there, "No one else can read it. It's in here," I said tapping my skull.

Chad frowned, "If it's in your head already—I don't see the problem."

"It's there. I just can't look at it. My mind's eye refuses to gaze upon it. I just get glimpses from the corner of my eye whenever I least expect them," I explained.

"Told you—wizard problems," repeated Cyhan.

"And that attitude is why he never asks you for advice on 'em!" said the huntsman, pointing a finger at the Knight of Stone.

"Just the way I like it," said the warrior.

"Weren't you the one advising him to talk to people instead of keepin' it all to himself?" rebuked Chad.

Cyhan belched before replying, "I just said it was his problem—I wasn't offering to fix it."

The hunter burst into laughter and I was considering retiring for the evening when he fixed me with a serious stare. "You should think of this thing like it was your quarry," he told me.

"And what's that supposed to mean?" I asked.

"You know why deer stand still when they hear somethin'?" he said cryptically.

My brow furrowed, "I don't think that really relates..."

"To keep from bein' seen!" Chad said loudly, ignoring my comment. "The eyes are tricky and they get bored quick. Most hunters rely on movement to spot their quarry. When you hunt from a stand, you're waiting on your prey to move—that's when you see them. If you're slip hunting, you hope to get close enough to flush them out, either way its movement you're wanting."

I decided to play his game, "Well this quarry won't be moving on its own, and I don't see how I'm supposed to 'flush it out'."

"You already know something, or you wouldn't be trying to learn more," replied the slender outdoorsman. "That's what you use. You follow the signs and markings. Once I learn where the deer are feeding, where they travel in the morning, I make sure I'm close by to catch 'em."

The 'when' of it all was deep in the past, but his words made me think of the door beneath my house in Albamarl. I already knew it was related to my hidden knowledge, but I had never spent much time investigating it. In fact I hadn't gone near the door in many years, possibly because of my subconscious dread. If it wasn't possible to force my reluctant mind's eye to look directly at the source of my anxiety, discovering what lay behind that door might force some of the knowledge out into the open.

"There's probably a place like that…," I ventured.

Chad looked at me intently, "But you haven't been there, have you?"

"Briefly, before I knew anything about it. After that I was always too busy. Over the last few years I've learned some things that made me uneasy about it, but…," I trailed off, leaving the sentence unfinished.

"But—you were too damned afraid to look it right in the face," he finished for me. Then he leaned over and patted Cyhan on the face to wake him up, "Hey! Wizard problems my ass—he just didn't want to face the truth. Pretty much like most everybody else in this place." Chad pointed unsteadily at the other patrons in the room. "Are you listening?" he added, once he realized that Cyhan had closed his eyes again.

I stood up to leave. "I'll take your advice if you make sure he manages to get home," I told the huntsman.

Chad nodded. "Big bastard can't hold his drink. That's what all that clean livin' gets him," he noted disapprovingly.

Clapping him on the shoulder companionably I made my way to the door, but as I left I heard the woodsman mutter again under his breath, "The big bastard ain't got no home neither—a bed, aye, he's got that, and steady work. Wizards ain't the only ones afraid to face their problems."

I mulled that over as I left, and decided that perhaps his perceptiveness extended to more than just keen eyes and ears. When I found my bed later that night, I could hardly sleep for the disconcerting sound of death's voice in my mind. Lately it had gotten increasingly loud, particularly during the quiet hours.

I was unable to test my newfound resolve for several weeks, for a seemingly endless array of duties appeared, preventing me from slipping away to the house in Albamarl. When a lull in my schedule did appear, Penny and Rose decided to take advantage of it with a trip to the capital, which suited me just fine.

The only fly in the ointment was the fact that I was hoping for an extended period of time alone. I could have had that easily enough, by confiding in my wife, but my reason for wanting it would have raised some alarms with her. In particular I wanted the house empty, just in case whatever I discovered turned out to be a more immediate and direct threat than a dusty memory or long forgotten misdeeds.

As chance would have it, the perfect opportunity presented itself on our second day there. Rose and Dorian were to visit her family, the Hightowers, that day and they had invited us along. It was a family occasion and naturally the children were invited as well. Lord Hightower wanted to see his newest granddaughter and he was probably also curious to meet our children too, since he had never seen them. It might have been a perfect day, but for my obligations.

"I can't make it," I repeated again. Penny often had hearing problems when she heard things that didn't fit neatly within her plans.

"Why not?"

I held up my hands regretfully, "I promised our King that I'd check on the portals at the World Road today; some of them have developed an odd shimmer and a humming noise. He worries that something might have gone wrong with them."

She waved her hands dismissively, "Tell James you'll look into it tomorrow. He'll understand."

I frowned, "He would, but I worry that something might be damaged. There's no telling what might happen if one of the portals discharged itself in an uncontrolled manner." Of course that was a complete fabrication, not only were the portals still functioning perfectly, but I had designed the enchantment to safely channel the energies they contained back into storage, should one of them be damaged unexpectedly.

It was a lie that I knew would be discovered eventually, had I not already planned to reveal the truth that evening. I merely wanted to make sure the house was empty during my planned exploration. "If things are in order I should be able to join you at the Hightower's home in the afternoon," I said placatingly, before adding, "I have a surprise for you later, something I should have given you almost a year ago."

She gave me a shrewd look, sensing something fishy in my manner and tone, but if she thought I was being deceptive, she withheld the accusation. Her intuition was still uncanny, but since she had taken the earth-bond over a year ago, she was no longer able to spot white lies as easily as she once had.

"I don't care about presents—you promise you'll join us as soon as you're free?" she said at last.

"Of course," I said, pulling her in close for a quick embrace. As always, the smell of her hair brought me a feeling of peace and security. It was the smell of home, for where she was—that was where I belonged. She allowed me a short kiss before pushing me away brusquely at the sound of Moira's laughter.

Our daughter was giggling as she looked up at us, while her brother could hardly conceal his distaste. "Ewww," he declared.

"I think they're jealous," I said, glancing at Penny mischievously.

The twins had heard that line before, and they reacted in entirely different ways. Moira smiled, nodding her head in agreement, while Matthew shook his head in denial. "No—no, we're not jealous at all!" he protested.

We ignored his objections and chased them both around the room, kissing and tickling them mercilessly once they were caught. Despite his insistence, Matthew was laughing and smiling the entire time. Not to be left out, Conall leapt to his brother's defense, or rather he leapt onto my back. It really did nothing to help his older brother's plight.

Squealing and laughing the five of us wrestled on the floor for several minutes before Irene started crying from her crib, either because the noise had frightened her, or perhaps because she was too small to join in the fun.

An hour later I bid them farewell at the front door of the house. Lord Hightower had been kind enough to send a carriage large enough to hold not only his daughter and son-in-law, with their two children, but my wife and children as well. I watched them board and Dorian looked back at me before stepping in behind them.

"Don't take too long, I can use all the support I can get facing old Lord Hightower," he told me with a smile.

"Don't worry, I'll hurry," I replied. "Take care of them till I can catch up," I added.

His eyes grew serious for a moment, "That will always go without saying."

I watched until they had driven completely out of sight, before turning back to the door of the house. It gaped open, staring at me blackly, and I felt a feeling of dread wash over me. The feeling was helped not at all by the dissonant sound of death, which had been omnipresent since we had arrived in Albamarl. At home in Castle Cameron it tended to vary, growing louder more frequently at night, but here it had remained strongly present the entire time. While I was beginning to get used to it, much like the voice of the earth, I still had no clue why it sometimes seemed louder and closer than at other times.

It couldn't possibly be anything good, I thought as I stepped through the doorway.

CHAPTER 40

We had only brought a couple of servants with us, and my first task after Penny and the others were gone, was to give them the day off, with instructions to return that evening.

With that done, I went to the bedroom and changed into what I called my 'traveling' garb. I had been wearing more formal clothes, the sort I'd be expected to have on if I were on my way to an audience with the king. My traveling clothes, by contrast were simple and functional, pretty much the same sort of thing I wore when busy in my workshop; trousers, boots, and a heavy wool overtunic. The main difference was the inclusion of my staff, my belt of pouches and a cloak. I didn't bother with the cloak since I was indoors.

The important distinction was the fact that I was ready for trouble.

Standing at the head of the stairs leading down into the bedrock beneath the house, I was filled with trepidation. My fear had become so strong it seemed almost a physical thing, palpable and unrelenting. To distract myself, I mentally reviewed my preparations.

I had called the dragon early that morning, commanding him to remain hidden somewhere within a few minutes flight of the capital. The figurine had provided no mental feedback though, so I couldn't be sure he had heard my instructions. Calling on Gareth Gaelyn for backup had seemed like overkill, but my fear made me excessively cautious.

I had my staff and pouches, which provided easy access to a wide variety of magical aids, devices, and weapons; everything from my iron bombs to the new flying device I had created. With those things and my own experience and abilities, I could confidently handle anything up to and including one of the shining gods. What could I possibly have to fear?

The house was empty, so come what may, I shouldn't be endangering any innocent lives, unless whatever was down there was so terrible that it drove me into the streets. *What will she think when she finds that two thousand years have passed?* The thought passed through my mind almost unnoticed. Mentally I grabbed at it and once again found myself empty handed. *She—could it be the woman from my dream?*

"If that's the case my greatest danger might be Penny," I muttered to myself with a half-smile. Gathering my courage, I descended the stairs until they reached the level space at the bottom, and there I faced the stone door.

The air was taut with tension, and the dissonance I had come to associate with death grew to the point that I found it difficult to concentrate. Interestingly it seemed to be strongest behind me, rather than before me, where the door lay. It was as if the grim reaper himself was looking over my shoulder.

"I've probably defied Lady Luck and pissed off Mother Nature so many times, that they've sent their boyfriend Death to collect me," I said aloud, though there was no one to laugh at my joke.

Ignoring the distractions, I focused my magesight on the door, seeking any hint of patterns or runes. The last time I had examined it I had had no knowledge of concealing enchantments, so I now had a better idea why I had sensed nothing beyond the door. As before, I sensed nothing, nothing but stone and more stone. It went on for at least forty feet in every direction, featureless and unchanging, before I noticed a difference. At some point beyond forty feet the stone became less homogenous, more varied and flawed, with frequent cracks and occasional changes in its composition.

The conclusion was obvious. The area behind the door was entirely cloaked in an enchantment, making it appear to be solid stone, when in fact it probably contained a room. *Why put a door here then? That's a dead giveaway that something lies beyond,* I thought to myself, *unless the purpose was merely to conceal the room from some powerful outside observer.* I shook my head, I really had no way to know at this point, and further speculation was pointless.

"Open!" I said loudly, wondering if it might be something so simple. Nothing happened.

Focusing my perception closely on the door immediately in front of me, I tried to find the runes that created the concealing enchantment. Generally such inscriptions would be small, and by their very nature hard to perceive unless you were looking for them. If anyone could find them though, it would be me. *My family invented enchanting, after all.*

I found nothing.

I was beginning to consider trying force, but a random thought stopped me. *Why had no other Illeniel wizard opened the door?* I couldn't be the first to wonder at what lay behind it. *Unless they already knew,* I thought. It might have been the sort of thing taught to each generation, something I might have known if I had received the same instruction every other wizard in my family had been given. My gut told me it was more than that, however. *They couldn't open the door.*

"But you can," said the voice of the earth, startling me. The words were a product of my own mind, but the meaning had come across clearly. While I heard the voice of the earth constantly, it was rare for it to direct anything resembling meaningful communication to me, unless I spoke to it first.

This door required an archmage to open. The conclusion was obvious, and I was surprised it had taken me so long to realize. *Otherwise they would have taken her.* Again I caught myself thinking strange thoughts, and I wished I could force the back of my mind to give me the knowledge I needed, but as soon as I focused upon it, my fear drove the secrets into darkness.

Ignoring my doubts and confusion, I opened my mind and began to listen, allowing myself to fall into a deeper rapport with the earth. What I discovered amazed me, for the stone behind and around the door seemed to have a separate identity. While it was still technically a part of the earth, it held a portion of itself apart, as if it had been given an ego or a 'self'. Not only was it separate, but it was deceiving me, projecting an image of itself as solid and whole, obscuring the truth behind an illusion.

Show me the truth, I ordered.

The stone responded immediately, *None but my master can command me.*

He is gone. I am his descendant and inheritor of his will, I told it, and then I put my hand against the stone door, lowering my shield and allowing the stone to come into full contact with my flesh.

Suddenly the illusion vanished, and I could see the room within, while simultaneously the door itself slid aside so that I could enter.

The room was twenty feet in diameter, circular and empty, except for the object in its center, an open stone sarcophagus. The scene was intimately familiar, for I had known what I would find here, just as I knew that the object in the middle of the room was no sarcophagus, it held a living creature.

Stepping closer I looked down upon her, Lyralliantha, the last of her kind, trapped eternally within a stasis enchantment. The woman inside was the most beautiful I had ever beheld, barring my encounter with the goddess Millicenth, and I discounted that immediately. The gods cheated. Her hair was silver, not simply white, but possessing an almost metallic shimmer, and while her eyes were closed, I knew that if they had been open they would have been an icy blue, just like all the children of her grove.

She was clad in a soft white gown that reached past her knees before revealing the smooth skin of her lower legs. Her hands and feet were slender and graceful, with short well-kept nails. Other than her unusual hair color and exceptional beauty, there was nothing that might have indicated her alien nature, except for her delicately pointed ears. Her eye color was slightly unusual, but it fell within the normal range of human color, in fact it was similar in hue to my own eyes.

Illeniel's promise rose up in my mind, the words of my long dead ancestor, *"This is the only way I can save your people. Rest here and I will return to release you— once it is safe again. I give you my word, I will return for you."* Except that he hadn't.

A feeling of terrible sorrow fell over me as I gazed upon her, and I spoke without premeditation, "Lyralliantha, last of the She'Har, you are alone in this world. It was never meant that you should endure thus for over two millennia. Your husband waits for your return— and your forgiveness." The words arose from someplace deep within my heart, and I knew as I spoke them that they were the key, the words that would release the stasis enchantment that held her in that timeless moment.

Yet nothing happened.

Puzzled, both at my sudden words and at their lack of effect, I bent my attention to the enchantment that surrounded her. In form and structure it was similar to the stasis enchantments I had created in the past. If anything, it was slightly less refined, lacking certain safeguards that I would have included. In particular it was constructed in such a way that if it were broken or forced, the backlash might kill the occupant. *That was deliberate,* answered the voice in the back of my mind.

As I studied the enchantment with my magesight, it became readily apparent why the spoken key had not had its intended effect. Woven around the enchantment was a second magical structure, something alien, while at the same time familiar. *She'Har spell-weaving,* I thought, recognizing it even as the phrase from my dream made sense. I had seen magic like it once before—when I had fought Timothy, the leader of the shiggreth.

"Starting to realize why you can't release her, animal?" said a voice close to my ear.

A jolt of fear and pure adrenaline ran down my spine, and if it had been possible I might have jumped out of my own skin, instead I reacted defensively. With a word, I created a new shield around myself while stepping sideways. I had fought enough battles that my reactions were more practical than panic stricken. Fear might drive me, but it was a foe I was used to dealing with.

"Who's there?" I asked, somewhat stridently.

The voice came again, though it seemed to have moved, and now it reached me from somewhere ahead and to my left, "Forgotten your old friend already? How sad."

I scanned the room frantically with my magesight and still found nothing. Whoever was there was invisible, not just physically, but to magical sight as well. There were only three people capable of such a thing, assuming the voice belonged to a person.

"Wondering why you can't sense me? Surely you've heard the phrase before, 'when a Prathion doesn't want to be found, a Prathion isn't found'."

The voice now seemed to be behind me, on my left side, as though the person taunting me was circling. The dissonant song of death was strongest in that direction as well. In a flash I realized that whoever this was they had been shadowing me, not just for weeks or days, but for months, possibly years. My entire life had been visible to them, and I had never even known they were there.

"It's taken you long enough to reveal yourself," I answered as calmly as I could. "You've been watching for a long time. I had begun to wonder at your sanity."

"Still lying, Mordecai? You should know better. Your ignorance betrays your bluff. If you had known I was there you'd never have turned off the lights to lie beside your wife, you'd never have left your children alone in my presence. How many nights did I lean over you while you cried like a babe from the night terrors, never knowing I was close enough to smell your fear? How many nights did I wait, wishing I could kill you and put an end to your accursed line?" said the voice from directly behind me.

Turning to keep my hidden opponent in front of me, I struggled to identify the voice. It was familiar and yet I still was unable to place it. It had already claimed to be a Prathion, but I knew all three of the living Prathion wizards intimately, and this voice belonged to none of them.

"If you wanted me dead so badly, why didn't you kill me?" I asked.

The dissonance, the voice of death that I had been hearing for months, continued to move, so—trusting my instincts I turned to keep it in front of me, even before its source spoke again, "I've learned patience," came the reply. "You surprise me with your movement, it's almost as if you can sense my location," it added.

"I can—now that I understand what you are," I replied.

"So—have you figured out my name yet, animal?" it asked curiously.

"Only the name that you've given me in the past, Timothy, but I'm certain that isn't your real name," I declared. As I did, it shifted and moved in a different direction, silently and without warning, I changed directions as well, keeping it before me.

"Interesting," it said, stopping for a moment. "It seems you really can detect me. I suppose there's no need for this then." A small figure appeared in front of me, resting its hand casually on Lyralliantha's resting place. "A pity your small mind can't remember my true name. *She* will recognize me," it added, glancing at the woman in stasis.

The memories in the back of my mind had returned to their former reticence, though the shiggreth's taunting kept hinting at secrets I should know. *He's a Prathion, yet in the past he said that the shiggreth were created from the spirits of the She'Har that died*, I thought, mentally reviewing what I knew. *Perhaps he's a shiggreth created from a dead Prathion? Walter's uncle?*

Even as that thought occurred to me, I knew it to be nonsense, for the body that the undead thing in front of me was using belonged to a small boy from Lancaster. A boy named Timothy, a boy that had been entirely normal as far as I knew. *Besides,* I told myself, *the Prathions were golden haired with ebon skin and red eyes.* The thought shocked me into stillness, as the implications of that statement ran through my mind. *Prathion was the name of a She'Har grove.*

That couldn't be correct. Prathion was the name of one of the five great wizard lineages, but somewhere, deep down, I remembered. It was originally the name of one of the largest She'Har groves, along with Centyr, Gaelyn, Mordan, and—Illeniel. Along with the knowledge came images, memories of the places connected with those names. The She'Har groves were something like cities, except that the place, the trees, and the people, were all part of one thing, one family. One fact still didn't fit, the fact that those names were now used in reference to the five great wizard families—*human* wizards.

"I can almost see the wheels turning in your head, animal. It's a pity, really. I had hoped you would remember everything before I slew you, so that you would understand the depth of your ancestor's sin. Perhaps I will tell you my name while you are dying," said the small boy.

"Then your patience is at an end. You sound as if you have already gained what you sought," I said, hoping to draw things out.

"We are here. Once you opened the door for me you sealed your fate, along with the fate of the rest of your wretched species," it told me.

"You want to wipe out humankind?" I asked.

The boy smiled, "I won't fail this time."

"You broke the accord," I said, and then I knew who he was, "Thillmarius Prathion." The words emerged without warning, but I could feel their truth resonating in my bones. *He was the reason she wanted the stasis enchantment created to kill her if it was broken forcibly,* I realized, as a wave of emotions began crashing through me. "You're the reason for this sealed chamber. You killed them!" I said remembering my dream.

"Correction, animal," he screamed back in rage, "I killed *most* of them. You ancestor was far more thorough, he slew all of my people—all but one." He gestured at Lyralliantha as he spoke.

"He destroyed you, you're dead," I mumbled, as a series of violent images cascaded through my mind. I was reeling in shock.

Thillmarius sneered, "Congratulations! I still am, but I intend to correct that." As he finished his statement his hands came up, and a wave of darkness flew toward me at the speed of thought.

My shield was ready, but it made little difference. The She'Har spell-weaving shredded it in an instant, and then it tore into my skin, ripping and slicing like a thousand knives. The last time I had fought the leader of the shiggreth, I had a Knight of Stone beside me, not to mention Walter. Without their help I would have been unable to survive long enough to trap Thillmarius underground, although I now knew that that tactic hadn't been successful.

Today I had no one beside me. A potentially fatal mistake on my part, but I wasn't ready to concede the fight yet. I had prepared for the possibility of this rematch, if only I could gain enough time to respond properly.

Experience had been an excellent teacher, and as the pain of my enemy's spell-weaving threatened to overwhelm me, my mind quickly sought refuge in the stone. The pain of my physical body receded even as I sent a spray of stone shards upward. Reaching out to the wind, I spun them into a twisting storm of razor sharp death.

The deadly spell-weaving fell away from my flesh body as Thillmarius was forced to defend himself from the destructive stone storm. Resuming more direct control of my human form, my eyes opened and followed his movement. "Enjoying the fruits of my training?" I asked, taunting the undead creature.

The stone shards had torn his small body, but the shiggreth's response was quick, and another spell-weaving flew from his fingers and lips, wrapping itself around him like a powerful shield and preventing further damage. I knew it would be only seconds before he regained the initiative, unless I could find a way to protect myself from his spell-weavings.

Reaching into one of my belt pouches, I withdrew a stone disk, the same one I had attempted to use the day the enchanted furniture had attacked. With a word I tossed it into the air above my head and watched as it split into a multitude of small pieces. Extending my hand, I began channeling power, feeding it to the enchanted shield stones, while in turn they began to spin and whirl around me with increasing speed, becoming a blur.

Another spell-weaving struck, but this time it skittered away harmlessly, unable to pierce the shield created by my stones. "Let's go outside. We both have too much to lose here," I told my opponent, indicating the still body in the center of the room. Turning toward the door I walked out and up the stairs, leaving a trail of blood behind as I went.

His first attack had left me with a collection of shallow cuts. The pain they caused might have been a distraction, but I kept my mind in an in-between state, partly connected to the earth and wind around me, which made the sensations of my human body seem small, almost insignificant. It was a technique I had practiced often since my battle with Celior and it afforded me numerous advantages.

The minor connection afforded me more power for my spells, while at the same time numbing my perception of pain. It also enabled me to control the environment around me in an automatic, almost unconscious manner that left my human mind free to cast spells at the same time. I had yet to come up with a marvelous name for my in-between state, but Penny, with her usual candor, had suggested I name it the 'idiot-trance'. She had explained that my lack of pain made me less concerned for my physical body and thus, less likely to defend myself. I knew the truth though; she just liked finding new ways to call me an idiot.

Her worry about defending my human body was a valid concern though, which was yet another reason I had created the enchanted shield-stones. Even as I left the underground room, I continued to channel more power into them with my human mind.

As I had hoped, Thillmarius followed me without protest, though I suspected he was preparing other weavings as we went. I led him to the front door and out into the street before he struck again, a probing attack meant to test the strength of my new shield.

"You'll have to do better than that," I taunted, while at the same time reaching into another pouch to touch the small figurine within. *I need you now,* I said silently, projecting my thought at the small statuette.

By the time I returned my full attention to him, it was almost too late. Thillmarius had sent his second attack into the base of the building beside me, and whatever he used, it turned a large portion of one wall and some of the foundation into fine dust, leaving the rest of the structure unsupported. It was in the process of falling on top of me, as I realized my mistake.

The neighbors are never going to forgive me for today. The observation flickered through the back of my head, while the more practical parts of my mind were busy figuring out how to prevent my imminent future as a pancake. While my enchanted shield stones had many advantages over my normal impromptu shields, it wasn't as easy to change their strength or the shape of the area they protected. They could probably stop anything Thillmarius might cast at me, but they would definitely fail if a building fell on me.

All this passed through my mind in an instant, and despite the timelessness of such adrenaline soaked moments, I still managed to do the wrong thing. Lifting my hand, I shouted a word and used my own power to brace the building. Such a move would have been fatal for most wizards, but as I had learned from countless other stupid moments in the past, I was the wizardly equivalent of a giant—and sometimes I was about that smart as well.

I understood my mistake immediately as the weight of untold tons of stone and timber made themselves felt against my invisible brace. Stumbling I gasped at the shock, but somehow I held it. The dumb part of my action was that I was now entirely consumed with the effort of holding the building up, it wasn't something I could simply stop doing when it became inconvenient. Given a second thought, I realized I should have called on the earth and allowed it to hold the building for me, keeping my own power free to respond to Thillmarius' next attack.

My foe was approaching rapidly now, charging toward me with a long dagger in hand. The blade was writhing with alien magics, and I knew instinctively that whatever he had put on the weapon would be able to pierce my new shield. Thillmarius had been one of the greatest lore-masters of his grove. Another bit of information had presented itself to me when I least expected it.

With my magic fully engaged holding up the building, I had no choice but to call upon the elements to defend me, and in my desperation I took a risk that I probably should have considered more carefully. I reached for that which the undead fear most, and the very thing that my ancestor had used to eradicate Thillmarius' body, two thousand years ago.

I reached for fire, calling to the small flames in the oven within the very house I was holding up. Opening my mind I spoke to them, I called them—and I gave them a home, joining them with my own spirit. What might have been an entirely innocuous feat of magic, if I were using my regular wizardly abilities, took on an entirely more deadly meaning when done as an archmage, for the fire infused my mind as well as my actions.

Roaring my hatred at him I sent spiraling streams of flame at Thillmarius, seeking to engulf him before he could reach me. The wind guided and goaded the fire to an incandescent heat, as it surged toward the undead creature.

Suffused with the fire's rage and desire for destruction, I laughed as I watched my foe stop, stunned at the conflagration racing toward him, but my glee was presumptuous. Reacting with incredible speed, Thillmarius wrapped himself within a slightly different shield that seemed to flow from his hands without effort. The ease with which he created spontaneous spell-weavings; magics that were as durable and as difficult to destroy as any enchantment I could craft—was simply unfair.

I had my own advantages though; in particular, I possessed a near limitless resource as an archmage, I wasn't limited to just my individual strength. The fire demonstrated that point quite eloquently as it engulfed the shiggreth's shield. The long dead lore-warden's defense held despite the incredible force I brought to bear, but even it couldn't last forever. Seconds ticked by, five, ten, fifteen, and with each passing moment the fire grew hotter while the wind whipped it into a fury, creating a sound not unlike a scream.

Inevitably the creature's shield failed, popping like a bubble as the flames rushed inward, to devour—nothing. Thillmarius wasn't there.

My own carefully crafted defense crumbled, as Thillmarius' knife severed the links between my enchanted stones in a gracefully complex stroke before plunging into my lower back. The monster had hidden himself and diverted my attention with a powerful illusion. I had to marvel at his skill, to be able to manage so many things at once, for the shield he had created for his illusory double had been quite real. Too late I realized I should have kept my attention on the source of the dissonant song of death, for it was the only reliable way I could be sure of his location.

"Did you think yourself a match for an elder lore-warden, *animal?*" he said sneeringly into my ear, as the blade sent waves of eldritch agony rippling through my body.

I was still in my 'idiot-trance' as my kindly wife had named it, and while my human form should have been incapacitated by the energies coursing through it, I was still largely able to act. Willing my human lips to move, I spat out my defiance, even as my elemental mind acted upon the stones beneath our feet, "I've got a collection of 'gods' at home. I really don't think you're that special."

Looking down, Thillmarius saw that his lower legs were fully encased in granite that had until recently, been street paving stones. Struggling to free himself, he tried to withdraw his blade from my back, to begin a new weaving, but I had the wrist of his knife-hand firmly within my grasp.

The child's body he occupied was no match for my adult frame, but the effort caused even more pain to shoot through my body. Showing his teeth, he growled at me, "Does it hurt? That body can't take much more before it expires, and unlike me—you can die."

"You really shouldn't piss me off," I bit back through clenched jaws. "Do you think it's that easy to hold all that back?" my eyes flicked upwards, and then I dropped the building on our heads.

Thillmarius' expression was priceless as he saw the stone wall and heavy timbers falling toward him, but I kept his hand firmly in my grip, and his feet were completely trapped. His body was crushed under untold tons of wreckage—while my own slipped through, stone and wood parting like water to let my human form pass unharmed.

Pulling free I left the dagger and the hand clutching it behind, while I used my now free magic to lift myself up and out of the pile of rubble, that had once been part of my neighbor's rather large and ostentatious home. As I climbed down from the top of the heap, I let my mind collapse inward, becoming once more merely human.

My physical condition was alarming, to say the least. The cuts I had received earlier had left me light headed from loss of blood, and my new stab wound had done terrible damage to my left kidney and some of the muscles in my back. I was still hemorrhaging, and my strength was diminishing with each passing second. Pain made it nearly impossible to move, and I already regretted leaving my 'idiot-trance', but it was clear that if I hadn't, I might have ignored my wounds until they left me dead.

Looking back at the wreckage I had just left behind, I prepared to finish what I had started. My wounds were dangerous but they didn't worry me too much. Given a moment's respite I could stop the bleeding, and with a bit more effort I should be able to restore myself to full health. Regaining my energy would take longer, but that was simply a matter of proper rest.

More important was eradicating the undead creature I had temporarily beaten. I knew better than to think Thillmarius was permanently defeated. My ancestor had burned him to ash and yet the magic that kept him alive had still preserved his spirit against the void, until first Balinthor, and then later, Millicenth, could resurrect him.

I had no way of unraveling the spell-weaving that kept his spirit and its eternal hatred tied to our world, but I could at least do as much as my predecessors had done, and destroy his body. Drawing my will inward, I focused my remaining magic and readied myself to turn the pile of rubble into a funeral pyre—even stone will burn if you get it hot enough, and I planned to spare nothing to make sure Thillmarius was thoroughly eradicated.

"Mordecai?!" came Penny's voice, yelling from a block away.

As I turned to look backward, the wound in my back caught when damaged muscles failed to do their job. Stumbling, I fell and found myself having difficulty getting back to my feet. *Shit, maybe I should have fixed my back first,* I thought silently, but I knew I had little time. My magesight, now that my focus had expanded, showed me that the carriage containing my family was returning, with Dorian, Rose, and the children still inside it. They were a few blocks further away but approaching quickly. For some reason Penny had chosen to run ahead, using her strength and speed to arrive sooner.

My attempt to stand didn't go well, so I quickly abandoned it. On hands and knees, I returned my attention to my fallen foe; I didn't need to be on my feet to incinerate him. My head came around just in time to intercept a heavy piece of masonry, as the pile of wood and stone exploded outward. I was fortunate in that the blow was a glancing one, otherwise it might have crushed my skull. Lady Luck wasn't doing me any favors though; her idea of 'fortunate' was more painful than being killed outright. I heard a snap, followed by blinding pain that sent me tumbling back as my jaw broke from the force of the impact.

Things became much more confused after that point, for I lost track of the world around me for an uncertain period of time. As my senses returned I noticed two things immediately; one, Thillmarius was now standing over me, and two, Penny was racing towards him at a speed that would have made a racehorse jealous. She had her sword in hand, and her skirts had again been hacked off. *And that's why we can't have nice things,* I said silently to myself, *because you keep chopping up your dresses.* Of course, I had to be silent, my jaw was a mass of blood and pain—speaking aloud wasn't an option. *That's going to make magic more difficult too,* I realized, not that I had much strength left.

My enemy didn't look like much now; his body had originally been that of a child, and it appeared to have been through some hard use—being crushed under a wall often had that effect. It was animated now purely by magic, and I could see that his bones had been shattered in numerous places, not that it seemed to bother him much. My chance to finish him off had disappeared, turning my hard won victory into a crushing defeat.

Gesturing idly with one hand, he sent a twenty pound block of stone flying toward my enraged wife. It shot toward her as if it had been fired from a siege engine, with bone crushing speed, but even before he had finished that weaving, I saw he had begun another spell weaving with his other hand.

Penny leapt skyward, taking to the air like a falcon springing into flight, rising over the stone and twisting in mid-air, to prepare for her landing. Thillmarius released his second spell as soon as he had seen her trajectory, sending a writhing mass of snakelike bands to intercept her as she came down. Her sword flicked out to strike the spell-weaving, but it flowed up and around it, catching woman and weapon alike in a tangled mesh of magic.

Penny screamed in anger as the tendrils of magic constricted around her painfully, but she refused to surrender, struggling with a strength that caused the bindings to cut into her skin and flesh. She might have torn free, but the shiggreth reached her first, putting his hand to her cheek.

"Relax Penelope, it will be so much less painful if you relax," he said, as his touch began to drain her life away. A shudder ran through her as she felt once again the cold touch that had haunted her for so many years after her kidnapping, and a look of wild terror passed across her face. It disappeared quickly though as she sagged downward, gradually losing the will or energy to fight.

An expression of delight and pleasure was on Thillmarius' face now as he followed her to the ground, and I could see some of his wounds healing even as he drew out her life, with one hand on her neck and the other on her bare thigh.

I might have roared my indignation, but my mouth was no longer cooperating. Drawing on my will, I sent a lance of force toward him, hoping to drive him away, but my magic dissipated the moment it touched his undead body. I cursed my own stupidity for wasting my last chance, as a wave of dizziness washed over me. My eyesight was growing dim and unconsciousness was approaching when I heard Moira's voice.

"Momma!" she shrieked, in a high tone that pierced my heart, and as she cried, I saw as much as felt her power awaken, blooming outward in a flash of aythar. The carriage had drawn close, and somehow she had gotten out before Dorian or Rose could stop her. The sight of Penny dying had driven her to desperation. Her call was a summons, a heartfelt plea to her mother to rise and resist the creature that was killing her, but it fell on deaf ears. Penny no longer had the strength to stand, much less fight off her attacker.

But someone else heard her cry, a different mother that Moira knew nothing of—and she answered instantly. Rising from the broken road, was the earthen form of Moira Centyr, the magical remnant of my daughter's actual mother.

Thillmarius was so surprised at her sudden appearance, that he released Penny and took two steps backward, but even caught off guard, his hands were already moving, preparing new attacks. He stood now directly in front of me, and I feared his next move would kill one of us.

The ground rippled and a wave of earth carried Penny back toward the carriage where Dorian and the others now stood. *I am fading already, this is more than I can handle,* said Moira Centyr within my mind.

Save them if you can, I responded instantly, pleading.

It might have been my imagination, but her gemstone eyes focused upon me for a moment before the world shook, and a massive ring of bedrock rose up around the carriage until it had formed an unbroken sphere.

Thillmarius turned and looked down, mock pity in his gaze. "So much for the cavalry, *animal,* but at least they're safe—right? Everyone gets a happy ending but you." He smiled, showing shattered teeth as he bent down to run his fingers through my hair. A cold wind passed through my soul, as I felt even that brief touch draw away some of my remaining vitality.

Drawing his hand back he spoke again, "I'm lying of course. Once I finish with you, I'll take that dome apart and give the rest of your family my undivided attention. It's just a pity that I can't keep you alive to see it; you're just too dangerous to ignore. I bet you wished you had learned that lesson before today—don't you? You almost won."

I struggled to speak but nothing worked, and I only managed to spit more blood upon the ground. My strength was gone, my magic weak and ultimately useless against the creature standing above me. My only hope was my abilities as an archmage, but I could no longer hear the voices of the earth and wind. They were drowned out by the dissonant wailing of the voice of death, loud and incessant.

The awful sound grew yet louder as Thillmarius reached down again, placing his hand on my neck. "What did you say earlier? You've got a collection of gods at home? Your boasting was meaningless to me. I'm the last lore-warden of the She'Har and my people *created* the gods. No matter what your bestial kind achieves, you'll never be more than animals in our eyes."

My last sight was his terrible eyes staring hatefully down at me. My last regret was that I couldn't respond with something clever before I passed away. *Stupid broken jaw,* I thought, and then darkness stole the world from me.

CHAPTER 41

In the darkness I saw a single light, but as I focused my attention it grew until I found myself sitting beside it, a lone candle in a darkened room. A table was before me, and sitting across it was another man, one I recognized.

"Hello," I said amiably.

"Hello," answered my twin with a smug expression. I could tell already that my alter ego was just as much of a smart-ass as I was, the arrogant bastard.

"Where am I?" I asked, deciding not to drag the conversation out.

"This is the end for us—or the beginning, depending on your perspective," said my other self.

"Listen," I told my doppelganger, "I know how much I enjoy being cryptic, but how about we dispense with the circumlocutions and just speak plainly. It won't be long before even this dream is gone."

"Not exactly," the other me replied, "Time is an illusion. In a certain sense, this conversation will last forever—in another sense it is already over—and for some, it has just begun."

I groaned, "I'm starting to wish it was already over. If this is the afterlife, please cancel my membership."

"This isn't the afterlife. You haven't died yet."

My eyes narrowed, "Then who are you?"

"I'm you," my other-self replied.

"Really? I thought you'd be more handsome," I shot back.

We both laughed at that; until I realized that it was rather pathetic, laughing at my own jokes with an imaginary friend—while I was dying. I wondered if Marc's experience had been similar.

"I'm here to offer you a choice," said my twin, bringing my attention back to the conversation.

"What choice?"

"Knowledge—or ignorance," my hallucination answered, and opening his hands he held out a small object toward me.

My eyes were drawn toward it, even as I retorted, "What difference will it make?"

"Exactly."

The object he held was a fruit, pinkish-yellow in color, with a high luster, and a jolt of recognition shot through me when I saw it. It was something the She'Har had called a 'loshti', a rare creation of their mother and father-trees. The best name for it in our language would have been 'ancestor fruit'.

"This is where it began," I said, lecturing my alter ego. "When our ancestor stole the loshti…" My eyes bore down on it and it seemed to grow in size. I had crossed the threshold—the door within my mind had opened, and now I chose to look into, to stare at, the knowledge that previously paralyzed me with fear.

Two thousand years of men and women struggling and living ran through my mind, the memories of my ancestors, stretching out behind me in a line that reached back to the point of my fear—the moment when my original ancestor stole and ate the loshti of the Illeniel grove. Looking deeper I saw the memories continued beyond that point, to alien thoughts and foreign dreams—the dreams of the trees. The trees we had slain.

The loshti was the vehicle by which the She'Har had passed down their collected wisdom, from one generation to the next. It was never meant for human kind, and yet he had stolen it anyway, in his quest for recognition—and power. It was the hidden place in my mind, the knowledge I hid from myself. It was what had lain hidden behind the name, 'Illeniel's Doom', for its theft and the knowledge it granted had led to the destruction of an entire race, and very nearly humankind as well.

The memories of the trees stretched out into the distance for untold millennia, making the two thousand years of human memories seem small in comparison. The knowledge of the loshti had taken root in the mind of the first human to steal it, but being housed within a being that was not of the She'Har, it had passed itself on to the next generation in a new way. From that point on, it had entered the first born of each generation of the new Illeniels, carrying with it the memories of each ancestor that had gone before—including those of the trees.

My fear had only partly been of the atrocities hidden within those memories. In large part I had been afraid of the alien, the 'other', tens of thousands of years of knowledge that would inevitably overwhelm my own humanity.

I gazed at my mirror image, meeting his eyes. "We were right to hide this. No one can live with such knowledge."

"You aren't living—you're dying," my other-self responded.

I knew now the nature of the spell-weaving that Thillmarius had used to preserve himself against the ages, against time, and against death itself. I still couldn't use it though—being human I was incapable of spell-weaving, but I had other abilities. Things no She'Har could do, even as vast as their powers had been.

Closing my inner eyes, I left the vision behind and listened again to the world, for it was still there all around me. One song stood out above it all, the dissonance that I had come to associate with death. I had first heard it when I brought Walter back from the void, but in the months that Thillmarius had stalked and spied upon me I had become intimately familiar with it.

"An archmage does not wield power, Mordecai," I heard again the words of Moira Centyr, *"An archmage becomes that which they seek to wield."* Opening my mind, I felt the death-song that Thillmarius Prathion had become, and I embraced it.

My eyes opened again on the physical world and I saw my foe's expression change to one of fear as I gazed upward at him. "What? That's not possible," he said, shocked as I reached out to him.

An outside observer might have thought that I had died and awakened, a new and ultimately empty shiggreth, as had happened to so many others. Nothing was further from the truth. My life still burned faintly, but it was changing, warping to adapt to my new song.

My hand passed through Thillmarius' chest, as if his flesh were merely an illusion, to touch his core, an intangible thing wrapped in the blackest of She'Har magic. Listening carefully I made it my own, and it unwrapped suddenly, leaving the undead She'Har's spirit unprotected as his ancient spell-woven curse shifted and wound itself around the source of my own life instead.

A look of horror crossed his face, and then his body collapsed, much like a puppet whose strings had been cut. Thillmarius Prathion, last lore-warden of the She'Har, and prisoner of his own hatred and death-magic, was finally free—his spirit passed on into the void, and mine took its place within his cage.

A shocking cold washed over me and I might have screamed, had it not been for my still ruined jaw. I was forced to settle for a miserable gurgle. *What have I done?* I wondered, as the world changed around me. Looking within, I found only darkness where the wellspring of my life, my vitality, and my power had been, a cold impenetrable shell had encased the center of my being.

The colors of the world were different now, intense and garish, at times both too bright and too dark—a medley of contrasts. I could still hear the voices of the earth, the wind, and all too loudly, the voice of death, but they seemed more distant now. My magesight had remained even though my native wizardry, made possible by my living aythar, had vanished.

To put it succinctly, I was confused as hell.

I was still lying, battered and bloody, upon the torn stones of the road. Tired and bewildered I closed my eyes—I needed rest, and the world could worry about itself for a little while. I had done enough.

I wasn't aware of having fallen asleep, but some time passed before I was startled by the sound of a voice nearby.

"He's still here," I heard Dorian say.

My eyes were still closed but my magesight revealed Penny, Rose, and my children clambering out of a hole in the stone shell that had surrounded them. It appeared that Dorian had been forced to hew and carve his way through the solid stone with his sword, a task that might have taken him hours. *How long have I been lying here?*

He stopped before reaching me, and his breath seemed to catch in his throat. "Don't come any closer, Penny. You shouldn't see this," he told my wife, who was now some twenty feet away.

"I'll be damned before I let anyone keep me from him!" Penny replied with her usual spirit, making a smile creep across my face—or it would have, if my mouth and jaw hadn't been a mangled mess of torn flesh and broken bone.

"He isn't breathing, Penny. He's dead. Take the children away, they shouldn't see their father like this," responded Dorian, in a somber tone.

I decided then that the charade had gone on long enough, and I opened my eyes to look at them directly. Dorian gasped and Penny ran toward me then. "He's alive! Someone get to the house, we need to send a message to Walter! He's going to need help immediately," she shouted, kneeling beside me.

Looking into her teary eyes I couldn't help but think how lucky I was to have her love, and I struggled to speak, to say just that—or at least make an inappropriate remark, but again my shattered mouth failed me. The gurgling that I did manage only served to alarm her more.

"It's going to be alright, Mordecai. We're all here for you. Walter's coming, and he'll make sure you stay alive until we can fix this, just stay with me," Penny told me with tears streaming from her eyes. "Please," she begged, "just stay with me—don't die! Do you hear me!?"

I'm likely to drown first if you keep crying over me, I thought, but it was impossible for me to express my words to her. To reassure her I reached up, resting my hand gently upon her cheek, and delicious warmth radiated from her skin, suffusing me with a pleasant sensation. Simultaneously, her eyes widened in shock and fear. More quickly than I might have believed possible, she bolted upright, leaping away from me. Her rejection was the most painful thing I had ever experienced, creating a loneliness in my chest that was immediate and unexpected.

Why?

"He's gone Dorian! It isn't him—he's gone!" she screamed in a heart wrenching voice. I had never wanted to hear such raw pain and emotion in her voice. It was the woeful cry of a woman that had just lost everything.

"What?" asked Dorian, puzzled.

Penny's sword was out now and she brandished it before her. "He's turned Dorian! He's dead—he's one of them!" she yelled hoarsely, with swollen eyes and a nose that dripped from tears. "Why!?" she cried, venting her grief at the sky.

I sat up, and my mind raced as I tried to figure out how to reassure them. I felt odd, certainly, and I probably had a concussion, given how strange the world seemed, but I wasn't dying. I looked to my friend for support, since Penny seemed to have lost her mind.

Dorian had approached already, sword in one hand while reaching toward me with his other, now un-gauntleted hand. I put up my own, thinking he meant to pull me to my feet, but as soon as our bare skin met he stepped away, a pained expression on his face. "It's true," he said, and his face twisted in a horrific expression of grief, even as his sword arm shifted—preparing to strike.

I saw death in his eyes then—the murderous resolve of a man who must slay his best friend, and there was nothing I could do to stop him. I gazed at him blankly, numb with grief and sorrow at the realization that they thought I had turned. *They think I'm one of the shiggreth now, but I'm not. It's still me.* Dorian's stance changed, and I knew what he would do—what he had to do—what we always did with shiggreth. *You cut them up and burn them.*

A sudden movement reminded me that we were not alone. Penny had caught our daughter, Moira, by the hand, but Matthew slipped past before she saw him. Running to me he was yelling, "Daddy! Don't hurt my Dad!"

Time froze then, as he leapt into my arms with the infinite faith of a child, as he had done so many times before. I caught him instinctively, and another surge of warmth ran through me, even as Matthew shuddered at the sudden cold—and then I understood the truth. *They're right, I've inherited Thillmarius' spell-woven curse—I'm one of them.*

Immediately I put my son down, trying to keep from touching his skin any further as I shoved him in front of me. He was still conscious, and he stood on his own— and despite the chill that he had just experienced, his faith never wavered. "Don't you dare hurt him, Dorian!" he commanded my friend.

I could see a war of emotions raging through Dorian's face as he tried to decide whether he could strike without endangering my son.

Penny tried to intervene, "Matthew, please come here," she said calmly, but the boy refused to move. Desperate she continued, shouting, "Matthew—now! Get over here!"

"No, Momma—Uncle Dorian will hurt him. Tell him not to hurt Daddy," replied Matthew anxiously.

Penny's next words broke my heart, "That's not your father, Matthew. It only looks like him."

I wanted to die then, but the sound of giant wings distracted me. Looking skyward, we saw a giant form descending. Everyone was forced to move back as the dragon, Gareth Gaelyn, landed beside me. Staring at him I saw the flicker in his eyes as he registered the change in me.

What is your wish? He said, projecting the thoughts silently toward me.

Take me away, I thought at him, unsure if my attempt to communicate would work without my magic. I stood and moved closer to him, hoping he would understand my motion.

Leave the boy, the dragon responded, *or I will not help you, bargain or not.*

I had drawn Matthew with me, pulling on the back of his shirt without realizing it. I was reluctant to release him—for he felt like the only thing I had left to save me from the darkness that now surrounded me. I held onto his clothes stubbornly. *I need him, you don't understand.*

The dragon roared, which sent even Dorian an involuntary step backward, while Penny instinctively sought to shelter Moira. Rose had already drawn the other children back into the stone sphere. Gareth Gaelyn's thoughts came to me again, *Trust me! Remember how I became a dragon. Release him before you destroy what you love.*

Unable even to speak the words that were crushing my heart, I lifted my son and threw him at Dorian, trusting my friend to catch him safely. The moment I was alone the dragon's claw caught me loosely, and with a great rush of air I found myself lifted, into the sky—staring down at the people I had loved.

Impotent and lacking even the capacity to cry, I was borne away by the dragon, no longer caring what might happen to me.

EPILOGUE

Penelope Illeniel, the Countess di' Cameron, and now widow of the late Mordecai Illeniel, returned to her bedroom in a state of dumb shock. A few short hours past she had left on a trivial journey, to visit Rose Hightower's family, never suspecting the tragedy that would befall her. Those hours seemed far away—they belonged to another woman, a woman whose life had not been rent asunder.

Her grief was so profound that, despite her initial outburst, she found herself now unable to cry, and her eyes were dry, though they remained swollen. She had not expected to return and find her husband dead, murdered by the undead fiend he had been pursuing for almost a decade now. The image of his shattered body, lying still on the road, yet haunted her. Each time her eyes closed she saw him there again, quiet and bloody—dead.

This can't be real. It will never be real, I won't accept it. This isn't happening. In her mind she saw his eyes open again, remembering her relief at seeing him alive. *But he wasn't...* As soon as his hand had touched her, as it had so often before, she had known. The cold touch, the bitter pain, those things she had learned well during her captivity among the shiggreth years before.

Despite the clear memory of his soul draining touch, her mind kept returning her to the look in his eyes—forlorn and haunted.

A knock at the door drew her attention for a moment. Lilly's voice carried through the wood, "Mi'lady, your children are asking for you."

What could she tell them? The enormity of it all threatened to sweep away her sanity. "Not yet, please! Tell Rose to give me a moment. I need to compose myself," she answered, in a voice that surprised her by its calmness. Surely it wasn't her voice? Those couldn't be the words of a woman who had just lost her husband—it sounded far too reasonable to be the voice of such a woman.

Walking to the bed she sat down, wishing for tears that would not come—anything would be preferable to the cold pain in her chest, and then she spotted something new. Resting on the floor, next to her bedside table, was a wooden frame. It seemed familiar.

She lifted it and turned it over in her hands, discovering it to be a large mirror—a mirror she had thought long gone. She laid it on the bed, and was shocked to discover that, while it appeared the same it had a difference, for a ghostly image stared back at her from the glass. The face it held was her mother's, from a time when she was young, a time when Penny and Mordecai had been children. Her mother's eyes seemed to stare into her own, and there was a faint smile on her lips.

How can this be? she thought.

A small slip of paper lay folded on the bedside table. Opening it she read:

Penny,

I am so sorry for leaving this so long. I repaired this almost a year ago, and in the chaos that later ensued, forgot to return it to you. I discovered it in the corner of my workshop last week, and have been looking for a good chance to surprise you. The image in the mirror was almost an accident, a memory that came to me as I was fixing it. I hope you don't mind. It seemed appropriate.

In spite of our busy lives, you should know that I have always been grateful for your love. You continue to amaze me daily, teaching me new things about myself, and showing me the depths that lie within your heart as you care for our children. Surely your mother must have been an incredible woman to have raised you—and it shows in the way you nurture your own sons and daughters.

Never forget how much I love you in return,

Mordecai

Sorrow found her then and Penny wept, clutching a pillow and shaking the bed with her muffled sobs.

The Story Continues In:

The Final Redemption

Stay up to date with my releases by signing up for my newsletter at:

Magebornbooks.com

Books by Michael G. Manning:

Mageborn:
The Blacksmith's Son
The Line of Illeniel
The Archmage Unbound
The God-Stone War
The Final Redemption

Embers of Illeniel (a prequel series):
The Mountains Rise
The Silent Tempest
Betrayer's Bane

Champions of the Dawning Dragons:
Thornbear
Centyr Dominance
Demonhome

The Riven Gates:
Mordecai
The Severed Realm (coming summer 2018)
More to be announced

Standalone Novels:
Thomas

9 781943 481231